THE WRITTEN SCRIPT

ANNALITA MARSIGLI

THE
WRITTEN SCRIPT

THE OVERLOOK PRESS

WOODSTOCK & NEW YORK

First published in the United States in 1998 by
The Overlook Press, Peter Mayer Publishers, Inc.
Lewis Hollow Road
Woodstock, New York 12498

Library of Congress Cataloging-in-Publication Data

Marsigli Alexander, Annalita.
The Written Script / Annalita Marsigli Alexander.
p.   cm.
I. Title
PS3563.A72255W75   1997   813'.54—dc21   97-19718

Manufactured in the United States of America

ISBN 0-87951-820-0

FIRST EDITION

1 3 5 7 9 8 6 4 2

In loving memory of I. M.
and for my father Giovanni Battista

ACKNOWLEDGEMENTS

With special thanks to Henry Clay Alexander Jr., Peter Mayer, Anne and Georges Borchardt and to the following friends for their invaluable help and criticism:

John Stoye, Magdalen College, Oxford; Milton and Shirley Glaser; Annelyse Allen; Evelyn Bates Owen; Patricia Bates Johnson; Lavinia Lorch; Nicolas Steiner; Katherine Nation

THE WRITTEN SCRIPT

THE RETURN OF IVAIN LA BAILLE

"Ars longa, vita brevis"
Hippocrates via Seneca

(Memories of September 1984 in August 1994)

IVAIN Jean Marie La Baille heard someone call his name. "How can it be?" he said to himself, "I'm just ashes and earth. A white mist in the morning sun." And the thought that he was thinking again, coupled with the sudden awareness of being alive, so surprised him that he added aloud, "Who is calling me back?" He opened his eyes and could not tell where he was, for everything was fuzzy and unclear. At first he believed himself to be surrounded by layers of smoke, broken up, here and there, by splashes of bright color. But, as he started to blink, he saw the outline of the earth immersed in various blue hues and above him a pale moon slowly vanishing as a single ray of the sun began to shine over the horizon. As he looked at it, he felt a tear running down his cheek. "I must be myself again," he said, but when he tried to wipe it away, he could not find his arms or his hands. So instead, he shook his head and heard the bones in his neck crack a little. "They haven't moved much in all this time," and he smiled as he worried about his spirit taking shape once more in the green fields he had once inhabited. His thoughts went back to his last day on earth. "In another life," he said to himself, "when there was time ahead of me," adding quietly, "or so I believed."

"Time was the key on that last morning in New York," he murmured to himself, "for on that day it looked as if time had changed speed. It was going faster than usual, as though there were fewer minutes in an hour." He remembered saying aloud, "Can there be too few notes in a fugue? And if so, how many notes less?" It wasn't logical. Logic was important to Ivain and science was logical not mysterious. Yet the silver clock on his night table was proving to him that logic, as well as science, was mysterious, for when he had looked at it, it was seven o'clock, and the next moment the small hand had moved to nine o'clock. Besides, it was ticking irregularly. A second would take forever to pass, while an hour went by in a second. Something was happening that challenged the daily certitude that the sun always rises in the East and sets in the West. "Is it me or the world that is out of sorts?" he mumbled to himself as he tried to find an answer in that sleepless, restless night he had just passed. He remembered how his wife France had woken him twice, talking in her sleep. And, when he asked her what was the matter, still sleeping, she had answered, "I'm tired." Alarmed, he tried to wake her, but she said she was cold, and so he covered her up and wondered whether he would be able to leave for Rome that very day. "If these unexplainable happenings keep on," he had said to himself, "I'll miss my flight."

Ivain La Baille was proud of the fact that, though he was a professor of Latin Literature at Columbia University, his real desire had always been to discover the essence of Julius Caesar, not just the historical Caesar, but also the Shakespearean character, and now the Roman Thespian Club was giving him a chance. He had already rehearsed the previous month with the Club's all-American cast in New York. He had worked hard for three gruelling weeks. He knew his lines, he knew his blocking, he knew his character. He must not miss it!

That morning he got up quietly and grabbed both his bathrobe and the clock, which was ticking normally now, and had gone to the dining room. There, he had opened his personal closet, where he kept his collection of "time gadgets" and taken out both a water-clock and a sand clock, and placing his silver clock between them he had set all three on top of the dining room table. He filled the first with water and turned the second upside down, shaking it a bit to loosen the sand. He then opened the glass door to the terrace and placed a thin silver stick near the shadow of the small, bronze Roman sundial bought in Pompeii years ago, when one could still buy such precious objects from street vendors, probably dug up the night before in their back yard. He remembered looking up, struck by the beauty of the morning. His apartment faced both Riverside Park and the Hudson River. It was at the point where the Tomb of the Unknown Soldier rises with its classical, eloquent echoes of past architectural glories: Corinthian columns and white marble. Farther away, the colors of that late September day were reflected in the calm water of the Hudson, which becomes swift during the incoming tides, twice a day. The water was suffused in red, brown and yellow reflections. "It is all too perfect," he said almost silently. "The beauty of the world is always troubling." And a sensation of uneasiness had gone through him like an icy wind. His eyes moved over the large terrace full of flowering plants and small trees, where both he and France would often sit at sunset. Sometimes he would tease her about her name. "What sort of parents would name a daughter after a country?" he would say. "A general who loved his country," she would sometimes answer.

He heard a noise in the living room which stirred him from his daydreaming, and he came inside the room once more, sat down at the table and saw a pot of hot coffee in front of him. Natalie, France's old nurse, must have placed it there when he was on the terrace, he thought. She was always doing thoughtful things for both of them. But lately he had become her favorite, and she insisted on serving him at all times, even when France wanted to help.

9

He remembered pouring himself a cup of coffee, but never taking his eyes off the three clocks. And he remembered how startled he had been to see it was suddenly eleven o'clock, and that the sand and the water had run out of their respective containers. His cup was full, and France, wearing a beautiful blue silk dress, sat near him intent on embroidering a red pillow that said something about love and happiness. He was all dressed up in coat and tie. Near him were his traveling bags, ready to go, and Natalie was somewhere in the room for she said, "You'd better drink your coffee, Mr. La Baille, or it will get cold."

"It's Mr. La Baille's second cup, Natalie," France said tactfully. His second cup? Ivain could hardly believe it. Where had time gone? How could he have missed it? What could have happened? He had tried to concentrate. At some point he was sure he had said to France, in an ironic tone, "Why is Fabian Pierce Alfred always calling you up?" And immediately afterwards he wondered why he had mentioned Fabian's given name, middle name, and surname in the same breath? Was it his old wish to be humiliated that made him say that? He even remembered France's answer, "You aren't going to be jealous of your own cousin now, are you?" adding, "You won that battle when you married me." He remembered thinking at the time that France was referring to the fact that she had been engaged to Fabian when they first met, but he said nothing. She had also said, "In any case, he's going to be at the airport today. Coming to see you off." But he could not remember what he said before that. So, he had gotten up, engulfed by anxiety, and had purposely walked slowly to the terrace to look at the sundial. But the silver stick had rolled off the stone and was lying on the ground. As he bent down to pick it up, he tried to steady himself so as not to appear too agitated by the discovery that on this day, time was getting ahead by leaps and bounds. There was no point, he felt, in worrying France unnecessarily. "After all," he thought, "there still could be a reasonable explanation for everything." He remembered once reading two definitions for the word "fugue" one of which could have applied to him now. A "fugue," besides being a musical term, was also a particular condition during which a person is apparently conscious or aware of his actions, but has no recollection of them later on. Could that be his case? He began to think things through. He could be suffering from a series of sudden and unexpected blackouts or he could have misread the clocks. "I could, yes, I could have," he said, trying to reassure himself. But for a moment he abandoned all pretense of being rational, and mumbled aloud, as he made a large, circular gesture with his arms. A deep frown appeared between his bushy eyebrows, which together with a strange smile on his lips, gave him a wild look; but since France was staring at him, he remembered falling into a stubborn, sullen silence. "I'm just trying out my Julius Caesar lines," he finally said aloud and smiled at her. "It's the end. I can never get it right!"

He had sat down, drank his coffee fast, then poured himself another cup, and grabbed a piece of stale toast that tasted like leather. As he chewed, he noticed that France was still staring at him. He looked into her light blue eyes, and he thought he saw a shadow of sadness passing through them. He felt sorry for her, though he did not know why.

"France," he said, looking away from her, "You had a bad dream last night, didn't you?"

"Yes," she answered softly.

"Won't you tell me what it was about? It might be important." He tried to coax her into telling him.

"Not now," she replied in a way that stopped him from questioning her further.

There was an awkward silence, and Ivain said that the dream must have been awful to scare her like that. But she kept avoiding his questions, though they were becoming more and more pressing. She lifted her eyes, and he saw they were full of tears, but she wasn't crying.

"Ivain," she had said, "please don't leave today. Please don't go."

"I'll be back in three days," he had replied to her. She got up, came to him, kissed him gently on the lips, and began to whisper sweet nothings in his ear.

"I love you and I'll miss you," he said, as he held her hands in his.

"If that's true," she replied, "postpone your trip for a day." She implored him now. He was not altogether surprised by her outburst, for he realized it must have had something to do with the dream, and though he was curious to know what it was, he knew instinctively she did not want to talk about it. He only said, "I must go," adding as he smiled, "Brutus is waiting." But, as soon as he said it, he remembered biting his lip, for he had made a frightful slip of the tongue, a ghastly mistake, and he morosely corrected himself, "I meant, Caesar is waiting."

"Can't Caesar wait a day?" she asked sweetly.

"Caesar does not wait for anyone," he answered. And, as he said this, he remembered that during the missing time, France had spoken about Caesar, too. What was it that she said? Something to do with the two novels he had just finished writing on his hero: *Caesar's Regal Rag* and *Caesar's Cosmic Rag*.

"Yes," she said. "Once they're out, you'll be famous."

He recalled she had used the word "fame" or "famous" and he now remembered his reply. "I've never thought much about fame." But he realized right away, that this was not true, for he had been obsessed with Caesar's glory, as well as his own. Every lecture he had given, every paper he wrote, and now the two manuscripts he had just finished, were all done with the idea of being recognized as the man who had important insights on Julius Caesar. He wanted his name to be linked forever with Caesar's. He wanted his manuscripts to be kept in a pretty room, in a shining mahogany case under thick glass, where a long line of people would come and look at them, while permission to examine them would be granted only to scholars. "Ah, vanity, vanity!" he muttered, looking straight ahead of him, uneasy at this view of himself. But, as he took a closer look at France, he became aware that she was in real distress, and taking her gently by the waist they went to sit together on the sofa.

"What's the matter?" Ivain asked. "I've left you many times before this but you've never been angry or upset with me. I'll be gone for such a short time. After my return, we'll go someplace together. We could go to our farm, or you could meet me in Paris and spend a few days in Le Plessis." He had gotten up and had begun to walk round the room as he spoke. "And, at Le Plessis, we can kiss under the trellis," he added, knowing that it was one of France's favorite spots where the ivy and the vines grew together in knotted trunks, making it one of the most romantic places he knew. "Near the pond too," he said. "Don't forget the pond. The weather has been so mild, the water must be covered with algae. Algae and wild ducks."

She was trying to listen to him talking about the trips they might take together. But it was as if she could not keep her thoughts hidden from him, for she interrupted him, saying, "I do remember the dream last night. I was frightened for you, that's why I didn't say anything." She fell silent, only to say out loud a moment later, "I've looked it up in my book." And to prove it, she pulled out of her sewing bag a large dark book, and leafed through it. "It says here, running horses mean passion, or the yearning for passion. A key that opens a door only opens a door to death." She had closed the book quickly and had gone back to her sewing, without lifting her eyes.

"And did you dream I was opening a door with a key?" asked Ivain somewhat alarmed, as he came and sat near her again.

"No," she replied. "In my dream I saw myself dressed in black, and going back to our home in France alone, and –"

"And?" pressed on Ivain, but she said nothing more.

He felt surprise at not being surprised by her answer. He seemed to have expected it. More than that, he needed to hear those words spoken clearly and loudly, like a death sentence pronounced before it could be executed. At once he began to wonder what would happen to France if he were to die. He felt terribly sorry for her, for he knew how dependent she was on him, and there was no one else to take care of her. It had been terrible luck that both her parents had died in an accident just a year earlier; as for his own parents – they had been dead much longer, so long in fact, that apart from a single conversation with his father about his search for "the kernel of truth," he could only remember moments here and there with them. "We are just two orphans," France would sometimes say, or "We are alone in the world," to which he replied, "Who isn't?"

"At least she would be well off," he thought. "More than well off." After all, with his money, she would actually be rich. "Immortality is the prerogative of youth," he said to himself and, as he remembered that it would soon be his own thirtieth birthday, he added "or at least of youngish people." The chances of his living another forty or fifty years were good.

He said to her, "You've always been so sensible. I didn't think you believed in dreams, and divination. So now you shouldn't think too much about this dream. Before you know it, I'll be back." But she was not listening for she added, "There's another part of my dream that I remember distinctly." She had taken a deep breath. "You see," she said, "after being dressed in black, I saw myself immediately afterwards dressed in a short white lace dress, and going to my own marriage." She paused for a moment. "The second part of my dream was just as awful as the first, for I don't see myself ever marrying again."

"Ah, the merry widow! That's more like it." Ivain had said ironically, because he felt she might be making fun of him now. A second marriage just didn't seem a likely occurrence, at least not for a long, long time, even if she was only twenty-five years old. And so, smiling, he had said, "Among so many unhappy omens, at last one that looks very good." But since she was serious, he continued, "Are you trying to keep me in New York through jealousy? Well, you won't succeed. Come what may, I'm going to Rome." He suddenly stopped, and felt like saying he didn't want to go. Felt like saying that he really wanted to stay near her, for in the last few hours too many unsettling thing had happened. And the lines came to his mind:

> "O western wind, when wilt thou blow,
> That the small rain down can rain?
> Christ, that my love were in my arms
> And I in my bed again!"

But instead he said, "Why are you so discouraging?"

She begged him to postpone his trip or, alternatively, to take a boat. "There must be some large, transatlantic ship that still goes to Europe," she said.

"But," he answered, "think of what happened to the Titanic!" and he laughed at his own joke.

Still, France was not the type to be easily put off, for when she pursued an idea she would not let it go. "Worse than a moray eel," he would often say to her, and now she began to talk of the walks they could take together at home.

"The Park on Riverside already has such a thick carpet of leaves that one's shoes sink into it," she said. "Or why don't we go together in a few days?" But finally seeing that nothing would dissuade him from leaving at once, she said, "Well, if you don't believe me, why don't you ask Mme Kamiska?"

"The tarot card reader?" asked Ivain, taken aback. He disapproved of France's consulting such people.

"Yes. She'll tell you what she told me the other day," France said.

"And what was that?" he asked, trying to sound casual.

"The tarot cards have appeared in an unfavorable sequence for you. First 'A Virtuous Roman,' then 'A Sea Wave,' 'A Trinket' and finally, the letter 'O.'"

"It all sounds like a lot of hocus-pocus to me," he said.

"You throw a short shadow, Ivain," she had replied, a bit too brusquely.

"That depends on where the sun is," he answered, appalled at the thought that in her dream she had seen a marriage immediately after a burial, and even though he didn't believe in dreams, the mere idea was irritating. "Besides," he continued, "since when do you consult such charlatans?"

"Since I've begun to fear the uncertainty of the future," she said, "but you wouldn't understand," and she turned around and started to fluff up the sofa's deep green silk pillows. That was a definite sign that she was deeply troubled, for whenever she was nervous, the house took on an extraordinary look of neatness, then everything shone and there was not a speck of dust to be found anywhere.

"But I do understand," he said, and felt rather affected by the way she was carrying on. Usually, she was not given to outbursts of this kind and, though he was in turmoil himself, he tried to reassure her by saying, "How many times do people have bad dreams which don't come true?" He stopped, "And anyway, I've a theory – all these bad dreams, all these bad omens only mean that something good is going to happen. It's always the opposite of what one thinks. Didn't you know that?"

And he laughed, but his laugh for some reason sounded empty, and he believed he heard an echo somewhere nearby laughing at him. France did not answer. She hid her face in her hands. He got up and was about to leave, when France, sensing this, pulled herself together and, with a noticeable effort asked, "Why are you going out so early? You have six hours before your plane leaves, and the airport is less than an hour from our home. Why such a hurry?"

"I have to go," he answered quickly, oppressed with a presentiment of disaster.

"But you aren't going to sit on a hard bench at the airport all that time, are you?"

"I just have to go, I don't know why," he had repeated, unable to describe to her the feeling that had taken over his whole person. There was no more time left to talk or comfort her, no more time left for him either. But secretly, he had made a plan to take a different plane than the one he was supposed to take. The day before, when he had gone to pick up his ticket at the Port of Call agency, he had asked for a list of all other carriers that left New York for Rome besides Alitalia. Why he wanted it puzzled him, even now, but it had been an impulse stronger than himself. Now he had answers, even though they would appear meaningless to anyone but himself. He knew that all the planes to Italy left in the afternoon or early evening. But he began to think that the chances of avoiding disaster were augmented if he were to go to Rome in a roundabout way, so as to fool fate. What if, instead of Alitalia, he took Air France, for instance, to Paris, and then grabbed another plane Paris-Venice-Rome? Or couldn't he try to get to Rome via Madrid, or Munich, or even via Sydney, Bangkok, or Cape Town? He had searched surreptitiously for even lesser known places. Was there a flight Ankara-Rome via Alaska, or Kabul-Rome via Cairo, or Buenos Aires-Moscow-Rome? He had a myriad of choices. He was free to choose. But there was an ominous feeling gnawing inside him. A feeling that would give him no respite, no matter how hard he tried to chase it away. It was not unlike carrying a little rodent in his belly, which was taking small bites of his innards. "I feel like that Spartan boy who tried to hide the fox puppy under his shirt," he muttered to himself. The inward pain was about destiny, for if destiny was closing upon him, it didn't matter which plane he took. That was the awful truth. So now he had the feeling that whatever plane he was on, something would happen to it that day, and to none others. Other planes might have engines that caught fire, might lose part of a wing, might develop a gaping hole in the pilot's cabin, but, ultimately, they would arrive somehow at their destination. It seemed to Ivain that even though on the surface it looked as if he was free to change planes, airlines, destinations and hours of arrival, in point of fact, France's dream, and his time gadgets, only pointed in one direction: a straight line toward some momentous, personal disaster.

This discovery made him sullen, but he tried, nevertheless, to think of something sweet and funny to say to France before he left. But, as his mind was a blank, he murmured, "There are fears that cannot be explained," and picking up his bag he started to walk toward the door. But before reaching it he noticed Natalie in a corner of the room, using the gift he had recently given her for her birthday, an inexpensive movie camera.

"What are you doing with that camera, Natalie?" he had asked, surprised.

"But Ivain," France had answered, "Natalie has been taking a movie of us since early morning. How come you've only just noticed it?"

He had been amazed once more, and felt like taking the camera away from Natalie. But before he could move, Natalie had come up and offered him a box of fortune cookies for the trip.

"Here, Mr. La Baille," she had said. "I baked them for you myself, as a going away present."

"Thank you," Ivain had replied, taking the box, looking at it, not knowing what to do with it.

"Aren't you going to open it and eat one?" asked France, who knew it would make the old woman happy.

Distractedly, Ivain had opened up the box and at random had picked out a cookie to find a small white paper wrapped up inside it. It said: "Confucius says you will enjoy a long and happy life."

"Look at this!" he said to France, laughing. "All your worries are for nothing. Confucius says so, and who are we to argue against what Confucius says?" Smiling, he had taken her hands into his. But he had quickly withdrawn them, because her palms were cold and clammy. At the time, he could not have guessed that had he taken any other cookie, he would have found the same message inside, for that was Natalie's thoughtful way of saying goodbye to him.

"Hurry home and you'll be able to see yourself in my first home movie, Mr. La Baille," Natalie was saying, as he had leaned over to kiss and thank her. At this moment he did not know that this was going to be the last time he would see Natalie alive.

He turned and kissed France on the cheek, picked up his bags with the intention of running out of the house, since he was suddenly overcome by a feeling of urgency, when he heard France calling, "Wait! I'll come with you." He remembered not wanting to wait for her, for the urgency that was overwhelming him had transformed itself into a sensation of speed. Speed gathering speed, feeding on itself, like a torrent of water that had broken through a wall and was rushing down to the valley below, leaving behind only rocks and stones. But he heard himself saying, "Come on or we'll be late." Why had he said that? What puzzled him most was that France had been absolutely right in telling him to wait a few more hours at home. There was no need at all for all his running, even if he had wanted to change planes. In fact, they arrived at the airport five hours before his own plane was to leave. So why had he pushed people aside to get the first taxi? And why had he begged the driver to hurry up, or else he would miss his plane? And why all the leaps, hops and skips even after reaching the airport? Then, he remembered how he stopped running, and standing absolutely still, he understood the meaning of everything that happened that morning, as if he were looking into a crystal ball. He even marveled at his own blindness up to that moment. Of course, it was madness for him to leave. One did not necessarily have to believe in omens and auguries. One did not have to believe in old ladies who read tarot cards, or in dreams, to know that all the odds were stacked against him. So, why take the chance? He looked at France, took her into his arms, and calling her by her nickname, he said, "Poucette, I've decided to postpone my trip. You're right. *Oculos habent et non videbunt,*" and he laughed hearing her clear laugh at his deliberate use of a wise saying in Latin. He also knew she was happy at his calling her by that very private nickname, for whenever he called her Poucette, they were both in a carefree mood. "I'll just go up to the counter and change my ticket." he added.

"Good," she said, "and I'll call up Fabian and tell him not to meet you here."

"Oh yes, Fabian. I had forgotten he was coming to see me off."

"But he wouldn't forget, would he?" she answered quickly. "You are more than a cousin to him. I think if he were not Fabian he'd like to be you."

He kissed her, whispering, "I love you."

20

It was amazing. Right away he had felt like a new man. A terrible weight had been lifted from his chest and he had begun to walk in a poised way toward the escalator. But before reaching it, he saw Fabian standing nearby, looking around.

"Fabian!" Ivain called out. "What are you doing here so early?"

"What about you?" Fabian replied, equally surprised.

"You know me," Ivain answered. "The anxious type. Always afraid of missing my plane. Always afraid of taking one."

"I know you too well," Fabian had said. "*Courage, mon cousin*," and he patted him on the shoulders to give him strength, but Ivain understood he had said it in an ironic tone. All at once, though, Fabian seemed to turn serious, so Ivain tried to lighten up the moment.

"Have you brought along your latest girl friend to see me off?"

"Of course not," Fabian said, looking around as if searching for something or someone. "I've serious doubts about her," he continued.

"Oh?" said Ivain. "No marriage in store for you?"

"I may still marry her," said Fabian. "After all, the only women worth marrying are the ones we have serious doubts about." Ivain smiled as they took a few steps together. He turned to him and said, "Fabian, do me a favor. France is calling your home right now. Can you wait here for her? I'll be right back – and keep an eye on my bags and my coat, too." And so saying, he left everything with Fabian, and walked on as he put his hand in his pocket and searched for his good luck piece, an ancient coin of Emperor Tiberius, but it was not there. Then he remembered he had left it with the family jeweler to be made into a surprise gift for France, but now he suddenly missed it. He shrugged his shoulders in a gesture of annoyance, but then relaxed, knowing that his cousin was there.

"Much better than a good luck piece." he said. He looked down at the floor and was about to step onto the escalator when he noticed an old woman with a dark scarf wrapped round her head standing in front of him. She stepped aside to let him pass, saying, "Once more, please." He wondered what on earth she meant but walked on, being careful to put one foot before the other on the escalator. He began to think that happiness was within his reach again. He imagined the warm embrace and passionate kiss he would receive from France upon returning home. He promised himself to open a good bottle of Bordeaux, from one of the better châteaux. And he remembered thinking how happy they would be together, happy as only two children who have a silly secret between them can be. And as he was being carried upward, lost in the most pleasant daydreams, he remembered hearing a loud shout. The shout had come before the shot, he was quite sure of that. He had felt a push on his side, but no pain. He turned around and saw France looking at him as she raised her hand to her mouth to suppress a scream, no doubt. And then he saw her trying to run toward him, but Fabian was pulling her back, away from him. He remembered falling down like an inanimate object on the step he was on, and being carried up the long stairway, until he reached the platform. There, someone pulled him off to the side. After that, everything was fuzzy. There were shadows bending over him, trying to lift him up. There was whispering all around, and the faint sounds of murmured words coming from far away. He could hear questions being asked. He could feel hands touching him. Someone was looking through his pockets. A voice near his ear kept repeating, "Hang on, you'll be all right." He wanted to say something, but found that he could not speak, as he began having trouble breathing. His chest had started to heave irregularly up and down. He was suffocating. "Don't be afraid. Don't be afraid," said the same voice, and at the same time he heard someone call for a priest or a chaplain. He knew he was dying and he knew he was not prepared for it. Everything had happened too quickly. He should have "lived his death more and died his life," as the popular French saying went. But it was too late. His mind had started to wander in long, shadowy corridors, full of childhood memories. Little cars, miniature trains, books, old photographs of his home in Rosay, and the warmth of his bed on the cold winter nights there. He thought he heard France sobbing near him, but wasn't sure. He did remember thinking how hard it would be for her to comprehend the horror of his sudden disappearance. "Like broken glass, our happiness is shattered in this instant," and felt like crying himself, but his body was beyond tears or laughter, or moving in any way. His mind drifted to his two novels still in manuscript form, hidden with his time-gadget memorabilia. France knew where to find them, he had made sure of that. His last words, whispered more to himself than to the world, were said as he thought of Julius Caesar: "My writing will survive. I am immortal, too." After that, there was nothing, just the abyss of the void. But now, someone was calling his name, and he was aware of being conscious once more.

MADAME KAMISKA

"The present does not exist – for it has a foot in the past
and a foot in the future, but only a shadow in the middle."

Mme Kamiska at Disneyland Paris

As soon as Ivain realized that his spirit had completed the
metamorphosis from thin air to a weighty corporeal shape, he
looked around and saw he was on an open country road which,
though familiar, he was unable to recognize. The road was surrounded by farm land that had already grown the year's harvest, and was shining with different hues of deep green, brown
and straw yellow. In other parts he could see the fields lined
with deep furrows, ready to be seeded for the following year.
Scattered in between the fields were clusters of trees, mostly
oaks and birches, and in the distance he could see the roofs of a
few houses above the tree line.

"What part of the world am I in?" he wondered, and raising
his eyes he saw a small stone house, directly in front of him. The
house reminded him of a humble French country place, the
kind often found in the Brie region. But this house had an air
of desolation about it, as if it had been deserted long ago, as if
no children had ever played there. He even wondered whether
it was inhabitable, since there were no windows, only a large
wooden door on the side. "Perhaps this is just a storage place for
a nearby farm," he said to himself, and felt sad that there might
not be anyone around to ask for information.

At his feet, a rusty bicycle had been left on its side. Near it,
scattered on the grass, were parts of a black telephone with the
handle still intact, a bit of torn cord still attached to its case and,
most remarkable of all, an eight-digit number still legible, four
times sixty-four. "It's an easy number," he said to himself, "easy

to remember." He repeated it as he turned around. He then bent down, picked up the bicycle, seated himself on it and started to pedal with vigor for he had a feverish desire to reach a still unknown place, pedaling as only a racing cyclist would pedal. But to Ivain's great surprise, not only did he not move a single inch forward, but he found himself going backwards. "This is a strange bicycle," he thought, but kept pedaling on and on anyway, not knowing what else to do. "I need time to think," he said to himself, "time to understand these inexplicable happenings." And while he was still pedaling, the phone, which was now quite a distance ahead of him, began to ring. It was an incessant, monotonous ring that tore through the crisp, thin morning air, and broke the spell of the pastoral scene in front of him.

"I'll never answer a broken phone!" he said resolutely, but immediately afterwards, he got off the bicycle and began to run to pick up the receiver.

"Who is it?" he asked.

"Where are you?" said a voice at the other end. "I've been waiting for your arrival." It was a woman's voice, both melodious and soft, full of hidden sensuality. It was a siren's voice. The same voice that had been calling his name just a little while ago, as he was descending through the clouds, when he was still in between two worlds.

"Who are you?" asked Ivain cautiously. "And why am I back?"

"Come inside the house, and I'll tell you," she said, and after a pause he heard sad, melancholic music coming over the phone line, notes that seemed to be played with a hollow reed; music that spoke of people and of a past that was unknown to him. But its sound was like no other sound he had ever heard. He was still listening, not quite knowing what to do, when the line went dead. Later on, he would learn that whenever he heard that same nostalgic music, the same lady was nearby. But for now, Ivain put down the phone carefully and started to walk toward the house, where he could see the door opening slowly. Suddenly he stopped. From the sky he saw a ball of fire coming toward him at an incredible speed. He stood still, as it passed so close to him that he felt a burning sensation both on his face and on his left arm. The following day, he would discover that the hair on his forearm had been singed and wondered why he had felt no pain. Now he looked up and saw that the fire had struck the wall of the house just ahead of him, giving it an orange glow. And as the fire died out, it left behind, imprinted on the wall, the image of an elderly couple. The woman was still handsome, with white hair pulled back from her face by a velvet ribbon, and she was spoon-feeding a man sitting next to her. She was smiling and was coaxing the man to eat, as he looked abstractly into the void. Ivain stared intensely at them, and all at once recognized France in the woman. How old his wife had become!

"But who was the man with her?" he wondered as the image disappeared as quickly as it had appeared, and Ivain found himself shaken and alone again. Hesitantly he walked toward the wooden door, not knowing what he would find behind it. The door, which had by now opened completely, invited him to enter.

Over the threshold, he found a large, red sign that read:

"Madame Kamiska, Theater impresario extraordinaire."
And underneath, written in smaller letters:
"Famous clairvoyant, ectoplasm savant, Tarot card expert."
and below that, written in even smaller letters:
"Serious Representative of the Cosmic Order."

He stood there, amazed at the thought that he was about to

meet the seer who had foretold his death, the one France had spoken about on that last morning. He was wondering whether or not to enter the house, when he heard the same melodious voice say, "Do come in. You're rather late, and I've other appointments."

But before entering he said, "What is this all about?"

"It's about Time!" she said, then modifying somewhat her first sentence, she continued, "It's about time you arrived. I've been waiting for you. Do come in."

Ivain entered a rather dark stuffy room, and though at first he couldn't see a thing, little by little his eyes got used to the darkness. He was surprised to find himself facing a wrinkled, withered woman, with thin gray hair and colorless lips. She was sitting in an enormous gilded chair made of wood which had been cleverly inlaid with white whalebone and mother-of-pearl shells, and she was wearing a loose flowery dress that looked like a tent. It seemed to Ivain that there was an aura of ancient memories about both the woman and the chair she was sitting in. "Just like the music I heard outside," he thought. "An ancient memory acquired through having lived for a long time," he whispered to himself, and then added, "An old soul, too," for he had noticed a slight hollow on her forehead, between her eyebrows.

He looked at her attentively, for her face seemed familiar, but he could not remember where he had met her. And though he would meet her many times after this first encounter, he was never sure of where he had first seen her until the very end of his second stay on earth, and by then it didn't matter any longer. He would run into her disguised as a beggar near his home on Riverside Drive, and he only recognized her after she thanked him for the change he had dropped in her lap. Once they came face to face when he realized she was the ticket seller at Vaux le Vicomte and, had he not been with his cousin and a young woman whom he wanted to impress, he would have returned his ticket. Another time, he would run into her playing the part of the seer in Shakespeare's *Julius Caesar*, and she became very angry with him on that occasion. He would even recognize her in the Park of Disneyland Paris. There she was underground, sitting in a rocky cave surrounded by gold pieces and precious stones. He would meet her in all those places, but not necessarily in that order. And then there were those times when she was just there, and other times when he wanted to ask for a simple explanation, and she was nowhere to be found.

Here in the old house, Mme Kamiska was surrounded by huge piles of old books stacked on the floor or lining the walls. There were illuminated incunabula, papyrus scrolls, historical tablets written in cuneiform or hieroglyphics, as well as Chaldean and Etruscan drawings on dried out sheepskin or parchment. As Ivain looked about he said to himself, "I must keep my eyes open and my ears sharp, for if it is some kind of game, I don't know the rules."

Immediately Mme Kamiska got up and approached him smiling, and it was then he saw she had only one tooth in her cavernous mouth. That tooth had been covered in both silver and gold and it hung loosely in the middle of her upper jaw and, as she breathed in and out, it swung like a tiny bell that made no sound.

"Who are you?" he asked.

"I am the daughter of Time," she said, as she held her hand in front of her mouth, ashamed of having lost all her teeth but one. Later on, Ivain noticed that there would be times when she would smile with a mouthful of teeth, while once she laughed and he saw she had none.

Now he murmured, "Are you really the daughter of Time?"

"Yes, I am eternal."

"Ah," he said. "That is forever."

"Not quite," she said, as she caressed an owl that had suddenly jumped onto her lap out of nowhere. "Eternity is the absence of time, therefore it's no time at all." She became suddenly serious as she deposited the owl on a wooden perch attached to the wall. Ivain looked up and was amazed to see that the owl was not moving at all, but had become absolutely still, as if it had been stuffed full of straw by a taxidermist in the last second or so. It was at this point, he was to remember later, that the thought crossed his mind that he was in the hands of a mad woman, but he tried hard not to show his fears, so he casually asked her, "How long is eternity?" adding, "I was always convinced that eternity was eternal."

"It lasts less than a second," she replied. "It's nothing. The void. *Le rien du tout.* Life, on the other hand is an eternity."

He suddenly felt distressed and would have liked to be able to get out of that house, out of that presence, but he did not know how. So he just blurted out, "How long have I been dead?"

"Ten years" she answered. He was silent for a while, then he said, "Is there a future ahead of me?" and as he spoke he realized his hands were trembling, so he quickly hid them in the pockets of his jacket.

"The future has already happened, therefore it's the past. Only you don't know it yet." And as she said this she moved her fingers over a small desk, as if looking for something.

"She is speaking in riddles, riddles I can't follow," he thought. "But where am I?" he wondered. "Why am I back?" he inquired aloud.

"Father asked for you," she said, "Father is Janus, the God with two faces who can look both ways at the same instant." And as she said this, she turned her head this way and that way, showing both sides of her profile, which to Ivain's immense surprise, were very different from one another. One being rather refined and classical, the other coarser and brutish.

"Yes," she continued. "Father likes to play games. Just now he was that ball of fire showing you the future. Hurling the future at you. That's how your sweet France will look fifty years hence. Still pretty, still pretty." Then, looking in the distance, she added, "But how time flies, doesn't it?" She paused for a moment before starting to murmur *sotto-voce* what sounded like an incantation: "As we get older, our souls get younger, and as we get younger our souls grow older, so that as children we are much wiser than as old hags." And she tried to say something else, but spoke so softly he could not follow what she was saying.

Ivain was suddenly more than afraid. He was terrified. There was something sinister in the face of Mme Kamiska which he now perceived, though he could not define. She must have noticed his fear, for she extended her hand, but as soon as Ivain touched it, he found it so cold he had the strange sensation of having burned himself, and quickly withdrew his own. He immediately regretted this act of impoliteness. What if Mme Kamiska took offense? "He should be more careful," he said to himself. But she pretended not to notice, and bending forward, began to talk about her Father.

"Father," she said, "is a young God, a Godlet, in point of fact. Two in one. You see, he was born as a Siamese twin with Space – the other side of his face – when the Universe came to be, and not before it. Before him there was the older God, his Creator." And then she added, "Father makes up for his youthfulness by being a fun Godlet. We've a lot of laughs together." She stopped for a moment, as if deep in thought. "Your sweet France – lovely girl. In fact, she's a favorite of mine." She paused now, searching for the right words. "The poor dear is having trouble gathering your papers for the Library room to be named after you,

In Memoriam," and she sighed. "It would be so good of you to go back and help her out."

"Ah," exclaimed Ivain, astonished, "I am remembered?"

"Remembered?"

"Yes," he continued, "The world remembers me?"

"You can see for yourself how the world remembers you, since you've a chance to go back. But, I'll be brief." And she immediately proceeded to be long-winded, talking about the different ways the world remembers the famous, and the infamous, ending up by saying, "If you wish to go back, all you have to do is sign this paper for me." And she tried to hand him a thin, transparent, golden page, adding, "This paper is a mere formality. Father is a stick-in-the-mud for this sort of thing. Everything has to be signed for. Regulations."

Ivain took two steps backwards, so as not to take it, but Mme Kamiska moved even closer to him, and held up the page for him to see. It was a small page with just two words written on it in large letters: "A Script" followed by an "X" at the bottom. Ivain looked at it from a safe distance, and asked what would happen if he refused to sign.

"Well then," began Mme Kamiska, "you can choose to become a shadow and roam the earth, or you can go back to where you came from."

He wanted to ask where he had come from, since he had no memory of the past ten years, but refrained from doing so. Instead he said, "And if I sign the paper, what am I signing?" and right away felt he should not have asked.

She pretended not to notice his impertinence and, looking away from him, casually remarked that her Father admired the theater as much as he, Ivain, did.

"Above everything else, Father would like to be a playwright. Consequently, he is always looking for new material."

She also wished him to know that – "both Father and I work

31

wonderfully well together and have actually founded a Theater Company." And, putting her hand in her large pocket, she took out a card which she handed him.

He read it quickly. It said: "The JanKam Co." He put it down on the table next to him as Mme Kamiska continued talking. "I've tried to help him by always being on the look-out for unusual situations and characters." As a dutiful daughter, she herself had always taken a role in all his plays, she said, her best having been that of the "tower guard," though she was supposed to be blind, and that of the "great orator," though she was supposed to be tongueless.

"The world is a stage, and the stage is a grand illusion, wouldn't you agree?" But Ivain, still trembling, said nothing. He just took out a handkerchief from his pocket and wiped his hands which had become moist and sticky, as Mme Kamiska continued, "Well? There is the Theater of war, the operational Theater, the political Theater and I could go on and on." But Ivain deduced that what she really wanted was for him to sign quickly and leave.

"And what does signing this paper entail?" Ivain asked. He was not about to sign his name on any document on the spur of the moment. He knew for a fact that any well-written play was always built around deceit. Since Mme Kamiska had spoken about the theater as her main interest, what deceit did she have in mind for him? And, though he realized he was not in a good position to demand anything, he decided to ask anyway. But, before he uttered a word, Mme Kamiska went on. "Back on earth, you'll be playing yourself as if you were alive, though you are dead and gone."

So that was the deceit! "How can I get away with that?" he said aloud, startled that she would even suggest it. If the world was anything as he remembered it, his real identity would be known immediately, and then how would he explain it?

Mme Kamiska was not perturbed in the least by his anxieties, for she replied in a quiet voice. "Always tell the truth. Leave it up to the others to find an explanation for everything. You'll be surprised at how creative people can be." Ivain looked round the room as he shifted his weight from one foot to the other. He was not in the best position to do anything. He was facing such an unreal situation. He began to wonder how far his limited logic would be of help to him.

"But what about 'the script'?" he asked humbly. "What 'script' is it? I am merely asking for my own information," he added, trying not to anger her. At first she said nothing, just stared at him, then started to mumble something again. He felt dizzy, as if he was going to fall down, and he steadied himself with both hands on the back of a nearby chair.

After a moment Mme Kamiska picked something off an old, three-legged stool, and held it up in her hands. "The 'script'" she explained, "is this floppy disk." And with that she showed him a small green disk. "Compatible with any Macintosh computer," she added.

In the silence that followed, her eyes wandered up, and she began to look at the many clocks hanging from the ceiling. None were ticking. They hung there, suspended, immobile, meant more to be aerial sculptures, with the long and short hands stopped at different times, than accurate instruments for telling time.

"As you know, it's not easy to write a play," she continued. "There are rules one must follow." And she took a deep breath, before going on. "Now, in exchange for living a second life, you could help Father and me by carrying this green disk with you." She stopped for a moment. "It will automatically record your actions and your words. And if we are lucky, at some point, we might have a polished and complete 'script.'" She fixed her eyes on him. "Well, what do you say?"

"My life, then, is a 'script' in the making?" said Ivain, and he tried to look into Mme Kamiska's eyes, but as the tenuous light had begun to flicker, he could not see her expression, he could only hear her voice which had somehow become monotonous, repeating words which sounded stale.

"Yes, yes," she said a bit too emphatically adding immediately, "you're going back as yourself, of course, but I'm giving you a different cover this time around." She paused before resuming. "You'll be a professional actor, named –?" and here she stopped and began again searching the desk in front of her, shuffling through the papers. Finally she asked, "What is Ivain in English?" and immediately answered her own question. "John, of course. So now you are John Elliab. La Baille spelled backwards. An inexact anagram, I'm afraid. One might even say a bad one. Perhaps we should add an O. to it. Yes, that's it! John O. Elliab. As John O. Elliab you have been offered the role of Caesar's understudy in Shakespeare's play, with the best acting company in town. You've accepted, but you can always get out of it if you deem it necessary. It's just a cover. But I imagine you are eager to play your hero, especially when I can promise you a triumphal success. Am I right?"

"Of course, of course." replied Ivain, a bit too anxiously.

"Ah, but to do justice to the great Caesar, you'll have to feel like Caesar felt at least once in your life." She paused. "Yes. Well, I'll give you that chance at the appropriate time, of course." He was silent. She quickly added, "And, through all this you will be close to France, naturally." Then leaning forward, pretending she was about to share a secret with him, she whispered in his ear, "Yours has to be a romantic story in the making, exquisitely passionate." As she said this, she moved away from him, only to come back to give him the paper to sign. He hesitated for a moment, but this time did not refuse it. He took the thin golden paper, held it carefully in his hands, staring at the words. By holding the page tightly, by not re-belling against the knot he was being offered to tie with the Godlet Time, Ivain La Baille sealed his fate in that instant, though he did not know it yet. At present, he just looked at it, held it up to the light and then turned it over. Many months later, as he ran out of the library room which had just been dedicated to his memory, his thoughts went back to that first meeting in Mme Kamiska's windowless house, where he had been offered a second chance at life if only he would sign his name on a golden page. He remembered how he had signed his name readily, believing everything she had told him. He had signed it even though he realized at the very last moment that the smile on Mme Kamiska's lips was full of mischief. He remembered having a passing feeling of uneasiness about it. There was something he could not quite see, but which was there never-theless, if only he knew where to look. But it was nothing he could put his finger on. It was just a sensation. Yet, his choices were bleak, that much was clear. And wasn't knowledge, whenever possible, better than no knowledge? At least he believed it to be so at the time. Also, Mme Kamiska had sweet-ened the offer, by saying "yes" to his one request, and he was grateful to her for that concession. But what the request had been, Ivain had often occasion to wonder, for he had immedi-ately forgotten it, and that memory haunted him throughout his second stay on earth, until the moment when Mme Kamiska revealed it to him again, and fulfilled that promise. As for now, she said, "Quite right – quite right. There are too many mysteries in the world." After that he had taken the pen and placed his name near the X, and Mme Kamiska had hand-ed him the green floppy disk. "Just keep it in your pocket, and go about your life, as you would do naturally," she said. "And forget you have it." He had held out his hand, taken the green disk and placed it in his breast pocket as she had suggested, promising himself that he would look at it as soon as the occasion presented itself.

"You are now on your own," she said. "Well, not quite," she added. "I've given you one of my best people to introduce you to your new life. She's waiting for you outside my door. Her name is Allegra Cagliostro. A genial name, isn't it? Perhaps you remember the more famous 18th century Palermitan Count, hum? Great friend of mine. I actually made him in the image of my Father. Father was very happy at the time. Exceedingly so." Then she rose to take him to the door.

"I think you'll find Allegra very pretty, even though she is a dead soul as you are. But that has certain advantages, as you'll soon discover. Oh, I mustn't forget to tell you, Allegra is not allowed to get in touch with me as long as she is your helper. You'll have to do that yourself," and pointing to the card she had given him, which he had placed on top of the table, she instructed him on how to reach her. "Just dial my name on any phone, with or without a cord, plugged or unplugged, and I'll answer if I am in this galaxy." And with that she handed him the card a second time, and this time he quickly took it, saying, "Thank you."

He was about to leave when Mme Kamiska stopped him by holding on to his sleeve. "Oh!" she said, "I almost forgot to tell you the one rule we have in our Company." And she lifted her bony fingers in the air to emphasize the point. "You must never, ever tell anyone your real name." Then she took a breath and shook her head from side to side.

Ivain looked at her, and after a moment of reflection, he asked boldly, "What happens if I reveal my true identity to France or anyone else?" to which she replied, "If you tell anyone your real name, everyone will quickly forget your second visit on earth, and you'll become vulnerable to death again – just long enough – to return to where you just came from."

This Ivain interpreted to mean a return to the void, and he silently swore never to tell a living soul he was: Ivain Jean Marie La Baille.

ALLEGRA

"If we do not like our feelings to be stirred,
we must keep out of beauty's way"

Po Chü-i

August 1994

IMMEDIATELY after Ivain walked out of Mme Kamiska's door, the house behind him disappeared in a cloud of dust, as well as the bicycle and the broken phone. At once he realized that only in the past, that particular house had been there, for in the present it was gone. "I am in a different linear time," he thought, as he found himself on the same road once more, only this time he recognized it as the road to the village of Rosay. It was the same road the Romans had walked down with their legions, their camp followers, and their heavily charged horses and mules in that period of history when Paris was called Lutetia. The same road where, as a child, he had come across both a large piece of a silver dagger inlaid with delicate gold flower buds, and a green coin. That night he had polished the coin, and the gold head of Tiberius had appeared in its glory and had decided his future for him. He was able to find out almost immediately that the aureus had been struck at Gaul Lugdunum, where there had been an important mint for coinage in all precious metals, established by Augustus.

Now, for some reason his eyes caught sight of something shining on the ground. He bent down and picked it up. He was amazed, for he was holding in his hand the same ancient coin of the Emperor Tiberius that he had found twenty-three years earlier. His surprise was all the greater for he remembered having given it to the jeweler, together with another ancient coin of the same period, to make into earrings for France. He recognized the frame it was in, since he had designed it himself, and noticed that the clip on the back was gone. He held it between his fingers, and played with it as he was overwhelmed with feelings of nostalgia for his past life, together with a feeling of joy, for soon he would be reunited with his wife in his old country house, Le Plessis.

"My good luck piece. I'm in luck," he said to himself as he put it in his pocket, and sitting down on a stone near the road, he buried his head in his hands, daydreaming of what he would say to France.

He was still holding his head when he became aware of a sound nearby, not unlike that of a child crying. He looked up and was surprised to see a woman, dressed in a yellow suit, sitting on the other side of the road with her head tucked in the corner of her right elbow. He got up, walked over to her and, bending his knees, brought his head close to hers. But, as she had not moved, he touched her arm gently, saying, "Here, let me help you. What is the matter?"

She looked up, and Ivain was surprised to see the most beautiful woman he had ever seen. She was a Nordic type, who reminded him of some glacier goddess, from a fjord undoubtedly, and even though her eyes were red from crying, her irises were of a brilliant dark green. She now pushed her straight, short, ash-blond colored hair away from her face, and Ivain saw that her skin was white, and had a transparent quality to it. All at once he remembered the words of Mme Kamiska and said, "You must be Allegra."

She nodded, as she turned her head away from him. He tried to think of something amusing to say to her, but the only thing that came to his mind was her name, "With such a cheerful name, how come you're crying like this?"

She looked at him. "I'm crying for you," was her reply.

"For me?" exclaimed Ivain. He made no attempt to hide his

surprise. Why be sad at such an extraordinary moment of his life? His first thought was for his wife.

"Has something happened to France?" he inquired, and immediately remembered her image on the wall as an old happy woman, so he realized nothing could be seriously wrong with her.

"Your wife is well, and has married again," Allegra said, drying her face on the back of her sleeve.

"Oh?" Ivain said, and he marvelled at the fact that France's dream had become a reality, after all. He wondered just how quickly after his death she had married, but did not ask, though he felt for the first time the dark sting of unrestrained jealousy.

"I'm crying because Mme Kamiska and her Father have deceived you, Ivain," said Allegra, all in one breath.

"Really?" Ivain was rather astonished at this statement. "In what way?"

"You've been had," she answered.

"How?" He moved closer to her.

"The 'green disk' you are carrying is not 'a script in the making.' It is a fully 'written script.'" And she added, "Very finished. Very polished. Very artistic." She moved her hands in the air in such a way as to form the image of a flower at the same time as she began to smile through her tears at his contrived expression.

Ivain looked away, and saw a boy with a small goat coming down the road. The boy stopped for a moment to look at them both, then walked past them as he talked to his goat about the tender clover they would find not far away.

"How strange," thought Ivain, "I'm equally surprised by a boy with a goat, as I'm about what Allegra has just told me." In either case he had no premonitions, no hints. Nothing. Everything seemed to be coming out of thin air.

"That's fine," said Ivain to Allegra as he began to suspect that something terrible was about to sink deep into his soul. "But how does that affect me?" And even though the answer was obvious, he still wanted to hear it.

"Everything has already been laid out for you. You're just going through the motions, and acting according to what is written down."

"In that case," Ivain said rather loudly, remembering the words of Mme Kamiska about how the future had already happened, "I'm just going to throw away the disk." He took it out of his pocket and with a large rotation of his arm attempted to throw it in the ditch by the roadside, but to his astonishment the disk made a perfect elliptical curve, and returned to its owner as if pulled by an invisible elastic string. "Not unlike those boomerangs used by the Australian aborigines," thought Ivain, "that once thrown in the air inevitably return to the hands of their owner."

"I am its magnet," he said in a whisper to himself as he tried once more to throw the disk away, only to have it back a few seconds later. Still, he did not give up the game for quite a while. He tried to throw it to the four winds – East, West, North and South, turning first one way then another way. He even tried to throw it up and down, clenching his fists tightly as soon as it was in the air, and finally he tried to lose it, by dropping it on one side, while turning his body in the opposite direction, but all to no avail. Inevitably he found the disk in his hand until, understanding at last the futility of the exercise, he put it back in his pocket.

Allegra looked at him with her sad, sad eyes. "It's a little game they play with the likes of us," she said as she got up and came close to him, so close in fact that for a moment he believed she was going to embrace or kiss him. "Please help me to end it all before it starts," she implored.

"How?" he asked with a certain gentleness in his voice, for he understood she was in the same position as he was.

"Help me return to my other life," she said simply. "I like you too much to go through this 'script.'"

"What's keeping you?" Ivain asked, as he felt himself becoming more and more angry.

"I'm here to do a job," she said quite casually now. "But it's not a pleasant job, believe me." She paused as if she was searching for the right, perhaps courteous words, to break some unpleasant news to him. "In some ways I could even say – it is awful. Terrifyingly so. And the sooner I'm out of here, the better for both of us."

"Oh?" said Ivain, trying to understand what was going on.

"We're dealing with the sort of creatures that dispense suffering as if they were handing out gifts," she explained.

"Oh" said Ivain again, not quite knowing where she was leading him.

"I'll need your help to get out of it." She was insistent now, as she placed her left hand on his arm either by accident or by desire, and he was surprised to find a sudden unexpected stirring for this unknown woman, whose skin seemed to emanate the delicate smell of violets and primroses.

"I'll do my best," said Ivain automatically, without giving too much thought to what he was saying, though he did wish to help save this lovely woman in any way he could.

"Then go and tell the first person we meet that you are Ivain Jean Marie La Baille, the Professor of Latin Literature, not John O. Elliab, the actor – and both of us will be back."

"I see," said Ivain, not quite prepared for what he had just heard.

"Do it," she said emphatically. "Do it," she repeated.

"Why should I say those words?" Ivain almost shouted, for it was the last thing in the world he wished to do. "I feel happy and contented here, and the grass is green, and the wheat is already cut or about to be cut," he continued, knowing fully well that those were *non-sequiturs*. But so was his appearance on earth again.

"You've studied the art of writing a play," she went on calmly. "You know there's only one way for this play you are in to end. Think for a moment," she added, as she looked at him. But he kept silent. "They'll create a situation in which you will have to say who you are. They'll place you in circumstances so emotionally overwhelming that you will have no choice," and she repeated, "no choice."

"And if I don't say it?" Ivain muttered to himself. "If I don't say my real name to anyone, but keep it hidden within myself? What then? This play, as you call it, this 'script' will never end. Won't that be a victory over the Father and Daughter Company? Won't it?" He looked away from her now, knowing that he would not be of any help to her cause. He had just returned and was not about to disappear. Not right away, in any case.

"Why fight? Don't you see it's useless? You can't kill Time." Allegra added loudly, and for the first time Ivain realized that she was a strong woman with a will of her own.

He began to have some doubts about her. He said, "Why are you telling me all this?"

"You're supposed to know right away that you are the leading character in your 'script.' As such, you are both actor and spectator," she said, "and I'm the one who has to tell you. That way," she continued, "you have the feeling that you can choose to stay or to leave. But it's only a feeling. Now, it's up to you, of course, but I strongly suggest that we don't stay a minute longer than we have to."

"Have you read 'the script?'" Ivain asked, looking in the direction of his home.

"I know the general outline," she said. "Every night, in my

43

sleep I get to memorize the lines for the following day. That's how it's done."

"Is that true for me, too?" he asked, quite astonished now.

"I don't know," she answered as she glanced at her long soft fingers.

"I see," he said. "And you wouldn't be able to tell me a bit more about my story, would you?" He tried to utter these words as if his life depended on it, which in fact, it did.

"No," she said, as she paused, and smiled. Then changing her mind, she said, "Yes. Yes, I can tell you that if you stay, our deaths are connected. You'll die first, and a few minutes later, I'll follow you." She turned, and when she spoke again her voice was full of sadness. "That is all I know."

"I see," Ivain said. "I see," he repeated, as he became lost in the songs of birds and the songs of crickets round him. But then, shaking himself, he tried to concentrate and understand how the two events Allegra had spoken of could be joined together logically. To do that, he needed to find out more, much more.

"We are in this together," he whispered to her. "You know more than you're telling me." He took a breath. "What are you hiding from me? And, why are you doing it?"

"I'm not," she stopped only to resume immediately, "hiding anything from you."

"I'll need more information from you before I can decide," he said. "Won't you share it with me?"

"No," she replied, though smiling at him in a flirtatious way this time.

"But you are so young –" and he was going to add, "you died too young," but at the last moment he stopped himself, for that was not very thoughtful on his part, and she might take offense. So, he just asked her, "Aren't you happy to be back here?"

"No!" she said again, and that "No" sounded like the crack of a whip in the clear August air.

"All right. Have it your way," said Ivain, resigned to the idea that he would not get anything else out of Allegra.

She had started to play with some blades of grass near her, picking them, tearing them out of the earth, and twisting them around her fingers, until they became rings round each one of them. Ivain stopped following her words. He heard sounds coming faintly from her lips, but his thoughts were elsewhere. Finally he said rather annoyed, "They think of everything, these people, don't they?"

"Yes," she answered as she looked away from him, into that space he had just come from.

That thought made him mad.

"Well, I am staying," he said resolutely. "That's all there is to it. I'm staying. And if, in this 'written script' there's a loophole somewhere, I'll find it. I've got to give myself that chance. I owe it to myself."

Allegra would not give up. She looked at him determinedly and said, "You will still have a chance in a little while when you see France. She won't recognize you, and she'll ask you who you are. Then you can either give up, or enter 'the script' and walk into center stage with both eyes open. Think about it."

Ivain was struck by her words. To begin with, he could not believe that his wife, his France, would not recognize him. That was not possible. How could she have forgotten him so soon? What was this woman up to? In any case, he was adamant to meet his wife again and see for himself. Later on, he would look back and realize that what Allegra told him was accurate, down to the exact moment he entered a life that was not his own, but seemed like his own; down to the minute details of how he combed his hair and cut his nails. This new life would take him into paths unknown to him, would lead him into discoveries he could not possibly think would pertain in any way to him or to what he had been. But there he was, desperately wanting to discover his past life in the present one, not knowing yet what was awaiting him. At this time he simply said to Allegra, "I've too many regrets about having died young. I'm determined to stay."

She looked at him and murmured a couple of sentences that again meant nothing to him, for he even forgot them. But those same words would come back and haunt him later on, though he could never explain to himself either his blindness or his unwillingness to hear her. Or alternatively, he heard what she said, but it did not make a dent in his perception. It would not have been any different had he been both blind and deaf; and there were many occasions when Ivain would wonder if it was possible that the Godlet had blinded him intentionally before meting out some sort of unthinkable and irrational punishment. As for now, he repeated to her, "I am staying."

"As you wish," she said and straightening herself she seemed to embody all the virtues of efficiency. As she got up she continued, "We better take my car and drive to the house. I'm supposed to have met you at the train station, picked you up and driven you back. I live at Le Plessis now. A month ago, I got myself hired as a secretary to France's husband, in preparation for your arrival. You and I are friends from New York, the city where you live, and where you just came from. Here's your ticket, your passport, and your wallet. Plus both your bank statements. And just for your own information, you have returned on a Sunday afternoon." She handed him some papers along with a brown leather wallet. The bank statements were open and he could not fail to see that both in France and in the United States he had generous accounts waiting for him. "More than generous," he thought, as he quickly put them away in a back pocket.

"France and her husband are waiting for us." She paused a moment, then breathlessly said, "Are you coming?"

He wanted to ask who his wife's husband was, but something made him keep silent. "There's always time for bad news," he thought to himself. Finally he said, "I would rather walk back to the house alone. I hope that's all right with you? I need to get my thoughts together."

"That's all right," she said, but he could tell she was rather annoyed. "In that case I better tell you a few things about yourself. You are an undiscovered actor. But, as the understudy of an important character, you're taking your role very seriously," and here she winked at him. "You're coming to Le Plessis to do research on the late Ivain La Baille's manuscripts and papers on Julius Caesar. You are doing all this in order to better prepare yourself for the part you 'hope' to be playing in New York one day. Do you understand?"

"My papers are here?" he asked, astonished.

"They were brought here by your wife. She wished to arrange them before sending them on to the Butler Library at Columbia University," Allegra said as she started to caress her neck lightly with her right hand.

"Why were they not left in New York?" He was rather perturbed. But why should he be perturbed, he wondered.

"The country is a better place to sort things out. I'm sure you would agree with that," she stopped, and seemed bored with the conversation. "More leisure and less noise," she added as an afterthought.

"Of course," said Ivain, rather irritated. After all, his papers were precious and France should not have taken the chance of losing them. "Are they all here?" he asked.

"Whatever is here is here, and has been put in a safe place in the living room," she answered him quickly, and turned her head.

"Well, that's a relief. Thank you," he said, smiling at her, and feeling his fears were out of place.

"Not at all," she said, then went on. "Now remember that

your name is John O. Elliab, but your friends call you Jack, I call you Johnny, and some people call you simply Jo! Remember also that you are walking part of the way because you said you needed the exercise."

She was talking to him as she, herself, started to walk toward a nearby place, half hidden by overgrown bushes whose name he could not remember. Then he heard the familiar noise of a car starting, and a moment later an old Renault came out of its hiding place, and as it passed him, Allegra shouted, "I've all your luggage in the trunk of my car, Johnny." Then laughing, she added, "You'd better get used to your nickname."

"Wait!" he said, and when Allegra stopped the car he ran up to her, "What does the O. in my name stand for?"

"It's up to you to find that out," she answered, and went off at a high speed, lifting a cloud of dust into the air.

He followed the car with his eyes, until it went out of sight, then sat down on a large, dark rock. He began to mull over the fact that he was Jack or John or Johnny O. Elliab, and under that name, he had the lead in "a script" written by a Godlet, and was playing the part that had been assigned to him. The thought simply horrified him. Why was he in this predicament? How had he gotten there? Yes, he had signed the paper, but was that all that there was to go on? He got up shaking his fist toward the sky as he shouted, "I am my own man. Do you hear me?" He looked around, but the countryside was absolutely still. Nothing was moving. There were not even the songs of birds or crickets anymore. He began to think of ways to prove what he had just said. "If I lift my right arm to my shoulder, and then my left arm to my other shoulder, and if I jump up and down a few times, then I'll show the Godlet that I am free to do such things as I please." And he began at once to lift one arm, and then the other one, and jump up and down until he lost count of his jumping. When he stopped, he marveled at the good shape he was in. He wasn't out of breath, and actually felt like starting to jump all over again, when the thought that this might be exactly what he was supposed to do stopped him. "This is too simple," he said. He should do something that was unexpected, something out of the ordinary that both the Director or the Writer had not thought of. He was supposed to be an actor, and as an actor he was free to improvise. He would improvise a speech on an absurd topic, at the same time as he would do a balancing act on a rope. Or alternatively, he would improvise an absurd balancing act on a rope, and simultaneously recite a well thought out speech. The possibilities open to him were infinite. But again he was seized by the feeling that, no matter what he did, that one act he would perform was the act he was supposed to do. In quiet desperation he lay down on the road and began to count anything his eyes rested on. Clouds, trees, blades of grass, pebbles. Then he realized that he could not go through his second life like that or it would be simply Hell, and then he thought that maybe he was sent to be in Hell. But as soon as he had decided that he could not possibly stay on Earth under those conditions, Ivain swore to himself, right then and there, that he would never give up his fight against "the written script" he was in. He would fight it subtly, more subtly. It would be guerrilla warfare, more than a declared war. He would make his hits against it when he was sure he had some small chance of success, and not one moment before, always remembering that the Godlet was a formidable opponent and the director a well-rehearsed instructor. He started to walk toward his house, trying not to let the despair that had entered his mind take hold of him.

Weeks later, when he had calmed down and was not any longer in the throes of that sudden, tormented discovery, he would look back and remember his walk toward his country house, and would wonder why he had not given up the struggle at the beginning, as suggested by Allegra. He never resolved the mystery except for the fact that he had accepted the challenge of "the written script". And from the first instant "the written script" had become the focus of his second life on earth. He would never forget he was in it. He carried it on his own person, as if it had been an amulet either in his breast pocket or, on elegant evenings, wrapped in soft indigo silk tucked in his yellow cummerbund. Moreover, he even began to feel the need to know it was there. It was a welcome reminder of his struggle, so that, instead of rejecting it, he tried to befriend it, analyzing situations down to the most minute details of his own words, as they made themselves known to him; paying attention to the sound and resonance of his own voice, all the while as he hid the horror deep down, within himself. Now, instead of pushing it away, he caressed it, cuddled it, turned it around, looked at it from every angle, to see if he could find a perfect sphere where there were only square corners. He hugged it, and generally nurtured it within himself as he would nurture a precious orchid found discarded in the desert's sand. He began to think of it as a friend he could sometimes share a secret with, as if it had been a person within a person, a soul within a soul, when in fact he ultimately knew it was his nemesis. But if he was going to walk outside "the script," he had to hide his motives and objectives. He began to fill his head daily with the most outlandish thoughts in the hope of finding that corridor through which he could escape. And he would lie awake at night and devise scheme upon scheme, only to refute them in the early hours of the morning, keeping all of them as ideas, so as to be absolutely sure that they were not part of "the script" – for it was the spoken words that counted, not his unspoken thoughts; actions and not inaction; awareness and not sleep; the ancient Egyptian God Ptah, and not the slumberous milk of red poppies.

ROSAY

"My book is myself."
Pascal

THE walk back to Le Plessis seemed to Ivain to have been the longest in his life, not because of its actual length, for he was only five miles from his home, but because he spent time looking now to his right side, now to his left, incredulous that he was actually back on earth. He stopped to gaze at an empty bird's nest as if it had been the first time he had seen one, then looked inside the hollow of a basswood tree, which had a large beehive in it, then at a spider's perfect web, marveling all the time at its maker's patience and precision.

"How wonderful it all is, but for the fact that I know that I am trapped in a strange and unknown story about myself, that is revealed to me as I live it," he whispered, adding, "if only I could be a child again, with all the privileges and carelessness of ignorance." And he touched the light, insubstantial threads of the web in front of him, placing his thumb a bit too closely to a large brown spider with a red cross on his back, that quickly bit him but, amazingly, he felt no pain. "Like the fire on my arms," he said. "No pain. Well, that must be one of the advantages of being a dead soul." And the fact that he was seeing and hearing again, and that his sense of smell and touch had returned, seemed such a miracle to him that for a while he forgot all about his predicament, lost in the astonishing beauty of the moment.

It was a peaceful and quiet summer morning, and with his eyes he began to explore the boundaries of a little wooded area near him, when, out of it rose a flock of golden pheasants and, flying low over his head, they landed on the other side of the road, near the dry bed of a brook. A brook he knew would come alive with the first rain of the fall. On another part of his walk he brushed against a wooden fence covered with blackberries, and picking a ripe dark one, he tasted the sweetness of the sun within. A few minutes later he saw a vast field of alfalfa, like a green river meandering in and out of a wheat field, swaying in the breeze that had just risen. In another field nearby, white and black cows, Holstein stock, lay as if painted on a bucolic canvas, under a few oaks and acacia or ash trees. And, upon discovering a tunnel that undoubtedly some child had cut through a bramble of thorny bushes, he could not resist the impulse of passing through it, though first taking the precaution of protecting his face with one hand, for he wanted to feel again, for a fleeting moment, the carelessness of a child. Throughout the walk he was accompanied by the repetitive coos of doves, the cries of swallows and the chirping of sparrows, which made him smile. But, upon hearing the cuckoo's song, still smiling, he put his hand in his pocket to see if there was any change there, for if he could find a few coins he could count on having money for the rest of the year, and he was happy to touch a two franc silver piece with the tip of his fingers. Later in the day, after he had heard the appalling news that was awaiting him at Le Plessis, he was to look back on this walk as the walk of a happy-go-lucky opium-smoking drifter, and thereafter believed that on that walk he had seen a halo around the sun, and a large rainbow on the clear horizon. He also believed that on that day, among the cows lying in the field, there had been one with two heads, and among the flock of golden pheasants, there had been a hawk holding a snake in his claws. Of the latter prodigy or portent he was never quite sure, though he never doubted the first one, and would sometimes swear by it. It also led him to meditate about the juxtaposition of identical time in two different spaces, for that morning at the exact time Mme Kamiska was giving him the "green disk" inside the stone house, and he believed himself to be the most fortunate of men, Allegra was already waiting outside at the roadside, ready to tell him how he had been deceived. And now he was walking leisurely, happily unaware of the disasters that were taking place at exactly the same time in a space so close, and yet so far from him. "Too many good auguries early in the day," he thought. "I should have prepared myself for unsettling news." And the moment he arrived in the sleepy village of Rosay, he began to see something was not as it should be, for the village was in turmoil.

He stood still, amazed to see people running to and fro, gesticulating with the palms of their hands high above their shoulders, while nodding and shaking their heads. He thought of Mme Kamiska, and suddenly becoming anxious, started to run toward Le Plessis, afraid it would no longer be there, but he stopped before reaching the gate, for there were a few police cars parked outside it. He lifted his eyes, and in the distance, rising magnificently above its surrounding wall, he saw his huge, old white house, beautifully proportioned, with its graceful verandas, large windows and its glass front door open to let the sun in. The very loveliness of his home made him feel troubled. He would have liked to ask someone why the police were there. He looked among the people who had now gathered in small groups of two or three, and quickly recognized George Villers, the carpenter, with his huge beret, and Edward Polaski, the man who forged iron with a dexterity known only to few, with his floppy muddy pants, and Claude Arc, biting hard on his cigarette and holding the villagers around him spellbound. But then, Claude had been the Mayor of the village for as long as Ivain could remember, and knew how to use words in a primitive but effective way, casting a spell on one and all. Claude Arc could talk as easily about birds and their habits as well as he could talk about the habits of men. Turning around he also saw Pierre Jean Boissy, the antique dealer with a shady reputation, who would always smile and pretend to be a friend in order to get to see the inside of one's house, so as – or so the villagers whispered – to rob it at a later date. "Not unlike those dogs that seem friendly and wag their tails, but when you go to caress them, they bite your hand," Ivain thought. Pierre Jean Boissy was talking to Bernard Faverolle, a painter nicknamed "Dudu Picasso," for he would take different objects from the master's canvases, and place them in his paintings as if they were his own inventions. Ivain, himself, had seen perfect copies of the master's vases, knives, pots and pans, glasses, fish, horses, dancing girls, lonely noses, large lips, and detached arms and legs placed in perfectly painted blue skies, as if they were floating out of the master's orbit into Dudu's personal one. "They deserve each other," thought Ivain as he looked at both men.

Two women passed by in the street. Aurelie Madeleine with a full bag of laundry on the back of her bicycle, and Josephine Lazar with her gray poodle in her arms, and they both stopped to join the group of men. Both women had been in the same class with Ivain in the elementary school run by Mme Fleury, and they knew him well, but now they nodded good day, without even smiling, treating him like a stranger who had no business in the village. He was amazed. How was he going to find out what had happened inside Le Plessis? He was afraid of approaching anyone, knowing fully well that the Briards had a natural distrust of outsiders, for in the not too distant past they had been used to living in châteaux where all their needs were taken care of. Inside those thick walls that once surrounded their ancestors, the Briards had made bread from their own fields of wheat, and wine from their own vineyards. Their butter and sausages had come from the herds of animals they had bred themselves. In winter they still knitted sweaters and bed covers from the wool of their own sheep flocks. Those were the Briards – lonely, unfriendly and mistrustful. Ivain knew this about them and now he pressed both hands behind his back and opening his fingers wide, he leaned on the smooth, highly polished wood fence that was facing the iron gate of his old house. He glanced around. A murmur of voices could be heard, like the buzzing of a newly flown swarm of bees, but that was all. Nothing he could string together to make a whole sentence. Out of the group, a man he had never seen before approached him. He was wearing blue jeans, a short sleeved shirt, and had a handkerchief tied around his thick neck.

"Passing through?" he asked, in a voice that betrayed curiosity more than annoyance, as he removed his handkerchief and passed it twice over his forehead.

"No," Ivain answered, trying not to betray his agitation. "I'm a guest of the family," and he pointed to the wrought iron doors not far from them.

"You've arrived at a bad time," the man said, and leaning forward he whispered in his ear, "a theft –" leaving the words suspended in the air, as if they were autumn leaves held up by a current of air, and then repeating them a bit louder, "a theft."

"Really?" said Ivain, trying not to lose his outward calm. "Were precious objects taken?"

"Furniture," the man said. "I think I heard the Mayor say furniture."

"Ah," said Ivain, "so that's what's all about. A theft." At that moment the iron gate opened from the inside and out came Jacqueline and Anatole Tibault, the maid and the caretaker of Le Plessis, whom Ivain himself had chosen the last time he had been in France. Anatole, nicknamed *la bonne bouche,* was a happy go lucky, fat man, whose belly shook every time he laughed, and Jacqueline, his wife, nicknamed *fillette*, was one of the thinnest women Ivain had ever seen. He was glad to find them still there. They both looked at him for a moment, but it was obvious they did not recognize him. They turned their backs and went straight to Claude Arc, to show him two small red ink drawings that they had just found lying on the grass in front of their gate-house. They held them high above their heads so everyone could see them. They were pictures of women draped in long, pleated dresses representing allegorically the muses of Poetry and Philosophy.

"These," Anatole said, "are tiny fragments of the riches the thieves stole from the house." And it was as if his words had the power to open a hidden cave where remnants of forgotten treasures had been left behind. Everyone now began to bring out of their pockets, or from under their jackets, little pieces of various and sundry objects that they had found outside the walls of *le petit château*, the name the villagers affectionately called Le Plessis. Polaski brought two brass knobs out of his pockets that must have belonged to some large piece of furniture, and a piece of a wooden leg that was undoubtedly part of an antique table, for it was full of wood worms. Everyone extended their arms and opened their hands to take and hold the objects, making some remarks as they passed them on to the next person. Then Villers came out with a small paper bag of glass fragments which had been part of the famous collection of antique Baccarat that the La Baille family had begun with Ivain's great-grandfather.

Not far away, a person was looking at the map of Rosay and explaining it to a farmer from the next village.

"See," he was saying. "There's the river Yerres, there's the island where once there was a boat house, there's the iron bridge that goes over it. And here are the walls of the house. The island, the left bank of the river, these fields and these farm houses, they all belong to the family." And he was pointing here and there, trying not to touch the paper with his fingers covered with black paint.

Aurelie Madeleine had more than laundry in her bag, and now she opened it up and took out remnants of Limoges plates, as well as little bits of crockery and earthenware, and pieces of white porcelain that once must have belonged to a larger set of pretty maidens being pursued by winged youths. Then a miniscule hand, a delicate shoe, part of a basket of roses, and a tiny pretty face without the forehead came out of the handkerchief of another person.

Some people were talking furtively and, from time to time, giving side glances toward Ivain, who had approached the group, and was now standing just behind the inner circle.

Claude Arc looked carefully at what was left of the objects, and inspected everything as if he, and not the gendarmes, were conducting the inquest. But that was to be expected. Few people, Ivain knew, had respect for the gendarmes of their village who were there, for the most part, to fill out the necessary papers on the daily car accidents on the highway, more than to solve any serious crimes. On the other hand, Claude Arc knew his village and its people well, and what he said was always taken seriously by one and all. Holding the remnant of the chair leg in his hand, he said, "As I see it, the thieves came with only one thought on their minds – to steal good furniture and good china. The murder was an unplanned event, I'm sure. Something that must've surprised them, too."

Ivain was appalled. Someone had been killed. Who could that person be? An acquaintance? A friend? Someone he knew well? He looked again at the Mayor who had paused for a moment only to resume.

"Now, I know for a fact that, though perhaps some among us may enter the house of a neighbor and take something or other," and he gave a quick look in the direction of M. Boissy, "no local people would dare steal from this family. And no one in this village, would murder to steal. But, I do think the murderer, or murderers, must have gotten help from a local person. How else would they've known when and how to enter the house? Someone must have told them that the proprietors were spending the night in Paris, that Anatole and Jacqueline were visiting their children, and that the only person left in the house wouldn't interfere." He stopped to light his cigarette which had gone out, and placed it again in between his lips.

"Someone must've had the house under surveillance, and known the habits of the people living there pretty well, I would say." He inhaled the smoke deeply, so deeply in fact that all the words in his next sentence came out accompanied by puffs of smoke. "And, if the perpetrators were *brocantes*, then they had great knowledge of antiques or they must have brought someone with them who knew real porcelain or glass or tables from copies. This is how it's generally done in these parts." Everyone agreed and nodded. "Now, no one would come to my house and steal 'cause, outside of my grandmother's old chairs, I've nothing that would interest the flea market in Paris." And he laughed a deep and heartfelt laugh which Ivain remembered a few days later, when someone told him that Claude Arc's grandmother's chairs had been taken while he was milking the cows and his wife was feeding the chickens. As for now, Anatole, leaning close to the Mayor, began to talk to him as if he were sharing a deep, dark secret, and Ivain moved a bit forward, straining to hear what they were saying.

"The theft," Anatole said, "is more important than we realized. Four antique bureaux were taken from the living room." He stopped and looked at his wife, who was nodding.

Ivain felt a shiver going through him, as if he had been touched by a cold, icy hand. He remembered Allegra's words about his papers. His papers were safe, she had said. They had been placed in the living room. Where in the living room? Inside a strong box? There was a strong box at Le Plessis, but not in the living room. It was in the library. "Oh no, no –" he said loud enough for some of the people to hear him and turn around. And just then Jacqueline started to talk, picking up where Anatole had left off.

"Madame is beside herself," she said. "The papers and manuscripts of poor M. La Baille are gone too."

"How come?" someone asked.

"They'd been placed inside the drawers for added security," Jacqueline explained in her simple way, without a trace of irony.

Ivain, listening in silence, felt his heart swelling inside him, its beats increasing wildly, as his eyes became red, though they shed no tears. He felt incensed that a great event that could have tremendous consequences for him could happen haphazardly. He would have liked to interrupt her and ask for specific details, but she had resumed talking.

"The only person who saw the thieves was old Natalie," she said, "and Natalie was killed near the alarm box. Her body is now on the late master's bed, waiting to be taken away." And as she said this, she wiped a tear away from her cheek.

Ivain knew then with certainty that all the happiness he felt at the thought of being back on earth had now vanished. People were still talking near him, but he was barely listening to what they were saying. Only an offhand comment, made by Faverolle, reached his ears. It was from this comment that he learned that the name of the owner of the beautiful manor was Monsieur Alfred. Monsieur had married the "La Baille widow" just a few weeks after the Professor's tragic death. It was only then, that Ivain understood that his wife France had married his cousin Fabian shortly after his death, as predicted in her dream.

After hearing the numbing news, Ivain sat down in front of a large stone, shaped like an oblong egg, used as a marker to delineate the end of one property and the beginning of another. He sat there, unable to think or move. His mind was a blank, penetrated only by the repetitious song of birds, the coughing of old people, and the buzzing of bees not far from him. It was in this place, surrounded by nettles, rose-colored eglantines and hawthorns, that shortly thereafter Allegra found him. She found a man overcome by consternation and afraid to come inside Le Plessis.

"Is all my writing gone?" he asked as he threw his arms into the air making a large circle.

"They have been stolen, yes – but that doesn't mean they're gone forever," Allegra replied, looking at him as she would look at a child who had lost his most precious toy.

"Where are they?" he continued, as he tried to control himself, knowing full well that his pain was apparent. He knew that she knew all about his pain, and though he was ashamed of it, he could not help showing it. She took his hand in hers, and spoke to him in soft tones. He heard her words floating toward him. "We must find a way to get them back. Someone has gotten them. It's just a matter of finding the thieves." And she looked at him with a look that seemed to say, "Why didn't you follow my suggestion when I first met you, before the plot thickened?" He got up slowly, as if his body had acquired a weight of its own, not corresponding to his real weight, and asked her if there was a Mac computer inside the country house. She shook her head, but added that she knew where to find one. "The newspaper lady in the next village has a Mac Classic," she said, "and for a few francs she'll let the customers use it."

"Will you take me there?" He was afraid of disturbing her, but he needed to know what was on that "green disk" he was carrying.

"Now?" She stared at him with a puzzled look. He said, "Yes, now," and was ready to apologize when she said, "All right," and turning on her heels, she walked toward the car.

On the way to the village they were both silent, though from time to time Allegra placed her right hand on his as she sighed deeply, and he found this to be not a displeasing show of affection. He even began to wonder about the inexplicable fate that had brought them together. Wondering about her name, wondering about her past. Wondering how she was related to that infamous Count. Was she his daughter or sister? But those were questions he did not feel he could ask her, though he realized he would have liked to know more about this woman, whose eyes seemed to look at him with a disquieting intensity from the very first moment they had met. But he did not know how to broach the subject, so he kept silent. Finally they arrived at the village, and Ivain saw the newspaper shop near the Romanesque church. The church was a handsome building done with large gray and burnt Siena colored stones. The same architecture and the same stones one finds in so many other churches in the region, but their large number does not diminish the grandeur of their appearance.

He got out of the car, and entered the minuscule store cluttered with newspapers, pencils, colorful gift wrapping papers, and candies. He paid a few francs for the use of the computer to a typical French country woman, with short, badly cut hair, and a smiling face. She took the money and put it immediately in a large pocket in her apron, and then pointed to the Mac in a corner of the room. He went to work immediately, concentrating on sliding the disk into the slot on the lower left side of the machine, and began to look attentively at the screen. Perhaps there were clues there that might give him a fighting chance. He waited a few minutes for the computer to warm up, and finally there appeared a single file on the desk-top that said: "A PLAY." Fascinated by this discovery and with a sudden nervous elation, he quickly opened the file, believing to have found the *sine qua non* without which he could never understand his present predicament. His future was hidden in there, he was sure of that. But what he saw left him perplexed. There were pages and pages of scrambled up letters separated in such a way as to make him think of words. But, if those were words, he did not recognize them. He went back to the beginning of the first page, where he noticed a single sentence in the middle of the page, and wondered if it might be the title of the play.

"Amkli jn jugnuk lihu eme idksl"

He looked at it, trying to understand in what language it was written. Were those English words hidden in a secret code or words written in an alphabet that had gone astray, and had been lost in past ages? In any case it was beyond him to decipher them. Yet, he was sure his destiny was there, facing him now. He began going down page after page again, and after reaching the end of page one hundred and twenty, toward the end of the file, he finally found words he could read.

Under the heading of "Predictions" he saw four phrases, which were the same that France had repeated to him on that last day:

"A Virtuous Roman"
"A Sea Wave"
"A Trinket"
"O"

In time he would discover what they all meant, discover the inner meaning of each and every one of them, and with it discover that the JanKam Co. had given new depth to the use of dramatic irony, but for now they were just meaningless words, floating on the screen.

Further on, he saw there were rules and regulations written down for the uninitiated in the art of play-writing. Ordinarily, Ivain would have thought this tedious reading, but now he concentrated on understanding the essence of every word, turning them over in his head, and trying to remember the first, second, and third meanings if there were any. He read carefully what he was seeing, as his eyes became clouded by a veil of tears, for he was sure that his life depended on it.

It started out by describing the different parts that make up a play, from the "Introduction," which is called "Exposition," to the "Main Deceit," which comes right after the exposition and engenders other deceits and complications in a formation of cause and effect, until the "Climax" is reached, and from there to the inevitable "Denouement," which led to the end. Period. It also went on explaining that, up until the "Climax," every possible road is open to the principal character, but after the "Climax" there is only one road that can be taken, which will lead to either a happy or unhappy ending. A marriage or a death, depending whether it is a comedy or a tragedy. There were references to different plays – Tragedies, Comedies, Tragic-comedies, Historical-tragedies, Historical-tragic-comical plays, Buffoon plays, dramas, melodramas, Commedia dell'Arte, and so on and so forth. And a note on how the three laws of unities of Aristotle on play-writing would not be taken into consideration in this one play. What play was that, he cautiously wondered? Then he remembered that Mme Kamiska had said his was a romantic story in the making. Was it going to be a romantic story? The authors knew the ending, but he, the protagonist, did not know it. He had to discover every passage as it came to be, and had to discover the intrigue of the play, as it played itself out, and the end, as it ended.

He looked again at the screen in front of him and, though it was now just a great blank, he realized he had not reached the end of the page yet. He took the mouse in his hand and went down the screen, and soon enough he found one last, unfinished sentence. It was a personal memorandum that Mme Kamiska had made for herself. It said, "Set him up, and –" then there was just a blank space, followed by some scrambled vowels and consonants that were meaningless. The first words that came to Ivain's mind were, "– and bring him down?" Is that what they were up to at the JanKam Co.? If they were following the structure of a well-constructed play, he would have to watch out for one set of words above all. His full name revealed to a living person. That was the key! How were they going to set him up so as to make him say those fateful words he did not know, for he could not conceive of any condition wherein he would ever say them. Torture was out of the question, since he had discovered the absence of pain on his morning walk. But he had to be careful not to let his impulsive character take over, or it would end badly for him. He was sure they, Father and Daughter, relied on that too, but he was going to surprise them. He was going to walk carefully, measuring all his steps and looking over his shoulder. With this in mind, he gazed at Mme Kamiska's words for a long time, as if it was a Gordian knot he had to untie or the Sphinx's riddle, but then he became bored and taking out the "green disk" he carefully placed it again in his breast pocket. He would never again look at the "green disk," until the night he knew with an absolute certainty what he would find in it, and when that moment came, he was not disappointed. As for now, he turned to Allegra and said to her he was ready to go to Le Plessis, and find out what had actually happened there. She winked at him, as if trying to give him courage, for she believed nothing had been irrevocably lost, and she said so out loud. "Besides, what value could his writing have for the thieves?" she went on. How did she know there were thieves in the plural? he asked, wondering what part, if any, she had played in it. But she replied that the bureaux were too heavy for a single man to lift all alone, and from what she had overheard, it must have been a well-organized band that had come in with a truck. He agreed, and tried to be pleasant to her on the trip back. He asked, "Why, out of all the souls out there, are you the one assigned to me?"

"Perhaps," she replied, "because I was once a shepherdess on Mount Olympus, or perhaps because I was once a court lady who could play both the clavichord and the flute, or perhaps because, I was a follower of Venus Ericina, from Mount Erice in Sicily, and Venus herself has taught me how to love men."

He looked at her in profile, and noticed that she was repeatedly biting her lower lip which had now become sanguine red.

"Love must play a great part in your life," he said to her, to which she replied, "I've often been told that I am a child-woman, or a woman-child, depending on where I am at the time." And she started to giggle and play with the car making it zig-zag this way and that way, going at great speed for she knew nothing could harm them. "I've also been told," she went on, still giggling, "that I'm one of those persons who can't stand rejection."

"She must be the worthy daughter of Count Cagliostro," thought Ivain, convinced that he was right. "If that's true, then I better stay away from her," and for the first time since his return, he felt his eyes burning, and a strange twitch around his mouth. Allegra's words had filled him with an irrational fear. She pretended not to notice his silence, and went on talking. "Rejection has always been my undoing." She glanced at him at the same time as she placed her hand on his left thigh, and pressed slightly down. Ivain blushed and felt again a stirring in his body as if it were resurrecting, but he stopped himself from responding in any way, for there was something in this woman

65

that was both dangerous and at the same time languid and inviting. He tried to concentrate on France. He was eager to see her again. The memories of his wife, whom he had left so young and so unprepared, still had a hold over him, as strong as ever. The fact that she was now married to his cousin could not be helped, he felt, for after all when one dies, one has no power over the ones that remain behind. But, no matter how much Ivain tried to rationalize his wife's new marriage, he could not stop a certain furtive feeling of anguish and depression from creeping up within him. After all, she had been his wife for a number of years, and should have waited at least two, three years before going into another marriage, not rush into it. And to marry his cousin of all people! Almost anyone else would have been easier to deal with emotionally. "But that is what happens when one is no longer around," he whispered to himself, and he concluded that up to that moment, everything he had left behind seemed to have had some unexpected change for the worse. And that thought did not make him happy.

LE PLESSIS

"The die is cast."
Julius Caesar

AFTER reaching Le Plessis, and leaving the car outside, Allegra took Ivain by the hand, and led him inside the wrought iron gates. Once inside his former property, he gazed at the gardens and at his old house and was suddenly overwhelmed by a surge of emotions that engulfed him with memories. Standing before him were the remains of old Roman statues he had collected with infinite care, and had placed on the front lawn in a perfect semi-circle. Now, some were missing their arms, some had only part of their legs and feet, and one had lost its head altogether, submerged as they were, by an abundance of flowery weeds that grew between the stones, in the cracks made by alternate winters' freezing and summers' scalding. Behind them stood some tall, cast iron vases, on pale brick pedestals. The vases had acquired a sheen of reddish-brown patina on their outer surfaces with green moss patches here and there, and were now filled with long, delicate rose geraniums that fell on each side in gracious abandon. Further back, there were the yellowish stone walls, ten feet high, encircling the whole property, still holding up well, though he could see a certain neglect in the variety of grass and small wild flowers, growing on its slanted roof top. But inside the walls, his favorite century-old ash, pine, maple and oak trees were still there, towering above him, and closer to the house, a few great round vases were filled with orange or lemon trees in clusters of three. He took a deep breath, and smelled their pungent perfume in the air. The whole place had an air of mystery around it, as if it had lived for centuries draped in a large spider's web. That feeling of nostalgia was broken only when Ivain looked up near the *lavoir*, or laundry house, toward the back of the English garden, and saw a well-dressed man talking to four or five policemen and an equal number of gendarmes. The man had his back turned to him, but Ivain recognized his cousin Fabian from the cut of his suit, and the way he had placed his left hand in his pocket, a habit he had since childhood. His first impulse was to run to Fabian to share with him the miracle that had been bestowed upon him, but on reflection, Ivain turned to Allegra and whispered to her, "I would like to say my last good byes to poor Natalie alone. Just one last moment with her. Can you get me into the house without anyone seeing me?"

"Before saying hello to your host or hostess?" she asked, as she cast a glance at the laundry house, whose simple beauty was partially hidden in foliage of different greens.

"Yes," said Ivain, "I love them both of course." He breathed deeply and continued, "But, I'll see them later on." As soon as Ivain said those words, he realized he was being paradoxical, since the word "love" had been said with a vague feeling of hate. But Allegra did not seem to have noticed it, for she smiled and said, "I'll be right back," and began to run toward his cousin. She reached him and, bending close to him, placed her hand over her mouth, cupping it to muffle the sound of her words, as she whispered something into his ear. He nodded a few times, though never turning his head around. Then Ivain noticed that their fingers were touching, just slightly, but enough to make him wonder. A few moments later, Allegra ran back to him, saying, "We'll have to sneak around the back of the house, and enter through the kitchen."

They began to walk together hand in hand, over the gravel, trying as hard as they could to tiptoe, as if they were conspirators, talking quietly, and answering each other with words that had meaning but almost no sound. His mind was elsewhere. What had Allegra whispered in his cousin's ear? Had she mentioned that the actor from New York had arrived? Had she told Fabian she had taken him to the village? Had she tried to find out if there was any news about the theft and his papers? He wanted to ask, but felt that if she had something to tell him, she would do so. She was not the kind of woman to hold back. As he was thinking these thoughts, he heard clear, light footsteps coming from the side of the house. Since they were near the kitchen door, he quickly opened it and, taking Allegra with him, hid inside it. But curiosity got the better of him and, going near the window, he slowly lifted a corner of the white curtain. He saw a few people pass by; among them was France. She did not see either of them, and walked straight toward Fabian. "Fabian's wife." Allegra said to him, as she held his arm, "Don't forget it." He did not answer her directly, but as he turned his back, he said, "I'm going up," and began to walk in the direction of his old room.

As he went through the house, he was amazed to see how much better it looked then when he had left it. Then it was in a ruinous state, with the fireplaces filled with the honey that dropped from the bees' hives inside the chimneys. He remembered how in winter, when a great number of bees died, they dried up in each room, and with the slightest breeze they would flutter away, leaving behind the delicate odor of honeysuckles and wild acacias. Now, everything looked well kept and immaculately clean. The ceilings had no more leaks, and though he had not paid attention when he had first come into the property, he was sure that the old slate roof had been replaced by a new one. Each of the eight rooms he walked through was decorated more tastefully than the one before it, all in the spirit of the 18th century, which was the era when the house had been originally built.

The architect had been a nobleman who, while travelling to Vaux le Vicomte, had lost his way, and having come across the village of Rosay, had been enchanted by the songs of the numerous species of birds he found there. "Many more," he wrote in a letter to his wife, "than in any other part of France." Not long after that, he had ordered his foreman to build a hunting lodge there, not to hunt the birds, but as a place to stay from time to time, to hear "the stories they had to tell of other times and other worlds."

As Ivain walked by the library, he stopped and looked in, and he remembered his father, for that was his favorite room. Often, he used to see him there, sitting on the large comfortable Tudor chair, holding a book in his hand, reading, always reading. The subject did not matter much, since his father's taste was eclectic. He read, or so he told Ivain, "to discover the 'kernel of truth' about the unanswered questions," which he tried to find in a singular phrase or in an unusual metaphor. He always read authors in alphabetical order, and when he died he had gone through the first half of those whose names started with M. The last book he read, Maupassant's short stories, was still open on his lap when he bent forward and died. In his life he had also had the time to go through all the works of Machiavelli, Mallarmé, and Malraux.

In the living room Ivain looked for the special corner that he associated with his mother, for when he was young, she used to hold him on her lap on the little white silk sofa, a sofa that had been placed in the attic long ago. Here and there he recognized a familiar object, and conflicting emotions would swell within him, but there was much that was missing too, and he wondered what had happened to a particularly memorable portrait or to a favorite china vase or to an old chess board. A beloved Hopper was missing and, with it, its silent New York streets and the red front of a store. The Guardis, with all the sadness of Venice, were no longer there either. Nor were the collections of drawings from Rembrandt down to Max Ernst.

His family's paintings had always meant much to Ivain, above all because they reproduced that absolute beauty that he could not find anywhere else, except in a museum, but then one could not touch or live with them, and that was a pity.

To distract himself from the oppression of those memories, he began to walk faster. He now reached the brilliantly shining oak staircase and his childhood came back to him in all its fullness. He used to run up those steps breathlessly only to be confronted by a dark corridor with a multitude of doors, all closed, and he never knew which one to open. That had been his childhood fear. That had been his later life's fear too, always trying to find the right door to open, until the very end of his life when, for a moment, he thought he had found it in his writing.

He looked up and saw he was in front of his old bedroom. He asked Allegra to wait outside, and went in alone, closing the door carefully behind him. Once inside, he tiptoed toward the bed, trying as hard as he could not to make any noise. There in his massive dark ebony bed, with elegant carved angels on each of the four posts, lay the dead Natalie. The contrast of the elaborate Spanish bed, with its canopy of rich brocade curtains falling on each side, and the frail body of Natalie on top of his old mattress, was startling. Old Natalie looked as if she had been caught dead in the middle of being very much alive, with her dress still spotted with blood at the height of her chest. All this was too much for Ivain and he was overcome by sadness. He sat down in a wing chair at the foot of the bed. He was not only overwhelmed for the loss of this dear, devoted family member, but also for all that he had lost that very morning. What was he going to do now? Why had he really been sent back? Why was he so aware of all the burdens of life again, when it had been so easy not being aware of anything? As he was lost in these thoughts, he noticed that Natalie's eyes were half open, and going near her, he gently closed her eye lids, saying, "Go gentle soul. Who would ever have imagined that your end would be as violent as mine?"

As he pronounced these words, he saw the shadow of Natalie rising from the bed and, smoothing down one corner of her dress with her left hand, she said, "Well, welcome back, Mr. La Baille. How good to see you here." Ivain was so surprised to see a pale transparent form that he could only say, "Natalie? Is that really you?"

"Of course, Mr. La Baille," she said. "I've decided to stay and find out what has happened to my recipes. You remember my special Pumpkin Pie? My Salmon Mousses? My unique Chestnut Cakes and Fruit Tarts? I can't leave until I find my own precious and unique inventions."

"Did you just come from Mme Kamiska's stone house?" asked Ivain, though he was sure of her answer.

"Yes," Natalie said, surprised that Ivain knew that place as well. "Nice lady, isn't she? She's given me permission to look for my work and to stay on as a shadow, as I requested. I wouldn't be at all surprised if my recipes got mixed up with your papers. And now they are gone too." Then she added, "Oh, Mr. La Baille, I tried so hard to stop those thieves, but there were three of them. What could I do?"

"You did too much, Natalie," Ivain said looking at her immobile form on the bed, where a ray of sun was now touching her face and moving playfully here and there, giving an incongruous form of life to her lifeless features. "You shouldn't have risked your life for me."

"I know how much your writing meant, and means, to you Mr. La Baille, and –" Natalie stopped, leaving Ivain with a feeling that she wanted to say more, but could not. Perhaps it was just his imagination, but she had looked at him in a way that seemed to betray that she knew his beginning and his end. Had she read all that had been written down? Would she have liked to have him partake of her knowledge? But she turned her back to him, and started to pass a hand over her transparent hair, that yet, within its transparency, still showed a fullness.

"What did the thieves look like?" Ivain asked, as he became aware that Natalie, too, must be part of 'the script' he was in.

"They were of medium height, dark skin, burned by the sun, with colorful handkerchiefs tied on their heads –" She stopped, then said, "You know, now that I think of it, they looked like pirates. Yes, pirates, with funny clothes, like one would wear at a masked party." She took a breath then added, "But I must be going. I must be going and start my search."

"Pirates?" repeated Ivain, "How strange." Then seeing that she was about to leave the room, for she had a leg already through a wall, he said, "Will we see each other again, Natalie?"

"Yes, Mr. La Baille, we will," she answered.

"Where?" Ivain asked with curiosity.

"In New York," Natalie said. "In New York." And she was gone to the other side of the wall. Ivain was still looking at the bed when he heard the door being opened and turning around saw Allegra come in.

"We've to leave this room," she said. "I saw the ambulance come inside the gate. The orderlies and the police will be here in no time to take the body to the morgue."

"Where can we hide?" asked Ivain.

"We can follow Natalie," said Allegra, as she began to disappear behind the wall. "This is another of the advantages of being what we are!" she said laughingly. Ivain, hearing steps in the hallway, pushed himself against the wall, and to his surprise found he was on the other side, in the guests' bedroom, which had been prepared for his arrival. He walked to the bed,

73

and sat quietly on the edge of it, thinking about old Natalie who had come back on a quest similar to his own, but had chosen to leave her body behind. Allegra broke the silence by saying, "Perhaps it would be a good idea if you came down with me and met your host and hostess."

"Not quite yet," he said, "if you don't mind."

"Do you wish to come into my room then?" She looked at him with a smile on her lips. "My room is the next one down the hall. Right near yours." She stopped, then began almost immediately. "Convenient, don't you think?"

Ivain had no desire to leave the comfort of his room, yet anxious to have answers, asked, "What exactly are your duties here?" He said it casually, not wishing to give undue importance to his words. She looked at him, sat on the bed near him, and started to unbutton the first button of her flowery shirt.

"Oh," she replied, "I'm sort of a man-Friday. I do a little bit of this and a little bit of that. And I can be a good business woman, if I need to be – like your cousin," and reaching in her skirt pocket, she pulled out a cigarette and played with it without lighting it.

"My cousin?" said Ivain in amazement. "How can you say he is a good businessman when he lost all his inheritance the first month he had it?" and he remembered how Fabian had bought stock in a private railway that had promptly gone bankrupt.

"He has become much better at it since he married France. I believe he has invested your money wisely," she said. "He seems to have acquired a sixth sense. Buying low, selling high – that sort of speculation." And she went on describing how he had started by changing a million English pounds for Mexican pesos, had sold them again for two million English pounds in a week's time. With the two million pounds he had then bought German marks, and had sold them for six million pounds in two days. He had then placed the six million pounds in American dollars, and within twenty four hours, he had made twelve million and he had gone on changing one denomination of money into another until he himself had no knowledge of how rich he was. "In fact," Allegra said, "he has increased what you left your wife by such an incredible amount that one could easily call him a modern Croesus."

"Really?" Ivain could hardly believe it, yet Le Plessis was bathed in what he used to call – the perfume of abundance. But there was another question on his lips, and he now asked Allegra, in a somber, almost sad tone. "Tell me, what's between you and my cousin?"

"I'm not in love with your cousin," she said, and as she talked, she lifted her skirt a bit, pointing with her index finger at the rays of the sun pouring into the room, as if to say it was too hot; but Ivain believed it was to show him her long, shapely legs.

"That is not the question I asked," said Ivain, rather cross more with himself than with her, for he knew she had seen him looking at her legs.

"Well, that's my answer to all your questions on the subject," she said. They were both silent for a moment until she added, "I did what I had to do to make your coming here more comfortable."

"You did all of that with my cousin for my sake?" His voice was full of irony now, for he had clearly understood what she was to Fabian. A mistress for whom just the barest touch of their fingers gave away the fact that he cared passionately for her. Somehow he felt that to be the case, but she did not reply. She looked straight ahead at a painting of the god Pan sitting among the nymphs that was hanging on the wall, right over the bed. "Don't look so sad. Let us talk it over in a more comfortable position." And she lay down across the bed. He did not move. So she went on, "France is so happy about your coming here because she thinks you and I –" and here she let the words trail, but Ivain did not pick them up, he just let them stand in the air by themselves, for he had no intention of becoming anything more than an acquaintance with this fellow traveler from the other side. On the other hand, Allegra attracted him, and in spite of all his good intentions, he was not sure he could resist her charm. In some ways, it would be more logical that he should yield to her, rather than fight her.

He got up and went near the window. The warm breeze of the summer wind touched his cheeks, and for a moment he thought Allegra had caressed him. He knew then that, had she done that simple gesture, he would not have been able to resist her. Later on, when he had made love with her until it seemed his veins would burst, he wondered if he ever had a chance of not being part of her. Venus instructed her in all the possible ways of making love, and then the Goddess told her one more secret that no one had ever discovered, and that only she knew. And yet when it was over, he realized he had never felt more empty or forlorn, for there was no tenderness, while at the same time desiring the sensation of that Olympic love again and again. He remembered pushing her away with the words, *Odi et amo*, and then pulling her back saying, *Amo et odi*, and, with the clear knowledge that their destiny was linked, he lost himself again into a languor that permeated all his limbs.

Now, after a long silence, as he wondered in what labyrinth he had landed, he said, "I suppose we'd better go and meet France and Fabian again." A love triangle did not interest him at all – or did it? "I am every man," he thought, as he tried to forgive himself. "As every man, I'm attracted to a beautiful woman, though I know she is as unreal as I am."

She opened the door and he followed her down the hall and down the stairway, until they were outside once more. Then Allegra turned right, and he stood still for a moment before turning his head the other way, and there, near the main door, was France. France, his France, his wife, whom he had loved and still loved. She was standing so close to him he could smell her sweet breath. He looked at her. Certainly the beauty of Allegra was nothing in comparison to France's, for hers was more distinguished and aristocratic, even though now she was dishevelled from what had recently happened. She must have been running for her clothes hung wet on her lean body, and her face was red. He took a moment to see what was different about France since the last time he had seen her. Her hair had become much longer and was streaked in a fashionable way, and her face had become thinner, making her features even more delicate than he remembered. She was at the height of her beauty, with milk white skin, so transparent that he thought she must have been the model for all the Sienese painters of the golden age. He remembered she was now five years older than he was. "How odd that is," and he felt like throwing his arms around her, felt like crying with joy in seeing how beautiful and young she still looked. For a moment the thought that France, too, had recognized him, and all was lost, passed through his mind. He met her gaze, ready to deny anything she would say about a resemblance between himself and her late husband. But he was shaken when she took a step backward and looked at him in a strange way.

"I have a feeling we've met before," were her first words to him. "You look familiar, but forgive me, I don't remember your name." Ivain was so surprised at what he heard that for a moment he believed she was making fun of him, that she was saying those words in an amusing way to tease him. But when he saw a frown appear between her eyebrows, he knew then that this was the moment Allegra had talked about. It was that instant in time when he would decide his future. Was he going to disclose to her his real name and leave immediately, or lie and stay? He thought of "the script," thought of all that the "green disk" implied, and looking at his wife, who was no longer his wife, but a woman whom he loved immensely, he plunged into "the script," by saying the fateful words carelessly, as if they were of no importance, "I am John Elliab." As soon as he said them he realized he had became an accomplice in whatever scheme Mme Kamiska and the Godlet had in store for him. That he was a willing accomplice in their deceit horrified him at this moment, and later on too, whenever he would think of it. What he had just done was nothing less than giving a hand to his heaven-sent antagonists. He was in point of fact helping them against himself. *Alea jacta est*, he silently repeated. "This is my private crossing of the Rubicon."

He had said the treacherous words once, and now he said them again. "John Elliab, your guest from New York. I presume you are Mrs. Alfred?" He said those last words with a smile, and as he said them, he shook hands with France, aware that there was not a moment of truth in this, their first meeting. "Oh, of course, you are Mr. Elliab." France said. "Allegra has talked so much about you. She calls you Johnny. May I call you Johnny, too?" She was being warm and welcoming as she pushed away her long hair from her face, where the wind was blowing it from behind. As he looked at her, Ivain began to think that, for France, life after his death could not have been so bad after all. And, in his heart of hearts, he wondered if she had been submerged with happiness in her new marriage with Fabian, until the recent arrival of Allegra – who must have brought with her obvious turbulence and whirlwinds that could not be ignored. "May I?" she asked again.

"Please do," answered Ivain, more and more surprised to see that France had no recollection of him. Presently, she looked at him and said, "Oh, I know why you look so familiar –" and at last Ivain's heart skipped a beat. "I must have seen you in your last play off Broadway, I think," she said it with a faint smile. "And you were very good in it, but I can't remember the title just now."

Later on, during his stay in Rosay, France would have moments of total lucidity, where she would turn to him suddenly and say that he was the spitting image of her first husband, to which he would inevitably say, "No, no. You're making a mistake. Memories sometimes play tricks with people. No two persons are ever that much alike, unless they are the same person," and he would laugh it off provocatively, as if to challenge fate. But fate was never challenged this way, for a moment later, France would inevitably forget what she had said, and go back to believing he was Allegra's friend who had stopped in Le Plessis on his way to New York. As for now, she continued, "I hope you'll call me France, and call my husband by his first name too, that is, Fabian. We're very informal here, quite casual in the way we live. Calm country life," she paused, "until today," and then repeated, "until today." She stopped and looked at the multitude of police and strangers who were walking about in the court-yard and in the English garden. "I don't know if you have heard?"

"Yes," he said, "I just did. And let me add how terribly sorry I am. A tragic event – or events, I should say." He found that keeping up the pretense of being a stranger in his own home and with his own wife was a strain, but not as big a strain as he thought it might have been. Besides, it seemed to get easier and easier as he talked.

"I suppose everyone already knows." France said, and he noticed that she was talking more to herself than to him, being as it were, in her own world where no one was allowed to enter. "We're a small village here in Rosay. We have the biggest house, and now we have this murderous theft on our hands. We can't stop people from talking." She stopped and he saw her looking away into space. "I lost my nurse today. She was more like a mother to me." She turned her face to look at him again. "I don't know how I'm going to go on without her. We're never prepared for death, but especially for violent deaths like this." She stopped for a moment, and looking at him, she continued, "It's the second time in my life that I am faced with such violence. I don't know if you heard how I lost my first husband, Ivain?" Was she asking him, Ivain wondered? He made up his mind he was not going to say anything, for he found his position there too uncertain for comfort, and so strange as to be almost unbearable. He shook his head. "No," he said, "no, I haven't heard." She looked up at the cloudless sky, then pulled a scarf out of her pocket, and placed it loosely around her neck. "Another time – not now – I'll tell you." She turned her back to him. At last she said, "Would you like to meet my husband?" At the word husband, Ivain could hardly refrain from saying something unpleasant, but held his temper in check. Paradoxically, he dreaded meeting his own wife's "husband," while at the same time he looked forward to seeing his cousin again. He nodded at her, and began to walk toward the tall figure standing near the pond, still talking with a certain ease to the chief of the gendarmes. When Ivain was face to face with Fabian, he saw that his cousin had changed very little. He was dressed elegantly as always, though on closer inspection his clothes were slightly worn. He was holding his jacket in one hand, and some papers in the other. Ivain looked again, but it was only when he stared at Fabian that he realized that his nose was slightly more aquiline and a bit longer than he remembered, and his skin looked somewhat darker, and full of freckles, due, without a doubt, to his spending more time in the open air. Still, his cousin's features were those of an aristocrat, with one exception. His large eyes had a sweetness that was particularly endearing. "In these last years," thought Ivain, "he seems to have become more of a country squire than the intellectual he always aspired to be." And he wondered if Fabian had left his small investment firm in Paris to become the writer of historical books, as he often said he would.

His cousin welcomed him in a singular way. He made the comment that he had seen him before, he was sure of that, but could not remember when or where. He specifically said, "I am sure it will come back to me sometime before you go back to New York. I have a wonderful memory for faces, Mr. Elliab." France corrected him by saying, "Johnny! Do call him Johnny. No need to stand on formalities with Allegra's friend, is there, darling? Besides, Mr. Elliab has given us permission, isn't that so?" Ivain nodded his head. "Anyway," she went on, "I expect Johnny will be with us for quite a while."

"I don't know," Ivain replied curtly, annoyed at hearing France calling Fabian with that particular word of endearment. "It will depend on whether or not the work of the late Mr. La Baille is returned to you." And as he said it, he emphasized the word "late" to see if there was any reaction on their part. But Fabian only said, "Well, we're all very hopeful. The chief here, –" and he introduced Ivain to the commander of the local gendarmes, "Chef Gerome Julien Perrot," who was nearby, seemingly out of breath though standing still. "Chef Perrot is adamant in his belief that if we place a few ads in the local and Parisian newspapers, and offer a reward, we'll have the manuscripts and the papers back in no time at all. The only problem, of course, is that the thieves are also the murderers, which means that they'll be extra careful, isn't that so?" And he turned to the gendarme who said, "The transactions for the La Baille papers will have to be handled with great secrecy. If those people give themselves away, they could get the guillotine." And here he took a deep breath as he shrugged his shoulders, trying to convey the impression that if the murderers did lose their heads, it would be one less problem for society in general, and for him in particular.

Getting his papers back was not going to be as simple as Ivain had imagined, or as Allegra had led him to believe. "My personal experience," continued Chef Perrot, suddenly becoming more friendly toward Ivain, "leads me to believe that if the ransom money is large enough, you'll get a response." But Ivain noticed that there was something in the manner the gendarme spoke that made him question his statement. Perhaps it was the way he had stumbled, almost stuttering on the words "large enough," as if to say, "How much money is all that worth? After all, the writing is from an unknown author, isn't it?" But the gendarme had not yet encountered the firmness of purpose of both France and Fabian, which was of such magnitude that it made even Ivain reel back when he heard it. "My wife and I are willing to put up three million francs to get the papers and manuscripts back."

"That's a great deal of money," said Chef Perrot. "I suppose for that amount you'd also like to know the name, or names, of the murderers?"

"No," answered Fabian. "For that amount we would just like to get all the writing back. I leave it up to you to find out the names of the murderers."

When Ivain heard these words, he felt a great surge of affection for his cousin, and he believed that France had done the right thing after all in marrying him. He was being kind and thoughtful. He had not forgotten him, though it was a mystery why no one recognized him. Mme Kamiska must have arranged it to be so. But, aside from that rather annoying fact, Fabian was exactly the same loving and caring man he had always been. Presently the chief of the gendarmes took his leave, and France and Fabian invited Ivain into the house to have a drink. Weeks later, he would discover that he had been welcomed so warmly by both husband and wife because France mistakenly believed that he was more than a trifle involved with Allegra, while Fabian thought they were only casual friends. Slowly, he came to realize that their singular beliefs were unshakable, and in time, as his relationship with Allegra took on a life of its own, it led him to face events that he could neither prevent nor foresee, and he clearly understood the trap within the trap that had been laid for him. Later on, he would describe these events as circles within circles, and himself as the hands on a clock that turn round and round as long as the spring is wound up. As for now, he followed his host and hostess meekly to the gray salon, decorated with stucco that had been patiently built onto all the walls – figure upon figure, rose upon rose, leaping dolphins among waves, and so on – three hundred years before, by an unknown Italian artist. Ivain looked closely and took in once again the beauty of the dancing young women, scantily dressed, surrounded by wreaths of flowers and fruits chosen with extreme care, to make the ensemble a delicate balance of decoration and art, and then sat down in the comfortable, white silk sofa that he himself had bought ten years before, and he felt for the first time, he had truly come home.

THE ANTIQUE DEALER: PIERRE JEAN BOISSY

"Am I a butterfly dreaming that I am a philosopher,
or a philosopher dreaming that I am a butterfly?"
Chinese reflection

THE first days in the country house passed peacefully enough for Ivain, as he tried to stay away from the many police officers who kept coming and going, always bringing the same news – that there was no news. No one had the remotest idea as to who the murderers were, nor was there even the slightest clue as to their identities. Chef Perrot would have found very helpful the description of the three men Ivain knew had killed Natalie and stolen his work. More than once he felt like saying, "Look for pirates!" but, for obvious reasons, he could not reveal what he knew. Besides, had he mentioned it, no one would have taken him seriously. "Pirates do not exist these days," he said to himself, "or do they?" He had heard that in the Asian sea some pleasure boats had been taken by force and the occupants thrown overboard, but was it true? As for his papers and manuscripts, they seemed to have disappeared into thin air with the rest of the furniture.

"Well, not quite thin air," Chef Perrot would say. "We know the route the furniture has taken." And he would proudly point out that first it had been trucked to Brussels, where it had been looked at by art experts, and then divided into three lots. One for Japan, one for the Emirates and one for North America. "Probably to Florida or to Texas where there is a big market for French antiques." He would say all this as he held a glass of cold, red Spanish port wine in his hand, which Fabian would make sure was constantly refilled in the hope, or so he said later on over dinner, of learning as much as possible from the commander.

In the following days, it was a rare night when the commander's face did not become redder and redder, and his speech more and more garrulous. France was sometimes present at these meetings, but more often she stayed in her room, where Ivain saw her sitting by the window, looking out over the well-manicured lawn, or reading or playing notes on the piano, bits of Chopin from different works, that pierced the clear air and seemed to him like laments for days that would not return.

It was painful for Ivain to be restricted to the role of mere spectator, and toward the end of his first week, one evening, as the sun was beginning to disappear behind the houses, he decided to take a walk in the village, and stop to see Pierre Jean Boissy. The antique dealer always kept a large assortment of objects that could be of interest. "Who knows what I might find there?" Ivain said to himself, for there was a small chance that some of the stolen items of Le Plessis had found their way to his home.

As he walked on the one main road of the village, Ivain became aware that, Rosay, though only forty minutes from Paris, was as far away from civilization as if it had been *la France profonde* (as the French say), or in some totally forgotten corner of the country.

The people of this village lived more or less in the same geographical space as the Parisians, but not in the same historical era. The same space but not the same time frame. And, while Paris was filled with a large population with a knowledge of satellites and computers, the latest art works, the most recent music and fashion, here was Rosay, at a stone's throw, so to speak, with people who still used candlelight to reduce their electrical bills, or who had no other way to heat their homes but old chimneys, walking daily to the near-by woods to gather dead branches from the ground. Most were farmers, and one of these families, the Le Clairs, was the embodiment of what farmers had been since time immemorial. They never took baths and they co-existed with fifty cows, five dogs, twenty ducks, and an indefinite number of chickens and rabbits. They lived in the most squalid and miserable way imaginable, so much so that Ivain heard that no one in the village would buy milk from them directly, and the Le Clairs could only survive by selling it to the state, which would then dilute it with the other milk they acquired in the region. "The most sophisticated people living near the most primitive," Ivain laughed at such a thought, but there it was. He stopped, struck by an idea. "Perhaps," he said, "living in Rosay is not so different from living in any other part of the earth, for wherever we are, we are still living within the echo of the first instant when the Universe came to be; living within the echo of an unknown past." And he thought he would have liked to see the birth of the Universe, he would have liked to see the first man who discovered "zero" in mathematics, and the first man who made the "wheel." But those were questions, and like so many other questions, he had no answers.

As he was thinking these thoughts, Ivain came upon the house of Pierre Jean Boissy, an ancient water-mill, near the river Yerres, and he knocked on the door amused at the small china sign that said, *Chien mechant et perspicace.*

M. Boissy welcomed him into his home, and surprised him by saying, "I never thought that any guests of M. and Mme Alfred would ever come to my poor house. Such fine people! And you, M. Elliab, such –" and he would have gone on and on, had not Ivain cut him short with, "I see the villagers have been talking." He took a breath, "I suppose it was inevitable."

"But M. Elliab, it's a compliment to our village to have an actor among us."

"I've come here, M. Boissy, to have a chat with you," said Ivain, as he took a closer look at the man standing before him. M. Boissy, or Coco, as the locals called him, was a man who looked closer to seventy than to his sixty years. Lean and bent with age, he had the unusual gift of having the whitest skin in winter, as transparent as the thin paper used to wrap delicate china, while in summer his skin darkened and cracked, parched by the sun as he swam in the murky water of the river and then baked on the river's banks.

The river passed partly by the side of his house, and partly under it, so that no matter where one was standing in the house, one could hear the flowing of the water swishing around and under one's feet. If there was a great rain, then the river's noise became turbulent and menacing, and Ivain, who remembered it from his visits to Coco as a child, was always a bit afraid of being inside that house. But, for the moment, the business he had with the antique dealer was more important than his childhood fears, so he began to look at Coco's appearance. It seemed to Ivain, that in spite of the surprise Coco had expressed in seeing him, he thought that somehow he had expected his visit, for he was clothed in a well-cut, dark brown velvet suit that had a certain elegance about it, and was probably not worn every day of the week. That suit, together with his long pointed face, gave him the appearance of a medieval scholar more than that of a small town antique dealer. He turned his face sideways and said to Ivain, "Well, I didn't know whether it was a friend or a policeman who had knocked at my door." He paused to catch his breath, and held on to a chair, "but I'm so old now that even those 'dog fleas'" – that was the word he used for the policemen – "do not scare me any longer. My skin is so burned out that they can't bite through it," he said, and in effect Ivain had to agree that his skin looked like cracked leather. He then began to talk immediately of his latest acquisitions, going on the supposition that the important foreigner wished to buy something. The word he used for the objects he had "acquired" was a word that in its vagueness could mean that he had either bought or stolen them, but in either case he was eager to sell them to M. Elliab. And then he begged Ivain to come and see all he had, and Ivain followed him into a room which seemed filled to the brim with all sorts of the most varied and strange objects. Lamps, braziers, ornate fireplaces both in marble and wood, books, boxes, all sorts of linen, from table cloths to colorful skirts, and tapestries. But on closer inspection, Ivain saw that the best pieces were statues and vases, the kind one finds in elegant gardens, and his thoughts went to his own Roman statues, and what a miracle it was they were still at Le Plessis. Then he was shown reproductions of well-known paintings which he would sell for a song, or so Coco said, adding that Picasso had painted them when Picasso was still a child, and no one had seen them, though his name was on the back. And, turning them over, he pointed to the name of the master, which Ivain recognized as having been written by Dudu Picasso himself. M. Boissy said all this in such a passionate, yet natural way, as to convince the most tight fisted man on earth to buy at least a few of them. But finally, seeing that nothing would grab the interest of his interlocutor, Pierre Jean Boissy brought Ivain near a cylindrical object which he immediately recognized as a hologram. He turned on the light and said that he, himself, had made that image, entirely from his imagination from a number of photographs.

"That person does not exist," he said, "yet it exists here in my hologram."

"How strange," thought Ivain, "that people alive can create imaginary people who seem to be alive, and perhaps will be remembered for a long time to come, while I, who have tried so hard to create a memory of myself, can't find anyone who even remembers me."

He put his hands behind his head in an unusual way and, looking at the old man, began to speak to him most politely.

"I've come here, M. Boissy," said Ivain, "in the hope that you would know something about the theft that took place at Le Plessis."

"Ah, yes," said M. Boissy, becoming suddenly serious, and at the same time disappointed, for he could see now that this stranger was in no mood for buying, and only wished information out of him. Not what he had expected. "I don't think there's one person here in the village who hasn't heard. Yes, it was most unusual. The murder made it unusual. In this part of the world there is never murder with thieving." He took a deep breath. "Thieving is more of a gentlemen's sport," he added, as if preparing an excuse for himself.

"I had hoped, M. Boissy," continued Ivain, "that you, who have a wide range of friends, could help me find the objects that have been taken from Le Plessis. More specifically, the papers of the late Professor."

"Ah, Professor La Baille," the antique dealer said. "Personally, I don't remember him," he added, and Ivain found his words strange since, in the past, he had often stopped at the water mill, but he continued to question him, nevertheless.

"I'm trying to help Mrs. Alfred recoup the papers that were lost. The papers being more important than the actual furniture for my hostess," said Ivain, who was momentarily distracted, for M. Boissy had begun to tap with his fingers in an annoying manner, tapping them on a table as if he were playing notes on an imaginary piano. It was obvious that for the antique dealer the papers were of little value, while the bureaux were of enormous importance. The old man did not answer him directly, but said, "How true is the saying that objects don't belong to one person, but at times, when they feel like belonging to someone else, they take off and go." And he laughed at his own words.

"What do you mean?" said Ivain. "What do you mean?" he repeated, without really knowing what he, himself, wanted to say.

"I mean, M. Elliab, that objects have a life of their own, and

89

often they wish to change proprietors, and we're only their humble intermediaries." And with that, he bowed a bit too low in front of Ivain, who felt uncomfortable and began to look around the room.

"That being the case," Ivain began again, as he pulled M. Boissy up from that servile position by putting his hand on his shoulder, "perhaps you could enlighten me as to where those objects have gone, and which master they are with now."

"Well," said M. Boissy, "sometimes they don't wish a master, sometimes they wish to end it all. Not unlike a person. They just wish to be broken up, or burned, or worse."

"What could be worse than that?" blurted out Ivain, now perfectly aware that he was fencing words with a master fencer, and was getting the worst of it.

"They could fall into the hands of people with no scruples and that's the terrible truth about objects that disappear from one's home. Just imagine all the letters written to one's lovers, or personal diaries? That sort of thing." And a moment later he went on to say, "It looks to me as if these events are giving you a great deal of trouble."

Ivain could see that it would be difficult to get anything out of M. Boissy, but he would not give up.

"Suppose," he began again, "suppose that among the objects that were stolen there were love letters *per se*, diaries, historical notes. Papers that would not be of importance to the person who had stolen them, but of immense importance to the man who could not write them any longer."

"Why wouldn't he be able to write them now?" M. Boissy asked Ivain, who began to suspect that M. Boissy was leading him by the nose down a rosy path. But he was not going to show him that he knew it, so he answered candidly. "Because they belonged to the late M. La Baille," Ivain said, as if he had not understood the antique dealer's teasing.

"Ah," said M. Boissy, "that would be a valid reason, or at least I cannot see one that is more valid than that."

"And let us suppose, M. Boissy, that among the stolen objets there were two large manuscripts which represented the *magnum opus* of the late Professor."

"Yes?" nodded Pierre Jean Boissy.

"How would one proceed to find them?" Ivain asked.

"By searching for them," he said, as if the answer would be obvious to a mere child.

"Where? Where would one search?" And since he was not getting any answers, he went on to say, "Would you have any leads, M. Boissy?" adding, "I could be easily persuaded in buying a great deal of what you have here if you give me the information that interests me."

"In that case," M. Boissy said, "I'll look around and see what I can come up with." And then he started to talk deliberately about other objects around the room, and Ivain understood that he was trying to get away from a conversation that was becoming too embarrassing. So he let him talk about his excursions in Italy, and how on one of these travels he had filled a bottle with the water from Lake Trasimene, and could he now offer the tiny blue bottle with that very classical water to M. Elliab? "This could help inspire you for your upcoming part," he said. So he knew. Everyone knew he was hoping to play Julius Caesar in New York, in the not too distant future.

Ivain took the bottle, shook hands with the old man and thanked him. But just before he left, Ivain saw M. Boissy pass a hand over his forehead as if he was thinking of something. Finally he said, "About the theft at Le Plessis?"

"What about it?" asked Ivain, stopping suddenly, not knowing what to expect.

"I just thought you should know there's a rumor going around among my friends. They're not from this village but know a few things here and there." He stopped, only to begin again almost immediately. "They're saying that M. and Mme Alfred set it up themselves to collect the insurance."

"What?" asked Ivain, not quite understanding the allusions M. Boissy was making.

"The word is – that M. and Mme Alfred stand to collect a lot of money."

"Really?" said Ivain. "How much can that be? After all, they are willing to spend three million francs to recover just the stolen papers."

"That is a lot of money," M. Boissy said, "But a small amount compared to the thirty-five million they'll be getting from the insurance company."

"Ah," said Ivain, taken aback by the great sum that had just been mentioned, and he began to walk around the room. "But the murder?" he finally asked.

"That was an unforeseen accident," said M. Boissy, looking out of the window distractedly.

"It doesn't make sense. They are so rich!" and by saying this, Ivain wished to imply that they didn't need to do this sort of thing.

"That will make them even richer, won't it?" M. Boissy added, with a touch of irony that irked Ivain and made him quickly say, "It's hard for me to believe it."

"Who knows? In any case, it's only a rumor and people are as envious here as everywhere else in the world. *Il faut de tout pour faire un monde. N'est-ce-pas?*" M. Boissy answered, and began to walk toward the door. He said good-bye to Ivain again, promising to keep him informed if he heard any other news, and he carefully closed the front door behind him.

Ivain left the water-mill with so many questions swirling around his head that he even wondered whether the water in the blue bottle had really come from Lake Trasimene. If so, it was Holy water for him, for he knew it must contain the last tears and blood of a great Roman army. "This is just fine," he said ironically to himself. "I'm holding the essence of the Roman spirit in my hand, but I am no closer to knowing what happened to my writing about those same Romans, than the day I arrived back on earth." And, with this relic in his hand, he began to walk toward Le Plessis once more, striving to keep his composure, and swearing to himself not to say one word to anyone about what he had just heard.

THE CHILDREN'S PLAY

> *"The life we lead is the script we are in."*
> *Allegra outside Mme Kamiska's stone house*

It was evening when Ivain left M. Boissy, but the light of the sun still lingered on, making the August day seem interminably long, just as in a few months, the night would close in by early afternoon. It seemed to Ivain that in France the days were longer in the summer than in any other place he had ever been, just as in winter they seemed to be shorter. He had walked briskly toward Le Plessis enveloped in dark thoughts. Once home he was welcomed back by Fabian who asked him if he would like to see "The children's play" in the Town Hall of Rosay, adding, "It would be nice to have you with us, since France is the patroness for this event." Before saying either yes or no, Ivain had a moment of reflection. Could Fabian and France be hiding something from him? Could it be possible that Pierre Jean Boissy's rumor was true? If so it would be such an enormous deceit that it would boggle the mind. "No, no," he said to himself, "I know my wife, I know my cousin. These are just dark calumnies provoked by the jealousy of small minds." The fact that they were going to get a large sum of money from the insurance was beside the point, he said to himself. So, though there was a moment of wonder in Ivain's mind, he quickly dismissed it, and accepted the invitation. He was happy to have a chance at last to see France at close quarters for more than just a few minutes, and to be able to exchange a few words with her. It wasn't as if he had not already tried to talk to her alone. But she had balked at seeing anyone, preferring to remain in her room, both day and night, to the point of refusing to come down for dinner. The excuse she had given was that she was mourning for Natalie, but Ivain quickly realized that her unhappiness also sprang from the presence of Allegra in her house. He knew France to be too clever not to have understood where her second husband's romantic interests lay.

"Every year," Fabian continued, talking to Ivain in subdued tones, almost as if he were giving away a secret, "France gives money to the school for different projects. Her favorites," he went on, "being the gymnastics show, and the one play that is performed in the summertime by the youngsters of our village." And tonight was the great occasion to see what sort of show the children had written for themselves.

After dinner Ivain walked alone with France from Le Plessis to the Town Hall, or the *Mairie* of Rosay, where the school theater had been set up. Fabian had gone ahead to see if everything was in order, and Allegra had excused herself at the last moment, and remained home on the pretext that she still had work to do for Mr. Alfred. Ivain saw that France smiled upon hearing that remark, happy to be without her presence for this one evening, and Ivain found her smile both enchanting and revealing. "Perhaps for me, too, this is going to be a perfect night," he said to himself. As they walked, Ivain asked France something he had been meaning to ask her since he had come back to Le Plessis.

"Mrs. Alfred," he began.

"France, please call me France," she corrected with a sweet tone in her voice.

"France," he said, "would it be too painful for you to tell me how your late husband died?"

She looked at him as if she had not understood his question, then she answered matter of factly, "He was shot by accident at an airport, in a cross fire between two factions of terrorists."

"Oh," said Ivain, "is that what in fact happened?"

She stopped and looked at him, as if wondering if he knew something more. "Yes. Why? Have you heard anything different?" she asked.

"No, no. Actually, I hadn't heard anything at all."

"The police, one policeman I should say – Officer Pellegrino – followed the case, and is still in charge of it. Well, he told me that Ivain died, 'because he was at the wrong place at the right time.' He was just destined to die like that, I'm afraid." She paused. "I saw the whole dreadful thing. I just wish I had been able to keep him home that day. I tried. Oh God how I tried! But I couldn't –" She turned her head as if she could not go on.

"I am sorry. It must have been particularly brutal for you," said Ivain.

"What isn't these days?" she said. "Sometimes I think we are passing through the darkest period of history."

Ivain was silent for a moment or two, then began talking again. "I suppose you have buried your late husband in Le Plessis?" She looked at him as if to ask, why all these questions. He felt he was not being too tactful, but there was no one else who would have known as much. There was Fabian, of course, and there was Allegra. But somehow he was also curious to see France's reaction to these specific questions.

"No," she said simply, "Ivain was cremated and buried in upstate New York, where we had, and I still have, a sunflower farm." She stopped. "Our caretaker buried him under a great oak tree that in the spring is surrounded by white daffodils and small, wild violets. The caretaker knew Ivain well and was devoted to the whole family. I felt it was better that way, I mean, to have him buried in our own farm, than in a cold cemetery." She took a deep breath. "I hope I made the right decision," she added.

"Those sorts of decisions are always very personal, but yes, yes under the circumstances, it was the only thing to do," Ivain said at last, after thinking it over. He wondered if she wondered what was going on in his head. If only she knew who he really was! If only she knew that he was thinking of his own self, now turned into a handful of ashes lying underground under a great big oak. He even remembered the exact place where the century-old tree was standing in the farm. His ashes had probably been placed inside an urn, and he was suddenly curious to find out what sort of urn he was in. Did France choose a little urn in the form of a Doric temple? Or was it a tiny Parthenon? Perhaps it was just a simple vase? But what was it made of? Alabaster or marble or opaline? Perhaps she had chosen a small box made of lapis lazuli knowing how much he loved that stone. Then he began to hope his urn had not been chosen among the ones that were extraordinarily expensive or it might have been stolen. A grave robber might put his hands on it, empty his ashes and sell it at a garage sale, for instance. An old Chinese saying came to his lips, "To be rich, dig up an ancient tomb; to make a fortune, open a coffin." The thought horrified him, and he tried not to think of it. Instead he reassured himself in the knowledge that someone attended his resting place. He did not have the courage to ask France any more questions about his burial, but he did continue to talk about his murder, though he could tell it made her uneasy. The words came to his lips naturally, as if he could not control them.

"By the way, did this police-officer in New York, this Officer –?" and here he pretended not remember his name.

"Pellegrino," she said quickly.

"Yes, did this Pellegrino ever find the culprits of this most unusual death?" he continued.

"No," she replied. "He's still searching. The case was never officially closed, though I've lost all hope they'll ever find the culprit or culprits," she said, stopping only to take a breath. "But, when I go to New York for the opening of the Library room, I'll give the police a call. The Officer always likes to hear from me."

Ivain was both puzzled and amazed. So, no one had been arrested for his murder. He would have liked to know more, much more, but there was another burning question he wished to ask: "Were all the manuscripts and the papers stolen, or were you able to save some?"

"I am sorry that you haven't been able to read anything of the Professor," she answered, as if to say that she had her own problems and right now his own were not as important.

"I wasn't thinking of my personal loss," said Ivain quickly, and he almost laughed out loud when he realized how incongrous what he had just said was. "I was thinking of how I could be of help to you."

She stopped, looked at him and said in a firm, hard voice which he had rarely heard from her, "Take Allegra away from my home! That's how you can help me." He was dumbfounded. Allegra was obviously the pawn he had to use to be able to get near France, unless he found a way to break "the script." That, of course, was his obsession, but he didn't have any ideas as to how to do it. Allegra was there. Now, he had to make the effort to get to know her better, he thought. But was it an effort? Was she not beautiful and available? He would have liked to say something more to France but they had arrived at the *Mairie*. He kept quiet.

He saw that a group of local people was already there, milling about outside, waiting for the play to start while they smoked a cigar or a cigarette and chatted loudly. Aurelie Madeleine was there with a cherubic-looking child in her arms, and a smaller one near her husband, who looked as if he barely had had time to change into good clothes. The other villagers were there, too. He saw Polaski talking to Villers, laughing from time to time with his high-pitched laugh, and he saw that Josephine Lazar was part of the group. Josephine Lazar had never married, and they were probably teasing her, Ivain thought. She had lost her looks, and seemed to have aged beyond her years. Ivain remembered her when he had run barefoot on the grass fields with her. How wonderful it had been to feel the soft grass under his feet! How they had laughed then. But now those were just memories, memories that made him melancholic and nostalgic.

There was a hush. Everyone had seen them coming, and they all said "Good evening" in their typical French way: *"Mesdames, Messieurs, bonsoir,"* and, after having acknowledged and repeated the "good evening" to everyone, Ivain and France went straight inside the building. The theater itself consisted of a large room with a rudimentary platform, lit by primitive lights. At each side of the stage there were worn out red velvet curtains. The chairs they were asked to sit on were ordinary kitchen chairs, hard and ungiving. But all the children's parents and their friends were there, and one could see that the air was charged with happiness. There was laughter and exclamations of surprise in seeing this or that person. Besides, this was a great occasion for the people of the village to sit with their benefactress, Mme Alfred, who was more talked about than anyone else in the village, mostly because she inhabited the big, beautiful house. Recently the talk had increased a great deal, due to the sudden and unexpected tragedy that had struck her household. Nobody in the village could remember a theft where there also had been a murder, and they called it: *un crime à l'Américaine.* The villagers felt real sympathy for her, and had come in great numbers to show their support.

The play which had been written by the children, with the help of their surly teacher, Mme Fournier, (a woman who tried to forget she lived in a small village by drinking Dom Perignon at every possible occasion), was about the search throughout the village for a lost kingdom called "Patoche." The whole premise for the play's success was that the people would recognize their neighbors, and laugh at each other's foibles. So, when they presumably reached the house of Claude Arc, they would say something like, "Nothing can be found through these 'Gauloise' clouds of 'Gauloise' smoke." Or when they were presumably entering the house of "Dudu Picasso," they would ecstatically say, "Could 'Patoche' be hiding among all these masterpieces?" And so on and so forth. This made the receptive audience laugh at every other little phrase and at specific gestures in which they recognized this or that child, for the little actors were dressed up as if they were going to a masked party. There were little queens from the Middle Ages, fairies with tall hats, pretty chimney sweepers, kings of Hearts, Clubs, and Spades and a little Pierrot.

In deference to their benefactor, undoubtedly, they also took the occasion of retelling how Le Plessis got the name of *le petit château*. Once, there had been a much bigger *château* in Rosay, a real *château*, with six towers and a drawbridge over a moat that surrounded it. But, due to a tax law that specified that one had to pay taxes on the number of windows and bathrooms there were in one's house, the owner of the castle, finding himself in a dire situation, had the whole beautiful structure dynamited, and went to live in his caretakers' home. That day the people of the village cried, and re-named the La Baille house, *le petit château*.

Halfway through this colorless evening a wild idea seized Ivain. He began to think that, although what he was hearing was a primitive script, it was "a script" nevertheless. It had been written down. It had been learned by rote, and entrusted to memory. It had been rehearsed. It had been put on for this one great occasion. So why not disrupt it now? What if he were to break into it? If this was a war to make his life his own again, then he had to start somewhere and this might prove to be just the combat experience he needed. He had to break the "fourth wall," which Ivain knew to be the imaginary wall that divides the players from the audience. What if he were to go through it, just as he went through the other, more solid stone walls? What would happen then?

He had an overwhelming desire to do just that, even though he realized that he would be provoking the anger of all the children's parents and friends, and above all, that of his host and hostess. Still, here was his first chance. He would walk up to the stage, and improvise. Maybe he would say that he knew where "Patoche" was and point to a specific place in space. Perhaps he could take one of the youngsters by the wrist and, with a wicked laugh frighten him. He opted for a third choice. Putting a hand in his pocket, he took out a white envelope on which he had written a couple of French words he meant to look up in the *Petit Larousse*. He now crossed them out and wrote the name of the school teacher on it, "For Mme Fournier." And underneath, "To be delivered immediately." Inside he wrote a little note for her which simply said: *Do ut des*. He was sure the school teacher would take him for an eccentric and not understand the meaning of his words, but he did not care, for they were meant for Mme Kamiska, not for Mme Fournier. Nevertheless, though, he felt guilty for what he was about to do, his need to disrupt the play was overwhelming and demanded immediate action.

He rose to his feet and saying aloud, "Excuse me, excuse me, but I've something I must do," he started to walk through the rows of chairs. People in the audience were obviously annoyed. The little actors on stage were momentarily distracted and looked out toward the dark room, as they kept on repeating their lines mindlessly, leaving them floating in the air. Something mysterious was happening, but they did not grasp its meaning. Neither did their parents for that matter. "Perhaps they think I am unwell," thought Ivain, who kept saying, "Pardon! *Excusez-moi*, but there is something I absolutely must do. Absolutely – *absolument*."

He was acting like a man possessed. A madman, in fact. But, if that was the case, then he felt that there was no need to explain or apologize to anyone, and he continued to walk over people's legs in a noisy manner. He walked up to the stage, mounted the one step of the platform, and found himself surrounded by the little ones. He looked around for the lead, Pierrot, and handed him the envelope.

"What is it?" said Pierrot, without outwardly showing signs of fear or anxiety.

"It's my way to enter your 'script.' See, now I'm a character in your play." Ivain said with a voice that reverberated in the small room, making sure that all the audience heard him. Everyone was listening carefully, that much he knew, probably still trying to understand if this character was supposed to participate in the play or not.

"But, what do I do with this envelope?" asked Pierrot again, with a serious expression that clearly showed he did not understand why this man was there on the platform with him.

"Ah," Ivain said to the child whose face, whitened by chalk, looked a bit scared now. "Make sure you deliver it to your teacher. It has an important message inside." And immediately after saying this, he turned to the audience and in a loud voice said: "Ladies and gentlemen, an unexpected stranger has entered the stage. The stranger is now part of this play. He is, in fact, the outsider we all wait to encounter in all the theater pieces. The one who comes in from the cold, so to speak, to change the routine of daily life. Do not be alarmed. This Pierrot is holding a letter to be delivered immediately to Mme Fournier. I do hope you understand."

"Lights, lights!" someone shouted. Right away the hallway was flooded with primitive, but effective bright lights.

Ivain jumped down from the makeshift stage and walked toward the back of the room. He turned around once and saw that the room was in an uproar. The little Pierrot was handing the envelope to his teacher, and a moment later he burst into tears. The other children followed suit and soon one could hear a single great lament that grew louder and louder.

There was a gasp from the audience. Words of outrage and indignation were mixed with nervous laughter. The parents were starting to get up and walk toward the stage. It was at this point that Mme Fournier, taking the letter from Pierrot's hand, opened it up and looking at the note inside, said, "There has been a misunderstanding. Please, please take your seats again. We will be back in just a few minutes, and begin the play from the beginning." And so saying, she calmly collected Pierrot, the queens, the kings, the fairies, the chimney sweepers, and left the stage as the curtain came down.

Ivain left the room and went into the corridor where he saw Mme Fournier taking the children into the mayor's office. He gathered that it had been made into a makeshift room for the teacher to dress up her little actors, and make up their faces with red and white powder, which was smudged all over their cherubic cheeks.

He stayed in the corridor long enough to hear the audience relax somewhat and discuss among themselves the turn of events. He heard one question over and over: "Was M. Elliab's intrusion part of the play or not?"

"If it wasn't, then being an actor didn't give him the liberty he just took," someone was heard saying. But since no one knew, they were all left in the uncertainty of the moment. Ivain did not care what the audience thought of him, except for the fact that he felt he had embarrassed his host and hostess, and he had been rude to the teacher. He decided he would make his excuses later on to the Alfreds, but he would go now to Mme Fournier and see if, somehow, she would excuse his behavior.

He stood at the door which had been left ajar, and saw the teacher talking calmly to the children, explaining to them there was nothing to worry about, for the stranger had made a mistake in handing them the letter. One of them wanted to know what was in the letter, but Mme Fournier seemed reluctant to say anything more about it. He saw her bend down over a little girl who was still crying; no doubt she was trying to console her with soothing words. The girl, who was dressed as a good fairy, nodded frequently and finally smiled. It was at this point that Ivain pushed the door open all the way, and entered the room. He had a sincere desire to apologize for what he had done. At the same time, he knew that he could not tell her the real reason behind his action.

When the teacher saw him, she asked the children to go through their lines quietly, that she would come right back. With that she went up to Ivain. "Who are you?" she asked, and immediately added, "Why did you behave like that?" He did not answer her right away, giving her time to say, "What is the meaning of this envelope?" and she held it in one hand, high over her head.

He said, "I am truly sorry," but could not stop himself from adding, "Have you ever thought that 'a script,' interrupted by a stranger, becomes another 'script'? Or, if you like, the stranger becomes part of 'the script,' so that 'the script' and the stranger make up 'a new script' of their own."

From Mme Fournier's expression, Ivain felt that the teacher must have thought she was dealing with a madman. It was only after he explained that he was the guest of M. and Mme Alfred that she relaxed a bit and sat down on the chair nearest to him. Ivain sat on the doorstep.

"You have no respect for what we wrote," she finally said.

"On the contrary," said Ivain, "I have such deep respect for the written word that I try to change it to suit me," and as he said it, he realized he was contradicting himself. He sincerely wished Mme Fournier to understand his position, but he did not know how to make it clear to her. After all, his actions were of the sort that could not be easily explained. "I hope you'll accept my apologies," he said.

"Does this have a particular meaning?" asked the teacher as she held the note he had written in her hand.

"No," said Ivain, "None whatsoever. It's meaningless."

"With all due respect to your greater knowledge of the theater," began the teacher with a tremulous voice that betrayed her annoyance at him, "I feel that you've humiliated us tonight. I really don't know how to go out and face that audience." She said these last words rather quietly, not wishing anyone to hear them.

"Say that it was all a mistake, my mistake," he told her, and stood up.

He felt badly for her, for he knew that he had ruined her evening. Still he had wanted to break "the script," and in doing so, he had changed the mood of ecstatic happiness among the peasants and their children. But, he was just at the beginning of his struggle. He had much to learn.

"I'm working my hardest to do my duty to the children, and to our patroness, Mme Alfred," she continued.

"I'm working my hardest to do my duty to myself," said Ivain, and this reply confused the teacher even more. But he felt he had to keep his thoughts hidden, even though she was not the enemy. She just happened to be in the middle of a war which she could not understand or even believe. Greatly disturbed, Mme Fournier turned her back to Ivain and began to talk softly to the children once more.

Left alone, Ivain's thoughts moved beyond the confinement of the room, into the room where he had first seen Mme Kamiska, and he wondered what she was thinking of all this. She must have gotten the idea by now that he would fight her to the end. Had he shown his hand too quickly? No. He gathered she must have known it. But the thing he was not sure of was whether he was doing what he was doing because it had all been decided beforehand, or was there still something that belonged singularly to himself? Had Mme Kamiska also foreseen the moves against herself with the knowledge that it was all important in the play she had written to have an antagonist? And he remembered how often he had told himself: "The more ruthless the antagonist, the better the play." How ruthless was the JanKam Co.? Was Mme Kamiska just playing with him, winding him up the way she would wind up a music box to watch the movements of the ballerina on its top turning and turning with her arms high in the air, and her leg straight in front of her? Was she watching the expressions on his face as he discovered the depths of happiness or despair as they happened to him? That he did not know, but admitting that she was behind all his spoken words, they still happened to coincide with what he wished to say at the time he said them.

He was about to leave when he saw the teacher near him. "Mme Fournier, don't think too badly of me," he said, as he walked out. He saw that she looked at him with a sad expression, and perhaps wished to say something, but he quickly turned his back to her and strolled down the corridor.

The following day, he heard that the children were inconsolable, that for the first time in years the play was a complete flop; that the parents could not understand what had happened, and the only thing that saved the evening was the decisive generosity of Fabian, who, in the middle of all this confusion, gallantly got up and said that his guest had acted on his advice, but had chosen the wrong moment to deliver the envelope; for he, Fabian Alfred, had decided to surprise everyone and give every child a thousand francs for their performance. By this gesture the evening, and the reputation of the Fabian Alfred's, had been saved. As far as Ivain's own reputation, he did not care. He felt elated. A small victory had been gained.

Much later on, France would ask him once as she spoke of the play: "Why did you do it?" And he had answered, "I did it to make a boring evening more interesting." She had been thoughtful and silent, and had never replied. The matter was dropped and never picked up again.

Outside on the street he found a strong wind, that not only tangled his hair, but flattened whole patches of sun-burnt corn in the fields, and bent the branches of the trees, scraping them against each other, making strange discordant sounds that gave the night a feeling of mystery and awesome power. He looked up at the sky and found it so dark, so full and so thick that for a moment he thought it was made of velvet, velvet that he could easily reach with his hand, cut off a piece and keep forever. He tried to scan the sky for stars, but could see none. They were all hidden behind the darkness of the clouds. The air was moist, full of mist, and Ivain thought that during the night it would inevitably rain, rain hard, and he felt a subtle pleasure thinking that he would hear it touch his window panes, knowing he was safe under warm covers. With these thoughts in mind he returned home full of joy. He had seen that any "written script" could be stopped in the middle, and his walk home was more at a saunter than at an ordinary pace.

He reached Le Plessis and opened the iron gate. He was surprised to find an open note laying on the ground in front of him. It was from Allegra and it said, "I am waiting for you in my room." He picked it up, and then looked toward the house and saw that there was a light on, in the upper floor, at the height of Allegra's room. He wondered if the note had something to do with Mme Kamiska. Was she angry at him? Was she going to punish him in some unforeseen way?

He ran to the main house, went up a flight of stairs, then walked down the long corridor until he reached Allegra's room. He stopped and knocked lightly at her door. Hearing a "Come on in," he entered her room. Inside, he found Allegra under a sheet so sheer he could see the contour of her body as well as the thin ridge of her underwear. After taking off his jacket and throwing it on the chair, he sat on the edge of her bed, and for a moment forgot why he had come. Then, remembering he wanted to share with her what had happened in the little theater, he said, "I've just had a first taste of victory over 'the written script.'" He recounted the whole incident, leaving out nothing, and as he went on and on, he realized that a strange, unexplainable happiness had come over him. It felt good to be there with Allegra, for she was the only one who knew his predicament and could sympathize with him. But her mind was somewhere else, though she did say, "Winning a battle, doesn't mean you'll win the campaign or the war."

"Do you know that for a fact?" he asked.

"No," she said as she started to caress his arm. But he was not interested in her caresses. He wanted to go on speaking about the play. She looked at him. "Don't be angry with me, for not being dressed up like you. It was just too hot. I find it more pleasant to be without any clothes on, under this sheet."

"She is being provocative," he said to himself, but pretending he had not noticed it, he looked about him, as if her seductive ways had not touched him one way or another.

"It is silly of you to keep the flame going for a woman who has another husband," she said in a little voice that seemed to be imitating that of a wind-up doll.

"She is still my wife," he answered, annoyed at her insistence.

Allegra would not give up, "Your love for her was in another life. This is the present. Why don't you exchange her for me?" And, as she did not get any answer from Ivain, she went on, "You may think you are who you were. But you're not." She stopped and looked at him. "Why are you laughing?"

"I didn't know who I was even in my other life," he said. "In any case it's easier for me to love someone who doesn't know anything about 'the written script,'" and as he said it, he looked at her as if to say, you are my partner in the situation I am in, and that kills whatever love there could be between us.

"But," Allegra continued "I too know very little of your 'script.' Remember that I get my lines during the night, therefore it's not my fault if I don't know what happens at the end of the play, nor in what circumstances you will reveal who you are, and to whom." She stopped, and started playing with her hair, pulling it first to one side of her face, then to the other. After a moment she said, "I only know that I have a great desire to be near you, and that you attract me more than anyone has ever attracted me, and I wish you would lie with me on this bed." And with that she pulled aside the top sheet, and opened her legs slightly so that Ivain could see that she was wearing finely made scanty underwear of white lace.

He was silent for a while, but then said to her: "Why, why don't you fight along with me?"

"Fight what?" Allegra said, looking at him as she had looked at him that first time they had met on the road.

"Fight the words that are suggested to you every night."

"But I can't," she said, lifting her short hair that had fallen on her face again, "I can't, because that's the nature of things, and

109

I belong to it. That is who I am, just as much as what you do and say is who you are."

"Don't you understand," he said. "You belong to them, and since my arrival you have often tried to seduce me for reasons that must belong to 'the script' and have nothing to do with desire and love. You're doing what you have to do mechanically, without knowing the real motive behind it. Don't you see that the meaning of it all still escapes both of us?"

"That's not true," she replied. "I care for you. I wish to be part of you, and that's something I feel within myself. I believe you feel it too, or you wouldn't have entered my room, taken off your jacket and sat on the edge of this bed," she said. Ivain looked at her and felt as sorry for her as he felt for himself. She was very beautiful, but he was leery about coming any closer to her. "Her mischief was perhaps done innocently," he thought, "perhaps even unknowingly." He asked her if she had heard from Mme Kamiska. She answered that no, she was not in touch with her. As a matter of fact, she was not, under any circumstances, allowed to get in touch with her. "But why are we talking about this person," she asked, "when all I want is to be close to you?" Ivain looked at her again, and he realized that she was hiding something under the pillow. He put his hand there and pulled out a small photograph of Mme Kamiska sitting on the very point of a half moon with her legs crossed.

"Why do you have this picture?" he asked.

"Because," she answered, "I always carry it with me. Sort of a good luck charm," she said. He looked at her again as she put the photograph inside a drawer, and he realized suddenly that he wanted to lie with her, kiss her, hold her in his arms, and touch those legs she had shown him time and again. He was about to bend down over her, when he heard a noise in the corridor. Fabian and France had come back, and as they passed her room, he heard two little knocks on the door. Allegra got up, wrapping the top sheet around herself, and walked toward the door. She did not open it, but said sotto-voce, "I'll be right down." And then he heard steps going down the stairs and other, lighter steps going into France and Fabian's bedroom.

"Where are you going?" Ivain asked Allegra, though he knew the answer.

"I'll be back later on," she said. "I have to go now. I don't love him," and then she added, almost as an excuse for what she had just said, "Have you seen how much hair comes out of his ears? A whole tuft. I try to cut it off every time I am with him. But it's no use. It keeps growing." She stopped for a second, only to begin again, "I'm not attracted to him. I'm only attracted to you."

"Don't go," said Ivain. "Stay with me tonight. Do what is not expected from you, as I did just a little while ago in the children's play."

"What makes you so sure that what you did tonight was not expected from you?" she said in a rather sibylline utterance as she put on some gray silk stockings that made her legs shine as if they were made of silvery powder. Ivain trembled involuntarily and whispered to her, "Do you know something that I don't know?" But she did not answer, and only said, "Wait for me here, I'll be back, and then I'll be yours. You can take me with you to the end of the world, and I'll come. I'm just doing it because I have to. There's no other way to explain it."

"You can stop yourself," Ivain said. "I'll keep you here, in my arms. I won't let you go. Stay! I need you." He begged her, as he realized that he liked her all the more because he had sunk to a new low in his own estimation. *L'amour à la boue*, that was his weakness. He wanted her because she was low, and common, and was humiliating him now. "How far will I fall?" he asked himself silently. He didn't know. He wished to stop himself, for he knew he could fall very far, but he couldn't do it.

Meanwhile, Allegra kept on dressing herself for a party that she could not miss for anything in the world. She put on a light blue blouse, decorated with tiny yellow flowers, leaving open the first three buttons, so that Ivain could still see the shape of her small pretty breasts that he knew would fit in the cup of his hand. He tried to touch her by opening his arms toward her, but she retreated, leaving his arms dangling in the air. In spite of himself, Ivain felt such loneliness at the idea of Allegra going to Fabian, that he now implored her without restraint. She answered him, "I would really like to. I would like to remain with you for thousands of years. We were made for each other. I've waited for someone like you all this time."

"Why are you going, then?" he asked her.

"I don't wish Fabian to be your enemy," she said. "He might be very important for you one day. You might need him." She stopped. "Besides," she continued, "I must prepare him for his loss, for he will lose me soon. Lose me completely."

"Really? Will he lose you to me?" he asked, and immediately decided that if her answer was yes, she would be less interesting to him.

"Of course," she said.

"That won't be easy," said Ivain, regretting he had wanted her so badly just seconds ago. "No one likes to surrender the person one cares about from one day to the next."

"Be careful what you say," she whispered, as she became pensive. "We're never alone. Someone is always watching us, even when we do the most secretive things, such as washing ourselves, for instance."

"Who is watching us?" asked Ivain, becoming suddenly suspicious.

"The shadows around us," said Allegra laughing. "Do you really believe there isn't an audience around us? We're on stage all the time."

"I don't see anyone," said Ivain looking around.

"Well then, if there aren't any shadows there is always the Godlet and his Daughter," she said, and she became sad, or so it seemed to Ivain, for revealing a secret that perhaps should not have been revealed.

"Do you realize," Ivain said, "that if we stayed together all night long, we would be praised, not condemned." And he took a deep breath. "We're not hurting anyone and we may even be helping France and Fabian's marriage."

"That's true," answered Allegra. "But it's too early for us to become lovers. I know that for a fact. We have to wait for another occasion. The occasion will inevitably present itself when it presents itself, and not one minute sooner. That's how it is." And then she went on, "Believe me – I have your interests at heart. I know what you need, and I'm trying to get it for you. I might even be able to help you." Ivain looked at her now, all dressed up and beginning to put heavy rouge on her cheeks, and a dark color of blue over her eyelid. Was she a friend? What was she up to? he asked himself. Could she be trusted? Was she sincere in her offer to help him?

"I'm sorry that you have to see me painted like this," she said at last. "I know you like a more natural woman, with her face washed only in cold water. But with him it's different." He knew she was referring to Fabian, though she did not say his name. "He needs to see a lot of paint and needs to see me dressed in a vulgar way to work up sufficient excitement these days. He also makes me walk up and down the room for a long time, asking me to move my bottom in a certain way, as if I were a dish. 'Chicken in aspic!'" She laughed at what she had just said, adding, "The normal does not interest him any longer."

"Ah," said Ivain, and his thoughts went to France. Would she too have to put up with those differences? He looked at her again. What did he really know about Allegra? Very little, he thought. Yet, he was tormented by the fact that he was both terribly lonely ever since the day he had come back to earth, as well as being physically attracted to this woman, not only because of her unusual beauty but because she emanated a sense of danger. "Not unlike the danger I sensed when I visited the Victoria Falls in Africa." And he now mused over those memories of his previous life, where he remembered he had to restrain himself from joining that incredible, attractive, transparent water that acted as a prism, transforming a horrible death into an irresistible rainbow of colors.

"If you go to him, I won't be here when you come back," he said and got up and was about to leave, when she said, "You will return to me. It is written. If not tonight, then another night."

"If it is written, then it is written in the wind," and he said it with more malice than Allegra's this time round. He then closed the door behind himself with a slam, ran into his room and began to mull over for the first time that, if he went back to her, he was really doomed. It was nothing that he could put his finger on. It was just something he felt inside himself, and with this thought in mind, he promised himself to be more careful from now on and not let his impulses get ahead of his good sense. But before closing his eyes, he remembered that history had gone ahead by leaps and bounds through the irrationality of men, not their good sense, and this thought disturbed him to the point that he could hardly fall asleep, and when he did, it was only for a brief fitful sleep.

DISCOVERY

"Expende Hannibalem"
Juvenal
(Combien de livres de cendres trouveras-tu
dans ce grand capitaine?)

On the fifth day of Ivain's return, he realized that there was still no news about the one all important matter – his own writing. Meanwhile at Le Plessis no one understood why he had created such chaos at the small theater, and he heard sentences whispered here and there, such as: "Our guest is a boor," or "Who does he think he is?" But ultimately his actions were dismissed by France and Fabian, as well as by the rest of the villagers, as being those of an extravagant or an eccentric actor who always wants his presence to be center stage, even at a small event such as the children's play of Rosay. It is true that, on the day following the incident, there had been talk between his host and hostess of asking him to leave, but Allegra interceded on his behalf, or so she said afterward, and calmed everyone's feelings by saying that it was just an innocent joke on his part, meant more as a funny gesture than anything else. France's only comment, repeated to him also by Allegra, was that – "If he wants to be an actor, and have a stage of his own, he just has to take a plane for New York, and not bother us any longer. – And," she had added, "when he buys his ticket he can also buy one for you as well. Good friends should be together." Ivain was surprised at the great anger that those words held in them, and he realized how unhappy France really was. But for the moment he couldn't help her out. "I should really begin to concentrate my attention on Allegra, then France would think kind thoughts of me," he said quietly, and promised to take Allegra out with him the first time he went walking around the grounds.

Meanwhile, alone in his room Ivain now took out his black wallet and realized that among the papers Allegra had handed him upon his return, there was also a short, abbreviated list. The list consisted of the most important historical events that had taken place during his years of unconsciousness. They were the highlights of what had happened in the world between the years 1984 and 1994.

As he held these notes in his hand, Ivain felt a sense of awe, for since his return, he had often wondered what he had missed in those ten years he had been absent. Wondered if what he had missed was of any consequence to his way of thinking. Could there have been something so startling in those years as to make him change his mind toward the way he felt about the world in general and toward France in particular? "Would these events have had any effect on the way I lived?" he asked himself, as he looked over the sheet of paper and read it line by line.

At first, he tried to control his feelings and looked at the notes with a certain detachment, the same detachment he used to have in his past life, for then the flow of history had only touched him tangentially, as the flow of water in a river on whose bank he might be standing. On those banks he sometimes imagined himself as seeing mutilated, unrecognizable bodies floating by, sometimes he believed he saw generals with shining medals on golden boats. Sometimes he thought he saw real heroes or heroines on rafts, or refugees paddling to get away from whatever horror was behind them.

But, as he read on, he became increasingly excited – hungry to know the direction the flow of history had taken. He tried to relate what he now read to his previous knowledge of this or that country, or of this and that person, and see if he could link together what was happening at present with what he remembered of its past. Some of the events were so stirring and touching, that Ivain felt his eyes filling with tears. The world had lived through turbulent and unpredictable times. "But when had it not?" he asked himself. "Hasn't existence on this planet been, at best, hazardous and unpredictable?" Still, it seemed to him that there was a definite return to a darker age, such as the one that had followed the ruin of Rome.

There were the not unexpected famines in various parts of the world, guerrilla warfare, terrorist attacks, disasters at sea, countries in the throes of exchanging one tyrant for another, as well as some extraordinary natural disasters. Strong earthquakes that had leveled cities and mountains, terrifying fires that had burned thousands of homes, huge floods that had turned vast territories of fertile land into lakes or made them part of the sea, and plagues raging out of control. But, out of all this information, three items stood out. The end of an immense empire, which had been broken up into small and large countries; the death sentence uttered by extremists toward an English writer for having written a book that displeased them; and the death of the widow of a late President of the United States who had been very popular both for her grace and her beauty. At first glance it seemed inconceivable to Ivain to think that an empire could collapse so suddenly in just the matter of a year or two, when it had seemed so solid and durable in his other life. But it seemed equally inconceivable, at the end of the century, to have a writer under a death threat just because of his writing. "Has nothing really changed from the burning of Giordano Bruno or Savonarola," he asked himself, "or from the trial of Galileo?" And he muttered under his breath, *Eppur si muove!* And as he said it, he thought of the death of the gentle widow of the slain president. He felt sorry that he would never again talk to her, for he had found her to be an admirable, sweet and caring person whenever he had met her.

He did not know it then, but later on, at the end of his second stay on earth, Ivain would find out that, of all the books that had been written on papyrus, or on clay tablets, or on paper, the inheritors of the earth would only find Allegra's brief list of historical notes. From these notes they would assume certain truths – which they wrote down and studied over and over, until they had memorized them. They assumed that the arches of the McDonald's represented a symbol for a temple of some sort where a variety of animal sacrifices took place. That the remnants of churches were places for the ritual sacrifice of humans, which they called "the small boned animals," in order to eat their flesh and drink their blood. They also assumed that the Empire that disintegrated had been called Atlantic, that the famines that took place had been due to the falling of a large meteorite in the desert of North America, and that the various terrorists were a religious sect, preaching peace and love on the planet "Earth" which they called planet "Ocean."

But for the moment, what surprised Ivain most about these events was the fact that the world had, in point of fact, gone on without missing him at all, and he assumed it would go on the same way when he disappeared again, unless he established himself as a worthy writer. France was the key, for she knew more about the fate of his papers than anyone else. Yet what could he do to get closer to her, short of revealing who he was?

This particular morning, Ivain, not able to endure the absence of his wife any longer, went into the formal garden in front of the house, and hid carefully behind the full leafed branches of a large wisteria. He was trembling with a nervous fever at the thought of being caught in an act that could be construed as voyeurism. But the need to get a glimpse of France was such that he overcame the terror of being discovered there. Later on, after he had seen a swarm of white butterflies with dark spots on their wings that looked like little ships with sails furled, floating on a current of air that brought them inside her room, he felt secretly tormented and he involuntarily trembled. It was only after Fabian discovered him there, and came near him to talk, that France suddenly appeared at the window, scantily dressed, with her hair wet from a recent shower, and with little beads of water rolling off her face, down her neck and below, below where he could not see, but where so often he had lost himself. The butterflies were now resting on the yellow cotton curtains that hung in the bedroom, and Ivain was grateful that Fabian spoke of that mysterious happening, as if it was a portent beckoning good tidings. Yet he was overcome with a feeling of shame even as Fabian was saying, "Perhaps now we'll get good news from Perrot. Perhaps now all will be well." That shame made Ivain try to explain himself, and in doing so, he found himself getting deeper and deeper into unlikely excuses. He had come "to see the wisteria." He had come "to see the apparition of those miraculous insects perceived from far away." He had come "to sit for a while on a branch of the low tree nearby." He had come to – and here he stopped. "What's the point?" he thought, "Fabian must know I came here to see the loveliness of France." But Fabian didn't say a word out of place, even if he had guessed the truth, for there was no shadow of reproach on his side, nor any doubts that Ivain had come there for any other reasons, except those he was now describing. As he listened to his cousin, Ivain wondered what was really going on inside his head and heart.

That night France made an uncommon appearance at the dinner table to be with her guest from New York and with "the other woman." She had gotten in the habit of calling Allegra "the other woman" to her maid Jacqueline. Ivain overheard her using that expression one day as he was passing in the corridor and felt a desperate sorrow for her. He stopped long enough to hear Jacqueline's response. "How little respect M. Alfred has shown his wife lately," she said, "and how easily he's forgotten the small niceties of life, such as bringing flowers, or writing notes to be placed under her pillow, as he often used to do." From this conversation, casually heard, Ivain deduced that France could not hide her sadness at having a husband who left her bed at night to go to another woman, but he also saw that she kept her sorrow to herself. Jacqueline and Anatole, meanwhile, would run the house – clean it, make the beds, serve the dinner. That night, they added a place for France, and seated her facing him. Ivain looked up, and noticed that her shame gave a moving yet stinging quality to her beauty. He would have liked to help her, for more than one reason, not the least of which was to be physically close to her once more.

The memory of the warmth of her body made him blush. It was in a confused state that he remembered – "My writing was the real reason I agreed to come back, not France. France was only a second thought in my mind, when I was standing in Mme Kamiska's presence." He sighed and, remembering his ambition, Ivain felt remorse, for he had placed fame and honor before love.

At the end of dinner France startled everyone by saying, "Johnny, would you be so kind as to go to the village with Allegra tomorrow, and place the 'ad' we spoke of in the newspapers?" She looked at him sweetly. "And don't forget to put in the amount of the reward." He nodded, and said he would do it first thing in the morning. "Oh, Fabian," she went on, "what a small price we're paying if we can get those papers back!"

"That's generous," said Ivain, thinking of the enormous sum they were willing to spend on him. But then, as he reflected, he felt that they were spending his own money, or the money they had inherited from him, so it was only right they were ready to give a large reward.

"I'll drive you first thing in the morning," Allegra said as she turned to him with a vague smile on her lips, so vague that he could not make out if it was a smile of happiness or of sadness.

"Thank you," Ivain answered her.

"There's no need to thank me. I am the one who should thank you," she said, and he felt that she was just being over-polite about the whole thing. The silence that followed was so enveloped in a sad aura, that he got up and, excusing himself, walked out to the front lawn. There, with an impatient move-ment, he took a few steps and, turning around, looked at the house, and was surprised to see that the space it filled seemed petrified in time. There was a sense of solitude and uncertain-ty about its beauty. Beauty that one day would pass, as he had passed, leaving behind just a few memories of what he had been, memories he was now impatiently searching for. He heard the night birds singing somewhere in the distance, and a young nightingale, just learning his musical score, beginning his chant much closer to him. He looked up and saw that it was going to be a clear night, and that the full moon would soon shine. "An August moon," he said under his breath, "it will be a red moon. It will have the luminous colors of the fires of the sun, caught and reflected in its glacial atmosphere, and it will be ours tonight, with so much light that we shall read by it." And he made a plan to come out later on, when everyone was asleep, to find out the exact path that the thieves had taken, undisturbed. But, changing his mind, he decided to embark immediately on this project. He made a conjecture that the thieves must have moved the objects out of the house through the large French windows, and then carried them into the back of the property. He started to walk in that direction, carefully avoiding the open windows of the dining room, where an in-decipherable sound of voices reverberated out into the night, and tip-toed on the small white gravel, made whiter by the ris-ing rays of the moon. He moved noiselessly, so as not to attract attention to himself. The gravel occupied a large space at the back of the house that looked like half a circle, and then continued into three little paths that led to the rose gardens, and beyond that, into the woods that surrounded Le Plessis.

Ivain was at a loss to know which path to take, but finally he felt a sense of powerful attraction to the one on the far right, and taking it, he began to look right and left for any clues he might find. In the formal gardens, where the bushes had been cut not higher than a foot, he found that many had been trampled over as if someone had passed through them in a great hurry, bending and breaking them, without much thought as to what they were destroying. "I might be on to something," he thought, and continued to walk the graveled path, until it abruptly ended in the wooded area that was covered with a thick mantle of ivy. There he cursed himself for not having taken a flashlight with him, for the rays of the moon, though filtering through the thick branches of the trees, scattered only odd patches of light on the ground. Here, Ivain began to walk more carefully, still trying to discover something, anything that would be of help to him in his search. He walked until he reached the stone wall that enclosed the whole property. He was surprised to find that in part it, too, was covered with ivy, so thick in places that it looked enormously tall, as if Le Plessis was a medieval citadel. He could see more clearly now, since there was at least twenty feet of space between the last row of trees and the wall. He started to walk close to it, almost touching the stones, checking for signs of anyone's having passed that way, and a little bit farther, he found what he was looking for. On the wall just ahead of him there was a ten-foot gap, where the ivy had been torn down. One could still see the broken, knotted vines scattered on the ground. Unquestionably, that was the spot where the furniture had been pulled up and pushed over to the other side where a truck had probably been waiting. He stopped and thought for a moment. The drawers must have been taken out beforehand to make the burden lighter. If so, perhaps some of the papers could have scattered on the ground. He looked around carefully, and sure enough, he quickly spotted bits and pieces of white paper, some as large as half a page, some much smaller. Trembling he picked up the one nearest to him, and by the light of the moon, he began to read what was on it. Fragments of sentences came out of it and remained motionless in the silent air. "– the Dictator, the great captain of antiquity – descendant through Aenea from Venus –" That was one of his best papers on Caesar in which he discussed what it must have been like to feel like a God, and descend from a God. Alexander of Macedonia had felt the same way, and the Pharaohs of Egypt, including Cleopatra. He read on, "– the great collection of enormous, gigantic bones, probably dinosaur bones dug up in all parts of the known Roman world and beyond, referred to by Suetonius as 'huge skeletons of extinct sea and land monsters, popularly known as – Giants' bones' – bones his nephew Octavian would one day proudly display in his collection at his sea-side villa at Capri, a collection perhaps begun –" and here the page ended, so Ivain finished the sentence, "begun, in my opinion, by Caesar himself, who would have been interested in discovering the thread between the fantastic creatures of the Greek myths, which these mysterious remains suggested, and the birth of his immortal nature. Those bones would have sung in his ears the songs of aquatic birds with immense wings. Bones that spoke of giant creatures roaming the earth with enormous powers, powers that only Gods would have had. Bones that were the living proof that Homer's sirens, that the one-eyed men, and all the strange creatures of Herodotus, existed." He stood there, trying to remember the rest of the paper, and how he had written it. Sentences and quotes floated by him, but that was all. He would need to sit down and think it out again. He would do it tomorrow, he thought, when he had more time. As for now, he bent down again, and pushing aside the ivy with his hand, he kept searching for more bits and pieces of his writing. Not far away he was lucky enough to find a full page of another paper whose title was, "I don't care to please you, Caesar, nor to know if you are black or white," which were the first two lines of a lost poem of Catullus. Again, he held the crumpled sheet of paper in his hand, and carefully folded it and put it in his pocket, wondering if he could one day reconstruct it, too. He searched for a while longer, but the shadows of the trees were making it almost impossible for him to see anything. At last, he started to walk back with his newly found bits of treasure which made him extremely happy, but for the thought that there was certainly some reason why he had discovered them. That reason had to be tied up with the green disk in his pocket, he was certain of that, and he involuntarily touched it. In any case his papers existed, and he would somehow either find them again, or rewrite them. He had time, all the time in the world, to do it. He would dedicate a thousand years to just one paper. Ten thousand, if needed, to a manuscript; and with these comforting thoughts in mind, he found that he had been walking aimlessly and in so doing, had reached the pond of Le Plessis.

The waters in the pond were transparent. It had rained hard the night before and it had washed away all the green algae. For some reason, the ducks had taken flight that same day, and the pond was now just a mirror of water, waiting for its inhabitants to come back, though it was full of the most varied kinds of little gold fish, moving silently here and there. The pond had always been one of his favorite places, both in his youth and later on when he was married, for he would often take France there, and together they would sit by its side and feel as if they knew what was going on in the world. He sighed at the memory and lifted up his eyes to see part of his large house in the background. Just then a window opened and Ivain saw the outline of a woman bending forward and with her slim open arms she pulled the shutters in. It all happened so fast that he was left wondering. Had it been France, or Allegra, or the maid? That image brought back the memory of how he had felt when he first saw France, with her disheveled hair across her face. That was all he needed to feel happy now. It was in this newly found happiness that he became aware of the presence of someone near him, and turning, he was startled to see France sitting on a small wooden bench they had often sat on together, looking out into the calm water.

She had not seen him, for he had stopped behind a large willow tree. "She remembers," he thought, "she remembers our special place." And, with a vengeance, memories of their past love came back to him. He remembered how she had run toward him that first time he had brought her to Le Plessis, and he had taken her up in her arms and lifted her up off the ground, only to put her down slowly as he was promising never to let her go again. He felt again the joy of seeing her hands full of daisy petals she had pulled off, asking the flowers if he loved her, or loved her not, and laughingly throwing the petals at his person, saying that the marguerites had never lied to her once, and that they said he loved her. He remembered his incredible pleasure at discovering her love notes, written on colorful paper, and hidden in different places, including the foot of his bed where he would find them at night, and his going under the covers to rescue them, bringing them up near his pillow, and reading them by turning on a small flash light so as not to wake her up. And he remembered her perfume which she had on even now. It was a perfume of a delicate white, spring flower, which after a while changed to the different scent of the violet when it is just picked from the ground. It was with these images in mind that he now felt the need to make his presence known to her. He shook a branch. She did not move. Did she not wish to talk to him? He shook the branch again, harder this time. At that she looked up toward him, searching to see who was there. She seemed to recognize him, for she said in a calm, soothing voice, "It's dangerous to be out with a full moon," and he did not know if she really believed it or if she was being ironic.

"Some people think that," he said, and then added, "I'm not one of them."

"Why did you leave our dinner table so suddenly?" she asked.

He replied, "Perhaps I just needed to be alone."

"We haven't been much help to you, have we?" she said, adding immediately, "you coming from so far away, and for so little. It seems a shame."

"A night like tonight makes up for it," he said, and going nearer to her, he stood so close that he could smell the faint odor of her perfume growing stronger and stronger at each small step he took, at the same time as he became aware of a sudden stillness that had engulfed the night, making the pond a place of arresting silence. The crickets, the birds, the frogs had all stopped their songs. Ivain and France were engulfed in a stillness that defined their surroundings. The only things that moved were the clouds across a full moon that shed such light that now one could read the scratches on the stones. The trees near and far had long dark shadows that were partly reflected in the water. The dark water of the pond also reflected the moon in its entirety, a large, tranquil shiny moon. A bird flew across the pond, there was no sound of wings, only a form which moved noiselessly and gracefully across the leaves.

"The great owl with yellow eyes," he whispered to France, as he bent down. Then he looked up and saw a cloud cover the moon and the sky became black, but then he saw the Chariot in that darkly lit green sky, and near it, the Pleiades and the North Star. There were fast moving stars crossing the Heavens, and for a moment, Ivain thought the whole sky was moving ominously away from the earth into a realm of its own. Then, as suddenly as the clouds had appeared, they disappeared, and the moon returned and canceled many lights in the sky as it dipped again in the waters of the pond. "Tonight, I will touch the moon," said Ivain, and as France looked on, he slowly walked inside the shallow waters of the pond and, putting his hand inside the circle of the moon, he touched it, and the moon dissolved into a million tiny fireflies, each one holding a lantern on its back, as they fluttered here and there, up and down, on their own waves. "This is what it must be like being God," thought Ivain, and still dripping wet, he walked out of the water. He went close to France, and touching her face with his wet hand, he lifted it up and, bending down, he first brushed his lips on hers, then he held her head with both hands and kissed her with all the force of a passion too long pent up within him.

She rose and for a moment Ivain felt she was going to stay there with him and it was all going to be like old times. But then she looked at him as if she had not understood his gesture, and turning her back to the enchanted pond, and to him, she ran back to the house.

"I am her husband," said Ivain, "yet, I am not her husband," and he understood that the two statements were at the same time both true and false. On an impulse, he had yearned to be close to her this night, to whisper things in her ear as he used to, words that would make her skin grow tiny little bumps, and make her shoulders shiver with love, but she was someone else's wife now, and she would be disloyal to her husband were she to kiss him too. Yet, wasn't he her legal husband? And was not her present husband betraying her openly? And then he remembered that he had been buried a long time ago, and that she did not know he had returned. How could she? Except Lazarus, no one had come back from the dead, he thought. Lazarus seemed more real to Ivain then all the heroes of the Greek and Roman myths, including Orpheus and Persephone, who had died and been reborn. Still, he realized that if he had had love in his heart for France when he first saw her, now, after this episode near the pond, his love had taken a leap forward and deepened. With these turbulent thoughts in mind, he went back to his room and, taking out all the large and small bits of paper he had found, he began to paste them on new, clean, white pages. Back in the garden Ivain did not notice that among the papers he had picked up were some torn photographs as well. He now looked at these remnants of his history. A face there, part of a head here, old people, young people, all smiling, for the photographs spoke of a happy past. Later on, he would identify in those torn bits his mother holding his hand, and his grandfather from his father's side – the man who had made the family wealth. "Built on," as Ivain would often say without malice, "his grandfather Homer's Chicago slaughterhouses." Putting down on a side-table the torn photographs, he took his pen out of his pocket, and said to himself he was ready to work; ready to reconstruct, first and foremost, his paper on the difficult friendship between Catullus and Caesar, and their times.

REWRITING THE MISSING PAPER

The best way to predict the future is to invent it.
Nicolas Negroponte

THE following day Ivain decided to begin a self-imposed isolation, and when he met Fabian having breakfast on the verandah, he told him of his decision.

"I hope," he said, "you will forgive my rudeness and explain it to your wife, my need to be alone for a while. You see, I have to go over the Shakespearean script I've brought along with me," adding, "and the worst thing is that I don't know how long it will take me to get it right. But, come what may, I must be ready for the September opening."

"I see," said Fabian, as he swirled a tiny silver spoon inside his coffee cup and, after putting it down, he asked him, "If I'm not mistaken, you are the understudy for Caesar? Aren't you?"

"Yes I am," and Ivain thought Allegra must have said something, since she was the only one who knew.

"And," Fabian went on, "understudies must be prepared to step on stage at any time, if the need arises."

"That is what I hope for. And that's why I trust you'll understand."

"Go right ahead," answered Fabian smiling. Just then Allegra, wearing a lovely colored shirt and a short pleated skirt, came into the room. She had been walking outside and wanted Ivain to go out with her for a short walk. After excusing himself to Fabian, Ivain got up and followed her. They reached a place where they both sat down on a patch of dry brown moss, burned by the sun. The moss looked parched, but Ivain knew that when the rain came in October, it would soak up the water as if it were a sponge, and turn again into a pale yellow-green carpet. How wonderful it would feel to walk on it again, and have his feet sinking all the way to his ankles in that soft rug. Remembering that feeling, Ivain was overcome with nostalgia for Le Plessis, and how much he had missed it, but he tried not to show it. Instead he asked her a favor. "Do you remember that 'ad' that France mentioned last night? Could you go by yourself and place it in the local paper?"

She said, "Yes, but why won't you come with me?"

Ivain began to explain to her that he was going to be out of sight for a while, but she should not worry about him. He also asked her to refrain from coming into his room. She said she would abide by his wishes, adding, "I'm going to miss you. I think I'm falling in love with you." Ivain looked at her. "Don't do that!" he said, and immediately regretted having uttered something that obviously hurt her. But what did the word "love" mean to Allegra, he wondered. He thought of her as someone who would be demanding, whimsical, and moody. But perhaps he had it all wrong. Perhaps she was just someone who had been badly treated, and still was, caught in "a script" not of her making.

He got up and left her there, sitting where she was, but before entering the main door of the house, he looked back, and thought that he had never seen a more lovely picture of a young woman. She was lying on her side now, holding up her head with one hand, while with the other she was playing with a long stem of grass, which she brought up to her mouth and passed lightly over her lips. She saw him looking at her, and smiled at him. "Does she know something I don't know?" he wondered. After that he walked back into the house, and into his room, and carefully closed the door behind him. Apart from Jacqueline, who would bring him a tray of food from time to time, no one would disturb him now.

Once in his room, he sat down at his desk, and began to work in earnest on the reconstruction of his lost paper. He began to write page after page, read and reread them, tear them up into little pieces, and begin the whole process once more. It soon became evident, even to himself, that to write the paper as it had been written years before would become his obsession. All his thoughts went to the personages he had described so long ago, and which now he tried to conjure back with the same language, down to the same words, wherever it was possible. But questions kept plaguing him. At what point had he described the feeling of the Roman populace? The circuses? The arena? The gladiator fights? The chariot races? Where had he written down what it was like being a Roman aristocrat in the Rome of that time? In which paragraphs did he describe the arrogant Clodius as dangerous? In which had he said *Cherchez la femme* ? No, he had been more specific. At some point he had written – *Cherchez la femme fatale* – thinking of Clodia, for Clodia or Lesbia, as Catullus liked to call her in his poems, had a sinister reputation. She was the most beautiful woman of her time and also the most corrupt, having slept with her brother Clodius, as well as poisoned her husband, or so Cicero had suggested in his *Pro Caelio*. He had tried to describe how Caesar must have known and admired Clodia too, for her brother Clodius was his dearest and most trusted friend, who for a few years ruled Rome as a tyrant, in the dictator's name.

He tried to remember how Catullus had loved Clodia, in spite of the suffering she had inflicted upon him, for his love for her was immense, and ultimately it killed him. At least that is what Ivain thought. It was the romantic in him, no doubt. Ivain again questioned himself as to where he had quoted some lines of one of Catullus' best-known poems, which he paraphrased to himself.

131

"Let us love, my Lesbia,
and let not the envy of old men
come between us –"

But again, he did not quite remember if he had placed it at the beginning of a page or at its end. The punctuation also drove him mad. It got to the point where he wondered what kind of quotation marks he had put before and after certain phrases. And finally he was uncertain if it had been in this paper that he had mentioned the genius of Caesar as a general. Where had he written up his brilliant use of the five reserve cohorts at Pharsalus against the cavalry of Pompey's sons? And what Caesar had said about Pompey, after the latter had won a battle against him, but not followed it up: "He does not know how to win wars!" for here, thought Ivain, Caesar was echoing the words of one of Hannibal's generals, right after the battle of Cannae had been won, who had said: "The Gods have not given you all the virtues, Hannibal, or you would march on Rome at once." But where had he inserted this particular passage?

All of these questions kept Ivain awake at night. He would toss and turn, and keep the light on, hoping to get back an idea or a word that he knew was surely in this particular paper.

Days later, when Ivain reflected on how he finished reconstructing his first paper, he remembered in detail all the difficulty he had had. He worked on it with an energy that was not human, and only stopped writing it when he found himself talking in soft monologues about what Caesar would have said to Catullus, or to Cicero or Clodius. Incredibly, in these monologues, with the help of his imagination, he was able to hear realistic conversations between his characters, able to close his eyes and visit Rome and, more specifically, the Suburra district where Caesar had lived. He even conjured up visions of all the cities that Caesar had destroyed in Gaul, and elsewhere, without having to leave his room. He did this through sheer will-power, having first made a great deal of notes on the humble beginnings of the birth of Rome, from Romulus and Remus, through its seven kings, through the greatness of the Republic with such legendary men as Camillus and Regulus, until the end of the Republic, which coincided with the twenty-three dagger thrusts into Caesar's body in the Senate, on March 15th of the year 44.

Finally, to make the paper look real, Ivain decided to write it longhand. This had the advantage of using the same handwriting as the late Professor's, Ivain mused, and it could be passed off as a first draft of the finished, more polished one, just as some painters do sketches on cardboard before painting them on canvas. To make it look as if it had been written on old paper, Ivain took some ordinary white paper, and moistened it so that when it dried, it was somewhat wrinkled. Then one night he went out and, taking a bit of dirt, he passed it over the reconstructed paper, as if it had been trampled on into the ground, near the wall where he had found the other fragments of his writings.

After a week of uninterrupted work, Ivain came out of his room, unshaven and disheveled with the finished paper in his hand. He made up his mind to keep for himself the fragments of his past work which he had found among the ivy. Why he took that decision was not clear to him until he visited his up-state New York farm, "Applebrook," when it became apparent what he had to do with them.

In the corridor, he asked a surprised Jacqueline where he could find M. Alfred. She had only the time to say, "It's so nice to see you out of your room, M. Elliab." Then, as there was only a curt, "Thank you for all you have done for me, Jacqueline," on his part, she understood he must be in a great hurry, and continued, "M. Alfred must be in his studio."

Ivain went downstairs and knocked at the door, and when he

heard Fabian's voice saying, "Come in, whoever you are!" he entered.

"Well, how is it going, Johnny?" Fabian said. "Do you feel comfortable now with your part?"

"Yes," said Ivain, "I used the time well." And he felt angry with himself for lying to his cousin.

"Good," said Fabian. "But don't think that in your absence we have been hopelessly idle. Perrot was here and we have found the way the thieves entered the house."

"Oh?" said Ivain. "Where did they come in?"

Fabian took him to one side of the living room and showed him a painted wall panel that actually opened up into a secret stairway. It had been Perrot who had found it, by knocking on the wall and getting an empty, hollow sound back. And it was only then, in his second life, that Ivain realized that the house in which he had spent his whole childhood had hidden its greatest mysteries from him. How much history it secretly held between its walls, and how little of it he had really known! He now followed Fabian down the stairs and found himself in a crypt filled with ancient medieval statues of kings and queens. Ivain realized immediately that what Fabian had found was a trophy of enormous value, having been saved from the revolutionary times thanks to the stratagem of hiding them in these underground vaults.

"Notice," said Fabian, "all the statues have their heads on them."

"Yes," said Ivain laconically, "the guillotine may have taken the heads off the people who inhabited the old house, but not that of their kings." They both laughed. Then they walked down long corridors, some half buried under the debris that had fallen from above. And Ivain realized that while he had been in his room rewriting his paper, Fabian had hired some laborers to dig farther down into the earth. He had dug through the dark ages, through the age of the Romans, through the age of the Gauls, down to the iron and stone ages. Fortunately, all this digging had been done quite a distance from the main house, and was stopped when the men had found the remains of a fortified tower, used, no doubt, to search for enemies coming their way.

"Here," thought Ivain, "soldiers lived and died to defend their feudal lord." And, still holding his paper in his hand, he retraced his steps and went up the secret stairway, followed by Fabian. When they were back in the studio, Ivain went to the window and was blinded by the sudden bright light of the afternoon sun. He closed his eyes, and still shaking from all he had just seen asked himself, "How many more secrets are there in this house that I have missed? How many lives do we need to live to understand it all?"

He remained near the window until he heard the voice of Fabian saying, "Well, what do you think of what I've showed you?"

"Quite an extraordinary discovery," said Ivain. "Who would have thought –?" and he let his words trail.

"I bet you that, if we dug deep enough, almost everywhere around here we could find amazing relics of the past."

"Humm," mumbled Ivain, still following his own thoughts.

"Would you like a drink?" asked Fabian, and Ivain, from the corner of his eye, saw he was pouring one out for himself.

"No, thank you," he said, still holding tight the paper in his hand. "By the way, Fabian," he continued, "I forgot to tell you that – I may have come across something important for the 'Ivain La Baille Room,'" and he handed the paper to his cousin.

"Really?" said Fabian, and with ceremonious courtesy he bowed forward a little. He took the paper from Ivain's hand, opened it up, and began to read the first few lines, stopping almost immediately.

"Where did you find it?" he asked Ivain as he turned it over.

"At the back of the park, in the ivy," said Ivain.

"Oh," said Fabian, "I bet you found it where we discovered a lot of torn pages from the Professor's papers," and with this he opened a red leather-bound brief-case and showed him large and small fragments that had been pasted neatly on gray cardboard. "I bet you found it near the outside stone wall in the back of the house?" He stopped and looked at him. "Am I right?"

"Almost right," said Ivain. "This paper was closer to the pond," he said, still looking away from his cousin, for he was feeling uncomfortable.

"Well, I am amazed we didn't discover it. I mean, both the police and I combed the place day in and day out," he said, "but if it is one of the La Baille papers, it's a great discovery. Much more important that those statues I just showed you. It would mean so much more to both France and myself," Fabian said. Ivain felt more encouraged after these words. "When did you find it?" Fabian asked.

"Oh, just last night," said Ivain, not wanting his cousin to think he had had the time to look it over. "I was talking a walk for the first time in a week, when I saw something shining in the ivy."

"Are you sure?" Fabian was questioning him to the point of feeling uncomfortable.

"Sure, I am sure," said Ivain, and seeing on the little side table near him a silver box, he opened it and took out a cigar.

"Do you have a light?" asked Fabian, again overly courteous, almost as if he was trying to be more than a gentleman, if such a thing was possible.

"Oh this?" said Ivain, looking at the cigar. "I don't smoke," and opening the silver box once more, he put the cigar back in.

"Do you have a light?" Fabian asked again.

And it was only then that Ivain understood his cousin's request. He was not asking for a light to light the cigar he had held in his hand. He was asking for a light to burn the Julius Caesar paper. At the thought of such a terrible action, Ivain shivered involuntarily. All the hours he had spent reconstructing it seemed in vain and lost now if Fabian was going to destroy it. Somehow, he must have made some major mistake for his cousin to realize so quickly that it was not an original paper, but he was afraid to ask. Afraid to say anything at all. His cousin was not in a talkative mood, and they remained silent for a little while. Then Fabian, taking out of his pocket a monogrammed handkerchief, began to wipe his forehead, though Ivain could see no reason for doing so. Then still holding the paper, he said, "Johnny, this is a fake. I don't know how it came to be among the ivy. Perhaps someone was playing a joke on all of us here." And without waiting for an answer he put away his handkerchief, and taking out a golden pen from his breast pocket, he began to underline different passages on the first page. Finally he said resolutely, "We must burn it," and with an elegant gesture, he threw it in the fireplace, which was not lit. This action, being exactly the contrary of what Ivain had expected, so confused him, that before he knew it, he was on his knees rescuing it, and shaking off the ashes that clung to it.

"Why do you wish to keep it?" Fabian asked him. "It's a forgery."

"How can you tell, Mr. Alfred?" asked Ivain, and then corrected himself, "How can you tell, Fabian?"

"I've read every thing of the Professor's," he answered, "and this paper was not there. Besides, I have the complete list of all the papers of my cousin," and he took out a notebook from his desk, opened it up and showed him the titles of all the papers. Every title was there, except for the title of this one paper. Ivain could hardly believe his eyes, but to say more would have compromised him. "Mme Kamiska," he thought, "must be behind this tricky situation. It must be written in 'the script' that this paper must never be part of the others in the Library room." After Ivain came to this conclusion, he gave up trying to save it, and putting his hand in his pocket, he began to search until he found a box of matches. He quickly handed them over to his cousin. Fabian took both the paper and the box of matches from his hand and began to strike one match after another for what seemed an interminable time, without being able to get any to catch fire. Finally Ivain understood that it was part of the dramatic irony of "the script," that he himself should do the job. But when Fabian asked him to help him out, he refused, and was about to leave the room when the next match that Fabian struck lit up immediately.

Ivain stopped to watch him burning, slowly and deliberately, his own words, while he heard Fabian utter what he, himself, considered a paradoxical statement: "This is a moment of truth over falsehood," and went on to explain that it was a moment of triumph, to save the reputation of his cousin, whom Fabian said he held in high regard. "I will not," he continued, "have a forgery placed in the Butler Library." He was talking fast, as if he had much to say. "Furthermore," he went on, "since that particular room will be dedicated to the true spirit of the late, and much missed Ivain La Baille, it is really an altar." So important was the project for both himself and his wife.

Ivain could find no fault with Fabian's way of thinking, and on the contrary found himself praising his cousin for his conscientiousness. Had he not carefully put aside all the little bits of paper he had found outside? Did he not file them as important fragments in the briefcase he kept near his side at all times, such was his fear that they would be lost too?

Still, he could not help thinking, "All my work has been in vain."

Besides, he wondered, what was his cousin going to think of him now? Might he think he had written the paper himself? Might he think he was somehow involved with the forgery? Might he think he had help from outside to please his host and hostess in some way?

Many days later, Ivain was still brooding over this incident. The one consolation he had was that, on the surface, there was no reason whatsoever for John O. Elliab to write a paper on Roman times, and pass it off as that of Ivain La Baille. That thought reassured him somewhat, though he felt all the guilt of a man who had done a disgraceful thing. But, no matter how much he tried to reassure himself, no matter how many times he would repeat to himself that the same hand had written the same paper twice, Ivain now felt diminished in the eyes of Fabian. It was a terrible feeling, and to try to regain his cousin's trust, he began to bring up as often as possible the incident of the paper. He would find excuses to repeat to Fabian the place he had come across it, as if, in the repetition, there was something akin to a sacred ritual that would cleanse the obvious offense he might have given. Then he would bring up the possibility that there may have been two papers on the same subject, that the one he had found was perhaps the first one the Professor had written, a bad copy of the real one. Inevitably his cousin would reply that he knew there wasn't such a paper, and that he should stop talking about it. "I don't understand," Fabian had added, "how this one has sprung up." Those were his very words, "sprung up," as if it had come from nothing. "And fortunately," he would add, "thanks to me, it has gone back to nothing."

These words, instead of lessening Ivain's anxieties for what he had done, only increased it. He now began to be obsessed with the idea that his cousin might know something more than he was telling. That obsession brought Ivain to write notes about small, insignificant events, such as what he had done that day, or what he would like to do the following day. The notes were always written in bad English, full of grammatical mistakes, and he left them purposely here and there, on table tops, on the seats of chairs, in the hope that Fabian would notice them.

"If he does," Ivain would reason alone, "he'll know without a doubt that such a polished paper as the one I've brought him, couldn't possibly have been written by someone like me. A person who should be considered practically an illiterate actor." But inevitably, it was France who would find these notes, and she would keep them in her handbag to be brought out as dinner conversation. There she would publicly show them to everyone, and laugh at her guest's written English.

"I've never been taught to write properly," Ivain would say in his defense. "Fortunately I can read and remember the lines of Shakespeare, and recite them. But the moment I sit down to write a sentence, I forget my own language." And he would cite cases of people he had known who could not say two words without stuttering, but were able to have hour-long telephone conversations without missing a beat.

On these evenings, Ivain's notes began to take on a life of their own, which he could not have foreseen. In fact, they became the only subject that everyone would talk about. In some ways it was a blessing in disguise, since Ivain felt they eased the pain he often had seen on France's face for having to sit at the same table with her husband's mistress. Still, Ivain could not be sure if these notes, besides having made a jester out of him, had lifted the cloud of suspicion from his brow. At one of these dinners, Fabian had remarked, "How strange it is to have someone speak English with such remarkable fluency and yet make so many common mistakes in writing it," while he looked straight into Ivain's eyes.

After that dinner, Ivain stopped writing notes, and stopped

making any more references to the paper. France saw that he was less talkative than usual, and she promised him that, since he had not had the chance of reading anything of Ivain's, she would show him a homemade film, taken on his last day in New York by their housekeeper. Fabian also stopped making hurtful remarks, and even promised to take him to the castle of Vaux le Vicomte in the near future, to see Caesar's marble bust. Ivain thanked both his host and hostess, and began to try to put behind him his own very personal loss.

Still, on the day his paper was burned, Ivain felt an immense sadness. That day, as he was to remember later on, was as dead as the previous ones had been alive with the thought of possible triumphs. Everything in his mind was now chaotic. What he believed would go one way, had turned out a different way. Events were taking on a mysterious life of their own. How much control he had over them, he did not know, and could only wonder silently about it.

That same night there was a huge storm with hail as large as pigeon eggs, and it beat down flowers and plants alike, not to speak of birds' nests that now lay here and there under the trees, like so many broken dreams. Everything was topsy-turvy and, as a final touch, he found a note on his pillow from Allegra asking him to smile more often. What she meant by that, Ivain pondered over all night long.

HOME MOVIE

"... if it be not now, yet it will come. The readiness is all."
                                                              Shakespeare

It was with trepidation that Ivain sat down to look at Natalie's home movie. France had excused herself, for Fabian was calling her to join him in the garden. Monsieur Jean Pierre Michel Delouche, the man sent from "La Forêt" tree nursery, had come and they would be discussing together which tree to plant in the fall, for it had become the Alfreds' common goal to plant at least a dozen new trees every year, and they tried to find ornamental and rare species wherever they could. Ivain, therefore, found himself alone with the movie already set up in the antiquated projector, ready to reveal its images on the large, white living room wall facing him. Before leaving, France had warned him about the projector. "Please," she had said, "watch this machine. It is not reliable. Once it broke down, and the film almost caught fire," and then she had added with the sweetest look, "It is the only film I have of my dear husband," and she had looked away, and he realized that she did not wish him to see her eyes filled with tears. After reassuring her, he pulled shut the gray silk window curtains, which had been elaborately embroidered, and turned off the light but, before pushing down the "play" button on the projector, he went back to that last morning again, back to those last moments of awareness before falling into the dark pit of oblivion and missing time. He remembered pouring himself a cup of coffee, and never taking his eyes off the three clocks in front of him. And then he remembered how startled he had been to see it was eleven o'clock, and the sand and the water had run out of their respective containers. Now, he had been given the possibility of clearing up that mystery. He got up and, taking a step, went round the projector, ready to start it. But instead, he hesitated a second, wondering if he really wished to see his past again. Curiosity, though, got the best of him, and on a sudden impulse, he pressed the "play" button, and standing there he saw his old dining room in New York appear on the blank wall of Le Plessis. He saw himself sitting in a chair near the table, in the act of pouring himself a cup of coffee. He remembered that he had come in from the terrace and how happy he had been to sit down and drink his coffee. He could see himself shivering even in the movie. It had been chilly outside. He now began to perceive and fill in the blank spaces of that time span that had oddly disappeared from his memory. He was able to do this because Natalie had begun to shoot the movie when he picked up the coffee pot on the table. He looked closely. He was amazed to see himself alive, when he knew perfectly well he was dead. Alive in a film which had been taken ten years before by a woman who was trying out a new toy, a machine she did not yet understand, or know how to use, and as far as he knew never used again. The shock of realizing how odd his present position was made him momentarily confused, and he felt unable to move, or think. He looked in front of him, and tried to concentrate on those images, though sometimes the angle of the picture was awkward and strange. He noticed he had not changed at all from those days. He could hardly believe he even had on the same English tweed suit, the same red colored tie, the same black suede shoes. He tried to look carefully at himself, hoping to find something different in his own present image from that of the past, something that would reveal the passage of time. A new wrinkle on his hands, little lines on the side of his face, a slight sagging of his flesh. He caught a glimpse of himself in a mirror on the wall behind him and saw his own reflection, but found nothing more than the same image in both time spans. The same heavy, bushy eyebrows, gray eyes, set far apart, white teeth, but not perfectly set, and a small, slightly aquiline nose. He looked the same as he had looked just before leaving for the airport, but was he the same person? He suddenly wondered which was the real image of himself – the one he was in the present or the one he was seeing in the past, or were both images false? Or perhaps both were real. Would the old self recognize the new self? Which was the real Ivain la Baille? Which one was the illusion? Or were they both illusions? Was he the real Ivain or was he an impostor? Or more specifically, was there an impostor? He thought of ancient times when, twenty years after the Emperor Nero had plunged a knife into his own throat with the help of the slave Epaphroditus, he was seen alive in Parthia, and so full of magic was his name to the Parthians that they began to worship him again, and gave him up reluctantly to Rome and to the Romans. Had the Godlet also written "a script" for Nero? Had there been a second life for him as well? He looked again at the movie, fascinated by the innumerable possibilities that were theoretically opened to him. And now he saw himself drink up the coffee, and then turn around to Natalie. "It's good to see you enjoying your gift. Hope it will come out all right," he was saying.

"Hope so, too," she had replied, and they had both laughed, and he had wished her well in her first outing in this new endeavor, ending up by saying: "Now, don't overdo it Natalie, or you'll be using up all the film just on me."

"Don't you worry, Mr. La Baille. I'll be coming in and out of the room." She paused, then added, "I'm just afraid I'm so bad at this – I might be taking only the table and not you sitting there." She laughed again out loud. He was now taking another sip of coffee, and was touching the water clock in front of him, bringing it slightly nearer to where he sat. Then a peculiar, inexplicable coincidence happened on and off the screen. Simultaneously, the telephones began to ring both in the living room of his New York apartment, and in the dining room of Le Plessis. It was the same monotonous, annoying and incessant ring that he had heard on the broken phone outside Mme Kamiska's door. The ringing, coming as it was from two opposite directions, made him turn his head now this way, now that way, and he was unable to decide what to do. It was as if that persistent ringing was beckoning him away from the present into the past. He began to wonder why no one, in either place, was picking it up. Where was France? Where was Jacqueline who was always in the house, since Natalie's death? He certainly was not going to do it for them – or was he? On an impulse, just when he had decided to pick up the telephone near him, the ringing stopped. Someone had picked it up, and there was no need for him to do anything now, but an odd thing happened. Though he had no wish to pick up the telephone, his right hand reached for it, propelled by a force that was not his own, lifted it up and brought it up to his ear. It was only then, as he was looking at the old movie, that he realized that this action had also happened in his past, for he saw his own image in the movie, looking absent-mindedly out of the window, with the phone near his ear. He was going to put down the receiver when he was amazed to hear a conversation between two people, whose voices sounded familiar. It was a conversation between France and Fabian, only it had taken place ten years before. At first the words were not clearly understandable. What he heard was a furtive murmur, a whispering, an ensemble of sounds that resembled more the musical notes in a flute and violin concerto, and he was left with the impression of birds' songs sometimes heard in dark, damp rainy forests. High trilling and low-toned warbling, like those sung by long-tailed colorful birds. It took a while for him to understand that they were musical notes from forbidden songs, therefore all the more sweet to the other listener's ear. Perplexed at first, Ivain soon discovered the furtive notes of deceit, for they reached his heart and there made havoc with his feelings, which in rapid succession changed from provocation to anger, and then to something resembling great love. His wife France, the most faithful of all wives, a Lucretia, for whom he would have gladly placed his hand on the fire if someone had suggested otherwise, was now saying and listening to words that left no doubt as to their meaning. Words that only lovers say to each other when their love is very young, or when it is still in that stage when each one lives only for the other. Broken up, tentative sentences. She was saying, "I can't see you any more. What we had – is all there is going to be between us." But Fabian's words were different, "Why are you so cold to me – if only we could always be together as we were the other day – I count the hours – all is forgiven – I know that your interest lies more on my side than with him – I've never stopped loving you – we'll find joy – we'll celebrate – we'll spend what we have and more – we'll live like kings – just say yes!"

Stupefied by this discovery, Ivain wanted to cry or shout, but found that he could not speak. He became aware of the complete silence surrounding him, broken here and there by an audible sigh. When the conversation finished and the lovers had put down their respective telephones, Ivain did the same, both on and off the screen. What he had just discovered was all the more devastating because he himself had always tried to be impeccably faithful. Accused sometimes of being cold toward the opposite sex, he even cultivated the impression, so as not to have to refuse unwanted advances and be impolite. He tried to think clearly, but realized that his thoughts were in great turmoil. Not only had France been unfaithful to him, not only had his cousin deceived him, but that last sentence kept ringing in his ear: "– we'll spend what we have and more – we'll live like kings!"

Spend what? His money? Could they both have had something to do with his death? Did they set him up at the airport? "No, no, that would have been too monstrous a thought," he said to himself. Still he would have liked to know more, but how? Suddenly, he decided that he would give it a try to change "the script" by getting into the screen, thus entering his own past. He got up and was about to jump onto the screen, when he looked up and saw he did not need to do anything. There in front of him was the living Natalie, smiling at him, and at once he realized that by the act of picking up the phone in Le Plessis, he had entered his living room in New York. He had jumped into the black and white light of those ethereal, transparent images, back into the past. Natalie was still rolling the movie and was smiling at him when he turned around from the window and smiled back at her. What she could not know was that, in those last few minutes, which had now become the present for him, an enormous yet invisible weight had come crushing down on his shoulders. He also realized that, for France and Fabian, talking so openly on the phone was an act that went beyond courage. It was an act that had a life of its own and could not be avoided or restrained. It was beyond human comprehension and therefore outside the laws of men. It had been decreed by higher authorities, therefore it was sacred.

Ivain felt the pain of the discovery reaching deep down into his bones. But the pain of the betrayal had just the opposite effect, for it did not conjure up a rage within him, but made him desire France even more. He imagined her making love to his cousin, and how they had dallied with each other. He realized that he had been humiliated, but his response to the humiliation was to want France more than ever before. Her body, which he had merely enjoyed in the past, now became an object of worship, since it was adored by another man. In overhearing what some of their pleasure consisted of, pleasures that he himself had refrained from taking with her, for he had placed her on a pedestal near his head and not merely at his feet, he now wished he had dallied with her in the same fashion. "For such is the double nature of men and women," he thought. "And such is the paradox of their love life. They always have to pursue what they can't have, finding an additional pleasure in anything that is hidden or forbidden." He looked down at his hands before philosophizing on love. "Love can only live on those fantasies," he thought, "for the mere act of love is extremely simple, therefore not enough to sustain the feeling of lust," which now, perversely enough, he felt overwhelmingly toward his wife. Only a complication of this sort would have awakened this strong, odd and inexplicable reaction in him; and though Ivain was not happy that France had betrayed him, he was not unhappy either.

He was thinking these thoughts, as he was moving round the room, when he realized that the reason he had not heard the conversation on that last day was because it had been decreed by the skillful writer that he, Ivain, had to learn the truth about Fabian and his wife at this precise moment, and not one minute sooner.

More than ever did it seem imperative for him to get out of "the written script," but how? – How? he was asking himself over and over, as he was being moved here and there around the dining room, like a piece of carved wood on a chess board. He was moving in a random fashion, pulled by invisible strings. He felt as if his body was really his own, but he was not in control of it. A higher form was in control, and he was just filling the space that had been given to him to play with. He tried to move his foot backward instead of forward, but he found that his foot would only go one way. He was just putting it down where the markers had been placed. There was no visible marker on the floor, no phosphorescent discreet light, but they must have been there for his feet found them without any problem. His arms, too, were being lifted by invisible strings, and his hands moved here and there, wildly at times, making strange circles. He had become a puppet, a perfect puppet made of flesh and bones, instead of soft cotton, velvet, porcelain or wood. He began to take notice of what he was doing. He felt himself taking two steps backward and a step forward, and a step backward and another forward, while his hands were moving up and down, following what he had said that day – years and years ago. His head turned now this way, now that way, and the same could be said about his torso, and the rest of his body. The perfect Marionette, or a Pierrot or – why not – Molière's *Scapin*? The Godlet must have observed well the Commedia dell'Arte, he thought, as he turned around and danced here and there. He even compared himself to the Japanese dolls moved by dark gloved hands, always in a hurry to go nowhere. He began to think of a way to get out of his strange predicament. If only he could make a gesture, either in the movie or outside it, a gesture that had not been written as a stage direction, not written in between dialogues, not indelibly set. But he would have to do it while the Godlet was not looking, so to speak, sneak it in on the sly, slip it in. Nothing big. He could pretend he was turning to the right and, at the last moment, turn left. Or shake his hair in front instead of behind. Do a hop while the Godlet was expecting a skip. Laugh when he was supposed to cry. Or less, much less. He had to be more subtle. Perhaps move his little finger up or down, add a pause, a discreet cough, a noiseless hiccup, a breath held in a bit longer than usual. A rapid batting of eyelashes as he turned his head. A sigh, or if not a sigh, a shiver, a voluntary shiver or just knit his brow. All would do equally well. But, in spite of his good intentions, he had to mouth words that had been said long ago. He now lifted his eyes and saw France standing in her nightgown in front of him. He was stunned by her beauty. He had forgotten how beautiful she had been. Her hair was loose down over her shoulders. Her nightgown was low enough for him to see the shape of her breasts. He approached her with almost the religious fervor of a new convert. He felt dazzled. Ten years had rolled off in a second. Here he was in her presence, the morning that he must go away from her and die. Die with the added knowledge that she was already in another man's arms.

"You look so pale this morning," she was saying. "What is the matter?"

At hearing those words, Ivain suddenly felt like shouting that he had heard the conversation between her and her lover; that her casual question to him now was intolerable, it was a fraud – outlandish in its brashness, but instead he heard himself mutter, "Nothing. Why?"

"You look like the shadow of your former self," she said. And immediately he knew that the Godlet was using his dramatic irony well. He wanted to say: "If I look as if I am the shadow of my former self, it is because I am the shadow of my former self," but instead he said, "Is it time for bread and honey yet?" and France replied, "Not as long as we keep Natalie here." And as she said that, she approached him and kissed him as she had never kissed him. Was she trying to make up? Was she feeling guilty? Her kiss did not give him joy. Instead he felt an incredible inner sadness, although he heard himself saying, "How lovely you are."

After that she left the room momentarily, only to come back fully dressed. Meanwhile, Ivain realized that even at this very moment, he was going forward in "the written script," by going backward like a shrimp. Yet what else could he do? He looked at the gift he had given Natalie, a flimsy camera. Yet, he owed it to her if he was now able to relive this moment in his past.

The fire was blazing in the gray marble chimney and was throwing off such heat, that Ivain felt like taking off his jacket, but no matter how many times he tried, he could not do it. This troubled him. "Why," he kept thinking to himself, "why can't I remove my jacket? Such a simple thing to do." But, he suddenly realized, it had not been written down. Both words and actions were all accounted for, as well as the stage directions. Yet, yet – if he could possibly add or subtract something, he could change the future. Even if only an "and" or a "but" he would not be dead now. A feeling of nostalgia for the life he could have had with France overwhelmed him.

Outside, the rain pelted down hard on the gray buildings of the city. He approached the window and began to look at the maze of chimneys sticking out of the roofs. They were of different heights and widths, some tall and round, some small and thin. They reminded him of pipes in a primitive stone organ where the wind and the rain played their own strange discordant notes. He felt himself turning around and walking toward the fireplace. France was chatting with Natalie, saying, "– you're doing great, Natalie, keep focusing on Mr. La Baille. It will be his home-coming gift. A nice surprise."

Up to that morning, he thought, his wife had looked pleased with herself, her marriage, her life. She was a contented woman, who had never asked much from life, but life had given her everything. Since they had had no children, he had become her child, her best friend, her lover. He thought he knew everything about her, yet he had discovered something he would never have imagined her capable of doing. He tried to reason out when Fabian and France became lovers. It had to be a very recent event, or so he thought. He looked at her and felt one thing above all. He wanted more than ever to live. She said casually, "Fabian just called." He heard himself say, "Why is Fabian Pierce Alfred always calling you up?" And she answered, "You aren't going to be jealous of your own cousin now, are you?" adding, "You won that battle when you married me." She had been silent for a moment before saying, "In any case, he's going to be at the airport today. Coming to see you off."

He tried to listen to her. She was saying, "– but please, Ivain, postpone your trip for a day," and her words suddenly sounded false and unreal.

He wanted to say yes! yes! with all his heart. He even tried to shape his mouth and utter those simple sounds – Y-e-s – and yet he couldn't. He heard himself say, "I must go. Caesar is waiting."

"Can't Caesar wait a day?" Again her words sounded different to his ear. Nothing would sound the same after what he had just discovered.

He wanted to tell her that – Caesar could wait a century, a millennium. He wanted to ask her questions, but instead he heard his own voice say, "Caesar does not wait," and he heard that the intonation of his voice was such that he might as well have said "Death does not wait."

She had started to play with a strand of her light hair as she talked of the autumn, of their walk together, of the color of the leaves. "Oh France," he said to himself, "if only you knew how much I wish to stay!" But the words he uttered had nothing to do with what he was feeling at the moment. Now he wished to confess to her that though today he would disappear from her life, one day they would be together again, that she would be able to nestle against him as she used to, and that his desire for her was more full of passion than ever. But instead he continued to repeat out loud the stale phrases of the past. He was beginning to feel that the situation he was in was both hopeless and desperate when he heard a strange sound coming from far away. It was as if there had been a siren alert, and Ivain began to look round and move as he wished. He was saying that "In the end, he would get it right, yes, that last line of Julius Caesar could be said with the right sincerity of spirit." As he said it he thought he had won, won over "the written script." It was the victory he had hoped for! Now he could reshape his life the way he saw fit. France was still his wife, and his writing would go on and on. But suddenly he realized that a bright light was in his eyes, and he was in front of a blank wall, for the screen had become a blank, and the room was filling up with smoke.

"Johnny! Johnny!" he heard France's voice someplace in the sudden darkness. And then again he heard her scream "Jacqueline, give us a hand!" and a moment later, "Open the window, Johnny, the film has caught fire!" He rushed to open the nearest window, and saw France trying desperately to put the fire out with her bare hands first, then with two pillows from the couch. At last, when she saw there were no more flames, France fell on her knees crying, for the film was now only a mass of dark cellophane crumpled up in a black knot. How had it happened? He looked at France as she was trying to control herself, but not being able to do so, she now cried without restraint. He helped her to get up. She was saying, "Where were you? How could you let this happen?" She paused, "Once before this machine gave us trouble, but we were able to put the fire out quickly. Now all is lost."

"Your hands," said Ivain, as he opened her palms and looked at them, but in that darkness he could not see very well. "You'd better put some ice on them," he continued. She followed him meekly out of the dining room into the kitchen, and let the cold water run over her palms and fingers into the kitchen sink, as Ivain crushed a few pieces of ice and wrapped them in two small towels.

"It seems that bad luck just follows me," she finally whispered, more to herself than to Ivain. "It's as if time is swallowing up all the memories of Ivain." She sighed, "Tell me, how long do you think a person can grieve? I mean grieve for someone one loved a great deal?"

"Are you talking about your late husband?" Ivain asked. But France did not answer him directly; she went on talking as if to herself.

"There is no dead person whose memory does not fade from the mind of man, is there?"

"I don't know," said Ivain, as he tied the towels over each palm, asking her to hold on tight. As he did this, he looked at her hands again, and saw that, though the skin was all red, it was not a deep burn. "A few days," he thought, "and she will be all right." And he was touched by her words and by the fact that she still loved his memory deeply.

Without meaning to do it, right after Ivain gave France the ice, he took her in his arms. It was for a moment only, but it was long enough for France to look at him with disquieting insistence, and he quickly realized he was once more out of place. He left the kitchen, went up to his room, and that night decided not to have dinner with France and Fabian, but to stay put, saying that he was not feeling well. He had made up his mind that he was going to give back to Fabian the immense pain Fabian had given him. Strangely enough, he did not feel as keenly the betrayal of France, though he realized she, too, had broken his trust. But Fabian – Fabian was different. But, wait! Ivain's basic honesty made him realize that Fabian must have felt, at some point, the same pain that he was feeling. Had he not taken away the woman he loved from him? Had he not married her knowing how much his cousin desired her? And following these thoughts, he also wondered if his cousin had tranformed that frightful pain into anger against him. He reflected on this, but could find nothing to reproach him with until this phone conversation. This was different. Fabian had tempted France. He had tempted her successfully, after she was married to him. Married!

On an impulse, dictated more by his wounded pride than by thought, Ivain made up his mind right then and there to seduce Allegra, the pearl of his cousin's eyes, the woman he visited every night. From now on, he was sure, this beautiful and strange woman would be his, if he wished it to be so. He planned to do just that at the first opportunity that presented itself.

THE SEDUCTION OF ALLEGRA

"Is it a wolf? No, it is just its shadow."

IVAIN was missed at dinner. Fabian and Allegra had eaten alone, for France had remained in her room with both hands wrapped in white gauze bandages. Jacqueline never left her side, and kept breaking up a large piece of ice into tiny bits for France to hold, which made the pain bearable. Then she even tried to entice France to have some broth she had made especially for her, but France would have none of it. At last the housekeeper left and went into Natalie's old quarters near the main entrance.

Alone in his room, Ivain was not sure any longer whether or not he really wished to visit Allegra's room. He leafed through an art book that he found on his night table, and as he turned the pages, he waited until he reached the period of the Renaissance before he was sure everyone was in their own rooms, and the house was completely silent. Then he got up and decided not to go through the corridor, but to walk through the wall, into the next room where he knew Allegra was resting. As he did this, he became aware that he was no longer sure of his intentions. Perhaps he was going to have just a chat with her, and not seduce her, as he had promised himself just a few hours before.

He entered the room and saw Allegra lying on the bed, still awake, as if she were expecting someone, and he knew immediately it was not him. Just that simple fact pleased him. He sat on the bed near her.

"I'm glad you are here," she said, looking at him somewhat puzzled.

"I'm glad I'm here, too," he said. "You're the only one I can talk to about what is really happening to me." And he began to tell her how his home movie had gone up in smoke. She said, "I have heard this from Fabian, and I'm sorry to know it's gone. What bad luck!" He appreciated her kind thought. He began telling her about the struggle he was having with "the script" and the struggle he had had that day in particular within the movie, when he had been able to enter but not move about freely.

"I felt so close to changing my life! I believed for a moment that it was within my reach, that I held the key in my hand. But, just when I thought I had triumphed, I realized I was out of the New York apartment, back in this house again." He fell silent for a moment, then began to say, "I was able to relive my own past. I was able to be actually there physically," he told her, "but that was all I was able to do. I couldn't change a comma or even a period."

She reminded him that he should have given up the struggle long ago, by saying his real name.

He said, "Never! They'll never make me say it."

"You should have," she said. "But now it's a fight to the end, isn't it?" and as she said this, she took his hand in hers, squeezed it a bit, and then caressed it, and for the first time, he did not pull it away. He became immediately aware that this small act on his part had not gone unnoticed, and still holding his hand, she went on to say, "Perhaps other opportunities will open up for you, and then you'll be able to seize them."

"You really think so?" he asked, hoping that she might tell him something new. But she made more general remarks, and Ivain understood that either she did not know, or she would say no more on the subject. But just the act of talking with her about the hopeless situation he was in, made him feel closer to Allegra than he had up to then. So he now lay beside her, and she let go of his hand, beginning to caress his arm instead. He realized that he was not in the mood to do anything, except lie there, perhaps even all night long. But she lifted her skirt and he felt her well-shaped thigh pressing against his own. Still, the desire was not there. If anything, he wished more than ever, to be closer to France. "Yet, in all this time," he remarked to himself, "I've not made a single dent in my relationship with France." In point of fact she seemed more distant and foreboding than ever. What was he to do? The only time she seemed to take an interest in him was when he was being flirtatious with Allegra. Perhaps the knowledge that he was interested in another woman made France feel more at ease with him, for she had to be aware of the way he was always looking at her. That fixed stare. That longing he could not hide. He was thinking all these thoughts and was actually about to get up and say goodnight to Allegra, when he saw the door opening a little bit, just enough to reveal a shadow. It was a figure of a man standing there. The door remained opened for a few seconds, then, as if everything had become clear to the intruder, it was closed again with care. It was obvious that the person outside in the corridor did not wish to make his presence known. But Ivain knew it was Fabian, and suddenly he felt he did not care what his cousin thought of him. On the contrary, his appearance made it imperative for him now to go through with his original intention. Besides, a nervous elation and lust that had not been there before suddenly shook Ivain's body, as if it had been touched by an electric wire. He would seduce Allegra more to make a point with his cousin, than because he was interested in her. By this mere act, the humiliations that had been perpetrated on him would be washed away. So, he turned over, and let Allegra undress him completely, at the same time as she was caressing him. She was taking over and commanding him to do certain things that would please her, or so she said; and it was at this point that he was surprised for she began to scratch his back with her long red nails. It was only a symbolic gesture because he felt no pain, but it made him feel incensed enough by her actions to begin to take more of an interest in her. He was surprised that Allegra started to put up some resistance. After all, had she not asked him to be her lover all these past days, weeks? And why had she undressed him now? So, why was she fighting him? And then he realized the fight was only a primitive dance of love, which he was part of, but which he did not know. Or perhaps it was a way to see how badly he wished to be one with her. Or was the fight just another way to say she wanted him, but could not say it except in the context of a fight? The way she fought him was with a smile on her lips, as if they were thieves trying to rob something of value from each other. At the end of the night, he would have the strange feeling that he had been more seduced than seducer.

For the time being, he lay with her on a bed that became soft and moist, and he lost himself in her little cries of pleasure, and in an ancient memory of his other body. He wanted to make love to her, but he realized that the only way he could do so was to let his imagination run free, and fill it with other images. He imagined himself tied down, unable to move; and it was France who was loving him now, not Allegra. It was only then that Ivain fell into a love spell. They went on loving without speaking. He was lost in his own fantasies which became richer and richer. He thought of forests, of birds, of nymphs near imaginary rivers, of colors that he had not seen for a long time, of mauve marguerites, and violet geraniums, green salamanders and, most of all, of the thickness and softness of France's hair. And then he felt Allegra's skin becoming wet under his, and she stopped struggling, and he was going to say something, but changed his mind, and kissed her instead, and the kiss was so long, that he thought he had reached the bottom of the sea, and would never come to the surface and breathe again. At the end of the kiss he did not know whether he was still himself, but he did not care. He kept kissing her until he felt he had nothing more to give. And then it was just a matter of losing himself, as one loses oneself in a tropical forest, where all is wet and dark, and the sun never shines, but where one can lie down and sleep forever. And it seemed to Ivain that he only woke up from such piquant love-making, when he heard the night bird song outside his window – "whoo, whoo," it was saying. He opened his eyes and sat up, but seeing it was still night, he lay down near Allegra again, wondering all the time how he could have missed her beauty, her warmth and intelligence and not slept with her sooner. In this way, he spent the night and did not know that the day had arrived until he was wakened by the raucous noise of the guinea hens under the windows. He got up, and taking a large, empty flower pot, filled it with water, and emptied it over his head. All wet, he went back to the bed once more.

He heard Allegra's voice coming from far away. "Why did you wait so long to make me part of you?" And he heard himself answer in a way he could not believe was coming from his lips. "How many times have you been with Fabian this way?"

"Not now," she said, almost begging him. "Please – not now."

"I have to know," he said, as he realized that his wish to be humiliated had surfaced in him again, stronger than ever.

"Why do you wish to torture yourself?" she said. "Why?"

"Was it once a night, every night since you have been here?" And as he said it, he felt that he could make love to her right away if she said, "Yes!"

"No," she replied. "But, please don't ask me. It was very rare that we did anything. We talked mostly. Don't go on."

He knew she was lying. "Just tell me how many times?" he

said again, hoping she would gratify him, hoping she would tell him all in graphic detail. He needed it, he realized, to get excited again.

"I don't know," she said. "I never counted them."

"All night long?" he continued. "Just as we – now?"

"No," she said, "tonight – tonight, well, I've never had a night like tonight. You meant everything to me, from the very first moment." She stopped. "You must believe me, I'll never go near Fabian again. I promise you that."

"I don't wish you to promise me anything at all," he said. "You're free to do what you like." And in his heart of hearts, he hoped she would go with his cousin again, and tell him about their night of love-making.

"But I'm not going back," she said, "I mean, I couldn't be with anyone else, after you and I had this moment together," and Ivain wondered if she was referring to what had just happened, or to "the written script."

"You owe me nothing," he repeated twice, almost as if he needed to believe it himself. And then he looked at her as she rearranged the large pink peonies in a crystal vase near the bed, and he thought of France. How much more he would have liked it, had it been France with him this night! But wait, would he really have enjoyed it more? Had not the night passed pleasantly? Had it not been wonderful to feel Allegra's young body under his own?

He would not be able to give an answer to this question for some days still, but every night he began to make it a habit to enter Allegra's room and leave it only early the following morning.

At present he walked toward the window just as the sun's rays were beginning to appear on the horizon. He saw birds darting by the windows to and fro, as if they knew where they were going. "How unlike me," he said to himself. One sat on a branch in front of him and began to teach exquisite notes to other smaller ones that were hidden in the foliage. Allegra wrapped a sheet around herself and came up, close to him. She embraced him with obvious happiness, which made him, for some unknown reason, terribly sad.

She said, "For me, the night just past has been the consummation of a marriage."

Those words had the power to frighten him, though he could not think of a logical reason why they should. "It's selfish of me," he said to himself, "to make love to Allegra, especially since I'm doing it for all the wrong reasons." He knew she was waiting for some show of affection from him, so without saying a word he went over to the table near the bedside and, picking a long-stemmed yellow wild flower that had found its way among the peonies, he gave it to her.

After that, he got dressed quickly and invited Allegra to join him downstairs for breakfast.

"I'll join you later," she said, as she walked into the shower, and closed the curtains behind herself.

Outside in the corridor, Ivain ran into Fabian, who was about to enter his own room. He stopped and wondered whether or not Fabian was going to forgive him for taking Allegra away from him. But his fears were dispelled, for his cousin stopped to say, "I gather you know how to entertain yourself these days," and winked at him.

"I don't know what you mean," said Ivain.

"Yes, you do!" said Fabian, laughing. "Don't be so modest," and he closed the door behind himself.

Ivain was surprised. "Fabian seems to be such a good sport about Allegra." he thought. "After all, not everyone would be so cavalier about losing a mistress, especially one to whom he seems to be so attached," and he wondered if inwardly Fabian might not be angry with him, in spite of his manner, for this was the second time he had taken a woman away from him.

But that thought did not stop Ivain from going down the staircase with a lighter step, as if he were flying through air. He went into the small breakfast room and there he found France, still with a few bandages on her hands, but feeling much better.

It was a different France than the one he remembered from the past days and weeks. She seemed as pleasant and happy as the sunny room they were in. Fabian had returned to her bed the previous night. She must be attributing her husband's return to his presence in the house, and to the way he and Allegra had become much closer lately. But was it just gratitude? He thought he saw something more behind that almost impertinent smile of hers. Could she suddenly see something else in him than just a passing actor? He had put to the test the theory that a man became more desirable if another woman took a keen interest in him. And now he became aware of the pleasant results. Seeing this new look in France's eyes, Ivain perked up his courage, and after breakfast asked her if she would like to take a walk with him in the countryside. She said, "Yes, I would love to."

He was happy.

They changed their indoor leather shoes for sturdy canvas ones, and began to walk outside the walls of Le Plessis, taking whichever little path they found off the country roads. Ivain was interested in talking about the writing he had left behind. What had really happened to it? The best way into the subject, he convinced himself, was to talk to France about writing in general, and then ease into his own. That night, alone in his room, he smiled thinking how much time they had spent talking about what was more laudable for a writer to do – write scholarly works, or works of fiction. History books and literary criticism versus novels, plays, short stories, and so on. It turned out that France was inclined to believe there was more originality and freedom in a work of fiction, while Ivain believed that both genres were equally difficult and equally singular, if well executed. Was Gibbon's *Decline and Fall of the Roman Empire,* a lesser masterpiece than Chekov's *Cherry Orchard?* or Turgenev's *Fathers and Sons?* Was Morris' *Shining Prince* less original and well written than Mishima's *Golden Pavillion?* Was Stoye's *Marsigli's Europe* less of an important book than Márquez' *No One Writes to the Colonel?* Was Kennedy's *Profiles in Courage,* less important than Bassano's *Garden of the Finzi-Contini?* Example after example was brought up, making the walk seem short when, in fact, it lasted all afternoon.

It was not until they were about to return to the house that Ivain found the courage to bring up his writing. He found out that France had not read his manuscripts or his papers. "But Fabian has read everything," she said. She also mentioned that – "Fabian has been thorough in making up a list of all of Ivain's writings. The list is now in his studio here," she said. The fact that France had not showed more interest in his legacy surprised Ivain, until she added, "It was so painful for me to pick up anything that belonged to Ivain. I still miss him. I loved him so!" And then they dropped the subject, and had gone on in silence for a while, each one following their own private thoughts.

At one point in the walk, Ivain stopped and looked at an empty space in front of him. He had recognized the spot where Mme Kamiska's stone house once stood. All that was left of the house was a small pile of pale yellow-brown stones, half buried by luxuriant vegetation. Nettles mixed in with tall thick grass and thorny bushes had grown over the foundations, which were barely visible. Shiny ivy clumps were trying to devour the ensemble. The force of nature, unforgiving, had taken over and covered whatever remained of the little house with a vengeance.

Ivain was still looking at it as if transfixed, when France said, "There was a house here once."

"Really?" asked Ivain with surprise, for he thought the house had disappeared a long, long time ago. He could not remember it even as a child, when he used to run about freely in the countryside.

"It was a peasant's house, used to stock forage, I think," said France and then she continued, "When we came to live here, Fabian used it for a while, then had it torn down."

"Fabian? Why would Fabian tear it down?" he asked.

"He said it served no purpose. Besides, we could use its stones to repair the walls at Le Plessis, which we did."

"How long ago was the little house torn down?" asked Ivain, and then he saw he had made a slip, which France picked up immediately.

"How do you know it was a small house?" she looked at him.

"I didn't know," he said. "I just guessed it," but he knew that he was blushing. He did not like to lie to France, or to anyone else, for that matter.

"It happened to be a small house," she said. "I liked it a lot. It had charm. It always looked so mysterious as if there was an unusual story connected to it."

"Perhaps there was," said Ivain. "Perhaps there was," and they resumed their walk, and France started to quote some poetry lines about the occult she remembered from her childhood.

What was so wonderful about talking with France again was the fact that she was a good conversationalist. Ivain had never been interested in women, however attractive they might be, whose conversation was only of the most superficial sort. Beauty was important, but beauty alone was not sufficient to keep him interested in a woman. He admired most those women who combined beauty with pleasant, educated conversation, and who were aware of what was going on in the world around them. With France he knew he could speak about art, literature, and music and always be surprised at her insights on those subjects. And he had to admit that in Allegra, Mme Kamiska had found an equally intelligent woman. There was no question that the JanKam Co. knew what they were doing when they chose that specific operative to be his companion and reintroduce him into the world. But when he found himself comparing the two women, France always came out on top, for besides her other attributes, she had a sweetness that always won his heart.

When they returned from their long walk they went into the living room, and France said to Ivain, "I've seen the way Allegra looks at you these days, and I think it would be nice if you gave her a little gift."

"How do you know how she feels?" asked Ivain.

"I observe," said France, "and since you arrived, she seems to be a different woman. A woman in love, in fact."

"Really?" he said laughing, not taking France's remarks very seriously. "That comes as a surprise to me."

"Well, you could give her a little souvenir for old time's sake," France said, and picked up an old silk sewing box that she had turned into a jewelry box, "Take something from here."

"Oh, I couldn't do that," said Ivain. "After all, they are your jewels."

"Go on, pick anything you like," she said. "These are not real; they're custom jewels. They are worth nothing!"

Ivain did not wish to give Allegra anything at all, but neither did he wish to displease France. He simply said, "I wouldn't know what to pick. I'm not good at that sort of thing."

"Well then," she replied, "leave it up to fate," and closing the sewing box almost completely, she continued, "Put your hand inside and choose the first trinket that your finger touches."

Ivain was still reluctant, but it seemed such a silly, inconsequential thing to do, that he decided to be agreeable, and play along with France. He placed his hand in the small slit of the box, and came out holding something that had wrapped itself around his thumb. It was a ring. It had a huge deep-blue stone in the middle, and it was set in what appeared to be a cheap metal alloy.

"Oh, you got a ring!" France said. "That will make Allegra happy."

"I don't know if I should give it to her," Ivain said.

"Why not?" asked France.

"A ring? A ring?" said Ivain. "She could misunderstand the meaning of my gift."

"Perhaps if it was a valuable one. But this –? This can only be taken as a nice gesture on your part," said France, adding, "Not unlike the silly surprises found inside those huge Italian chocolate eggs."

"Perhaps you're right," said Ivain. "A friendship ring." And, though he did not say so out loud, he thought to himself that he was going to think it over carefully before giving any such gift to Allegra.

VAUX LE VICOMTE,
IN FRONT OF CAESAR'S BUST

"Si vous n'êtes Romain, soyez digne de l'être."
Mme Adrian Proust

THE ride from Le Plessis to Vaux le Vicomte was so short that when Fabian stopped the car, they were all astonished to see the castle standing in front of them, in all its magnificence. It had begun to rain. Thin, light rain, drizzling down so lightly as to be almost invisible. It was through this veil of rain that Ivain now saw again Vaux le Vicomte, and he realized that it looked different from the first time he had seen it with his mother and his old aunt Franny. Then he had been a mere child of seven or eight. Now he looked at it in a different light, as if he had never noticed the heavy cut stones or the large vases, or the corpulent statues which decorated its ornate facades. It now seemed to Ivain as if the castle existed only to emanate a sense of power and wealth.

As he looked at it, he noticed droves of young Japanese women coming out of its front entrance, all dressed in the same clothes, and each one holding up a white and black umbrella over her head, chatting away. Some hid their laughter behind the other hand. Soon they were moving in one column toward the exit, and for a moment Ivain thought of them as delicate, exotic flowers in the formal gardens of Fouquet's castle.

Fabian bought the tickets to enter. But as Ivain passed near the ticket window to go inside, he looked up, and realized that the person behind it was no one else but Mme Kamiska herself. He stopped, not knowing whether to go on or return to the car. He lifted his hand and touched his face, then he saw Allegra ahead of him, making a sign with her arms to join her, and it was at this point that Mme Kamiska said, "Perhaps you should go on and be part of the group. You might learn something about Caesar you don't know yet."

"Perhaps you're right," he answered, still pondering what to do. But not wishing to disappoint Allegra he moved on, not without first asking himself, "What is Mme Kamiska doing here?" On an impulse, he had gone back to the booth where she had been selling the tickets to ask for an explanation, but when he looked in he saw a different woman in her place who handed him a piece of paper with a message scribbled on it. He took the paper, put it in his pocket and wondered if it had all been a mirage and if his mind was playing tricks with him.

Allegra and Fabian, with Ivain between them, began to walk briskly toward the entrance of the castle. They stopped once when they reached the large moat surrounding it, and marvelled at the fish inside the muddy waters. Red and grey carp as large as small water monsters. Finally, after passing through the small gardens just before the entrance, they went through the main doors, and walked straight to the only large room Fabian and Ivain had been interested in seeing from the very beginning of the outing.

It was the large oval room that held the marble busts of the Caesars. The room was magnificent, even with its unpainted imposing cupula, which the painter Le Brun had never been able to start. Le Brun had lost his patron Fouquet before he had had the chance to paint it, for Fouquet had been sent to a miserable dungeon in Piedmont by order of King Louis XIV, on what was later described by historians as "the whim of an absolute ruler."

Allegra, after looking briefly at the sculptured marbles of the two Octavias, the sister of Augustus, and the wife of Nero, said she wished to visit the chamber where Molière had given his first play, and would they excuse her? Gallantly, Fabian said they would both miss her. Allegra smiled, but not at him, at

Ivain. She smiled in a flirtatious way that could not possibly have escaped the keen eyes of Fabian, and, before walking out of the room, she looked back at Ivain once more.

After she left, Ivain and Fabian started to walk toward the bust of Caesar. In his eagerness to reach it, Ivain walked quickly, so quickly in fact that Fabian noticed it. "Johnny, what impatience you're showing!" he said. "But who can blame you?" he went on. "You must take a good look at the man you'll be personifying so soon."

Ivain stopped brusquely for he had arrived in front of Caesar's marble bust. "I'm glad we are alone," Fabian continued, "for no one else can understand what you are feeling at this moment," he said.

"He had more delicate features than I thought," Ivain replied, "but just as powerful a look as I suspected."

"The forehead," chimed in Fabian. "Don't forget to look at how high the forehead is."

Ivain felt that Fabian was making fun of him, but staying with the lighter tone, he said, "Perhaps it was even higher. I've read somewhere that Caesar was almost bald. My make-up man will have to be extremely good."

"Yes, he was baldish toward the end of his life," said Fabian. "That is the reason he always wore a crown of laurel. A privilege voted by the Senate, which by that time was doing what Caesar wished."

Ivain was taken aback by that remark. He remembered that in his other life he had never discussed Caesar with Fabian. Fabian's interests lay primarily in finance. He considered himself to be an astute investor, though at the time of Ivain's death, that had hardly been the case. Then, his main interest in all conversation had been "hot tips" on stocks, together with the art of buying and selling futures, or derivatives of different money denominations. Alternatively, his cousin liked to talk about France, too. He kept going over her great attributes, such as her kindness, her thoughfulness, her ability to make a room cosy just by her mere presence. Now that Fabian had France as a wife, Allegra as a mistress, and as much money as he had once only dreamed about, Ivain wondered if his cousin had taken more of an interest in history in general, and in his own manuscripts in particular. He was curious to know how much his cousin really knew about Caesar, without letting on how much he himself, as John Elliab, knew. So he began a sort of imaginary dance with Fabian, where words and sentences could be taken as *double entendres*. Smiling, he said, "You seem to be rather anti-Caesar. Is that a fair statement?"

"No, not really," said Fabian. "I recognize his genius, but to play him on stage, as you will, you must know the limits of the man. By that I mean, the best moment and the worst moment in Caesar's life."

"And what is, in your opinion, the best moment of Caesar's life?" asked Ivain.

"His death," answered Fabian, as he looked at his fingernails and touched them with his thumb one by one.

"Why his death?" Ivain was puzzled by that provocative answer, and he began to think of Fabian as a person whose soul had died and been replaced by another Fabian, a Fabian he did not recognize.

"It came at the right time in his life, and it was memorable."

"Why do you think it was the right time?" Ivain said, resuming the conversation after a pause. "After all, his death began a civil war and, indirectly, other civil wars as well, and Rome never became a Republic again." He stopped and looked again at the statue. "It seems to me that his assassins did not achieve what they had hoped to achieve, neither for themselves nor for Rome." He lowered his head and said, "Are you by any chance on Brutus' side?"

"No, no," said Fabian. "But Shakespeare was. And you are playing Shakespeare's Julius Caesar, not mine."

There was a silence. Ivain had often thought about this particular point, but had come to the conclusion that Shakespeare would not have called the play *Julius Caesar* had he been for Brutus. On the other hand, calling it *Marcus Brutus* might have displeased Queen Elizabeth, who did not look kindly on regicides, for Caesar, though he never wore a gold crown, was *de facto* a king. Besides, had not Sophocles called his play *Antigone*, and not *Creon*? Was that not enough to show where the sympathies of the author lay? Ivain looked around the room at the other statues and began to recite in a muffled voice – "Augustus, Nero, Claudius, Vespasian, Trajan, Hadrian. Don't you see," he finally said to Fabian, "how many men became Emperors who could't have been Emperors had there never been a Julius Caesar?" He took a breath. "Shakespeare knew that Caesar was larger than life, and admired him for that."

Fabian said, "In my Latin, not in that of Cicero or Livy, I would say of Caesar *Cupiditas Vincit Omnia*." He stopped to smile at his own cleverness, adding, "There is also a famous verse by Licinius Calvus:

Bithynia quicquid
et pedicator Caesaris umquam habuit."

and looking Ivain straight in the eyes, he continued, "Do you understand Latin, by any chance?"

Ivain was about to say, "Yes, I can even speak it," when he caught himself and said instead, "No, no, I'm just your average educated actor," and as he said it, realized he had almost given himself away.

"That last saying implies that Caesar made another king as well. The King of Bithynia." And Fabian now laughed at his own coarse joke before going on, "How do you propose to play a patrician who used the plebeians to gain a crown? How do you play a man larger than life?"

"Humbly," answered Ivain, astonished at how much his cousin knew, and feeling that it would be so much fun now to be able to talk to him about every detail of that part of Roman history, but he refrained from saying anything that might give the impression that he knew too much.

"I only wish I could have read the Professor's ideas on this great man, and not know just a few things from that paper I found – the so-called 'I don't care to please you, Caesar –'" Ivain continued in a whisper, "The one you said was unfortunately a fake," and as he said it he felt a pang that his beautiful work of scholarship had gone up in flames.

"I glanced through the manuscripts," said Fabian at last, as he took a cigar out of his breast pocket and played with it, passing it from one hand to the other. Ivain's heart skipped a beat, but he tried not to show his emotions. In that, he only succeeded partially because his right eyelid began to twitch. He wished to ask for more explanations, but he had to be careful. He went back to his own writing and remembered how he had begun one of his manuscripts, a work of fiction on Caesar's life, in which he had spoken of the year Caesar was born as being the only year when the swallows would make their nests outside cow barns or horse stables, choosing instead corners on walls of ordinary homes. In that same year, there had been an invasion of dark flies, larger than usual, that seemed to come from Africa, brought by the sirocco wind. The warm African wind also brought with it a thin layer of red dust that covered all of Europe. Those had been the portents that had marked the beginning of a memorable life.

Fabian now began talking on his own, without any prompting, and with each word he said, Ivain's amazement kept increasing, for he felt he had read his manuscript.

"Really?" he finally mumbled, "And what did your cousin write about Julius himself?"

"Oh, he considered Caesar a God. He did not take into consideration the darker side of his nature," Fabian said promptly. "His pronounced vices, for instance. The power he had to corrupt anyone and everyone at his will. The many love affairs he had with both men and women. And his cruelty –" Ivain was looking at Fabian, not understanding how he could possibly be saying words that were so far from what he had written down. Fabian was actually turning his thoughts around, for Ivain remembered specifically the tragic consequences of the siege of Alesia, in which thousands of people died of thirst and starvation outside its walls, in front of Caesar's army. He remembered writing how Caesar had given orders to storm cities only because they could be plundered for their riches. He remembered how he had stolen thousands of pounds of gold from the Capitol and had it replaced by bronze – first dipped in a bath of gold. True, he had also emphasized the genius of Caesar, for was he not the best Roman orator after Cicero? The best historian? In his opinion, better than Livy or Tacitus. The greatest general, and one of the most humane when dealing with his enemies? And, above all, Ivain remembered how he had tried to give a balanced opinion of the man who, yes, was his hero, but like all heroes – flawed. He loved Caesar all the more because he had flaws – unlike Cato, for instance, who seemed to have none, or Marcus Brutus, for that matter, who was always talking about virtue, virtuous, virtuousness.

As Ivain was deep in these thoughts, Fabian turned to him, and putting his hand on his shoulder, winked and said, "As Caesar, how will you play the husband of Calpurnia? Tenderly? Coldly? Indifferently? Perhaps as the passionate husband? Or will you be the sort of husband who respects the deal he made with his father-in-law, the powerful Lucius Piso?"

Ivain looked at him and saw that Fabian had tightened his mouth, making his lips look like two thin slivers, paper-thin. He himself took up the provocation by retreating within himself, as a snail retreats into its shell. He wished to say, "I'll play the husband to Calpurnia as you play the husband to France: with a mistress I adore on the side. Cleopatra, for Allegra!" but instead he said, "I don't know yet, for Caesar had many women he loved, Calpurnia being just one of them." After that, he moved away from Caesar's bust and walked toward the large door-windows. He was angry at his cousin's words and needed a moment to collect himself lest he make a slip.

From where he was he could see the best of Fouquet's gardens. They were simply spectacular with many fountains spurting water from dolphin's mouths held by sea gods. He saw a workman with a large pair of scissors in his hand trimming the bushes, which looked impeccable. The workman was doing it with perfect grace, as if it were a ballet which he had rehearsed over and over. Just at that moment the man looked up, and Ivain saw a face that looked both angular and full of wrinkles. A face that could have been the same face since time immemorial. "Can one cheat time?" he asked himself, "and if so, can I do it?"

Fabian had again come near him and was talking quickly, more quickly than usual about something that Ivain was not following. He still thought of his cousin as a puerile man, incapable of formulating complicated thoughts. But later on, in the Library, he would realize that he had not estimated him correctly, for he was much more intelligent, clever and well-read than he had ever given him credit for.

So Ivain turned round and, interrupting his cousin, said, "The point I'm trying to understand is: did Caesar deserve to be assassinated, and if so, was it for Brutus to express the moral justification for his murderers?" He paused briefly before starting again, as he felt his face becoming red from anger. "Why did Brutus really join the assassins?" and without waiting to hear his answer he said all in one breath, "Do not tell me it was to save the Roman Constitution, for the Constitution may or may not have had much to do with the thrusts of Brutus' sword into Caesar's breast."

Fabian seemed to have been taken by surprise by the intensity of these questions, but he quickly said, "Do you really think that Shakespeare's *Julius Caesar* is only about Brutus and Caesar?"

"Yes, I do," said Ivain. "It is a duel between those two principal characters that are fighting on both a personal and a public issue. Is Rome going to become a Monarchy, or remain a Republic? I don't think that the play can be fully understood unless that relationship is clear. For me, as an actor, the question is: was it regicide or parricide? for Brutus might have been Caesar's son."

"Brutus was only one of the plotters," said Fabian, "though perhaps the most important. But Caesar was killed by twenty-three thrusts of different daggers. In my opinion, those daggers pierced through his toga because he had celebrated five triumphs through the streets of Rome into the Forum. In four out of the five, he had rejoiced in the slaughter of Roman citizens." Monotonously he recited: "the Gallic, the Alexandrian, the Pontic, the African and the Spanish." He stopped, only to begin again by saying, "And here, if I may say so, I'll tell you what, in my estimation, was the worst moment of Caesar's life."

"Yes?" said Ivain, waiting impatiently for his answer and considering his cousin much too polite, more than the occasion called for.

"It was at the battle of Mundi where, thinking he had lost the battle, Caesar considered suicide and was about to plunge his sword in his own breast. But then one of his generals brought the news that he had won yet another victory." Fabian stopped only long enough to look back into Caesar's marble eyes, which somehow seemed empty and forlorn now, even to Ivain.

"You mean, you identify with his pain at Mundi?" asked Ivain.

"No, I mean, it was too bad he did not kill himself then and there. You see, the world would have been a different place now." He stopped. "All this is in the manuscripts of my late cousin," he added.

Ivain was shaken. He had never written anything of the sort, though, of course, he knew about Mundi and the dark thoughts of suicide that had crossed Caesar's mind. But Fabian was mixing up his own manuscripts with perceptions that had nothing to do with his writing. How could he be so confused? He had no idea. What history books had Fabian been reading? He could only wonder. Obviously the portrait Fabian had of Caesar was so contorted that Ivain thought of it as a tall tree, whose trunk and foliage could never be seen since it was totally covered by too much growth of some abundant ivy.

And as he said these words, he looked sideways at Allegra who had come back into the oval room and was walking toward them. She had taken off her rain coat and was now showing her white dress, almost transparent in its lightness. She was smiling at both of them, and as she came closer she said she felt she could live in Fouquet's castle forever. She felt happy there, she said. "There's something that reminds me of a memorable night that I've passed here."

Ivain guessed that she had been there in one of her other lives, and tried to make a sign to her with his hand, hoping she would not go on talking about the past. She could say something that might give away the inconsistency of her being. But she went on.

"Perhaps it was when Fouquet gave his first and last party

here. Then it seemed that all the world was at his feet," she said, as she looked at Ivain. Fabian laughed and squeezed her hand.

Ivain, annoyed at seeing this, turned to Fabian, and asked him, "What did Professor La Baille look like?" And the answer he got from Fabian, as Fabian was staring at him, was memorable. "He was good-looking on the whole. Not too tall. Oh, a good deal shorter than you, I would say, and much heavier. Yes, much heavier. His hair had almost your color, but perhaps a shade lighter, and his eyes were much smaller and darker than yours." He stopped and, looking at Caesar's marble, he said, "I miss him."

Ivain was astonished that his own cousin remembered him so differently. Were people's memories so tenuous that a mere ten years would cancel the memory of one's features?

They walked out together, silently this time. The weather had changed. The wind had picked up and pushed the rain away. Here and there the sun's rays were coming through, giving the whole valley an eerie feeling. The light also reflected on the newly washed leaves of different trees, making them shine in unexpected ways. The small, spidery rose geraniums were falling in a careless manner from the antique bronze vases that were to be seen all around them. A profound sadness overcame Ivain. "It is a sadness provoked by the fact that I've memories," he said to himself. "If only we didn't have a memory, how much happier we would be." He did not realize that he had said this loud enough for Fabian to hear him, and he heard Fabian answer, "How true, but how few have that privilege." Ivain blushed at his own unbearable nostalgia, a nostalgia that would not leave him. Then, as they were about to leave Vaux le Vicomte it happened that an image from his childhood came back to him, with details he had forgotten, or perhaps did not wish to remember. He stopped and looked at the castle again and all at once saw it as he had seen it the first time, when as a child Aunt Franny took him by the hand and his mother said, "Look Ivain! The castle is immense. It is solidly built." But his answer had been, "No, no. It's not solid at all. It's light. It floats!" and he remembered his mother taking another look and saying, "You're right. It's the evening light of the sun coming from behind that gives the feeling that it's made out of – of –" and she could not find the word until Ivain had come out with it and said "air!" And then his mother had agreed and said, "Yes, yes. You are right. Air and clouds!" And his aunt sucked in her lips, and stood there for a moment before bending down and kissing him on the forehead. That was how he now saw Vaux le Vicomte – air and clouds. Involuntarily, he touched his forehead and remembered the kiss.

DISNEYLAND PARIS

"You are all here to traverse life as apparitions and be gone."
Mme Kamiska's message at Vaux le Vicomte

As the manuscripts and the rest of his writing were nowhere to be found, and as there hadn't been any answers from the discreet notices placed in the local newspapers, Ivain remembered what Mme Kamiska had told him to do in case of an emergency. He could dial her name on any phone. "Even one that has been out of use for a long time," she had told him, "with or without a cord, working or not working." And she had promised she would answer him if she were in the Milky Way Galaxy, and not somewhere else in the Universe.

He had kept this information hidden within himself, for he felt the less he dealt with Mme Kamiska, the better off he would be. But he was now so shaken by the burning of his paper and the unknown destiny of his other works, that he felt not unlike an actor who needs his director to explain this or that passage in a difficult play.

He went into the garage and, after making sure no one was around, picked up an old phone he found there and dialled the word K-a-m-i-s-k-a on it, using the numbers corresponding to each letter. Keeping his anger and resentment toward Mme Kamiska to himself, he hoped that his voice would not betray any emotion, for he did not wish to discuss "the written script" he was in at this time. On the contrary, he wished to act as if the cunning trick she had played on him did not matter.

Immediately on dialling her name, he heard the melancholy music coming across from seemingly very far away, and soon after that he heard Mme Kamiska's melodious voice, which reminded him of a tropical song-bird with colorful plumage.

She started to tell him about the place she had just returned from, where a tornado had sucked up a great gulp of water from the Atlantic ocean and deposited it and its harvest, on a thick forest in Central America. And then she told him how the inhabitants of the nearest village had woken up, to see all the branches of the trees hanging with fish – sword-fish, salmon, sole, mackerel as well as dolphins. "Moreover, there are manta rays, as large as enormous flags, wrapped so tightly around tree-trunks that they draped them in their dark-bluish colors. And there is a great gray whale impaled on twenty gigantic bread trees and sycamores, sprouting orchids from her enormous mouth." Mme Kamiska laughed a little as she said those last words. She would have undoubtedly gone on with her astonishing story, had not Ivain interrupted her, as politely as he could, by saying, "I see, but closer to these shores, would you happen to know who the thieves are that have stolen my papers and my manuscripts?"

She was quiet for a moment, then seemed to be quite understanding, and said something resembling a sibyllic utterance. "Look in today's obituary column in the American papers. You will understand, I'm sure," and with that, he heard a click, and the music stopped shortly afterwards.

Immediately Ivain went to the house and, seeing both the *Herald Tribune* and the *New York Times* on the coffee table, he leafed through the pages until he got to the obituaries in both newspapers. He could see nothing extraordinary in either of them, except for one small item that appeared in both papers. A man had died the day before in a car crash in California. According to the brief account he read, he had been one of the designers of the "Pirates of the Caribbean" exhibit at Disneyland. The words were "– one of its creators." Since Disneyland was only fifteen minutes away from Le Plessis, Ivain went straight to Allegra's car, and seeing that she was about to take a walk, he asked her if she would let him borrow the car, so he could drive to Marne-la-Vallée. She not only said yes, but with a tender look, she said, "I'll take you there," adding all of a sudden, "I adore you. You are my idol! Just say it once that you love me. Just once!"

Ivain looked at her, and was so frightened by this outburst of emotions, that he said nothing. He could not deny that he found her smile irresistible and charming, and that first night unforgettable; still he did not wish to complicate his life with a love that could become difficult. Or to put it in another way, there was the possibility, even the hint, that it could be a great and unique love; but the idea that it would go on for conceivably a million years, restrained Ivain from actively pursuing what was an obvious invitation from a woman who was both beautiful and graceful.

Allegra did not seem to mind the fact that he had not followed through with that famous first night, when he had lost himself in her beauty. He still entered her room, whenever he lusted for her, but not with the same *élan* as that first time and not with the same interest, when the act of giving had been made more complex and more intense by the discovery of France's and Fabian's betrayals.

At present, Allegra gave him the keys to the car, without waiting for an answer to her passionate words for his silence had been painfully eloquent. She just sat herself languidly next to the driver's seat, but made a point at each curve of the road of sliding toward his side and leaning against him. He tried to move away, but that action was both awkward and obvious. Then he thought it would be better to let her be as close to him as she wished. That way he would not anger her, and at the same time he did not have to exert such an unnecessary struggle to move to the corner of his seat while driving the car. Also, there was something reassuring in the knowledge that such rare beauty could be so enchanted by his company, though he must never forget that she got her lines and cues every night for the next day, and undoubtedly also her directions as to which movements to make and at what point. "She is the fly, and I am the sticky fly-paper, and she is stuck on me," he said to himself, and for lack of anything better to do, at the next curve he, too, began leaning on her, and together they made a very odd twosome indeed.

When he arrived at the entrance of Disneyland he realized it was some sort of holiday, for he saw a great number of people waiting on endless lines trying to buy tickets to get into the Park. Discouraged, he turned to Allegra who, taking him by the hand, said, "We don't need to wait. Follow me," and she went to one of the gates, and passed through the bars to the other side, and soon Ivain found himself walking with her toward the road to "Adventure-land" where the "Pirates of the Caribbean" lived. They took the principal road, then another road that cut in half a make-believe American town, realistically portrayed as only an unreal set can contrive to do, for it was filled with quaint signs of different stores for clothes, food, ice cream, and where all sorts of Americana souvenirs could be bought. Ivain stopped to look around and take in this extraordinary bit of American soul grafted on to a typical French countryside, and as he looked about here and there, he was surprised to see so many older people in the crowd, without any children at their side. He became bold enough to ask a couple who was standing near them why they had come to the amusement Park.

"Because, young man," the man with white hair replied in a heavy German accent, "we were never young. We never had a careless youth like your Swiss yodeling boys. First there was the great war, then there was the other war, and afterward there was the reconstruction, and then more work – to become a great nation again and what have you –" and here he stopped to pass his right hand over his forehead, already shining with little beads of perspiration. "What I mean is," he continued, "we are rich now and have time on our hands, and so we come here to become children again," and he laughed. He was still laughing when Ivain felt a push from behind, looked round and realized there were a great many people moving forward, like a sudden surge of water in a dry torrent, so both he and Allegra began to walk at a quick pace and soon lost the old couple in that immense crowd, though they still could hear the old man's laugh. After a while the pushing from behind lost some of its intensity, and they were able to take a side path and found themselves almost alone. The path was paved and went slightly uphill, meandering in a curved line here and there, until they came upon a shiny lake that held an old replica of a wrecked Spanish galleon painted red and black. On the front of the boat there was a mermaid sculptured in wood, with a blue fishtail, holding a small harp in one hand. This ancient boat was standing very still and filling a space that seemed to have been taken from a past century. Ivain stopped and marveled at the furled white and red sails that still hung from its robust masts. Marveled at its whole design, so well-conceived that one might think that if Marne-la-Vallée were not so far from the sea, not so far from Britanny or Normandy, this could be a seaworthy vessel, one in which a few mariners could sail and discover the New World again. The only discordant note was the strip of water the boat was floating on. It was too small for such a large boat, even though an attempt had been made to place sand dunes here and there. "Only a huge hurricane would have had the power to have landed it here," thought Ivain. He looked at the waters it floated on, and though glittering and trembling they reflected the grayness of the cement underneath. "Is it real?" he asked himself, and then answering his own question he said, "It is if it seems so, for I have no other way to determine what is and what is not." And so saying, he hurried his step toward the Spanish-looking fort, and toward the pirates' cave, for he was eager to see what was below the tunnels, deep within the earth. They reached the entrance, and Allegra turned to him and excused herself saying that, if he did not mind, she would prefer to see "'Sleeping Beauty's Castle', for," she went on, "it reminds me of the one I slept in for a thousand years."

"Not at all," replied Ivain, as he wondered what country would have built such a palace. Egypt? Syria? Babylon? The New World? Or was it there in France, in the same place? Perhaps one day she would tell him, then he wouldn't have so many questions and so few answers. And he followed her with his eyes, until he lost her among the crowd below where he was standing.

As soon as he was alone, he entered the dark, cold tunnel and began his descent toward the lower part of the cave. As he walked, he realized there was no one round him. "That can only mean," he thought, "that I am in the right place, and Mme Kamiska has arranged it so that time is standing still." He walked down a steep path of packed earth, until he came to a dark place with a river, and on the river there were boats waiting. "For what?" he asked himself. "For a dead soul like me?" he whispered, but before he could give any answer, a handsome youth dressed up in a green and red striped costume, wearing a black patch over his left eye, welcomed him and helped him into the boat.

Ivain pulled out a five-franc piece and gave it to him, saying sotto-voce, "Here's my silver piece, Charon!" The young man, though not understanding the meaning of his words, thanked him nevertheless, "Not many people are as thoughtful as you are, sir. Thank you." And giving him a hand, he helped Ivain move to the front of the boat which immediately began to glide forward on the dark waters. "Thalassa! Thalassa!" shouted Ivain, and immediately corrected himself by saying under his breath – "No. No. This is no sea. It is the river Styx!" But it was too late, for he had shouted "Thalassa!" loud enough for his words to reverberate with their own echoes through the stalagmites and stalactites, through the rush of the waterfalls, through the smoke of the burning town, through the sound of cannons and pistols firing, the clash of iron swords, the meowing of half-drowned cats, the barking of tail-wagging dogs, the endless braying of the donkeys, the drunken songs of the pirates themselves, and through the silent screams of the women being pursued by rude, untamed men – round and round within the inner court of their house, in an eternal circle as their town was being sacked.

The boat that was carrying Ivain was not going at such speed that he could not enjoy the various scenes that appeared here and there, on each side of the river, as if by magic. What surprised him most was that no amount of money or time had been spared to make the false look like the real, with the result that the various robots, whether cats or dogs, men or women, were moving and laughing, singing and struggling, in such a way as to seem more real than the warm-blooded creatures they were supposed to copy. In good conscience, Ivain had never met any creatures more alive than the ones he now encountered, for in these machines there was life, while in the Park above, there were only real people impersonating the fake ones below, and faring poorly in the comparison. "Perhaps the day has arrived when we'll just be happy with machines surrounding us," he said, and the thought that he could stay below the ground and enjoy the pirates' singing for hundreds of years to come, did not displease him in the least. "On the other hand," he said, "perhaps I am witnessing the ideal pirate for I may have stumbled into Plato's cave where such pirates like to hide." For a donkey here gave the illusion of being the ideal donkey, and the same could be said of all the other creatures, and of the fire which was the ideal fire, as well as of the malicious and not so subtle cruelty of the pirates, partly hidden under a loud laugh while pretending to be drunk, though Ivain knew better than to believe it.

The end of the very last cave was filled with various pieces of gold and jewelry, and guarding this treasure was what looked like a human skeleton with a black Napoleonic hat on, enhanced by two white crossbones on the front of it. "Perhaps," thought Ivain, "this is to leave the traveler with the moral *dictum* of: Ill gotten money comes to no good, or perhaps to suggest just the opposite: that some lucky man enjoyed great riches until the end of his life and beyond." The possibilities were endless, and in thinking so Ivain arrived at the end of his underground trip.

He got out of the boat on the same side where the trip had begun, and decided to return to where he had just come from. He had not yet found what he was looking for, though what that was – he didn't know. He saw the same polite youth who had helped him before to get into the boat, and again was asked if he wanted to sit in front, to which Ivain replied, "Yes, thank you," and taking out another five-franc piece, he gave it to the young man who gave exactly the same answer as the first time, and as Ivain sat down, he wondered if the young man was a robot, too. But before he could answer, the boat had already left the dock, and was on its way into the channels of the underground river. He again moved easily on the water, this time wondering whether his second trip was an entrance or an exit. As an actor he should have known that every exit is an entrance in some other well-defined place. Ordinarily such entrances or exits would have been included in a stage direction, but here there were no directions, only the sounds of rushing water, and the cacophonous sounds of a city in the midst of being ransacked.

Ivain went through the second trip in a shorter time than the first one until the boat came to a full stop and, as he looked about, he noticed innumerable tiny white boats on the water bobbing up and down, scattered here and there around him. He realized they were made out of paper, similar to the ones children played with in a pond or in a small brook, and light enough for the wind and the current to take away. He bent down and, picking one up, he was surprised to see it was made out of a written page. Curious to see what it said, he opened it up and, as he began to read it, he saw that it was a page taken from his unpublished manuscripts, the ones that he had left in the time gadget closet on his last day on earth. Ivain trembled at the thought that the underground river was filled with little paper boats like the one he was holding, and, stretching both arms, he tried to catch as many as he could. Before long, he had his hands and pockets full. The rest were carried off by the current.

He was still astonished and perturbed by this discovery, when he became aware that the boat he was on had stopped in front of the last cave, the one with the treasure, only this time, sitting near the skeleton, was someone whom at first he thought was a specter, until he realized it was Mme Kamiska. She was wrapped in a voluminous gray silk dress, and wearing a green corsage of red cupped flowers at the height of her neck. Ivain felt an immediate desire to shout out loud – "How dare you make little boats out of my best writing!" But then, remembering what Allegra had told him sometime ago, that Mme Kamiska hated confrontations, he calmed himself and felt it was better to use diplomacy and ask in a polite way what was happening to all his writing. To do that, he left the boat and, wading through the water which was only a few feet deep, he steadied himself by getting hold of a round stalagmite that stood between the boat and the cave. He then helped himself by holding onto a few stalactites that came all the way down from the ceiling, and in this fashion he walked unsteadily toward Mme Kamiska.

To reach her, he had to step over the various treasures, for she was sitting among huge, skillfully worked, elaborate gold plates, silver goblets, various precious stones – rubies, emeralds, sapphires and diamonds, and she was surrounded by immense amounts of pearls, precious chains, bright colored swords, gold stilettos, and even a Bohemian chandelier, hanging in the middle of the cave's ceiling. Everything was enclosed by thin transparent spider webs.

She saw him and, smiling, said, "Oh, there you are. Come closer, closer." Ivain did his best to push aside the spider webs and reach Mme Kamiska, and then he sat down near her. Looking around him, he was amazed when he realized that all the gold was real, as well as the many highly polished large plaques of moonstone that reflected everything within the cave, and later on he was to discover that they had belonged to the Emperor Domitian, in the first gallery of mirrors the world had ever known.

Mme Kamiska explained that the objects near her were of great value and, seeing a beautifully made centerpiece statue of Hercules, smiling, she said that it was the very one that Hannibal always carried with him on all his campaigns. Then, pointing at some elaborate mosaic mounted on soft carpet, she announced that it had been part of Julius Caesar's campaign paraphernalia. Ivain felt a shiver as he looked at the running white horses mounted by elegantly dressed knights and, standing in their midst, the towering figure of the war God Mars. He couldn't help thinking that Caesar had actually walked over it, and had sat on it. Then with his left hand, he picked up a gold coin which came from Alexandria, when Alexandria was the center of the world, and with his right hand he picked up another one from Constantinople, when Constantinople was the center of the world, and one from Athens when Athens was the center of the world.

It was at this point that Mme Kamiska made a remark about time and, more specifically, about present time, and he made a note of it. He saw that, as she was making that remark, she was leafing through various books that lay open on her lap, and before he said anything, she volunteered the information on what she was doing. Apparently, Mme Kamiska thought that the pirates were not showing enough of the cruel side of their piracy, so to speak, therefore, she was looking up some forgotten archaic laws: Hittite and Sumerian, Trojan and Arcadian, written in secret codes that only she could read fluently and with the proper rhythm. These ancient laws were known for their creative cruelty, almost exquisite in their subtlety and poetic in their phrasing such as – "the clear light of the moon, the light of the rising sun, and the stars of the north horizon." What was interesting in these laws, so she said, was that in their brutality exceptions could be found, as if a ray of kindness remained within their reach, which was the reason she found them so inspiring – such as: "You can kill a milking kid, but you shall not boil it in his mother's milk."

It was after reading off her notes to Ivain that Mme Kamiska confessed being the originator of all the scenes Ivain had just seen, for she had suggested them at night to their human creators in their dreams. She also added, "I am pleased with the effect everything is having on your visit here. It means I've done a good job." It had taken her a bit of time to paste it all together, she said, but she had done it; though as he could see, she was still trying to improve it.

Again, Mme Kamiska would have gone on with her fantastic stories, had not Ivain interrupted her in as polite a way as he knew how. "Mme Kamiska," he began, as he took out some of the papers from his pocket, "I'm impressed by the lovely songs you have given these outlaws, but how come there are many paper boats in the water, with my writing on them?" And, though Mme Kamiska seemed annoyed at not being able to finish the description of her elaborate projects, she said, "Oh those. You mustn't worry. Those pages are just replicas of your original manuscripts which are right now in Orlando. Yes, yes, they are in Florida safe and sound." In so saying she took one of the little boats that Ivain was holding in his hand, and after carefully unfolding it, she wrote a phone number on its margin, saying, "Do not call up directly, but have someone in your household make the call and offer the reward money. I'm certain you'll get everything back, for pirates always like to have lots of money around them in thick, round bundles tied with red elastic bands." Then she added, "Do not delay. Time is of the essence in this case." And, she looked at Ivain who was nodding, without knowing why he was nodding. "Yes," she continued, "A stitch in time saves nine." And after saying that, Ivain understood that she wanted to get back to her books. He got up, thanked her, turned his shoulder for a moment, and when he turned back to say "Thank you" again, Mme Kamiska was not there any longer. Only the skeleton remained among the treasure that once again had turned into *papier-mâché* and tin. The saying "Everything that glitters is not gold" came to his mind, even though just minutes before the metal was gold, and all the stones were precious.

Ivain was still thinking about what had just happened when he reached the river again, and there waiting on the dark waters was his boat. He waded once more into the cold swirling river and was about to pull himself into the boat, when he heard far away the various sounds of the places he had just left behind. Later on, when he calmly recollected what he had done, he realized that it was the memory of those sounds that gave him the impulse to disrupt "the written script" of the pirates. What if he were to stop the cat from meowing, for instance? Or the donkey from braying – what then? Would that not be a victory over one, seemingly eternal "script"? It is true that theirs was mechanical, a simpleton's "script," made up mostly of one easy line, said over and over every twenty seconds or so, while the one he was in himself was immensely more complicated in comparison; but that did not make the pirates' 'script' less of 'a script'. The more he thought about it, the more he felt that the robots' lines were said with a lot more élan and éclat than his own. These machines were perfect actors every time, and they were doing a Sisyphean labor which they did not mind at all. He stopped himself, momentarily afraid that Mme Kamiska might be greatly offended by this act, but his will to break "the script" was too strong, so he began to walk against the current upward, trying to reach the place where the greatest mêlée was going on, where the pilfering and pillaging, the plundering and sacking of the city was at its most fevered. He began to walk through the water, encountering first the thunder and the cascades around him, but paying no attention he continued on his path. On one side he saw a nest with a white sea gull in it, motionless, so he passed on, walking through the cross fire from one side of the river to the other, imagining the air heavy with gunpowder. Still he walked on, even when he came to a waterfall where he could pull himself up by hanging onto the bolts sticking out in the middle of the fall, placed there to hoist the boat up and down. He even walked in waters where the images he saw became confused. He walked through a labyrinth of petrified polyps, with huge tentacles, seen through a few transparent rays of the sunlight, radiant in the darkness. It was at this point that he thought he could decipher words written in the bright dust of those rays. Words that might have the code to understand his destiny, and put an end to his endless doubts and suspicions.

On the way back to Le Plessis, he tried to remember whether in the cave of the pirates he had seen first the town on fire, or the public selling of the town's women, or the three pirates singing a song accompanied by an accordion and a banjo and a braying donkey. It all became confused and unclear. One thing did stand out. The moment he saw the three pirates singing, he remembered Natalie's words, and was amazed to see they fitted the exact description of the thieves! Without hesitation, he began to look for wires or electronic buttons, and having found them hidden in a box behind a cardboard rock, he pulled them apart, stopping their singing in the middle of a phrase, and leaving all the figures, including the donkey, with their mouths open, unable to move. Not happy with that, he stopped two duelling pirates by taking away their swords, and throwing them on the side. Then, going back into the river, he saw a basket full of chickens and began to exchange the wires hidden in their necks with other wires laying nearby, so that the chickens began to sound like the three little piglets not far away. "Oink, oink," he heard, while at the same time he saw the piglets clucking like the chickens, "cluck, cluck, cluck."

Then he saw a stairway whose first steps were lapped by little waves of water, and on top of the stairway he saw a door. He took that stairway and ran up, two steps at a time, and without knocking, opened the door to find inside three sad-looking people, identical to the three pirates whose technological life he had just ended. They were sitting around a table, each with a beer glass in front of him, and kept repeating the same line over and over, as if in a chant: "You spoiled our song. You spoiled our song." Ivain quickly closed the door. "Of course," he said. "It was Mme Kamiska with her father the Godlet, who orchestrated the theft and Natalie's death!" He was sure he had recognized the murderers in those three men he had just seen. "Fabian and France had nothing to do with it. The antique dealer's 'rumor' was just a rumor to throw me off." And he shuddered to think that for a moment he had doubted his cousin and his wife. Angry, he now went back into the river where he reached the Blue Lagoon, and saw that all the tables at the restaurant were empty. On top of a wooden board he found a dish full of hot fried potatoes, picked one up and ate it, as he laughed out loud, saying, "This is a new 'script.' It's mine and no one else's."

He left the cave through the restaurant and walked outside into the hot humid day, where he saw that the line to enter the pirate's cave was now a mile long. "It will never be the same," Ivain remarked, and was walking ahead, pleased with himself, when he heard a voice behind him saying, "We are not amused," and turning around he saw that the Disney Parade was about to begin, and Queen Victoria was standing majestically erect on top of a flowery decorated green car, saying this line over and over. His intuition told him that it was a strange Queen Victoria he had just seen, but he tried to put the thought of Mme Kamiska out of his mind. And he walked on, thinking how much more difficult it would be to get out of his own "script." If he only could find the wire that could make him take his own destiny into his hands, and change it at will, without having to follow a path already paved over for him! He had this idea that he was walking down a road with many smaller roads leading off on each side, but he could not choose a road other than the one he was on now. And that thought made him sad and morose.

It was in this state of mind that he reached the Disneyland

gate. Allegra was there, waiting for him, chatting away with Minnie, Daisy and Mickey. Still upset, Ivain, with a sudden movement, tore off the head masks of the three cartoon figures, and underneath he uncovered three frightened midgets, who quickly ran away screaming, "Give us back our heads! Give us back our heads!" To a child who began to cry, Ivain gave the limp masks of all three characters, saying: "Life is never what it appears to be."

That relatively simple gesture suddenly compensated for all the bitterness Ivain had felt up until that instant. He was able to walk out of the Park with Allegra, laughing and feeling that in some remote corner of this Universe, the underdog had taken a tiny bite out of the giant, and in his euphoric state, Ivain touched his pocket and felt the box with the ring he fished out of France's sewing box. Turning to Allegra he said, "Let us stop in a coffee shop. I've a little gift for you." He astutely realized that in giving Allegra a ring, he would get France's full attention. He wanted this more than he had ever wanted anything before. He never gave a thought to how happy the gift he was carrying in his pocket would make Allegra, and what consequences could ensue from it, for he had convinced himself he was giving away an object of no importance.

THE SURPRISE ENGAGEMENT PARTY

"Theater is all about lying, and life is theater."
Mme Kamiska backstage in New York

THE last two days were the best days Ivain had had since his return. Fabian called the number that Ivain had given him in Florida, and received assurances that the papers and the manuscripts were in good hands, and that he could come and get them as long as he paid the promised reward. To make sure that they were really Ivain's original manuscripts, Fabian asked the thieves to read him a page, seemingly chosen at random, but in reality a page of which he had one half in his hand. That fragment was one of the few that Fabian and Chef Perrot had found at Le Plessis in the days following the infamous and murderous night. Later on, Fabian would say that when at the end of the telephone line he heard the man say he only had half of that page and read it to him, Fabian knew he had to fly to Florida as soon as possible. At lunch, he was happy to announce: "Ivain's *magnum opus* will be there when the Library room is dedicated." Ivain was extremely pleased that events had turned out for the best after all.

Following a cheese soufflé lunch, Ivain, elated by the good news, took a walk alone in the countryside, only to come back around the middle of the afternoon. He was surprised to find that most of the villagers were outside the gate, dressed in their best Sunday clothes. At first he had a feeling something terrible must have happened. But then he said, "No, that can't be," for everyone was smiling. He wondered what the occasion was. Claude Arc winked at him, and Edward Polaski and George Villers kept saying, "That's great! That's just great!"

"What's so great?" he said to himself. He turned round and saw Dudu Picasso saluting him, and nearby Pierre Jean Boissy, who said, "Now is the time to buy something from my collection, eh?" He stopped and looked at the ground, shuffling his feet nervously. "I haven't found out any more about the missing papers," he continued, "but at the water-mill I've many beautiful gifts for the pretty lady." And he added with a whispering voice as if he wished to make him his accomplice, "All new aquisitions." But, since Ivain did not know what "lady" he was referring to, he just waved his right arm in the air, and walked on.

As he entered the gate of Le Plessis, he was surprised to hear, somewhat in the distance, the sound of people talking and laughing, and love songs being played over a loudspeaker. He wondered what it was all for. Curious, he walked toward the English gardens at the back of the house, and there he found a large number of people who, as soon as they saw him, almost in one voice said: "Here he is!" and *"Le voilà!"*

They touched him, and congratulated him, though he could not understand why. Then there was a clapping of hands, and all eyes were on him, and he felt he was on stage again, but he did not know which play he was in or why those people were so cheerful. What were they doing there? It was some sort of surprise, but for whom? A good-bye party perhaps? And was it in his honor? All these questions came to Ivain's mind almost at once, but he knew he had to wait for the right answer.

He looked around, smiling at everyone, though a bit lost, and he felt happy and somewhat reassured when Allegra came near him, and embraced him. Among the guests he noticed that the local aristocrats were well represented. He remembered them from before, when first his parents, then both France and himself, used to invite them over for elaborate picnics and dinners that went on into the following day. He noticed how well dressed everyone was. Costly fabrics: silks, elaborate Swiss cottons and light muslin. "Overdressed," he thought, "betraying their provincialism, for as always, they wish to appear more Parisian than the Parisians."

A white-gloved servant in a grey uniform served champagne on a red lacquered tray, while another one passed around a silver tray filled with delicate *petit fours*. He took a glass of champagne. It was of a good vintage, which he immediately recognized as Veuve Clicquot. Fabian and France had gone a long way to make the party a special occasion, and they were lucky with the weather too, for the sun was shining in a cloudless sky, but it was not too hot.

Once more he thought that the setting was too perfect, and he felt uneasy. What little drama had the JanKam Co. thought up for him now? He involuntarily trembled, and swore to himself to be careful, and look about him before making a move, even the smallest one. He did not have to wait long for the answer to his question. He saw Fabian step on an elaborate wooden stool, holding a glass carefully in his hand, and heard him say in a loud voice: "Silence, please! Just for a moment!" And when all the guests had quieted down, he continued. "As you know, tomorrow we are all leaving for the United States. I am going to Florida. Orlando, to be more specific. Johnny and France will be going to New York, where Johnny will be the understudy for *Julius Caesar*, and France will put the last finishing touches to the Library room at Columbia University, named as you know, after her late husband. As for Allegra – she will remain here for a day or two to clean up my desk, and then join Johnny in New York City. But, do not miss us too much because we'll be back soon." And here there was loud applause, and Fabian patiently waited until it had quieted down. Then he began again.

"Today we are giving this surprise party for a particular reason. It's in honor of the engagement of Johnny to Allegra. Even though Allegra had often spoken to all of us of how much she loved Johnny, it was with pleasure that we all looked at the ring her fiancé gave her just yesterday." Here Fabian had to stop again, for there was great rejoicing, and Allegra once more kissed Ivain on the cheek, who just stood there, unable to move. Fabian silenced the guests with a gesture, then lifting his glass he said, "And now, here's to both of you. Happiness, and a long life to enjoy it!" There were cheers again, and good wishes. Some of the guests were congratulating Allegra, others had come up to Ivain, who was standing in the middle of the crowd, not yet believing what he had just heard. When Fabian's meaning finally dawned on him, he was appalled. He looked at Allegra and saw her laughing happily as she held her hand high to show off the ring on her finger.

"How did this ghastly misunderstanding happen?" Ivain wondered. Yet, he remembered being absolutely clear with her, no question about that. He went over what he said to her at the coffee shop, "This is a little gift. A present for you, just to show we've become good friends. Fellow travelers in a nether world. Neither here nor there," and he remembered he had taken her hand into his: "Wear it and think of me when I'm away from you." How those words could be twisted into an engagement, he could not fathom.

Ivain felt his situation, at this particular moment, to be extremely dangerous. He was bound to make a mistake, but under the circumstances he could not let this lie go on. He knew that what he was about to say would not make Allegra happy, but felt he had to tell the truth. Later on, he often wondered whether he should have waited a day or even a week before saying it. He wondered why he had not been silent and let the whole thing slip into oblivion. Why did he feel compelled to tell the truth? Moreover, as soon as he realized the depths of Allegra's anger, he debated with himself for days why he had fallen into the trap, a trap that had been carefully laid out for him. But wonder as he might, he could never arrive at a reasonable answer, except to say that everything was part of "the script" he was in, and he was following it *verbatim,* even though it seemed as if the words he was saying were his own. So now he tapped lightly on the champagne glass he was holding, with a little silver spoon that had his initials on it, I.L.B, and then, putting down the glass on a nearby table, he looked round. Everyone fell silent and all eyes were on him.

"I am afraid," he began, "there's been a terrible misunderstanding. Allegra and I are very good friends. In fact, I consider her my best friend. Yesterday, I gave her a ring as a token of that friendship, and today we are here to celebrate our friendship, not our engagement."

There was an audible gasp among the guests. He looked at Allegra. For a moment she seemed lost. He could see her lips pressing together until they turned white. Then, either by accident or volition, she let the glass she was holding slip from her hand and shatter on the stone near her feet as she ran out of the garden, out of the main iron gate, screaming. On an impulse Ivain ran after her, calling her name aloud.

Once outside Le Plessis, he looked for her. What path had she taken? What road? Dudu Picasso pointed to the left, Anatole Tibault to the right, Jacqueline was shouting something he could not hear. Finally he began running in one direction, then changed his mind and ran back, and then ran straight ahead. He thought all was lost until he saw her red and blue scarf trailing on the left side of the road he was on, which led into a field and into a cluster of trees nearby. He followed that trail, running as he had never run before. He searched among the trees, he searched farther on into another small forest, and then near the river, but she was nowhere to be seen. Finally, he sat down and realized that she could have gone through the wall of a number of houses, and could be hiding anywhere. It was futile for him to look for her any longer, though he still believed that if he could talk to her, he could explain himself and perhaps she would not feel such anger. If not, then he had made an implacable enemy. Yet what could she do? Was he not beyond sickness, pain and death? Still, he continued to look for her, and instead of taking the main road back to the house, he chose a new path in between the fields. He was surprised to find that the old Briard house that had been there when he was a child had been redone in a more modern style which did not improve its appearance. If anything detracting from its original style. He also noticed that, almost attached to it was an immense net that covered what could easily have been the length and width of a large stadium. He immediately realized that it was a bird cage, used to raise pheasants and red-breasted or golden partridges to sell to the hunters in the winter months – and he was amazed to see that now it only held about twelve to fifteen large crows, trapped under it. The crows had feathers of deep dark iridescent colors which in the evening light changed to blue and green tones. They were flying around pitifully, trying to get out of that enormous trap, but fly as they might, they could never find an opening anywhere. They would land here and there and look for something to eat or drink where there was none and then they would once more begin flying to nowhere. Some were already so weak that they could not move any longer, and one or two were lying on their sides. Ivain came up to the net and, putting his fingers in between the cords, stood there and stared at the sad spectacle, wondering why no one would open a side door to let them out. He walked around the net to the other side, where he found a man on a tractor passing nearby, followed by a large dog, part Labrador, part Cocker Spaniel with large, dangling fuzzy ears.

"Is this your farm?" Ivain asked.

"No," replied the man, "I just work here. I'm a farm hand."

Ivain looked at him more closely. He was surprised to find that the peasant had a certain beauty in his countenance which sharply contrasted with the rough way he spoke. His face was finely chiseled. He had a small straight nose, and a well-shaped mouth. His eyes were large. His irises were of a tone of light brown rarely seen, and though his skin was burned by the sun and covered with freckles and wrinkles, that did not diminish an apparent elegance, all the more unexpected in such a person as the one sitting in front of him.

Ivain asked, "What work do you do?"

"This is the end of the season," said the man. "We're just about to turn the earth over and disinfect the place for next year's crop."

"A breeding ground of beautiful birds for the pleasure of the hunters," thought Ivain, and he remembered how, as a child, he used to follow the hunters, who pretended to hunt wild birds in the forest. They would free fifty or sixty bought pheasants at a time, having first placed their heads under their wings and swung them around to make them sleepy, to be sure they would not go far and therefore escape the hunters. "Hunting is the national sport all over Europe, but the French are masters at this game," mumbled Ivain morosely, for he hated hunting. "It's more fun to kill here than elsewhere." But, as it was August, all the partridges and pheasants had already gone.

"What are these crows doing in the net?" Ivain asked the farm hand. "How did they get there?"

"We left the net open so they would enter. Then we closed it. Now we're just waiting for them to die," said the farm hand as he took a breath. "No water, no food," and he winked.

"Why are you doing this?" Ivain asked, once more amazed that hidden under such a pleasant face was such an unpleasant and insensitive nature.

"We want to teach the other crows to keep off the fields. It's an example. A lesson," he said, and turning his head in another direction he pointed to a tree nearby where a crow had been crucified, and hung with its head on its breast. "Like that one," he said, "crows only understand that kind of talk. Here, I'll show you," and, taking a wounded crow he had hidden in a small sack beside him, he threw it on the ground so that his dog could finish it off. The bird, though wounded, defended itself bravely, jumping here and there, but in the end, the teeth of the dog proved too much even for his large beak and for his one good claw, and he fell down, letting the dog tear him apart, throwing one last quick glance at both Ivain and at the man in the tractor. Ivain was appalled by what he had just seen and heard. "Would you free the rest of them if I pay you?" he finally asked.

"Why spend good money on this rubbish?" the man said, looking at him in a strange way. "They're better off dead, just like the rapacious ones, or the owls. One hooted last night on my window-sill." He paused as if he had thought of something, then began again, "There'll be a death in the family, unless I find it and kill it." And with that, he started his tractor again and went his way with the dog following him, wagging his tail.

Ivain looked at the imprisoned birds again and felt pity for them. He would have liked to tear the net apart and free those intelligent creatures, but he knew it would not be any use. The peasants of Rosay would find other ways to finish them off, just as cruelly.

"I feel trapped like these crows," Ivain said to himself. "I too am in a net, and for the moment I don't see any way out," and thinking dark thoughts, he walked briskly toward home.

Later on that night, after he heard what Allegra said to him, he got up quietly, and taking a sharp kitchen knife, went back to the net with its imprisoned crows. He felt he had acted cowardly during the day, and now tried to make up for it by cutting the net apart as he shouted like a madman, "We're all part of 'the script,' but we don't have to make it worse for our fellow creatures." He heard a shot in the night. It might even have hit him, but what did it matter? Was he not immortal this time around for as long as he wished?

That same afternoon, when he returned to Le Plessis, he found Allegra packing her car, ready to leave. He went up to her. He could see she had been crying.

"Allegra," he began, "You're a charming, fascinating woman, and –"

"My fascination or charm must be wearing pretty thin, since you don't care for it," she answered.

"I don't know what came over me. Please forgive me." He came close and tried to touch her, but she pushed him away.

"There's nothing to forgive," she answered as she continued to pack her car. "You humiliated me both publicly and privately. You made me look like a trollop, a simpleton, or worse, a spinster who would grab any man just to have a husband. I've nothing more to say to you."

He looked at her with apprehension. He wanted to say that it had been madness for him to behave that way, and out of character. He wanted to remind her that it was not his fault or hers. He wanted to say that no one could have predicted this sequence of events, for they were all in "the written script." And finally, he would have liked her to join him in fighting it. "But how could she?" he thought, "if up to now I've not been able to change it in any meaningful way?"

He tried again. "Please listen –" he began. He would have liked to keep up the friendship. But it was too late. It was all too late. She looked at him with hatred. "There's no place for reason left now," thought Ivain, "and yet in her uncontrollable rage and temper there has to be also tenderness somewhere.

But will I find it?" He wondered. "The ring –" he started to say.

"Yes, the ring," she retorted. "Let me tell you about the ring you wish everyone to think as a worthless gift. I had it appraised. The jeweler has never seen a more magnificent sapphire. In his own words – a priceless jewel. No, Ivain, what you gave me was an engagement ring, not a trinket!"

"What?" he said, "What?" he repeated, as if he had not understood Allegra.

"Don't pretend to be surprised," she said. "You knew all along what you were doing."

Ivain could not believe his ears. "A priceless jewel? – Not a trinket?" He was not sure what surprised him more, the fact that he had given Allegra, "a priceless jewel," or that it turned out not to be "a trinket?" Where had he last seen the word "trinket" written down? And then he remembered that it was one of the four words he had found when he had first searched the floppy "green disk" for answers and clues. He should have stayed away from any charms, talismans and baubles that were of little value, and could be called "trinkets," he said to himself. But how could he ever have imagined such a thing happening, especially after France had tossed the sewing box under his eyes with such ingenuousness and candor?

Allegra had already gotten into the car and had started the engine. The window on the driver's side was all the way down. She put her head out and her last words to him were: "I hope you rot like the crows in the Brie!" and then added those incomprehensible last words to him – "Never forget for a moment that I loved you madly!" and she said it in such a way that the word "love" had never been more filled with "hate."

Ivain was dumfounded. Allegra knew about his encounter with the doomed crows? He deduced she must have been hiding nearby. He looked at her again, and this time he could not believe that he had never before noticed that the roots of her hair were dark, and her eyes too far apart for her to be really considered a classic beauty. Besides, they were too large for her face, which gave her a sort of waif-like look. Also, the paleness of her face for the first time reminded him of the paleness that he associated with a person who has just died, for he could not find even the tiniest shadow of a vein anywhere in her skin, and with horror he realized that there was nothing attractive about her, and that it had all been a terrible mistake. How could he have ever thought of her as extremely beautiful? He now saw that she was merely ordinary, when before she had been extraordinary; that she was plain when before he thought her a splendid Goddess. Besides, he became suddenly aware, she was not refined and did not have the style that interested him. What he had found in her just a couple of weeks ago was unexplainable, for she was just the sort of woman he always ran away from, had always been frightened to come too close to. She was not at all what he looked for in a woman, and the fact that he had been her lover distressed him more than he could even permit himself to say now, either aloud or silently.

He pulled away from her, trembling with an irrational fear, as Allegra put the car in gear and left in a hurry. "Where was she going?" he asked himself, as he leaned against a sack of trash that had been left on the sidewalk, just outside Le Plessis, wondering if he would ever see her again. He did not know then, but he would see her only once more, briefly, before he died, as she had predicted when they first met outside Mme Kamiska's house. But while he was staying in New York City, he would receive from her various written messages, always unsigned. Once he got a card with a large heart drawn on it, pierced with various pins and needles of all sizes. Another time, through the mail again, he received a piece of cardboard on which circles within circles had been painted to represent a primitive target practice, whose center had been pierced with holes made by bullets of different caliber. Many times the phone would ring, but when he picked it up, no one answered, though he knew someone was there. He even received a book by express mail with no return address, and when he unwrapped it, he saw it was further wrapped in three kinds of soft paper, pink, cherry red, and burgundy red, each tied with a blue or turquoise ribbon. The title of the book proclaimed boldly that it was all about the close relationship between love and hate, but when he opened it, he found only blank pages inside. Days later, whenever he thought of these objects, he would convince himself that they were really objects of love, that the sender had just not understood the meaning of either his words or his gift. He would swear that the large heart was really filled with tiny diamonds, and that the target was only a map with holes made by the arrows thrown by the winged child Eros. He even convinced himself that he had read poems in the empty pages of the book that were as beautiful as those of Sappho, or Ronsard, or Byron.

But for the moment, as he remembered the image of Allegra, he was overwhelmed with sadness and hopelessness, and he began to mull over this most recent event. "To think that all this has happened to me," he said to himself, "because I went to the airport six hours ahead of time, got killed by accident from the cross fire between two warring factions of terrorists, whose names or nationalities no one knows, then after ten years of unconsciousness, I went on to accept what was described to me as a diary – a blank 'script' – to fill with this new life of mine, only to find it had been otherwise decreed. And now I've just made another unpardonable mistake in humiliating Mme Kamiska's own operative. Oh – if only I had waited ten more minutes at home with France, I wouldn't have been on the escalator just when those people were shooting at each other, and I would be alive now, tucked in bed with the only woman I ever truly loved."

NEW YORK – DETECTIVE PELLEGRINO

"The Professor's death? A riddle hidden in a Chinese box."
The police answer to Ivain's question

The following day, as Fabian, France and Ivain were driving to Charles de Gaulle, he heard Fabian say, "Johnny, it will be good for you to be in the city. Staying here would only remind you of yesterday's unpleasant event. And you're welcome to live in our apartment." He then took France's hand in his and said, "Darling, I'll be back from Orlando as soon as possible, and I'll call you every day."

The disastrous event of the previous day made it difficult for Ivain to act in any reasonable way, but it was driving him to the edge of distraction. All night he had been up, wondering why he was not more attentive to the utterances of people around him. He now marveled at his own stupidity for not having linked "trinket" immediately to something dangerous and sinister. "The fact that I have not been able to pick it up is an ominous sign. It does not bode well," he thought.

They arrived at the airport a bit ahead of time. They all sat down to have a cognac before leaving for their different destinations.

Ivain now tried to find out all he could about the ring. He turned to France and asked her, "How come there was such an expensive jewel in your sewing box, among all those other trifles? How did it get there?"

France stared at him with a blank look. "I don't understand it myself," she said. "I have no idea."

It was Fabian who made clear to both of them what had happened. "You see, Johnny, I gave that ring to France, thinking nothing of it. I found it in my mother's drawer after her death, mixed in with all sorts of trivial objects. I truly believed the ring to be a bagatelle." He stopped to take a long sigh. "This dreadful misunderstanding is all my fault. I'm so sorry it ever happened."

"The party was a horrible mistake," echoed France. "I truly hope you'll forgive both of us." After that France and Ivain said good-bye to Fabian, whose plane was leaving before theirs. Before boarding, Fabian had come close to Ivain, and said, "Will you ever be able to forget this awful experience?" and Ivain replied, "It's not your fault, or France's. Please do not think for a moment that I hold you responsible. You've been a gracious host, and I'm in your debt," and Fabian had embraced him, with a warm strong embrace and Ivain felt it was a great pity he could not share his secret with his cousin whom he loved so dearly.

★ ★ ★

As soon as Ivain arrived in New York, he immediately made a telephone call to Petronio Pellegrino. He was the police Officer France had mentioned in their walk from Le Plessis to the *Mairie* of Rosay. "The Officer," she had said, "who was in charge of Ivain's murder case."

He called the Officer, and found he had been promoted to "Detective" with "Homicide." On the telephone Ivain introduced himself and, with the excuse that he was a friend of the late Professor La Baille's widow, "in whose apartment I am staying," he asked, "Could I come to see you?" and explained, "I'm curious to know if the Professor's death is still unresolved, or if there have been any breaks in the case." Did the Detective know the name of the murderer or murderers? he asked.

At first the Detective seemed reluctant to talk to him, and Ivain sensed a feeling of distrust. "But distrust was built into his training," thought Ivain, and he could not hold it against him.

To reassure the Detective, Ivain gave him the phone number of the apartment on Riverside Drive and asked him to call back and speak to Mrs. Alfred herself. After that, there was no problem, and Ivain made an appointment to go and see him that very afternoon.

When Ivain arrived at the police station, he found the Detective in a small office. "Having lunch, though it's late," he said laughing. And in fact he was dunking large pieces of Italian bread into two eggs sunny side up, still in a small ceramic frying pan. He said he cooked all his meals himself, on an electric plate he had brought with him to police headquarters, and pointing to a corner of his office Ivain saw the hot plate, still smoking from a bit of butter that must have fallen on it. Pellegrino excused himself for continuing to eat, and offered Ivain a chair on the other side of his desk.

Between one mouthful and another, the Detective managed to give Ivain a lot of information. He said he had looked carefully into all the possibilities of how the Professor had come to his tragic death. "Solving this murder has been a full-time job for me," he continued, and pointed to a large file of papers on top of his desk called "The La Baille file" and underneath it, in capital letters, was the word "Adjal."

"Adjal?" said Ivain. "What is it?"

"An office joke," answered the Detective. "When we couldn't find any lead at all, one of the junior officers baptized it Adjal." He cleaned his mouth with a piece of paper towel. "Something to do with the predicted hour of one's death, I think," he said, laughing again. "You know how it is," he continued, "if we didn't do a silly thing once in a while, there's enough here to go mad in a day." And he began to repeat slowly, "rapes, suicides, accidents, missing children, husbands killing wives, wives killing husbands, and so on and so forth," he muttered as he continued to eat unperturbed.

Ivain was struck by that word "Adjal." It must have been Mme Kamiska who had suggested it. Not a bad word, he thought. Again, "dramatic irony" was at work here and he knew she knew he knew.

They went on talking. Ivain kept expressing curiosity about the file. The Detective had asked himself the question, time and again, how the Professor came to be killed by that bullet and made a witty remark about it, adding, "It has been a mystery for whom the bullet was really meant," he said. "And that, my dear sir, we've been unable to explain. For the moment, there's still no real, serious lead in this murder," he said, and continued to describe what they had found up to date, including the terrorist trail, though nothing had come of it.

As he was talking, he would open the file, and take out a piece of paper from time to time. He had a handwritten report in the folder that described in detail the intimate relationship between the wife of the "deceased" and the "deceased's" own cousin, both present at the airport at the time of La Baille's death. He had put a note in parenthesis when he had found out about this love affair, through an anonymous tip left on his answering machine, which on closer inspection proved to be true.

"Such relationship, which might or might not have been known to La Baille," he said, "was something that had to be looked into."

He bent over Ivain, as if he was imparting a secret that should have remained one. "Personally I've often wondered if the husband knew." he said, not without some malice, Ivain noticed. "So my question was and is: Did the Professor know?"

For a moment Ivain felt like saying, "No, the Professor did not know, nor did he suspect." But before he uttered a sound, the Detective had resumed talking. "From my discreet investigation, I've found out that the La Baille couple was on the whole a happy couple. Their only concern, as far as I could find out, was the lack of a child, which Mrs. La Baille confided to me she thought was due to her husband's sterility. How she came to that conclusion is unclear to me. I think it was more of an assumption on her part than a proven fact, since it turns out, I believe, she was the one who had the problem." And he took a long breath. "In fact she hasn't been able to have any children with her second husband as well," he said. "Frankly, for a while I thought that she started the love affair with Mr. Alfred to conceive a child. But this assumption is neither here nor there. They were lovers, that's the point. Lovers before the Professor was married to her, and lovers afterward. I believe the affair had only begun again a few days before the Professor's death. 'One time' Mrs. Alfred confessed to me 'a one-night fling' with Mr. Alfred after her marriage to Mr. La Baille. And that was provoked, she explained to me, because she'd found out that the Professor was seeing someone else on the side." He stopped, only to resume right away. "To tell you the truth, I was never able to prove this part of her story. Personally I doubt it. When you look into the life of a person, as I've done, you can tell right away whether someone is a Don Juan or not. You know what I mean?"

"In your opinion, then, the Professor was not having an affair?"

"He was not that sort of man, not at all. A bit on the prudish side, if anything," said the Detective laughing, and Ivain was struck more by the word the Detective had used than by what he had said. "Prudish is such an old-fashioned word," he thought, in view of the fact that, since coming to the police station, every other word he had heard around him had been profane. In contrast to the French police in general, and to Chef Perrot in particular, who were inordinately polite, though probably not as well trained, the New York police were irreverent, boisterous and crude. "But then vulgarity was becoming part of city life," he thought. "Yes, people were getting more ill mannered than ever before."

"On the other hand," the Detective continued, "I had to question whether the lover of the Professor's wife, who also happens to be his cousin, wanted to do him in." And as he said this he got up and, putting some change into a nearby machine, got a Coke can out of it, so cold that it was covered with white frost. He opened it, and began to sip it slowly as he repeated almost to himself, "He had a motive, that's certain, and time." And here he stopped and looked at him with apprehension. Did he expect a word of encouragement from him? Did he expect perhaps a word that could open a new door to the case? But Ivain remained silent, moving his fingers up and down the side of his chair. With a nervous gesture, Detective Pellegrino set the Coke on top of his desk, lit a cigar, and continued. "You see, I have to ask the question – Could Mr. Alfred have fallen madly in love with Mrs. La Baille? And if so, could he be acting alone, or could they be in it together?" He stopped as he filled the room with puffs of smoke. "As you know most murders are done by someone close to the dead person in question. The murderer is almost always known to the murdered." Here Petronio Pellegrino went on to describe how he had felt obliged to question both the wife and the cousin of the deceased, in view also of the fact that the widow had married "the aforementioned cousin" so quickly after her husband's death. "I found it very unusual. I found it even disturbing that Mrs. La Baille would not wait a reasonable time for mourning her husband's tragic death. A husband whom she said she loved immensely. But," the Detective said, "we cannot put a widow in prison just for remarrying quickly. There are no written laws about how long one should wait after the death of one's own husband, are there? That is something between her and her conscience. Besides," he went on, "I quickly came to the conclusion that neither the wife nor the cousin of the deceased had been either directly or indirectly involved. Who to blame for that fatal bullet, is still an unresolved question."

After that, he handed Ivain a written summary of two and a half pages, which Ivain read quickly. Then knowing that there was nothing more to say or do, he got up, shook Detective Pellegrino's hand and left.

Outside, in the street, Ivain mulled over the report he had just read. In it there was nothing that he had not known. Everything was there wrapped in a veil of mystery. Toward the middle of the second page, though, Ivain now recalled, he had come across a sentence that struck him as incongruous. "At 12:20 the Professor was alive on the escalator, with one hand on the rail, and the other apparently in his pocket. At 12:35, the Professor was dead, with both hands across his chest." He was amazed by the simplicity of what people around him saw, as written up in the summary. Yet for him, those fifteen minutes had been filled with the most varied and strange remembrances. Seemingly for the world, he had done things that living people do when they are barely alive, yet still living. Apparently he had smiled to the old man who was holding his hand. The name of this person with his address was written there in parenthesis, in clearly legible letters, demonstrating the efficiency of the investigation. He had also tried to say a few words, but what had been heard were just discordant sounds, which no one could clearly identify. Above all, he had done something totally unexpected under the circumstances. He had kept smiling, as if this were a festive occasion. He stopped now in the middle of the street, and looked up, struck that – so close to death – he had smiled, which seemed paradoxical. "Yet," he said to himself, "the truth of the matter is that as long as one is alive, one will do what living beings are known to do, however incongruous. Therefore a smile, or smiling, is a sign of life." And then he remembered a friend of his, whom he had visited in the hospital when he was close to death. He now remembered how surprises he had been to find him trying to conjugate irregular German verbs. He was repeating either *"ich werde sein,"* or *"ich verschlinge."*

"Why," he asked him, puzzled at this effort "are you tiring yourself in such a way? What use will this be to you?"

"Because," his friend had answered weakly, "I'm still alive," and as he said it, he breathed his last, saying *"ich habe – verschlungen."* At hearing this Ivain remembered he had first cried then laughed. He had actually laughed so hard that the doctor on duty insisted on giving him a tranquilizer, which he refused. He was then accompanied to the front door of the hospital and asked to leave, at which point he started to laugh again, and did so until he reached home.

"Life remains life," thought Ivain outside of the police station, "in its seemingly minute details, until there is no more life, until nothing more can be learned. And then all one's knowledge disappears like a phantom with the first crowing of the cock and the first ray of the morning light."

JULIUS CAESAR

"The best of all mankind."
Shakespeare

Two days after his arrival, Ivain took a walk alone on Riverside Drive on the side of the Park, along the long line of cars that were always parked there. Since he had come to New York, he had been trying to get in touch with Mme Kamiska, but when he dialed the numbers corresponding to the letters of her name, he had only found an answering machine that asked him to leave a message, for she was in the Himalayas, drinking waters which were supposed to lengthen a life, or so it was believed. At first Ivain found the message so perplexing that he did not know what to make of it. "Wasn't Mme Kamiska eternal? And if so, what could such waters do for her?" But, overcoming his apprehension, he had left a message, suggesting they meet on one of his daily walks, preferably when he was alone, so they could talk more freely. On this particular morning, he was surprised to find that up and down the street, all the car windows had been smashed, the pieces laying on the ground. Shaken by this discovery which pointed to a ubiquitous and increasing vandalism in the city, he looked closer and became aware of the presence of a person. To Ivain this person looked like a homeless tramp, dressed in dirty, tattered, mauve rags, with two squirrels on one shoulder, and sitting on a carpet of shining pieces of glass. Ivain stopped struck by the scene, for the glass on the ground reflected the rays of the sun in a myriad ways, as if there were an infinite number of prisms. Astonished by the beauty of all this light, he walked up to the man who was bending over and carefully picking up the glass, one piece at a time, and putting them in a tin can. What looked like a poor, lost human being, lifted his head and stared at him, and under all the grime and dirt, Ivain recognized Mme Kamiska by her toothless smile. Many days later, after he, Ivain, had laid down with France, on a soft grass dell that seemed made for illicit love and for lovers, he remembered this moment, but remembered it differently. He was not sure any longer of what he had seen, for it seemed that not only the ground, but the trees as well, were covered with glass and shining as if there had been an ice storm the night before, and not just nameless thieves searching for loot. He thought he remembered the branches of chestnuts and beeches bent down under the weight of icicles. He even believed he saw tropical plants there, cut out of pure, brittle ice that made a crackling noise, and spiders spinning pure shining threads for their endless webs, and red robins sitting on crystal nests. He remembered the sun's rays filtering through the branches, giving an impression that the whole world was made of glass, ice and light. That is how he remembered New York too, as the city of light and ever shining sun.

Now he looked at Mme Kamiska and, bending his knees, he asked what she was doing on Riverside Drive when he thought she was somewhere in Asia.

"Oh," she replied, as she continued to pick up the glass fragments from around her feet, "I had to postpone my trip for I had forgotten about last night. See how beautiful these tiny glasses are? They are props for another play in another planet, in another galaxy." Ivain was curious to know more, but did not dare to ask for there was a personal favor he hoped Mme Kamiska would grant him. Something that he believed would change forever his "written script," so he kept quiet. But Mme Kamiska volunteered anyway and said, "What is glass on one planet is a diamond on another planet, and vice-versa. This glass is a priceless stone in Sigellium."

"And where is this planet?" he blurted out.

"Ah, that is a question. And questions will have to wait – for the answer will come when it will come, and not one moment sooner," she said. Then, seeing that he was disappointed, she took out of her rags a large *Atlas of the Universe*, and opening a page she pointed at a picture with two round halves of a planet.

"But this looks like Earth!" cried out Ivain as he recognized the masses of land.

"Look again," she replied, and when Ivain pulled the book nearer to him, he saw that though the continents looked the same, they had different names written on them. North America, for instance, was the land of Lilliput, South America was the land of Oz, Europe was the land of Daddy Jones, Africa was the land of Gondour. And he saw that cities, though in the same place, had different names too. In the place of Rome, New York, Paris and London he saw Heliopolis, Emerald City, Atlantis, and Kadath. And Asia was Orfena and Australia was Kravonia. And there were names such as Dilectable, Has, Kunlun, and Morgal for mountains, and Spoon and Telhearna for rivers. Amazed at the discovery that all the imaginary places he had read about were real in another part of the universe, he was tempted to ask for more details but, realizing that Mme Kamiska had almost filled her tin can with diamonds for Sigellium, he closed the atlas and handed it back. It was with an unusual effort that Ivain came back to the business of the moment. It was his intention to ask Mme Kamiska to find a way for him to play Julius Caesar on its opening night.

"That's tonight, isn't it?" she asked.

"Yes," said Ivain.

"And do you feel you are prepared for it?" she inquired.

"Yes," he said again, adding "I've been practicing my lines all along. I know them well – and as for the character – well, I'm beginning to feel more and more like Caesar."

"But, are you Caesar?"

"No, I can't say I am quite the great Caesar. Perhaps one day –" He was tentative now, for he would have liked to feel like him.

"One day you certainly will," she said. "As for now, go home and prepare yourself. Do remember that on stage you'll have the same blocking as you had in your previous rehersals in New York, with the Thespians. I'll arrange everything," and with that she stood up, and holding the tin can tightly with both hands, she took a few quick steps, and was soon out of sight.

Back in the apartment he was greeted by France who said his theater director had sent him a note by special messenger. And as she said this, she looked at him for the first time as she used to look at him when they were husband and wife. Was she falling in love with him again? He wondered.

Certainly Ivain felt closer to France, and it was harder and harder to be under the same roof, and not in the same bedroom and not the same bed. That apartment had so many tender memories of his own past, though once more he found that many personal items were missing. His historical books, his collection of walking sticks as well as his collection of rare stamps, and all his pipes. But, still, those walls were full of the echoes of the resplendent parties they had given there, of intimate dinners, and of intellectual arguments which always ended with France's affirming that "Feminine intuition was worth a hundred books of philosophy, or of literature for that matter," which always made Ivain laugh. And that was that.

But now he turned away from her in turmoil for he was afraid his good luck meant inevitably bad luck for the leading actor. *Mors tua vita mea,* he whispered under his breath, but France heard him and, looking at him, wondered what it all meant.

"Is it Allegra again?" she asked.

"No, no," he said as he opened the note. He read it quickly.

The leading actor, a famous name in the American theater, had lost his voice unexpectedly, the note said, and it went on to inform him that he, Johnny, would be opening the play this very night, and would he be so kind as to go to the theater as soon as possible. Later, at the theater, he would find out that many doctors had been in and out of the leading actor's apartment on Fifth Avenue and could find nothing wrong with him or his vocal cords, yet the poor man could not as much as whisper, and had to write everything down on paper. Throughout the day, he had been drinking hot camomile, mixed with honey and mint leaves. He also submitted to having a large white linen handkerchief, filled with hot mud and spices, placed around his neck which his Haitian maid said never failed to cure people with his affliction. Moreover, the same maid, noticing with increasing anguish that nothing was working, had gone to Central Park and had picked leaves and moss to do a voodoo rite she had learned in her native Port au Prince to take away the "evil spell" cast on the great artist she served. That he was suffering from an "evil spell," she was sure, she said. On hearing the story, Ivain could only marvel how right this Haitian woman had been, and felt sorry that probably few people believed her. While all around town theater people were calling each other up and saying, "How odd this sudden turn of events. How odd." Ivain knew better, and was thankful that Mme Kamiska had arranged things so well for him.

He quickly told France of the note. She seemed tense, and turning away from him began to walk toward her room.

"Wait!" he said, and taking her hands into his, he asked her to forgive him for having upset her, that she was the most wonderful creature in the world and the last person he wanted to hurt, that it had been a month of uncertainties for him for reasons he could not explain just then, and that, yes, of course he was happy and ready to open Julius Caesar on Broadway. As he said that, he gave her the note to read for herself.

France was still mesmerized by it when Ivain left for the theater. He felt elated thinking about the clever stratagem he would use to break out of "the written script."

He walked down Broadway all the way to the Vivian Beaumont Theater at Lincoln Center. He passed many stores, some of which, he thought, did not differ much from those in the Suburra district in Rome. There all sorts of vendors would leave their wares outside: sandals from Italy, transparent clothes from India, boxes within boxes from China. He walked past well-dressed men and women, but they were the minority. Most of the people he met looked miserable, human beings of all colors and nationalities, begging or standing, swaying and reeling from too much alcohol or too many drugs. "What a wretched experience life is for most people," he thought, and pulling out of his pocket one dollar bill at a time, he started handing them over to everyone who asked, running out after ten or twelve blocks. There were also young women at various corners ready to sell themselves, as well as young men who were on the search for someone to notice them. Some even tried to give him a card, but he answered everyone with a standard sentence, "Too early in the day, for God's sake! Try me tonight." And he walked on, concentrating on what he was about to do. He went over the script carefully, and at least on that score he knew that he was going to do well, and not forget his lines, for he had been practising since the day he returned. Every day in Rosay he had stood in front of the large mirror in his room and mouthed the lines, making sure that they were said naturally, but powerfully, to represent Julius Caesar as he must have been: humble and arrogant at the same time, magnanimous and cruel, forgiving and unmovable, generous and tight fisted. Always alert to his enemies' moves except for that one slip at the end, and even that slip was due to a single moment of blindness, since he had been given ample warnings from both his wife's dream and the seer's words, that some tragedy around his person was afoot. Later on, just before entering the stage, he was both imbued and touched by grace, when he suddenly realized that to find the greatness of Caesar he would have to concentrate on the weakness of his character, not on his strength. He would concentrate on the faults, not the eloquence, of the man. He would remember the path traced by the Gracchi, Marius and Catiline. He would walk that road as he spoke the words of Shakespeare.

He put out of his head all the Stanislavski preparation of the actor's studio which he once attended in his previous life, though he realized that some moments in the script had been found through his past experience. The wish to be crowned by Mark Antony in front of the Roman populace, seemed very close to the wish to be president of his class at Harvard, and to his disappointment when he was flatly rejected. But apart from this moment, he could find no similar situation in his own life.

When Ivain arrived he went to the director. The director seemed beside himself, and greeted him with the words, "Can you get ready right away? The make-up artist and the dresser are waiting for you." Ivain was amazed to be greeted in this familiar way, since it was the first time he had laid eyes on the director, just as the director had never seen him before. But he felt so happy to be given the opportunity to play his hero at last, that he nodded consent.

He walked down a long corridor where he saw an old man with long white hair and red cheeks, dressed in a rich but tattered blue velvet costume, coming toward him. "I am the soothsayer, Caesar," he said aloud, and then added in a whisper, "Well, the Ides of March have come." And with that, he took both his hands in his own and kissed them unexpectedly before

Ivain could take them away. In the strange man Ivain recognized Mme Kamiska at once. "Mme Kamiska!" he said. "You! Still here?"

"I always take a part in my Father's plays," she said, and then after a short pause, added a line about life and theater, which Ivain thought he had heard before, but did not know where. After that she ran down the corridor, saying loudly: "We'll see each other later, after those that must die are dead." He stood still, stunned by this apparition for the second time in the same day.

He walked on until he reached another long corridor, and there he found a door with his name on it. He opened it, and saw the dresser waiting for him, holding a white toga with a violet border. In the dim light that came from the small window, he could make out the long, thin table in front of the large mirror, with all the make-up kits that would be used on his face, neck, arms, hands, legs and feet. The table was cluttered with small and large containers, powder boxes, colored pencils, brushes, combs, hair brushes, puffs. There was also a series of colored bottles, each prettier than the other, with silver tops, filled with mysterious liquids, and creams, oils, balsams, Kleenex, linen towels, and other larger cotton towels. Under the table there was an assortment of expensive objects of every description – tall vases for the flowers that were inevitably sent on opening night, bracelets, silver canes, long pearl necklaces, and a large assortment of swords and scimitars. There was even a gold plated ashtray. He sat down and the makeup artist, who had been hiding behind the dresser, began to open different jars of creams and pastes, and his face took on the hue of a pale red brick as his eyes were highlighted by a dark pencil and his lips accentuated in scarlet red. As he was looking at his own face being transformed in the mirror, he thought of this speech and that speech, and tried to remember all the words of the immortal Shakespeare. And then he mused, was Shakespeare really Shakespeare – or the Earl of Southampton, or Bacon or Marlow? Questions, always questions. And he wrote them down on his list.

Just before entering the stage, he had a moment of fear. Might he not forget words, cues, whole speeches? He felt the full force of the shame and humiliation that would crush him, if that were to happen. But then he thought of how much he had longed for this moment and, regaining control of himself, he walked out into the stage lights and with an imposing presence began:

> "Let me have men about me, that are fat,
> Sleek-headed men, and such as sleep o' nights:
> Yond Cassius has a lean and hungry look,
> He thinks too much: such men are dangerous."

Later on he was particularly effective and convincing when he rose up to the lines:

"Cowards die many times before their deaths –" et cetera. His overall performance was powerful, forceful, and excellent. And when he came to the end of his part, he had grown into a superlative Julius Caesar, towering above all other Caesars in living memory.

Then it happened. Suddenly, unexpectedly. Decius had just finished saying, "Great Caesar," and Casca had lifted his hand holding the dagger saying, "Speak, hands, for me," and as the hand had come down with the dagger, and he was being stabbed repeatedly by the conspirators, he was now supposed to say his exit line:

"Et tu, Brute! Then fall, Caesar"

But he did not say it, neither did he fall.

He had been stabbed, he had seen the knives, the vials of

225

stage blood had all burst on his white toga, drenching it with large blotches of red liquid, but he did not fall and die. The surprise in the eyes of the assassins was immense, and they began the ritual of stabbing him with their fake daggers all over again. He heard the voice of Casca repeating, "Speak, hands, for me." And Brutus whispering to him "Et tu Brute! Et tu Brute!" The points of the daggers were beginning to dig into his flesh as the blades disappeared into the sheaths that covered them. He knew the script well. He knew perfectly well this was where Caesar, mortally wounded, dies. Yet, he kept standing among the shining blades. Standing in a pool of vermillion blood, standing, not falling to the ground, refusing to utter the last lines of the script.

The conspirators, alarmed, tried to murmur in his ears the words needed to go on with the play. They murmured them once, then once more, then again, as Brutus, in desperation, tried to trip him by playing with his feet, and kicking him. Aemilius Lepidus, Trebonius and Cinna, conspirators too, pushed him from the side and from the back, but Ivain would not fall on the floor where the marked X had been clearly painted.

He would not die.

Finally, there was total confusion on stage. Everybody began to ad-lib, "Take this Caesar, and that Caesar, and Caesar dies, and Caesar must die." But, there was nothing that would make Ivain's Caesar die. There would be no deaths tonight, not even the mimicked death of the stage. Nothing at all. He kept standing there, head high, looking contented to have escaped the conspiracy alive. Finally, Brutus, with a puzzled and angry look on his face, took Ivain under one arm. Then Casca, following Brutus' lead, took the other arm and Trebonius pushed him from behind, and in this way Ivain was pulled off stage.

As soon as he was backstage the arms that held him up released him all at once, and he fell to the ground with a thump, all crumpled up, as if he had been a sack of old shoes. He got up, and went straight into his dressing room without answering the chorus of angry questions behind him.

"Would the play go on anyway?" he mused to himself. He opened the door slightly and waited to hear the words "Liberty! Freedom! Tyranny is dead! Run hence, proclaim, cry it about the streets." And indeed, in the good tradition of the theater, he heard Cinna making a try at it. But there was no dead body lying on stage, in fact there was nothing on stage resembling a body! How could the conspirators dip their hands in Caesar's blood? They never got very far, certainly not as far as Antony saying those famous words:

"Friends, Romans, countrymen, lend me your ears;
I come to bury Caesar, not to praise him."

The audience had began to murmur and tiny peals of laughter were beginning to be heard, first muffled, then bold and loud. The play began to acquire a heightened sense of unreality, making it in some way more frightening and more comical. Finally he heard the whole audience laughing out loud, and the director ordering the stage hands to bring the curtain down. Then, somewhat more distantly, he heard voices clamoring for the return of their money. Voices which said they had come to see how a great man dies as his blood spills out, and they had been greatly disappointed. There were bloody clothes, bloody stains on the floor, but that was all there was. Caesar had left the stage alive! And Ivain had broken the first rule of the stage – thou shalt not tamper with "the script."

In his room he began to look round. It was total confusion. On an impulse, he bent down and picked up the gold ashtray to discover that what shone like gold was really only cheap paint that had been cleverly brushed on. So nothing was what it seemed to be, either in real life or on stage. He looked up at the long blue curtain at the end of the room, and near it he saw a few hangers for his clothes. The room looked more like a bazaar in some Middle Eastern town than a dressing room. But Ivain's state of mind was such that he didn't mind the disorder, but rather welcomed it, for his thoughts were on what had just happened. He felt intoxicating happiness, a well being that came from the realization that an important goal had been attained and from his certainty that something extraordinary would follow. He congratulated himself over and over again for having been able to change "the script." He had finally done it! He had been able not only to change Shakespeare's play, but also to change history itself – to change what had been Caesar's end, for Caesar, tonight, lived on. He would live to make love once more to Cleopatra, he was sure of that. Or to return to Calpurnia first, to reassure her he was alive, and then run back and make love to Cleopatra. Or he could go directly to see Mark Antony and together make immediate plans to sail to Egypt and proclaim Alexandria the new Rome of the Empire. He would forget Parthia for the moment. No more wars, only the love and luxury of the Orient where he would fulfill the belief that he was the God Amon. He would graciously let the conspirators live, but they would have to go into exile in Lutetia, far enough from Alexandria to be safe from their daggers. He would order Marcus Varro to organize and collect all the important Latin and Greek books. Lake Fucinus would be drained and there he would build a number of magnificent temples, so many that he visualized a time when it would be called the Valley of the Caesarian Temples. He would employ a hundred thousand slaves to open a passage through the Isthmus of Corinth. And these were just a few of the plans he could now carry out.

In these pleasant suppositions and daydreams Ivain spent what seemed an infinite time, though it was just a few minutes. Then he became aware that the room was dimly lit, but he did not bother to light the brass lamp on the table. A blast of cold air came from the open window, and Ivain sensed that someone was in the room. He turned around and saw France standing near the door which she was closing gently.

"Why? Why?" she began. "You were so good –"

"I didn't feel like dying tonight," he replied simply as he got up, tip-toed to the window, closed it and tip-toed back to his chair.

"Johnny," she began, "when you go out of that door, say anything, but not what you just said to me. You'll ruin your career," she added. "No one will ever employ you as an actor."

"I am proud of what I did," he insisted. "I did it deliberately."

"Why?"

"Because I identify with Caesar," he said smiling. "And Caesar had a beautiful woman waiting for him." And as he said it, he tried to touch her, but she recoiled.

"It was the chance of a lifetime. It was your chance." She looked as if she was about to cry.

"I've given Caesar a chance, too," he said, looking at her. "Now he can return to the streets of Rome and the night is his."

"I don't understand you," she said simply.

He could see she was in pain. Her face was contorted. She was trying not to cry. It was a pity he could not say more to her. He tried to regain his bearing too, and look into her eyes. Tried to tell her what he knew he could never tell her. He began to say something, but immediately stopped, just closed his eyes and pushed his head back. Everything was in turmoil. He was living with his own death. Living with the thought that he was just a handful of ashes buried somewhere in his old family property. Now he had some time. Time is limited. It has a beginning and an end – or it would not be. Therefore he had to keep silent, if he wanted to remain close to her.

He got up and told France as gently as he could that he would meet her back home. She left him by the side door, not before going near him and kissing him. "She's falling in love with me again," said Ivain to himself, happy that everything was working out as he had predicted. Allegra was, of course, a nuisance, but she was not a danger for him, no matter how many crazy schemes she thought up, for he was untouchable. After quickly taking off his make-up and dressing in his own clothes, he opened the door and was not surprised to see the director in the corridor pacing up and down.

"You are fired!" he said.

"Thank you," answered Ivain, as he descended the staircase and heard the director still shouting in the corridor, "You'll never have another job! Do you hear?" Ivain laughed as he walked toward the back entrance that opened directly onto the street, convinced that the director would have no trouble finding another understudy for his part. Besides, he was sure that the principal actor had recovered from his ailments, just as quickly and unpredictably as he had fallen ill.

Outside the theater he saw an old hag, whom he recognized immediately as Mme Kamiska, for she had changed back into the ragged, mauve costume she wore that same morning. She did not look at him, but he clearly heard her say in an angry tone: "Your exit line? You forgot to say your exit line!"

"I didn't forget," cried out Ivain. "I deliberately broke the sequence of 'the written script.' And don't expect me to follow it again to the letter, for I'll change pauses into speeches, and speeches into pauses. A sneeze into a yawn and a yawn into a sneeze. The dead will rise up and live, the living will fall down and lie still. And lovers will laugh hysterically in all their love scenes. That's how 'scripts' will be played from now on!" He said all this defiantly, almost deliriously so. She only replied, "We'll meet again."

"Where?" he asked in a loud, brassy voice.

"At the foot of Pompey's marble," she answered, as she quickly turned the corner, melting into the darkness of the night.

TRIUMPH

"Non omnis moriar"
Horace

Nᴇxᴛ day, following Julius Caesar's first night, Ivain found himself both unemployed and famous. As soon as he woke up, he had the feeling that something extraordinary was happening. He could not describe this feeling except as a halo around himself, that protected and irradiated everything with its own light.

His stage action on that opening night of *Julius Caesar* was the talk of the town. All the newspapers in the country, as well as those abroad, spoke of the "un-death of Caesar" and what consequences it could have for our own times. The best writers in town, and out of town, began to write essays on the philosophical and historical meaning of this act, and Ivain, though he did not understand how it had all come about, accepted the accolades in good humor, and with graciousness. In any case, he began to suspect, that in spite of the terrible rage of Mme Kamiska, or perhaps because of it, people had begun to take notice of him as a personality, and not just another actor. The intelligentsia of New York tried to outdo one other in praising him for his *coup* at the Vivian Beaumont Theater. Actors praised him for his courage, and both men and women tried to touch him.

There were innumerable large sacks of mail that kept arriving every day, sometimes ten or more. The first day he opened as many letters as he could. That afternoon he counted two hundred proposals of marriage, not to mention the large number of strangers who wished to be friends, or simply pen-pals. After a while he just let the mail sacks accumulate in rows in all the corners of his bedroom until there was no space left to walk about or even to get to his bed.

The few great hostesses in town who had either great wealth, or beauty, or social position, started to squabble over who would invite him to which dinner or to which cocktail party. Ivain was in demand everywhere. There was always a television crew following him around town, and everyone said that what had happened to John Elliab was a phenomenon that could not be easily explained. Some even ventured to say that the event had something of the miraculous and the mystical.

Charitable foundations, as well as good-hearted individuals, asked to use John Elliab's name to raise funds for such different causes as helping to stop famines in Asia or genocide among certain African tribes, as well as for the introduction of human rights, and the end of the death penalty.

To all these appeals Ivain said yes, and to help them out he not only opened his wallet and gave his ready money away, but also wrote generous checks.

France, who had watched him with pride, finally said to him, "You will end up a poor man if you keep this up." But she said it with a smile full of love and he had replied, "I hope you will support me then," and they fell into each other's arms, kissing for a long time, silently happy that Fabian was still in Florida and would not come back until the night before the Library opening.

This was undoubtedly Ivain's moment of glory. He went everywhere, and wherever he went he was a sensation. He was the people's idol. Crowds waited outside his house to get a glimpse of him. Some even put a tent up in front of the Tomb of the Unknown Soldier, near his home, and slept there all night to get a glimpse of him in the morning. He heard people talk about him in the street, as if a revolution would soon take place and he was at its center.

A few days later, in the editorial page of a major newspaper, he was called the man who had saved Caesar's life. That this act of defiance in a familiar theatrical role took on a life of its own, was totally unexpected to Ivain. What he expected was to be called an outcast, to be derided and punished in one way or another. But instead Ivain was becoming as famous as Caesar himself, and the whole world called him affectionately "Julius' Savior," soon changed to "Savior of Iulius," and almost immediately shortened to simply "S.I." which in some languages means "yes."

But it was not all smooth sailing for Ivain. There were innumerable times when strangers would come up to him in the street to congratulate him on one hand, while on the other hand, trying to trick him into saying that last line of the play. Sometimes they would tease him – Would he please say it for their sake, so they could become instant millionaires? – for a rich San Francisco billionaire had promised to make a millionaire many times over the first person who was able to make John Elliab say what he had refused so far to say. And not all of the approaches were friendly. One night he found himself surrounded by young thugs who seemed ready to kill him if he continued to stubbornly refuse to proclaim *de facto* Caesar dead. Another time he was hit with a crowbar, then shot at by a gang who had pulled him into a dark alley. Both the beating and shooting stopped only when a car pulled up, and he quickly got in. It had been France who had come searching for him. In the car she explained she had gotten an anonymous phone call from a woman whose voice she did not recognize, who had told her precisely where to find him.

She now quickly glanced at him and said, "You must be suffering terribly. Look how torn your clothes are!"

He said, "You saved my life tonight." She took another look and in total disbelief said, "Johnny, you've no bruises, no cuts, not even a scratch! How did you escape being hurt by those horrible criminals?"

"I'm just lucky," he replied, but he saw she was looking at him differently. He had hoped he would bleed somewhere, for the sight of blood would reassure France. But his skin was intact. Still she kept looking at him, and asked for the first time a question she would repeat again. "Who are you really?" He looked away and remained silent. She stopped the car, and took his face in her hands and kissed him. He heard her say sweet, loving thing into his ear. "I know it's wrong," she was whispering, "but it seems as if I can't live without you. Hold me close."

He pushed her gently away. "Let's wait," he said.

"Wait for what?" she asked, showing she was irritated by his manner.

"Let's just wait a while," he said rather mysteriously. But he felt happy that she had begun to take notice of him in an amorous way, "like old times," he said to himself, "like old times."

From that day on, as France became more and more attentive to him, word began to spread among the people that there was something not of this world about "SI." These voices spread the rumor that John Elliab could raise the dead, cure the blind, and transform women into birds with webbed feet and scaly skin, for no human being could endure what he had endured at the hands of those thugs, and still not say that all important Shakespearean last line.

The effect of his great refusal now began to show itself in ways that were unpredictable, and a cause of concern for all around him. He could see changes that, though at first subtle, were becoming more evident with each passing moment.

The stock markets around the world were behaving more irrationally than usual. The price of stocks and bonds would go sharply up and down in long, straight lines on every chart in a matter of hours. People bought and sold property on the spur of the moment, and they married on whims, sometimes after just having met a stranger at a movie or on a train or in a bar, only to separate immediately or fall in love forever. In the street, it became a daily spectacle to see people laughing aloud, only to cry without restraint moments later, and when they were asked the reason for this unusual behavior, no satisfactory answer was given. "I don't know," they would say, or "I was thinking of something, but I don't remember what it was." Peasants were becoming owners of the land they tilled from one day to the next. Rich people were becoming poor overnight, and had no explanation for it. Many murderers would confess to heinous crimes and ask forgiveness from the families of the victims, while people who had been considered saints would hold public orgies in the main square with no regard for anyone's opinion. There were servants who were served by their masters. Prostitutes who began to work for charitable foundations, while quite a few pious society ladies could be seen standing at corners of the city's darkest streets lifting their skirts or showing their breasts with impunity.

Moreover, the weather seemed to follow the general topsy-turvy pattern, for the sun had never burned more hotly in northern cities, while in the tropics there were reports of snow storms. In the savanna, an African tribe had apparently seen a pride of lions grazing on grass, refusing to eat any kind of meat, even of the gazelle or zebra which had been left for them, as an offering. There were also reports of fish flying over land, while birds were seen swimming for hours in ocean waters. Whether all these reports were accurate or not, it was not known, but historians seemed as affected by these strange happenings as they had been in ancient times. History books were beginning to be rewritten with slightly different endings, which Ivain knew would become odder still the longer he could let Caesar live on through him. Besides, there were tangible signs that the technological age would be replaced by an Earth age, in which people spent most of their days finding and planting edible flowers and exotic fruit, and lived side by side with the animals which up to that moment they had hunted down almost to extinction. Greed was being replaced by generosity, envy by kindness, cruelty by goodness. It was beginning to look like a different planet altogether, for some asked whether the sun had begun to rise in the West and set in the East. It was not unusual to hear questions such as: "Would the day still be divided into light and darkness? Or, would there be only darkness?"

It became apparent that everything was in the process of changing, and would do so until Ivain pronounced those last sacred words of the Shakespearean script. Television had hourly reports on the obvious lack of progress on this subject. Entire days were dedicated to talk shows. It went as far as having an obscure religious group declare John Elliab, or "SI" their idol for he kept growing in the popular imagination by leaps and bounds. It was as if the world had become fixed on this one event and waited for an epiphany to settle it one way or another. A wit even said that the world was waiting to see if "SI" was going to turn into "NO." But Ivain was immovable.

A few days after that famous opening night, Ivain remembered that among all the requests he had gotten on those first days of his triumph, one had stood out from the rest. It came from a group of noisy, rambunctious Italian archeology students. The students had approached him as he was going out of the front door of his apartment house. They said: "Mr. Elliab, if you let us use your name on our fund-raising brochure we will make you an honorary citizen of the Roman city of Claterna," adding, smiling, "You can even be its Mayor!"

Ivain wanted to know more about this ancient city, whose name he did not recognize. He said, "I'm late for an appointment." But he did give them a rendezvous for a few days later at the Meadows in Central Park.

When the day came, toward evening, Ivain decided to walk from his Riverside apartment to the Meadows. On the way there, he noticed how many things had changed in his absence, especially in the Park. There were new trees, flowers everywhere and a feeling that it was well cared for. There were many more wild ducks swimming in the reeds of the Central Park lake, and even a pair of swans. He raised his eyes and saw a pair of blue egrets building a nest on a treetop. The closer he came to the Meadows, the more clearly he saw himself as someone standing at the center of the world, for that was the way he perceived New York to be at this moment, not unlike the new Athens or the new Rome of old. All round the edge of the park, in what seemed to be a perfect circle, rose the tallest and best known skyscrapers of the city, clustered together so thickly that they looked like a forest of sequoia trees that were reaching for the clouds. They reflected the light of the falling sun. Some were bathed in red light, some in deep burgundy, some seemed to be on fire, and one looked as if it had the same dark hue as the stones of the Egyptian pyramids. A large numbers of bicyclists passed by, and for a moment he thought the Park had come alive with fireflies, until he realized what he was seeing was only the flicker of red lamps behind their bicycles. He reached the gate of the Meadows, and saw a man trying to fly a beautifully handmade pterodactyl, the reptile-bird of the dinosaur age. It had bones made of light white wood, and its body and wings were covered with shiny dark paper. The man had a remote control in his hand, and two young helpers with him. Ivain could not hear what the man was saying, but gathered that he had asked the young people to run with the bird until they got up enough speed to make its wings rise. Then Ivain saw, as in a miracle, a pterodactyl in flight, like a glider going up and up until it stood still and immobile in the air for a moment; then suddenly it turned and looked as if it was going to plunge toward the grass. It was heading straight down, when Ivain saw with startling clarity the direct effect of his refusal, for the pterodactyl began to take on a life of its own, and flapping its enormous wings took off, flying higher and higher, until it disappeared behind the tallest building of the city. Everyone rushed screaming toward the direction taken by the great giant, and Ivain was about to join in when, turning around, he recognized the young archaeologists from Italy who had just arrived at the Meadows.

Without saying anything of what he had just witnessed, Ivain sat with them on the grass and found out that the city of Claterna did not really exist. They told him that Claterna was a phantom city, whose traces had recently been found under a large tract of land in the northern region of Emilia-Romagna. There the students had dug up a large tract of land during the winter months, and found the remnants of the foundations of a city that had once stood. So far they had recovered some small fragments of Roman and Greek ceramics, and some red tiles that had been dated from an Etruscan roof. They had not yet come across any important artifacts. But, that a Roman city existed on this site, had been a surprise to everyone involved, for no ancient source referred to it. Ivain gave them his blessing and a check, and the students made him instantly the Mayor of Claterna. They even gave him a round medallion with the name of the city written on it, and near it they fastened a large bronze key with some ordinary brown string.

"As the first citizen of Claterna, the key to the city is now yours," they said. He thanked the students and, putting the decorative medallion and key in his pocket, he started to walk back to the Riverside apartment, proud to be the new Mayor of Claterna. He was walking quickly, when all at once he realized that there were innumerable fireflies everywhere around him, lighting the darkness of the night with their tiny lanterns, and he began to suspect that they had come into existance out of those flickering bicycle lamps in the Park.

Ivain was now sure of one thing, for he saw it clearly in his mind. The disruption of "the written script" was having an improbable, unforeseen, and unpredictable impact on the world as a whole as well as on his own person in particular. He knew for a fact that this state of uncertainty could not go on forever, or he would change the Universe in ways that might slip from the hands of the JanKam Co. He even began to think of his antagonists as thrill-seekers, who had jumped out of an airplane, and were waiting too long before opening their parachutes. Billions of years and billions of worlds must have bored them to the point of seeking these perilous feats! If he won, everything would be different. His life would become his own once more and he envisioned himself growing old with France at his side. But he also knew that a reversal was possible, and that it could happen fast. Perhaps it was already on its way. Therefore he was aware that he was in great danger.

This terrifying aspect of his present situation was brought unmistakably to his attention when he received an unsigned, hand-delivered note, in which he read the following words, written in an almost illegible scribble, around the edge of a crumpled piece of paper:

"Beware, someone close to you is also Mme Kamiska's mole on earth."

He realized the note came from Allegra, and wondered if he should take it seriously or just put it aside. Was this another of her cruel missives, or was someone close at hand really betraying him? If so, who could that person be? He thought of M. Boissy, the theft at Le Plessis, the insurance money, and then Fabian and France. Could one of them be a mole? Ivain thought for a moment and could not find any proof of this. But why was it so important that he should have this information at this particular moment? Could it be a diabolical move by his antagonists to throw him off balance, and make it easier for him to reveal his real name? It would be interesting to see how the JanKam Co. intended to accomplish this feat, for he was more than ever determined not to give in.

The very next day, one week exactly after his victorious opening night of *Julius Caesar*, Ivain was expecting another remarkable evening. He felt elated. He had already enjoyed one triumph as John Elliab, but now another, more personal and more significant, was awaiting him, in the unveiling of Professor La Baille's room at the Butler Library. No one at that gathering would know who he really was. But he, Ivain La Baille, knew. And that was all he needed to make him feel sure he would be remembered for years to come.

THE LIBRARY OPENS

"Il est tombé à la baille"
*Fabian shouting in the night,
after the Library Opening Reception*

THE day Ivain was waiting for all this while finally arrived. Columbia University had made a special arrangement with the director of Butler Library to close the building that Sunday afternoon. This was done in preparation of the ceremony which was to be held between six and eight o'clock that evening. Meanwhile, at his apartment on Riverside Drive, Ivain finished a quick lunch with France and, unable to stand the long wait until evening, he decided to take a walk to Columbia and "just hang around," he said. If she thought that was rather odd on the part of her guest, she said nothing, but kept working on her embroidery. "It calms me," she had once told Ivain. "Every stitch calms me. It's therapy." It was only when she saw he was about to leave, that she lifted up her eyes and said: "In a way, I wish I could be there with you alone, though we couldn't have held the party without the two manuscripts Fabian brought back yesterday." And Ivain wanted to say how sad it was that Fabian had not brought back any of his other papers. Apparently they had not survived, except in the fragments that he and his cousin found at Le Plessis.

There was something else Ivain had wanted to ask France for a long time, but had not had the courage to do so. He would have liked to visit his grave, which he knew to be in upstate New York. And now, seeing that she was so well disposed toward him, and that her attitude was becoming more and more friendly, he asked her about her farm, the farm well known for its enormous sunflower fields.

"Oh those!" she replied. "Our caretaker says they are at the height of their beauty now. It is one of the serendipitous gifts of nature."

"If I ask you one favor, will you grant it to me?" he began, smiling at her.

"That depends," she replied, smiling too, stopping her embroidery while she looked at him.

"After the ceremony tonight, will you take me there?"

"To Applebrook?"

"Yes," he replied. She was silent for a while, as if she were thinking. Was it about Fabian, he wondered? Would he be angry with her? With him?

"What a strange idea," she said at last, looking at him in the light of what he had just said. "Why would you wish to go there?"

"To see the sunflowers with you," he had replied, knowing that he was lying a bit.

"I don't know," she finally said. "You see, Ivain's ashes are buried at Applebrook, and now I always feel so sad when I go there." She stopped for a moment, only to add, "I go on a sort of pilgrimage on All Souls' Day, in November."

As soon as France spoke those words, Ivain's desire to go to Applebrook increased immensely, as well as his curiosity.

"Well," he began, "you could tell Fabian that you wish to go tonight to pay a visit to your late husband's grave, to tell his roaming soul, if indeed it is roaming, that you have kept your promise."

"Ah," she said. "I had not thought of that. Of course Fabian will agree. He won't be able to come himself unfortunately. That I know."

"Really?" said Ivain. "Why?"

"Oh, I thought I had mentioned it to you. After the ceremony, he's flying back to Florida for a day or so, to finish paying off those horrible people. To tell you the truth, he didn't tell me his plans until this morning, and very casually at that. Perhaps he wished to spare me the details, for he said it only in passing. In any case, as you see, he is always working for his poor cousin's best interests." Here she stopped and took a long breath that was akin to a sigh. "He'll be back the day after tomorrow," she continued. "But so will we. We can spend a couple of nights there, and come back early in the morning."

"I see," said Ivain. "So it will be just the two of us. You don't mind, do you?"

"No, I don't mind," she replied. "I don't mind at all –"

"And Fabian?" he asked.

"Neither will Fabian, when I explain why I'm going there." She took a breath. "Oh, I'm sure he'll understand."

"That's settled then," said Ivain, as he walked toward the door. "When the Columbia ceremony is over, do come back to the apartment. And if you can get the car ready, I'll meet you back here as soon as possible."

"Would you like me to take you there now?" she asked, almost imploring.

"No. But thank you anyway," he said. "It will be good for me to be alone for a few hours." And with that, he opened the door and left.

Once outside he walked quickly up Broadway, all the way to 116th Street, finding pleasure in walking out in the crisp air of September. Again he found himself walking among people of many races and nationalities and again he pulled out of his wallet a handful of one dollar bills, and gave them out until there were none left. "All the world must be represented in this walk, and Babylon must have resembled New York," he thought as he approached his old hunting grounds.

He recognized the first large buildings of the University, and stopped to look at them. They were imposing in their structure, massive, and solidly built. He looked around, and remembered specific events that had happened in each of them with a sense of sadness for a lost past. Students running after him in search of a better grade. Students asking for the postponement of a paper. Students asking for explanations for a passage they had not understood in class. Professors stopping him to ask him to sign petitions for prisoners of conscience in practically every country in the world. And then there were the letters of recommendation for jobs, as the young pupils became teachers themselves in some far away state. Washington, Arizona, Wyoming, or even Hawaii or Alaska.

He entered the main square, and at the back saw the library. Butler Library, with the names of famous people carved on its stone architraves, under its cornice, in large letters that no one could miss. Cicero was there, Horace and Virgil. Demosthenes and Homer as well. He looked about himself. The square with its large matron, the symbol of his Alma Mater, sitting on the large comfortable chair, was almost empty. There were a few students walking to and fro, from one building to another, and a few others lying about on the grass, reading or talking quietly to each other.

He walked straight toward the library, even though it was closed for the afternoon, as he well knew. He went up to the tightly shut bronze doors and rang the bell and waited there on the threshold. And then he decided to go right through them, just as he had gone through the wall in Le Plessis, when he had first arrived there. Later on, during the reception, he heard a student, who was serving drinks talking to another student who was serving salmon and cucumber and cress-salad sandwiches on soft, white bread, saying that he had seen a flash of light near the decorated bronze door that same afternoon. Ivain wondered if what he had seen was his passing through to the other side. Could a supernatural action be visible to other humans? And if so, was it just an instant of energy tranformed into light?

Once inside the bronze door, Ivain wanted to go straight to the room that in a little while would be dedicated to him, but something detained him. He heard a strange noise coming from the main section of the library, from the room with the open shelves. It reminded him of the noise the wind makes in October, rustling in the hedges or passing through the last dry leaves on the trees. He stopped and decided to go and see who could be there at that hour. He opened the door and was amazed to see the room filled with strange people, people dressed in various clothes, from the Greek kiton to the Roman toga, Japanese kimono and Indian sari, as well as others dressed in modern clothes as he was, and others again, in clothes he had never seen before. Everyone was looking through the shelves, or leafing through books, and putting them back and taking others out. He looked more carefully, and realized that all those people were transparent, in fact they were shadows. They were all running about, frantically searching for something, and what that was, he did not know. He was mystified by these comings and goings, until he heard a voice near him.

"Didn't I tell you we would see each other again, Mr. La Baille? Everyone comes here sooner or later."

He turned around and there was old Natalie in front of him. He was so surprised to see her there that he just stood without making any movement. She was dressed in the same way as the last time he had seen her in her bedroom, when she had been lying there dead, clothed in her beautiful Sunday best.

"Natalie!" he said, "what are you doing here?"

"I've been looking for my recipes," she replied, "and lucky for me I've just found them."

"In the room dedicated to me?" Ivain asked, and added, "You know, today it will be opened."

"I'm so proud of you," she said smiling, "but believe me, I searched that room from top to bottom, and I couldn't find my recipes there. Nothing doing. No, they were in the philosophy section of the main library, in a folder that said 'I eat therefore I am.' I don't know how they ended up there."

"I'm happy for you, Natalie." said Ivain as he smiled knowing that the title of the folder was meant for him. Natalie in her innocence had not understood it. "And what will you do now?" he asked her.

"I'll be leaving soon. Going back –" she said quietly.

"Oh," said Ivain. "I'll miss you, Natalie." Then he stopped. "Wait! Don't go yet," he said. "Tell me first, who are all these people? What are they doing here?" he asked, looking around himself, not wishing to say the word "shadow," fearing he would embarrass Natalie. But she replied very candidly: "These shadows are doing just what I was doing. They're looking for their lost work. They're lucky to find a fraction of it. Sometimes nothing more than a sentence is all that remains of their life's work. Most of the time, there's nothing at all. Even their names are forgotten." And then she went on to explain that there were different groups of shadows. Shadows from the past. Shadows from the present, and shadows from the future.

"Natalie," began Ivain, unable to hide his surprise. "You mean to say that there are people here who have not yet died or even been born?"

"Yes," Natalie said. "That is what you are seeing. The ghosts of the past, present and future," she continued. "All those who thought they'd left something important behind. Look at them now!"

"Ah," said Ivain. "Poor shadows! They are not as lucky as you and I have been."

"So much of what survives is chance," said Natalie. "Whimsical chance at that. Some minor poets are here with all their works intact. But over there – Sappho," said Natalie, as she pointed to a woman who seemed cut in Attic stone. "The best of them all." And bending toward Ivain's ear she said, as if she was sharing a secret, "I've heard her sigh every single night."

He began to walk with Natalie to other parts of the library, and in every room stacked with books there was the same sorrowful sight. He noticed that the shadows were often grouped in coteries. The Literature corner, the Philosophy corner, the History corner, and so on. In one of these corners he recognized the people from having once seen their marble busts or portraits. Dante was there shaking his head, as well as Boccaccio, leafing through various books. Virgil was standing near Dante and trying to console him, though he seemed inconsolable. What had Dante lost? Was there another masterpiece besides the *Divine Comedy*? At the other corner of the room Socrates was standing near Seneca in deep discussion over a book which they kept looking at. Ivain also saw a myriad of other ancient and modern writers in the middle of the room. In a few seconds, he counted ten standing in a semi-circle – including Sophocles, Euripides, Camus, Dostoyevsky, Pushkin, Faulkner, and Proust.

He heard someone saying that in Buenos Aires there were good libraries, that in the Sahara desert there were tombs of kings still undiscovered, where scrolls might one day come to light. One shadow was crying because he had discovered his books written on bronze scrolls inside the cavernous tomb of a lost Egyptian Pharaoh in the Valley of the Kings, but no one had discovered it yet, and he didn't know how to get word to the living in order to begin the excavation. A few were desperate because their work was lost forever under the waters of the Aswan Dam.

In another room, he was particularly struck to see some people he knew well. People who, in fact, would be present at the

Library Opening in just a few hours. They too would follow the fate of Natalie, become shadows and search for their work. One of them in particular made his heart fill with pity. He recognized a well-known society lady, known for her mythical beauty and taste, looking for her secret diary. At first he wished to go nearer, but then he felt it was better to leave quietly, and was about to do so, when standing near the doorway, he recognized Julius Caesar himself. He was dressed in a beautiful white toga, whose folds had been pleated with immense care so they would fall in a precise, yet natural way. He held a book in his hand, but was not looking at it. He was looking directly in front of him. At first Ivain thought Caesar was looking at him, but turning around he saw the shadow of a younger man just behind him someone he did not recognize. Ivain would have liked to speak to Caesar, to ask him about particular incidents of his past, but he felt like an intruder and, repeating softly Dante's line – *Nel mezzo del cammin di nostra vita* – went out of the door, saying to himself, "There are only questions, just questions, and that is the real torment of our daily life." Soon he was standing in the middle of the University square, having said good-bye to Natalie, lost in his own thoughts.

Later in the the afternoon, he began to see people arrive, well-dressed, with clothes that spoke of renowned tailors and stylists from Italy, France, England, as well as from the United States. He knew that it was time for him to go in, and welcome them together with France and Fabian.

The elegance he found inside astonished him. Undoubtedly there were all the people who counted in the New York aristocracy, or so he thought. This may have been partly due because Ivain La Baille had been described as a genius in his field, and partly because his untimely death had made a stir among the great ladies of the city, who, toward the end of his life had begun to compete for his presence at their dinner parties. They came also to see their latest hero, John O. Elliab, the man who had dared to disrupt the immortal script of Shakespeare. Now he heard broken sentences again: "The city lost so much when the Professor died" – or "passed away," (the most common euphemism for death) or "went into the great trip of the beyond, from which there is no return" – (another euphemism that made Ivain almost laugh aloud). Everyone there was busy praising either the late Professor or the great actor, as they went from ebony case to ebony case looking at the few fragments of papers that were left from his past life, and looking at the two manuscripts that were in the process of being published. "That was the only real monument to his own memory," thought Ivain.

A bouquet of red roses came, brought to him by one of the waiters. Ivain quickly opened the note that was attached to the bottom of a stem. It said, "'Congratulations,' Mme Kamiska." He put the note away, as he involuntarily shuddered, and told the waiter to keep the roses in the kitchen.

Then he turned around and began to chat with this lady and that lady. The great lady herself, Mrs. X, was there, and was seen shedding a tear when the late Ivain La Baille's name was mentioned, and he found it all the more incredible since he had just seen her as a shadow in the adjacent room. Then she came up to him and said: "I was in the audience for the opening of Julius Caesar. I thought what you did was very brave. I have been meaning to ask you, would you have done the same if you had been playing on the stage the part of my late husband?" Ivain looked at her, still beautiful in her sixties, and without hesitation said: "Yes, definitely yes. After all, he had you to come back to." Then he turned round again and realized that he had seen practically everyone present, in the halls of the library. They were all shadows searching for what they had left behind.

The great families were well represented. Many members of the famous Four Hundred were present. Besides, there were benefactors from among the great captains of industry and the great names in politics, including a former president of the United States. Outstanding luminaries and professors were there too. Not to speak of the ladies whom no one knew, whose husbands had recently given large sums of money to the library. The latter had scaled the social ladder, to be present at functions such as these; to mingle with both established society and the best and the brightest of the city. It was the most resplendent group of people that Columbia University had ever seen under its roof. They were all there, and Ivain could consider himself lucky to be remembered in such an extraordinary way.

Ivain was immersed and lost in these thoughts when he heard the murmur of two distinctive voices coming from behind a nearby column. He did not see who was talking, but inferred from the tone of the voices that it could only be senior Librarian and Fabian. What surprised Ivain was what the Librarian was saying to Fabian. "I would think two – perhaps three years at most – then I think we can do it." Can do what? wondered Ivain, suddenly interested. "It will be the same room, only we will add first the incunabula that you have so generously given us; then little by little, all the rest –" the voice continued in a whisper.

"Very well," he heard his cousin answer.

"Eventually," continued the Librarian, "eventually we will rename the room." He paused as if he was following a thought. "I think that will be best," he said.

"That will be perfect!" he heard his cousin answer. "Absolutely perfect," and then they talked about the library's latest acquisition. A gilded copper astrolabe with the Farnese coat of arms on it, and a sphere of the earth, with all the other planets and the sun rotating around it. The latter had been found in a town near Padua, and was at least four hundred years old. "It has been a great find," his cousin was saying. In such way they went on discussing how many more acquisitions were planned for the following year, since Fabian would continue to be their principal benefactor.

Ivain could not believe what he had heard, and to make sure that he had identified their voices, he circled round the column to find both the Librarian and Fabian confabulating as only old friends can. He joined the conversation for a few minutes, then left them, and for the first time began to look around the room, and go from case to case, where his fragmented papers were carefully exhibited. Some had only a page. Some showed only the titles of his papers, others displayed broken pieces of paper well pasted on grey cardboard. As he was looking at them he had a growing sense that he was staring at something he already knew, and had known for a long time, but had not had the courage to look at, and now it was about to be made clear to him. And as often happens with major discoveries, he realized in a second, that he, who would never write a sentence with a split infinitive, had just seen one in front of his own eyes, in one of the fragments with just two lines. He was so astonished by this discovery that he walked straight to the ebony case that held his two major manuscripts, carefully guarded under a glass top. Earlier in the week, he had asked senior Librarian permission to look at the MSS, a permission he had obtained through the intercession of Fabian. So, Ivain now opened the case, picked one up and carefully opened it at random. He began to read it. This was not his writing. These words spoke of Caesar as a God, and it went on and on in that vein. It was just sheer adulation, and badly written too. He counted the word God or Divine as referring to Caesar five times on the same page. This was not his manuscript. It had been changed. He was absolutely sure of that.

He lifted his eyes and saw the Librarian near him. "Where did you get these books?" Ivain asked him.

"They arrived from Florida, yesterday. Just in time for the opening," he replied rather seriously, with a look that betrayed annoyance more than anything else.

"How do you know these are Professor La Baille's manuscripts?"

"Whose manuscripts could they be? They have his titles on them, don't they?" He was getting upset at Ivain.

"That doesn't mean anything," continued Ivain, adding, "I think you are displaying two fake manuscripts." He had blurted out those words, not knowing why he had done it. They had just come out of him almost against his will.

"That is an outrageous accusation! What proof do you have to say such a thing?" the Librarian answered as he polished his glasses which had for some reason become white with mist.

"I happen to have read some of the late Professor's papers, and this book betrays a completely different style. Not at all like the Professor's."

"Perhaps he changed it," the man said laconically. "In any case there are no more original papers left from the Professor except for a few broken up fragments. How one can tell the style from fragments is anyone's guess. As you know, everything was either destroyed or lost in that theft in France. We've no idea what his style was like, except from these manuscripts." He ended the talk rather abruptly and was about to leave when Ivain stopped him.

"Have you read them?" He could see he was exasperating him.

"I haven't had the time," he answered. "They just arrived, and with the opening tonight, and what have you – I haven't had the time. In any case, you and I have to take the word of the people who most loved the Professor and who most wished to remember him. That is – Mr. and Mrs. Alfred. We have no choice, do we?" he said in a rather petulant way as he turned his heel on Ivain, who rested his hand on the glass case, and felt the cold of the glass go through him like lightning going through the core of a tall tree.

Again Ivain opened the glass case carefully, and carefully picked up the other manuscript, just as the President of Columbia University was preparing to give a matter-of-fact speech, more to remind the distinguished guests to keep up their generous donations than to talk of the late Professor. Ivain only heard a few words here and there – "Ivain la Baille would have been so proud to know he had a room in this famous library – that will be preserved forever – he is truly among the immortals – your checks have made all this possible, and will make other equally important rooms in the future possible."

Ivain heard this as he held the manuscript in his hand. He held it as if it were a reliquary. What he realized immediately was that this, too, was not his work. It took him a minute or so to comprehend that the sentences were at best obscure, at worst undecipherable. He started to read another sentence. Who wrote in such a ponderous way? He counted a paragraph that went on for twenty lines before coming to a period. He looked again at the title of the books. The titles were his: *Caesar's Regal Rag* and *Caesar's Cosmic Rag*. In both books he had meant rag as a joke, as an irony of fate, of what Caesar had to overcome to become Caesar. The books were all nuances and double entendre, written in a witty and amusing way. While what he was reading now was as ponderous and heavy as a brick. The style seemed vaguely familiar. And then he understood. It was the work of his cousin Fabian! Fabian the Benjamin of the Godlet! Fabian who had done Mme Kamiska's work! For a moment Ivain juxtaposed the terrifying evidence that was staring him in the face, with the fact that, in his other life, his friendship with his cousin had been more real and touching than even the greatest love he had ever felt for a woman, including the love he had for France. Yet, he now became convinced, with a sense of total awareness that only the true innocent can have, that the "Ivain La Baille" room would one day become the "Fabian Pierce Alfred" room. This very room, which had been created out of his work, his talent, his money! In the final analysis, Ivain concluded, in that room the only thing that he could call his own were the titles now affixed to the false manuscripts. His thoughts went back to the tantalizing titles of those known and unknown authors described in Diogenes Laertes. He remembered reading the list of titles of books that had disappeared. And then he thought that just a little while ago, he had seen the author's shadow, searching for them. What had their books been about? Ivain wondered, and felt akin to them. Like those unknown authors, nothing of his remained on earth but vague memories, vague notions, suffocating in a deluge of other memories and other times. Once he had been a man who breathed and walked and talked. Now, he realized he had been stripped of his life's work, his wife, his home, his furniture, his memorabilia and finally, his life. And then it came to him, the full revelation, and it was as clear as the moon reflected in the pond of Le Plessis. What about his life? he asked himself. Had it been a life? There were tantalizing hints, shadowy leads, alluring notions, false starts, gnawing memories, but nothing to hold on to. Nothing certain. The few hints that he had once existed were now scattered like sheep in some lost field he did not know. And he, Ivain La Baille, who had always tried to be a conscientious teacher, a hard working writer, a good actor, a faithful husband, who had loved a beautiful woman, and been loved by her in return, could not prove to himself or to anyone else that he had ever walked the earth. The realization of this verity made Ivain drop the manuscript on the floor. He excused himself and walked out of the door. He wanted to run out in the fresh air of the night. He wanted to scream, to curse, to cry. But, without trying to explain himself to himself or anyone else, he left.

He ran through the long corridors of the library as he cursed himself for having signed his name on Mme Kamiska's paper. Had he not come back, he would have been a man who died young, with the sweet illusion of his own immortality still fresh on his lips. He would have died thinking that somehow, through men's memories and through his writing, his life would be prolonged after his death, would go on by itself and acquire a life of its own. Now he felt like a sleepwalker in an unfathomable night. He reached the door and, still running, went out, where he saw the rays of the full moon filtering ominously and silently through the branches of the trees on Campus Square. He noticed the odious beauty with which they reflected their silver light on the early September leaves, making mockery of his pain. At any other time he would have been enchanted by this vision, but now it just heightened his despair. "All this loveliness," he thought, "all my knowledge, my ability to speak many languages, my writings, my love for the theater, my Roman studies – what are they for? What were they for? What do they amount to?"

He lifted his eyes, and saw a huge wave on the horizon, and he remembered the prediction – "a sea wave" – and at the same instant he realized that the mountain of blue, turbid water was beginning to move toward him. He had dreamt about it time and again, but now he could actually see it with his eyes open. It was higher than the highest skyscraper, and it was of a deep blue color, with green and yellow touches here and there that changed continually as it moved, as if rays of light were escaping from its sides. But the frothing crest remained a brilliant silvery shine, highlighted by the moon's rays, and it was rolling toward him. It was a massive wall of water, and when it was close to him he saw many dark green wrinkles going up and down its side, as if criss-crossed by a myriad of rivulets, and he was transfixed by the sheer majestic beauty of this monstrous power that was coming inexorably his way. He had just time to give one last look before the light disappeared, before he was engulfed by a darkness that he never knew existed. But more than darkness engulfed him now. Ivain felt entirely covered by the weight of an immense ocean. The huge mountain of water, the great wave, had broken on top of him, and he felt its weight over his head and shoulders. It was a pain that he could not stand, yet he somehow survived as he was rolling in its depth – rolling until his head was spinning and his ears were bursting – yet, he rolled on and on, to a depth of despair and forlornness never known before.

All that was his was either burnt, lost, stolen, or forgotten. He shook his head, and found himself lying on the cold stone near the sculpted bronze statue of the Alma Mater, and through his half closed eyes he perceived first the outline of nocturnal forms that seemed to wander aimlessly here and there, then he saw the guests pouring out of the library into the Square. The party was over. All those people were going on with their lives as if the world was still together, and not under an ocean. The women touching the pearls, rubies, sapphires and gold adorning their wrists, neck, hands, and hair. The men talking amongst themselves, being ever so polite to their perfectly groomed women, and to each other. Broken sentences and words floated toward him "– the next dinner, our next meeting – such a lovely evening – such a great man – whether or not – say yes, – yes, yes, yes –"

A few minutes before he, too, had believed in that world. Now he felt the utter folly of his ideas, and the loneliness of an outsider. For a moment he became delirious, dreaming that he and France had drowned in that last big wave, and had been cremated together, their ashes giving forth an exquisite fragrance of musk and pine trees.

But then he remembered that he was dead, that he was already a little box of white ashes, and that there were no more deaths to be feared since it had already all happened, and already all forgotten. That thought overwhelmed him so, that he clutched at the side of the Alma Mater stone pedestal, when he heard someone asking, "Where did John Elliab go?" and it was Fabian who answered, "*Il est tombé à la baille! Il est tombé à la baille!*" which Ivain recognized as French slang for "He has fallen in the water!"

"How appropriate. Fabian too has not forgotten the use of dramatic irony," he said.

Later on, when he got up, he realized that the University Square was empty, left in its own solitude, filling a space that had become for some reason the essence of nostalgic thoughts. He wiped his face with a large handkerchief, and on an impulse then and there he made a momentous decision. He, Ivain Jean Marie La Baille, would reveal his name and true identity to France in order to have and to hold in his hands the final proof that he had lived, and had been part of the living. The paradox within this decision did not escape him, for the very act of knowing whether or not he had dreamt his existence, implicitly held the certainty of his final oblivion. But before saying that fatal string of words, he would find a Macintosh computer and look again at the "green disk" he had been carrying on his person. This time he knew what he would find in it, since he realized he had just crossed the "Climax" of whatever play he was in, a play whose part he had never learned, whose lines he had never known, but which he was discovering as he was pronouncing and clearly enunciating them. He also knew that from the "Climax" onward, the path ahead of him was linear and continuous, until the moment he reached the end of the play. He was now in a straightjacket, he realized, unless he could still find a way to break out of "the script."

THE GREEN DISK

"I have been Dr. Cupilius' wind up doll."
Ivain's comment after looking at the green disk

Iт had become quite dark, and the street lights were lit, as well as the lights coming from the rather squalid stores along upper Broadway. As he turned a corner of the avenue he saw a copy store which he knew had a computer, a Mac Classic, which was rented out to help needy students write a page for an overdue paper, or a quick memo for the next class. When he reached it, Ivain looked through the large window and saw there was no one in the small shop except a workman, slouched over a chair, half asleep. He entered, and without saying anything, left a ten dollar bill on the counter. He turned and walked quickly toward the computer, then stopped. He suddenly had a great fear to look at the disk, that disk for which he had signed his name on that golden paper in Mme Kamiska's house. The disk he had been carrying with him all these months, but had never checked again, for he knew he would only find the same notes, and the same scrambled vowels and consonants that were meaningless. But now it was different. After what had happened at the library opening, Ivain knew that the JanKam Co. had nothing to lose by letting him see the intricate plot which they had set up around him. On the contrary, that knowledge would enhance the play, for it was an added subtle pleasure to draw attention to their cleverness on a predestined victim. He turned on the machine, overcome by a shadow of despair that would not leave him as he began to contemplate the idea that there might be "something" on the disk which he had not seen. "Something" that he had overlooked from the first moment. "Something" behind the jumbled up alphabet letters, perhaps even behind the machinations of Fabian. Without thinking, he mechanically took the disk from his breast pocket where he always kept it, wrapped in soft indigo silk, and pushing it into the slot of the Macintosh, waited for it to appear on the screen. He needed to know quickly.

Again he saw the file that said: "A PLAY," but when he pulled it up, he saw that, for the first time, there was a file on "Ivain Jean Marie La Baille." Curious, and at the same time startled, he opened it. Under the same title he saw: "A comedy," and near it in prominent letters, "Working titles" – "The Complete Written Script," or "The Final Version of the Written Script," And then simply, "The Written Script." Underneath these suggestive titles were the initials of the author G.T. and, in minuscule letters under it: "The author thanks his daughter Mme K. for all her help both as an actress and a delightful director." It went on and on, in superlative terms that were so sweet and mellifluous that it made Ivain sick, and he actually felt faint, so much so that he put his hands on each side of the machine, to hold himself up.

At the beginning of the page there was a list of characters. Then a note as to who was the principal character, or protagonist, and who was the opposing character, or antagonist. It was simply his name versus that of the Godlet. Bending over, he looked further down the page, and saw that his life was all there as a play. The play was divided into scenes, each one having a number in the French way, that is, each scene was numbered with the entrance or exit of a character. And it was divided into two acts. Act one was about his first life on earth. From his birth to his premature death. Act two was about his return to earth.

The plot was the romantic story of a man who, ten years after his death, returns to earth as an actor to play Caesar in the Shakespeare play of *Julius Caesar*, and to help his helpless wife gather together his papers and manuscripts to ensure his fame for posterity. He read on with consternation about his meeting with Mme Kamiska, which was written down *verbatim*, followed by the one with her operative, Allegra Cagliostro, in which she revealed to him the real nature of the "green disk" he was carrying on his person. He read all about her imploring and begging him to leave this world immediately for the thin air he had come from, by saying his real name to the first person he encountered. All this should be said as if Allegra were reciting litanies, so the stage directions advised.

His refusal, as he now found out from a note inserted by the director, had been expected by the Godlet, who astutely predicted his move to fight Heaven itself. The Godlet had counted on Ivain's anger at the great deception played on him. Continuing to read on, he saw it anticipated the temptation, seduction, and engagement with Allegra. He saw it also predicted the love that France would begin to feel for him again, and it foretold how her love would grow for him as he got closer to her rival Allegra. He stopped and looked down the page. Everything seemed to be there, including the description of the scene he was in at the moment, "the script" continuing to add on with every movement he made, and, for a brief moment, he wondered which of the two versions of "the script" he was in was true – Mme Kamiska's, that "he was in 'a script' in the making," or Allegra's, that "he was in a written script?"

But, somehow Ivain knew instinctively that there was more to the text than he was now reading. And he had a flash of intuition that the real plot was hidden in the subtext – the subtext being actually the true story, only one became aware of it too late, because it ran parallel to the apparent story, but hidden under it, like an underground river. So, he went to File, and in File he found Print and in Print he pressed "Print Hidden Text." And then he saw all the pages with the scrambled-up alphabet letters realigning and becoming legible. And, as the paper came out of the printer, he saw the Godlet's true construction of the deception played on him.

It had started with a young man who, mad with rage and jealousy for having lost to another man the woman he truly loved, had gone to see a famous seer, Mme Kamiska. He had proposed to her a plan which was going to be of mutual benefit.

At first the seer was not convinced. It was only when Fabian had made the remark that his cousin's most important thought was: "To be famous, and therefore to be remembered after his death" that the attention of Mme Kamiska perked up, for she had said, "Now, my dear, you have given me something we can work with – the tragic fault of vanity," and she had promptly accepted the task for herself, as well as in her Father's name. Unfortunately Ivain's last words at the end of his first life, as he lay dying, were fateful to him, as he now realized, for he had said, "My writing will survive. I am immortal, too." Those same words had confirmed the wisdom of the author's endeavor. Out of this plan had come "The Written Script," which was so cleverly constructed, that the knowledge Ivain had of being in it, far from being a hindrance to the play was, in fact its cornerstone. He also saw that the play had been written in such a devious way that, with every step he took to break out of it and live, he was actually taking a step closer to saying his real name, and dying. In a side note he read the following statement as recorded by the Godlet – "This is the beauty of it," Mme Kamiska had told Fabian in one of their sessions, as she coached him on how "to pretend" to be in love with Allegra. "The feeling Ivain La Baille must have is of breaking out, when he is actually being pulled in!" and the writing went on down the side, "He must feel as if he is running away from a falling stone, only to find out that he has been running toward it."

He stopped reading for a moment, and lifting his eyes he said, "Like the bicycle," and remembered how hard he had pedaled to go forward, and how astonished he had been to find out he had gone quite a way backward. Right at the beginning he discovered these clues to his future, such as the bicycle and those other enigmatic words he had seen in the floppy disk. If only he could have understood their meaning then! Had he only known what the "trinket" was, he would possibly have figured out that Fabian's passion for Allegra was only Mme Kamiska's ruse to make his wife jealous and depressed. And he had fallen for it all! His antagonists had counted on France's retreat to her bedroom, depriving him of her presence. They had correctly predicted and written down that he, Ivain, would want to talk to her, and to do so he would have to go through the tortuous path of Allegra's possessive and perverse sense of love. He lifted his eyes toward the ceiling and took a moment to admire his opponents' well-thought-out moves, before resuming his reading.

As he read on, Ivain thought at first that he had two antagonists: the JanKam Co. in the clouds, and a man on earth. But he realized that they were one and the same, for the will of the masters coincided with the will of the servant. They wanted him to return to earth to find out that nothing that was his remained. Fame is a pact with Time, and in his case, that pact had never been signed. It had been just a bit of drollery combined with an unparalleled jealousy for what he had had.

"Oh!" said Ivain, "Oh!" And he kept repeating it, fascinated and repelled by these discoveries.

At last, in the subtext he came across the greatest deceit of them all. It was when he found the actual title of the "script," still in the hidden text, that the mystery was revealed to him.

He found it by going back to the very first page of his life on earth, a page decorated with geometric symbols, resembling those found on early Greek vases. There, among the elegant angular lines, which had been painted in both gold and silver, he saw in bold letters the title:

"Amkli jn jugnuk lihu eme idksl"

which before his very eyes changed to become:

"Ivain la Baille does not exist"

and underneath in smaller letters – "A Written Script." Again it gave the name of the author, as well as "His thanks to his daughter Mme K. and the revered and most helpful co-author Fabian Alfred" and it continued in superlative terms, sweeter and more mellifluous than the first time round, which made Ivain so sick that he stopped reading. What was the point? He knew the end. The end was a given. He had the singular distinction of having lived through life's greatest irony: "coming back from death only to find that he had never existed." He had been the puppet of the Godlet who had two faces. A phantom character in a phantom play. Perhaps the only person walking about who had the right to call himself a true citizen of the phantom city of Claterna! And he wondered how his life had been worked out in detail by the master writer of all playwrights, with the help of Fabian who must have signed a contract with Mme Kamiska too, though he had not seen it. But Ivain was sure it existed. He was also sure he was going to discover it soon enough, or the pleasure of his makers and creators would not be complete, nor would "the script" be finished. He passed both his hands over his hair twice, and pushed it back. And then, after a pause, he did it again.

"How strange," he thought, "that I've never felt so intensely the joy of existing as I do now that I know I've never existed," and then immediately after mumbled to himself: "Expect only your worst fears to be realized, never your dreams." But he said it in such a way as to say: even that is wonderful, because the alternative would be not to know what it is all about, even though we forget it immediately. But for one moment, we know that we don't know. That's the wonder of it all. That's what it comes down to. But, what was this feeling of happiness that kept surprising him? Was there some cohesion, some order to all these mysterious feelings? Would there be some answer to all his questions? He tried to think back over the whole unusual experience of this new world he had come to know. He had put up a good fight against Heaven itself. He had fought courageously, if he could be bold enough to say so, or perhaps presumptuously enough to contemplate himself as chivalrous. He had given his all to breaking "his script," and now – the only weapon left, was to reveal his name. Reveal who he really was. At that moment the Godlet's play would end. But for a short time, he would become a real person again, not just a fictitious character.

Paradoxically, he had to die to prove he had existed. But he needed that proof for himself. He could not go on not knowing. He thought that, just as in the dark corridor at Le Plessis, there had been too many closed doors, and though as a child, he had almost always found a knob, he had never been able to open the right door. Similarly here, the end had taken him by surprise, or perhaps he was exhausted by the search. "I'll never know the real reason why I couldn't escape from 'the script' and make my life my own," he said, "but –" and here he admitted his defeat, "'the script' has held me in its grip. It has molded me with its own carefully chosen words, accurate pauses, pointed punctuation – colon, semicolon, dash, commas, periods. Period." He continued: "In the final analysis, I have only stated and enunciated the words, in a well-performed and resonant way." Ultimately he could be thought of as a good actor, if one wished to be kind to him, and assess his elocution and movements; or, if one wished to be unkind and find a different epithet, one could just say that he had been a marionette, a *burattino*, a *fantoccio*, *Fagiolino*, *Pulcinella* or *Arlecchino*.

He remembered the names of the marionettes from an Italian *burattinaio* or puppet master, who had passed through Rosay in his youth. Never had he thought he would be transformed into one himself. He had felt that same mocking sting once before when he entered his own "Home Movie," but there he had felt that the act of becoming a marionette had been a temporary state, while now he knew with certainty that it was a chronic condition. As he said this under his breath he realized that the papers that had come out of the printer were turning to dust in front of his eyes. In a desperate effort, he tried to take the "green disk" out of the computer by placing it into the "trash can," but the "trash can" would not return it. And finally the small floppy disk, which contained all that he had been, all that he was, disappeared with a sloshing sound, as if swallowed up by a gluttonous monster. He shook the machine, and pounded on it with his fists. But it was all futile. Why go on? But he would not give up yet. In the few hours that followed this discovery, Ivain would have time, retrospectively, to contemplate the depth of his maker's cunning cruelty, and clearness of intent.

The only question now was to choose the right place, the right time, and the right person – to share this very private truth of who he was. He would show the JanKam Co. how wrong their hidden title was! He knew he had existed in his past. He would show them he would exist again in the present, though it might be for a moment only.

THE SUNFLOWERS AT APPLEBROOK

"Mee thinks I have the keyes of my prison in mine owne hand,
and no remedy presents it selfe so soone to my heart,
as mine own sword."

Donne

Oɴᴄᴇ again outside in the street, Ivain noticed that the light of
the moon had disappeared behind a cloudy sky, and a cold wind
had come up out of nowhere. He began to walk briskly toward
his apartment on Riverside Drive, for he felt there was one
more thing he had to do before revealing his name, namely –
to confront France. "Maybe," he said to himself, "she's part of
the JanKam Co. too, and if so, I'll have nothing more to do with
her. I owe myself that much." But a moment later he would
waver, and tell himself that he would never stop loving her no
matter what side she was on. "She is all I've got in this life. She
is all I had in my previous life, though I didn't know it," he said
to himself. But then he remembered the last postcard he had
received from Allegra, where she spoke of a "mole" on earth,
and at the same time he thought of the "green disk" with the
sickening "thank you's" his cousin Fabian had gotten from the
Godlet. All this made him wonder if it was possible that there
were two moles on earth.

"It's true that France knows Mme Kamiska," Ivain began to
reason in a voice that reverberated up and down the Avenue of
Broadway. "But that in itself does not make her treacherous,"
and he continued talking aloud, even though a couple of obvious drunks had stopped to listen to him, as they swayed from
one side to the other. "It is also true that France is always going
to see Mme Kamiska, but that is only to have the tarot cards
read, or the tea leaves studied, or her dreams interpreted." And
then he paused, when he noticed the two men appearing to nod

approvingly while he spoke. He looked at them, and burst out with, "The weakness of the flesh!" and the two drunks, thinking he was talking about them, said almost in an angry chorus, "Brother, aren't you weak as we are?" and then began to walk away. But in reality, when Ivain had uttered those words, he was thinking of France and Fabian and the conversation on the phone he had heard at Le Plessis. Still hoping that France was not involved with the JanKam Co. he said, "The weakness of the flesh is one thing, but to be thrown to the wolves to be devoured is something else." And he resumed walking as fast as he could, soon breaking into a run toward his home and his wife.

He arrived at the apartment and found France lying down on the sofa with her eyes closed. As soon as she heard him come in she sat up, and he saw she was all packed and ready to leave for the country.

"Wasn't it a great party, Johnny?" she said sitting up. "Ivain would have been so proud of what we have accomplished in his name," she added, then stopped and, looking up into his eyes, she questioned him. "Where did you disappear to? Fabian looked for you, but then he had to leave for Orlando," she said.

"That's all right. I didn't expect him to be here," Ivain replied as he took his jacket off.

"We can leave right away," she said. "The car is parked just outside the door."

"Yes, I saw it when I came in," he replied, and he put his right hand in his pocket and took out something which he held in his hand, adding, "Before we go, I need to ask you something."

"Oh?" She had gotten up and had come near him. Her delicate perfume made him feel faint. But he had to know. "Whose coin is this?" he said, and he opened the palm of his right hand which held the shining coin of Emperor Tiberius.

As soon as France saw it, she gave a little cry of joy. "Where did you find it?" she said. "I've been looking for it everywhere."

"I picked it up outside the ruined stone house. Remember? The one both you and I looked at not far from Le Plessis?" he said. "The house Fabian had bulldozed."

"Oh, that house!" she said with a puzzled look. "Well then – Fabian must have lost it there."

"Fabian?" asked Ivain. "But wasn't this coin one of a pair of earrings made up especially for you?"

"Yes, that's right," France said, "But how would you know that?" and she looked at him with amazement.

Ivain tried to think quickly. "Oh, I believe Fabian told me once that your late husband gave you a pair of earrings made from old coins. When I found it I wondered if this could possibly be one of them. After all, it's nicely mounted. Am I wrong?"

"No," she said smiling, "You're right." She picked up the coin from the palm of his hand and looked at it. "I never went inside that house," she continued. "Fabian was the only one who used it. I don't exactly know what he did there. He would go over in the morning and come home at night." She stopped and gave the coin back to Ivain. "Once he told me he was working on a book there. One not unlike those of my late husband."

"Really?" said Ivain. "Are you saying Fabian wanted to be a writer?" And then he realized that Fabian had rewritten his manuscripts in that old stone house.

"Well, he certainly wished to try his hand at it," said France. "But I don't think he was very happy with the result. In any case he never talked about it again, and he had the house torn down."

"How long ago did that take place?" asked Ivain.

"Oh, perhaps three or four years ago," said France. "But what is this all about?"

"Why would Fabian have this coin?" asked Ivain.

"When I got remarried, I gave both coins to Fabian," France said. "Oh, I know it may seem like a strange thing for me to do, but, you see, it was the only gift he wished from me. I never understood why those particular coins – and not something else. Perhaps they reminded him of his cousin." She took a few deep breaths, "So, though I really didn't want to part with them, I had them made into cufflinks for him." she sighed, and then as if she had remembered something, she went on, "Wait! I can show you the other one." She ran into her bedroom, coming out a little while later holding a red suede box which she opened, and there was the companion of the Tiberius coin made into a lovely cufflink with its back pin intact. So Fabian had lost it, or dropped it on purpose, near Mme Kamiska's house!

One final thing Ivain wished to do before leaving. He asked France if he could make a long distance phone call. She nodded and said, "Yes, of course."

He picked up the phone, dialed the eight-digit number he had seen on the derelict phone outside Mme Kamiska's house. Four times sixty four.

France was close enough to see what he was doing, and now looked up at him in disbelief. "But Johnny," she said, "that phone was disconnected long ago. You're dialing the number that used to be in that little stone house." She stopped; the phone was ringing. When France heard that she added, "Someone else must have that number now." But Ivain did not think so. A man picked up the phone on the other end and said in an almost perfect French, "*Oui? J'écoute.*"

It was Fabian's voice, but Ivain wanted to be sure, so he said, "Who is this?"

"Monsieur Alfred," the voice said, "And who are you?" Ivain put the phone down. France had heard the exchange and was amazed.

"What does this mean?" she asked.

"It means that you are innocent!" he said at last as he pulled her closer to him.

"I don't understand." She was looking at him, and fidgeting with the suede box.

"It also means that Fabian is not in Orlando, but with an old lady," he added.

"You are joking, aren't you?" she said as she pulled away from him, though she was smiling now. "This is your sense of humor, isn't it?"

"Yes, that number belongs to someone else now," he said, and added "another family." He did not wish her to be frightened of something she had nothing to do with, nor could she understand.

He breathed a sigh of relief, knowing that France had been a stranger to all the intrigues against him. Her only weakness was that of a person who trusted the world too much. He felt sorry for her, and also wanted to protect her. He looked at the coin in his hand and said: "Do you mind if I keep this in my pocket as a good-luck piece?"

"Not at all," she said. "You found it," and she gave him a kiss on the cheek.

The ride up to Applebrook was wonderfully warm and cozy. He could see that France was in love with him all over again, like the first time, and he was happy about it. He loved her too with the same intense feeling, and he kept holding the steering wheel with one hand, while with the other he brought her head near his, and kissed her hair, and stroked her neck, as he gave quick glances at her delicate profile.

They arrived late, but the light of the moon was shining again, as clearly as on that night near the pond at Le Plessis. Frank Luini, who was both the farmer and the caretaker of the property, had been expecting them and came forward to welcome Mrs. Alfred and the gentleman with her. Ivain noticed he had grown very old, and walked with difficulty, so he went over to him. He would have liked to greet him as he used to, but to avoid embarrassing the old man, who might not understand, he just shook his hand.

He let Frank Luini help France with her little bag. They all entered the farm house, and France showed Ivain his room saying, "When Ivain came up here, this is the room he liked the most, isn't that right, Frank?"

"That's just so, Mrs. Alfred," he said. "That's his old bed. That's where he slept, all right." He spoke with an unmistakable New York accent, which Ivain remembered and found so endearing in him. Besides, it always made him smile. He now put down on a chair near the bed the little overnight briefcase he had taken with him. Inside was a new shirt, a toothbrush, and a razor. France now excused herself by saying, "It's been a long and wonderful day, I hope you don't mind if I leave you," and with that she retired into her room saying, "Good night" to both of them.

Frank Luini asked Ivain if he was hungry and would like some fruit or some of his homemade cider. Ivain just said, "No, thank you," and as he said it, he remembered the memorable dishes of hare and rabbit, in wild herbs and wine sauce, that Frank used to cook for him. Turning round he asked for the front-door key. "We don't use any keys here," Frank Luini said. "The door is always open."

"Like the old days," thought Ivain.

He looked up and saw that Frank Luini was about to leave. In fact, he said, "Is there anything more I can do for you tonight? If there isn't, I'll be going." He looked at him sleepily and continued, "The world is out of place these days."

Ivain knew it was due to his breaking "the script." Still, he was eager to hear how it had affected his upstate farm. Frank then gave a litany of events that were outside the normal experience of his long life. A chick was born with four legs. A small water snake had changed in front of his eyes into a boa constrictor. A pig gave birth to five piglets with two heads each. A mushroom had grown five feet tall and ten feet wide, with huge spots on its white skin, the likes of which he had never seen before. "Who has ever seen a mushroom with blue spots?" he asked, adding that strange birds he had never imagined existing now came to feed near his aviary. "A black one as big as a horse landed in the fields yesterday." And the little lake had a large flock of loon birds. He ended by saying that he thought he was going mad because he had heard a cow talk, and a neighbour bray like a donkey. "I need to sleep," he said. "I've been overworking these past weeks. I feel I'm going nuts." And with that he got up to leave. Again Ivain stopped him because there was one thing he wished inordinately, and that was to see his burial place. Could he ask this tired old man to take him there, at this hour of the night? Should he not wait until daylight? he said to himself. But he decided he would go ahead.

"There's one thing I would like to do tonight, if I'm not asking too much," Ivain said. "Would you show me where Professor La Baille is buried?" Ivain said, and he saw that Frank Luini was taken aback.

"Now?" he asked.

"Yes, now," said Ivain, "if you're not too tired."

The caretaker thought it over for a moment, then said, "I'll take my large flashlight and show you," and with that he returned in a few minutes and they began to walk toward the large, knotted old oak tree, a little way from the house. Ivain walked behind Frank Luini, but he already knew where to go, since France had told him where she had buried his ashes.

It had always been a favorite tree of his, for he had often played the recorder sitting there. Telemann, Couperin, Purcell and Rameau would come alive under its abundant and luxuriant foliage. And as a child, he remembered swinging from its lower branches, and later, climbing almost to its top to save a stray cat. Both he and the cat fell down, fortunately on a pile of straw, so both survived the fall without a scratch.

"I buried Mr. La Baille here," Frank Luini began to say, as he halted near the oak tree. "And I take care of this ground every day," he added.

"And how long ago was that?"

"Oh, it must have been about ten years. The widow – Mrs. Alfred now, didn't know where to plant him. So, I suggested this place." He rested his arm on one of the lowest branches. "Mr. La Baille came here often, and I would hear him play his flute from my room over there," and he pointed in the distance, "or some instrument like a flute. He would play modern music. Jazz. Nice, very nice."

Ivain was startled. He had only played classical music. Never jazz. But he said nothing. Instead he took out of his wallet a twenty dollar bill and gave it to Frank Luini. But as soon as he did that, he realized he was thanking him for the trouble of digging his grave, something that Frank Luini could not possibly know. Anyway, the old man took the money and thanked him.

Ivain next asked him to point out the exact spot where he had buried the Professor. Frank Luini began to search with his flashlight among the roots of the tree, some of which had pierced the earth and were growing above ground, as he was saying, "It wasn't easy to dig a hole here. Look, there are small and large stones everywhere. It took quite a long time to dig it. I got calluses on my hands, but I got the box down there, between those two roots," he said. Ivain went round the tree twice, then asked Frank Luini if he would leave him alone since he wanted to say a prayer. The old man wanted to leave the flashlight with him but upon hearing Ivain's reply – "the moonlight's enough –" he said "Good night" and just as he began to walk away, he shifted the flashlight from one hand to the other, lighting for a moment his face, and Ivain saw his eyes were red.

When he remained all alone, by the tree, Ivain looked around himself. On the ground there were still dried-up violets and celery stalks brought there by Frank Luini every day. The offering of celery stalks to the dead was an ancient custom, dating from the time of Homer, and kept up by some ancient Romans too. So France still remembered what he had once told her, and had asked Frank to continue the offering on his grave. Sweet France, who had fallen in love with her husband again, without knowing him: therefore that forbidden love was all the sweeter.

He took a piece of wood and made a circle on the earth, round the place Frank Luini had pointed to. Inside that circle he placed carefully in a pile all the little bits and pieces of his own writing found among the ivy at Le Plessis. Then he took out a match and lit the first page that came under his eyes. He held it in his hand until the fire caught on. He could read words here and there. It spoke of "a great empire," of "the white marbles of Rome," of the "Pantheon" and in each of the words he had written he saw his own style, his own imprint. As the fire caught that first page he was holding, he put it down near the others saying: "Go and vanish, as I too will soon vanish from this land, and join you."

When the fire had burnt out, he began to dig up the earth with his bare hands, but seeing that he was not advancing quickly enough, he found a stick nearby. With this he was able to move the earth more easily about, and then he lifted it out and put it on one side. At last the stick struck something hard, and he renewed his effort. The top of the box became visible and little by little he was able to free it all and lift it clear of the ground.

Here was the box that held all that he had been! It was quite ordinary, made of wooden planks held together by iron rings. He tore off the top plank and saw a crystal lid. He lifted it and was amazed to see how white ashes can be. They were whiter than white as the light of the moon reflected its own light back. He brought his fingers to his mouth, wetted them, and put his hand lightly and carefully inside the box. He touched his forehead with his own ashes. For him it had been Ash Wednesday every day. Suddenly, a puff of wind blew close by and scattered the white ashes into the air. They spiraled up and up and up, whitening everything they touched, not unlike a sudden volcanic eruption, only to fall and settle on the green moss and over the recently cut timber nearby stacked up in a huge pile. Some, lighter ones, fell gently downwards, and he was covered with white flakes of his own self from a different time and a different space. One fell on his lips, and he tasted it. "Mud," he said, "it has the taste of mud," and softly he repeated as if it was a prayer – "moss unto moss, mud unto mud," and putting the empty box back into the hole, he covered it again with earth as best he could. Then he slowly went back into the house, and fell into a deep sleep without a single dream.

The following day he woke up late. It was early afternoon, and he could hardly believe that he had slept all that time. France was waiting for him downstairs, and asked if he wanted some soup. He apologized for being so late, drank the soup, and asked France if she would like to show him the property. She looked at him and said, "Of course," and they both went out.

He saw that she was going to take him to the oak tree, but he took her by her waist and said, "Poucette!" then was silent for a moment, only to repeat "Poucette, let us go toward the lake." She turned around and looked at him with a puzzled look.

"I have not been called that for a very long time, and that was by a man I loved very much."

It looked as if she was beginning to understand who he was. Now the only thing left for him to do was to say his own name.

"Who are you?" she was asking, as she started to look at him in a different way, half afraid, and half joyful.

"I am the man who married you once, long ago," he said.

"Ah," she said, though still not understanding, "Won't you tell me your name?" They had arrived at the lake, and he was looking at the numbers of loon birds, dipping in the water, disappearing for a while, and then reappearing some distance off. They seemed to be playing all the time, to know only the joy of living. Just looking at them made him happy, and for a moment he forgot about himself. Then he looked at France still standing near him, waiting for an answer to her question.

"I'll tell you my name," he said, "after a walk with you through the sunflower fields." He looked at her. "Then you'll know. I promise you that."

He took her hand and together they began to walk toward the fields. He heard France's voice as if through a dream coming from very far away, and he listened to his own answers as if they were wrapped in mist. "I realize I don't know much about you –" she was saying, "I don't even know where you live in New York, when you don't live with me –" and a moment later, "Why are you saying you live where I live? – how can that be? – yes, those are the words I used to say to Ivain – yes, that is the same expression, – yes, it looks as if you knew him too – but where did you meet him? And how is that possible? Perhaps you remember him because you are my guest – You saw his photographs – no – there are no more photographs of him. Why are you so mysterious?" And then added – "You say you have lived a long time in my apartment, in my bedroom with me – then, why don't I know you?"

"She can't identify who I am even now. How sad," thought Ivain.

She stopped walking, and told him of the prediction Mme Kamiska had made to her right after Ivain had died. She had said: "One day, my dear, you will see your husband again. He'll come to you, but you won't recognize him until he reveals his name," and looking at him she now asked again, "Who are you?" And he simply said, "I am your husband who has come back to be a little while with you."

At first she seemed reluctant to believe him, but soon there were so many things that in retrospect she remembered about him, that reminded her of Ivain, that she asked again, "Why won't you tell me your name, then?" And she wanted to say more but could not go on.

Ivain, knowing as a certainty that as soon as he said his name, it would be the end of his second life on earth, and knowing also that the situation was becoming unsustainable, with a supreme effort said, "Let us walk first."

It was mid-September, the time of the year when most of the sunflowers would have been cut down, but this year they had huge pointed green leaves, and round light brown circles, tinted by a yellow crown around the darker middle, so soft that when one touched it – it dissolved under one's fingers. The sunflowers were all turned in his direction. "The eyes of the Godlet," Ivain thought to himself, as he began to walk toward them.

It was a primordial walk that Ivain took in that sunflower field that lay before him. France followed closely behind. But it was he who took the first tentative steps in a forest of stems, smaller and higher than himself. It was a walk from prehistory to the present. It was the stone man walking into the ages ahead of him. Walking out of the ages altogether into the galaxies, into the Universe. The sunflowers spilled over the horizon. They went as far as the eye could see and beyond the gaze of man, creating the illusion of suns and stars brighter than any suns or stars ever seen. Where there had been nothing there was now something. Where there had been unconsciousness there was now consciousness. Where there had been blindness there was now sight, and Ivain now felt he was walking among the constellations, millions of suns, billions and trillions of stars. And then he became a Godlet among the suns and the stars as he had once become a Godlet in Rosay when, bathed in the moonlight, he had actually touched the moon as he was now touching the suns. He was the primordial mover. With one hand he bowed the flowers and at his touch the biggest and the brightest fell this way or that way, opening a path for him. It did not matter that a soft warm wind had risen, that the sea of flowers had started to sway to and fro all around him, for Ivain felt as if he was their maker, their originator. He was the Godlet of the sunflowers, the Godlet of the suns, the Godlet of the Universe for one brief "now" that he was finally able to perceive and possess, and make his own.

They had come to the end of the sunflower field, and Ivain looked at France and was about to reveal his real name, when he suddenly stopped. He thought that perhaps it was foolish on his part to give up all the time he could have in the world, just to prove to himself that he existed, that he had existed. Didn't he know for a certainty, that once he revealed his name, no one would ever remember him? Didn't Mme Kamiska say so when he had first met her? What reason was there to doubt her word? An old Japanese proverb came to his mind and he said softly, "Is it not better a day more on earth, than a thousand beyond it?" And he thought of all the books he could write, all the places he could visit, all the discoveries he could make, all the women he could love and be loved by in return. Such thoughts were seducing and almost irresistible, yet he turned to his wife and said in a simple and natural way. "France, I am Ivain Jean Marie La Baille." He said it all in one breath, and right away felt different, as if his body had acquired an immense weight, while just a moment before the force of gravity was not there. And immediately afterwards he felt a sharp pain on his left side. "Pain," he said, "I can feel pain. I am mortal again!" and taking off from France's jacket a tiny gold bee pin, he pricked the back of his hand and saw a drop of blood run down the side of his wrist, and he quickly added: "I exist. I am!"

Immediately upon prounoucing those words, the sky that had been without a single cloud darkened, and it looked as if night had come. But a moment later, the sun shone again, and it was day once more. France ran into his arms. She was looking around, saying, "What is happening?" Then they both noticed that every single sunflower had fallen to its side, laying flat on the earth, wind-bent by a sudden gust that had come out of a calm balmy day. It was sad to look at such destruction, when just moments before there had been so much beauty around them.

As he held France in his arms, he said, "Don't be afraid. We are safe," and immediately realized that nothing more was going to change in the world, because, by saying his real name, he had not broken the sequence of "the written script" he was in; on the contrary he was following it to the letter. It was then, and not a moment sooner, that he understood fully the implication of what he had just done. His overwhelming desire to be recognized and to be known as the man he was coincided perfectly with the will of the Godlet to end the play he was in.

"Victory in defeat!" he mumbled to himself as he shivered in dismay. "The end of the play as written in the 'green disk' has now become self-evident to me," and after a brief pause, "How clever!" he said.

France looked at him, and by her amazed expression, he knew she knew who he was. They were both silent while they looked in each other's eyes, as they used to in the beginning, when they were young and in love. "This is my first moment of truth with France since my return," Ivain thought. "No more pretentions, no more make-believe, but the sincerity that only imminent disaster brings with itself, and makes visible." He was relieved and anxious at the thought they could now be close again, as they once were.

His manuscripts did not matter any longer. Fame did not matter any longer. It was not so much, *Après moi le déluge*. He still cared what the world would be like after he had gone, but what memories of him remained in men's minds were not important. He understood how foolish he had been to ever entertain the idea he could achieve immortality. He knew now that it was unreachable; dispensed as grace is dispensed, here and there, in a whimsical way and for an uncertain time, that sooner or later disappeared forever. Beyond that, it no longer made a difference. Not now, not ever.

He was still immersed in these thoughts when France came closer to him and said: "I knew you would come back, Ivain, for Mme Kamiska had promised me that I would see you once more."

"Mme Kamiska? Mme Kamiska? Why would she grant you this favor?"

"Because I've been carrying a great burden and wished you to forgive me. Fabian and I – while I was still married to you. Do you understand why I couldn't live with myself after your death?" She was silent for a moment, then added, "I too saw the home movie of Natalie, and then I knew you knew."

He said nothing.

"I made love to Fabian not out of lust, but to get even with you. For you see, I knew you had a lover – your secretary, Miss Cavalcore."

He wanted to say: "No, no – that is not true. I've never had a mistress or a lover apart from you. You're mixing me up with Fabian!" What was France talking about? Who could she possibly be referring to? Was she referring to something that had happened in this life or the other? He was confused. Which of his two stays on earth was real, anyway? Both or neither? It is true he had made love to Allegra Cagliostro, but Allegra was not his secretary. And though he was not proud of his actions, he would never have had a lover while he was married. Perhaps Mme Kamiska had thrown Allegra in his arms to show that at the right time, any man can succumb to any woman for one reason or another. Had he too betrayed his wife? Anyway, who was this "Cavalcore" woman France had mentioned? Ivain now felt himself blushing as France went on speaking in detail about her personal life. "Then I married Fabian, not because I loved him, as you may think, but because he convinced me that we owed it to you – to build a monument to your name and to your memory. That is why I said, 'Yes' and that is why I couldn't rest until yesterday, when the Library room was finally dedicated to you. It was out of –" She was about to go on, but Ivain shook his head. He gently put his fingers over her mouth as he remembered some of the words in that last phone conversation she and Fabian had had before his trip to Rome, the one he had discovered by accident or, more likely, because he was supposed to. He knew her to be the more innocent party in all this story, and besides, he felt she was the only one in the world he wished to be close to. He just wanted to spend his last hours on earth as peacefully as possible. Soon enough, he realized, he would rejoin that immense ocean of unconsciousness, where there was no pain, but no happiness either.

The thought that happiness could exist, and existed for him now, made him paradoxically unhappy, for he could not benefit from it for long. So, he lay on the ground, and for no good reason remembered his walk on Riverside Drive where he believed he had seen a world full of ice, icicles and snow. He shuddered as he pulled France down near him. She smiled as she realized the night was theirs. She said: "I'm older than you now. Did you know that?" He looked at her beautiful face and answered, "It has always been my dream to be near an older, more experienced woman." He kissed her, and in such an embrace they waited for the night to cover them, for the morning seemed to be a long way off. He looked at his watch and became aware that Time had changed direction again. Now, a minute took forever to pass. He was silently grateful for this unexpected gift from the Godlet, and he tried to find the reason for his life in those hours of tempestuous, chaotic, and at times tender love-making; thinking of himself as a May butterfly that lives one day only, but who can say it has not lived? And when the night melted into the first rays of light, Ivain knew that his love for France had increased immensely and bore no resemblance to the earlier one, though he could not explain to himself why he felt that way. He also understood that it was going to be more difficult than ever to leave her behind.

THE RETURN

"There is not enough time. There is no more time.
There is going to be the absence of time."

Ivain La Baille, talking to himself

September 1994

As the fateful words "I am Ivain Jean Marie La Baille" had already been uttered, when morning came Ivain knew he had to die. "It is strange," he said to himself, "all these past months I thought nothing could touch me, that death happened to other mortals, but not to me since I was not mortal, but now I know that I am mortal again." And this thought made him cry silently at first, then laugh aloud. It was a laugh with a note of rueful mourning in its uncertain sound. "I'm now condemned for what I've said. I just hope that I'll stand up well to this predicted death." And he added, "I've gone through it once, I can't be a coward now. My courage mustn't give way. And if it's harder than the first time, I must be ready for it." France meanwhile had woken up, and was staring at him. He took her hand into his as he remembered the night they had just spent, remembered the tender loving and the many sweet words they had said to each other. He realized that his approaching disappearance would be hard on her, and tried to prepare her for the very thing one is never prepared for.

"Shortly I will be going," he began. "I want you to think of this time together as an unexpected gift." And then he repeated more than once, "I must go away."

"Where to?" she asked, though he knew she knew the answer.

"I must go back to where I came from," he said smiling.

"Will you die again?"

"Hardly," he said. "Am I not dead already?"

She smiled through her tears, but he could see she was beginning to lose control and he felt it imperative that she should not. He remembered the vision on the wall of Mme Kamiska when he first returned to earth, the image of France as a sweet old lady near the fireplace, with Fabian at her side. As he looked at her he said, "You have a long way to go yet. You'll live for a long, long time," and as he said those words he realized that he had never loved her more. She had been the only grand passion of his life, and nothing else really mattered. He just hoped she would be strong for the sake of them both in this last trial of his second life.

"I want to go with you," she answered desperately, and he saw her bare feet turning white from the cold stone they were standing on. He could see the cold traveling through her body and leaving it pale white. Before the coldness reached her hands he took her hands in his and smilingly said, "Borrow the warmth from a dead soul, and keep this coin as a souvenir of our love." Giving her the coin of Tiberius, he kissed both her hands.

During the night he told her he had to return, but that was all. He did not mention Fabian or the Library room, or anything that might spoil the intensity of their feelings. Now she must have realized that he would not stay much longer, for tears began running down her cheeks. She cried without making a sound. By returning to her he had altered the unalterable, it seemed. He looked at her, and discovered that she was as beautiful as the first time he had seen her, in the halls of the Philosophy building at Columbia holding the hand of his cousin Fabian. As beautiful as when she laughingly challenged both of them to catch her, and ran along the darkly lit corridors, chased by them both. But it was he who found her breathless and red in the face, who had kissed her in that empty classroom, taking in the fullness of her beauty. Her beauty was not of the caliber that made men or women turn their heads. It was the sort of beauty more admired than envied. Both he and Fabian had fallen in love with that sort of beauty, but it was he who got her to swear "eternal love" near Rodin's *The Thinker*, and it was he whom she married.

Now, from the look on France's face he knew she was thinking about her imminent loss, and the fact that he was going back to that same place which could not be clearly defined, and was therefore all the more frightening to her.

"I will have one hundred thousand copies of your unpublished manuscripts printed, and send them to the best libraries of the world," she was saying. "You will be famous and remembered. Your words will live on after you!"

For Ivain the paradox was too much. He almost burst out laughing – refraining from doing so only at the last moment by biting hard on his lower lip until a drop of blood appeared. His books had been burnt, or were floating away as little paper-boats in the underground rivers in Disneyland. The mediocre manuscripts at the Library were Fabian's. Poor France! And yet it was her destiny to believe she was doing her best for his own memory. It was at this moment more than at any other that he felt tempted to reveal to her what Fabian had done. The theft, the destruction of his manuscripts, his pretended intrigues with Allegra, and most of all, his terrible jealousy and pettiness with their catastrophic consequences. But Mme Kamiska and the Godlet, together with his cousin, counted on his rediscovered love for France, and they were right. He was not going to change, even for a few minutes, that picture of happiness he had seen on the wall. He was going to remain silent, even though he realized that if he told her the truth he might change the future, and in doing so break through the inner walls of "the written script."

"If I tell her who Fabian really is, she is bound to leave him.

Then the Godlet's play would not work. But they knew my deep love for her, and they were right."

His life didn't matter any longer. Nothing really mattered except the fact that he was at this moment living his own life, even while he prepared to die as best he could. He wanted to be prepared for the pain above all, for pain more than death frightened him. But it wasn't up to him to choose. He looked again at France, trying to remember her like this – in a light blue wool sweater and flowery skirt. She looked as if she was still trying to understand what he had told her, almost surprised to hear what she had known would happen. He understood her fears and wished somehow he could have protected her from too much suffering, but he also knew that it wasn't possible. His final words were spoken softly, and as tenderly as they could be, while trying to brace her for the inevitable.

She lay down again on the cold stone, trembling, and he lay near her. She looked at him and said with a frown, "Please, don't lie there as if you were dead."

"But I am dead," he answered smiling.

"Don't pretend to be a spirit who has come back," she continued as if to reassure herself.

"But I am a spirit who has come back," he said, and as he said it, he felt that the oddities of his present life were too much even for him, a living oddity.

"I don't understand," she said finally, and planted both her elbows firmly on the musk and verdurous pasture, resting her chin in her hands and looking intensely at him, waiting for his answer.

"Neither do I, actually," he replied as he bent toward her.

"I can see through you," she began as she moved slightly away, then stopped a moment later to say, "at least I think I can."

"I am still here," he said laughing. "Right now I am flesh and blood. I won't disappear so easily. I am quite sure you'll know when it happens."

"I see you falling down on a long stairway, over and over again –" she began.

"That's your memory reliving the accident as it happened the first time," he said. Then he silently touched her lips with his fingers, and she responded by holding his hand to her mouth and kissing each finger gently. He now heard his own voice as if coming from far away, telling France in a soft tone to remember she had to be strong, that she had been happily married to him once, and was married now to a good man who would take care of her, as she would take care of him; that she should think of him as an apparition outside time and space, or as an aberration from both these dimensions, who had come to help her in the search for his manuscripts. Now that this had been accomplished it was only natural he should go back.

France had not replied. He now gathered she was feeling numb from the staggering discovery she was about to lose him for the second time. She was just looking around, aware of the cold air of the morning, dimly noting the mist that hung on the lower branches of some pine and maple trees. The dew on the ground had an icy color that made the green grass under it look all the more opulent and rich. He helped France to sit up, but she fell back overcome again by the absurdity of the unknown and unknowable, until Ivain took her by the arms and pulled her up. He held her until she stood firmly. After that they began to walk together along the rural road.

After a little while, he heard the noise of cars approaching behind. They stopped, and he turned around to look. Coming slowly toward them was an ordinary, yellow New York taxicab. Right behind it, there was another car with "Applebrook" written on its side. Ivain saw Frank Luini at the wheel, bowing his head to both of them as if to say he had come to be of help, if help was needed.

Both cars stopped nearby. From the taxi a woman got out. It was a new, younger Mme Kamiska though her hair still had hues of gray and on her lips she wore pale white lipstick. As she stepped out of the taxi she said, "As we get younger, our soul grows older."

"Mme Kamiska!" France almost shouted, and then turning to Ivain she said, "Ivain, we are saved! My friend will help us now."

Ivain, remembering the old withered and wrinkled Mme Kamiska, was so amazed that he could say little. But he realized at once that the person who was supposed to save him was the person who was going to make sure he would disappear. "This is too strange," he murmured. "Just like all the rest of my life." And then an unexpected tear fell on his hand. "There," he whispered looking at it. "This tear is the last defence of my intellectual life. The only weapon I've left for my last battle." He looked at France. She looked frail and defenseless. But Mme Kamiska spoke to her in quiet, reassuring tones.

"My dear sweet girl, how is your late husband Ivain La Baille? As you have seen I've kept my promise." And she laughed, a little laugh, almost like that of a child. "But," she continued, "I'll be brief since we have no time to kill. I'll take your darling sweetheart under my care now while you go on with Mr. Luini to meet Fabian who is waiting for you at this address." And she showed a crumpled piece of paper to the caretaker who took it, and after changing glasses, held it up close to his eyes. "Hurry up, hurry up," she added to France.

"Oh Ivain," France said, "I almost forgot. This came for you a few days ago. Here!" she said as she took an ordinary envelope out of the little white bag she had tied around her waist, and handed it to him. Ivain was holding it as France said, "Thank you. Thank you for everything, Mme Kamiska." And then the question. "But will I see Ivain again? Will I? Will I?"

At this, Mme Kamiska took out a pack of cards from her pocket. They were tarot cards, but not the usual kind one finds in small shops that carry the secrets of the occult. These cards were larger than ordinary playing cards. They were elaborately designed with figures of men and women set against classical architectural backgrounds, with Doric and Corinthian columns. The cards had specific words written at the top of each picture, which could be interpreted in different ways, depending on the order in which they followed one another. All this Mme Kamiska explained to Ivain and France. One said "The Soldier," another "A Friend," another "The Old Lady," another "Riches," another "Misery," and so on and so forth.

"My dear, it takes subtlety in my kind of work. Finesse would be a better definition. But after so many years – " and she let the words trail, as if to imply that the cards held no more secrets for her. As she said this, she held the pack in her hands. "Pick one," she said to France, fanning them out in front of her, "for I'll give you the other one to make it easier. Here!" and she handed France a card that said "A Friend." France took it eagerly, but was hesitant to pick the other one. She even looked around at Ivain in a furtive way, as if to say, "What if –?" but in the end she did what she was told. She picked quickly and did not turn it around immediately. Mme Kamiska carefully reshuffled the pack when she announced in the whisper of a voice, "Now look at it and tell me what you got, remembering that 'A Friend' followed by 'The Stranger' brings bad luck. But if you have 'A Friend' followed by anything else, you will see your beloved Ivain again before you know it," and she winked at Ivain as if to say, "Aren't I clever?"

France held one card tight in each hand, and with the help of Ivain who took her hands into his, she turned with some hesitation the one card she had picked. Her face became radiant and she smiled with relief.

"A Friend" was with "The Virtuous Roman," and she handed the cards back to Mme Kamiska. But in that instant Ivain saw that on the back of that last card, the word "Stranger" was designed with such skill that each letter seemed to be a stalk from a different flower, so that it looked more like a painting than a word. France had not noticed this. Instead she had turned to Ivain and whispered: "Darling, I remember now the name of the play you were in Off Broadway. It was called *The Written Script*, and you used your *nom de plume*." She then added as she kissed him, "You were very good in it." and hurriedly got into the car which was now in front of Mme Kamiska's taxi. As she passed by him, he noticed that her smile was both luminous and clear, reflecting a happiness that was not to be theirs.

When Ivain remained once more alone with Mme Kamiska, he felt a sharp pain in his stomach and an unnatural twitching began to bother his left upper eyelid. He passed a finger over the eye, trying to stop it, but he only managed to scratch himself with the envelope in his hand. Looking at it, he noticed that under the name Ivain La Baille he could see the shadow of his other name: John O. Elliab, and under this, written rather elegantly – "delivered by hand."

He decided to open it quickly before getting into the cab. He did not know why he had this need to open it then and there. It was as if the instinct of survival had taken over and was telling him to do so. He had gotten a foolish hope in his head. "Perhaps," he thought, "there may be a message here that will save me. Perhaps I'm in 'a script' that ends with a *deus ex machina*. Perhaps I won't have to die." He tore the envelope apart, while Mme Kamiska waited patiently for him by the side of the car. He looked at what was inside and for a moment was puzzled.

It appeared to be a thin, golden paper with a shining knot in the middle and on each side of the knot, the paper opened up to resemble a fan. On the fan there were words intricately painted, as well as designs of blue butterflies and iridescent scarabs. On the actual knot there was one single legible word, but written in such small lettering, that Ivain had to bring the paper near his nose to read it. It said: "The Faustian –?"

"Ah –" he said, and quickly put the paper down, as he understood its meaning. He had seen the same golden paper before, and even held it in his hand. It was the paper Mme Kamiska had used for his contract with the JanKam Co. Only this was a different contract. It was between Mme Kamiska and Fabian, and it was put into his hands because he, Ivain la Baille, had to see and touch the instrument of his cousin's betrayal. He knew that there was a reason for this punctiliousness, for this courteous formality, but he did not yet comprehend it. Later on, he would understand, and for an instant marvel again at the cleverness of his opponents. At present though, as if compelled by a force stronger than his own will, he opened up the fan just enough to read the signature on the X, while on the other side he saw what he had been exchanged for: France, and the erasing of his name and memory from Earth. The exact words being "Pursuing this goal with the same enthusiasm, and single-mindedness that Pharaoh Tuthmosis tried to erase the name of his Pharaoh step-mother Hatshepsut."

"It is all so clear," said Ivain. "So clear!" he repeated, thinking of his cousin's insincerity, which was so Machiavellian that for a moment he did not know whether he should look upon Fabian with awe, or with disgust, or both. "What subtlety in his lies!" Ivain now whispered under his breath, blushing as he remembered how easily Fabian had burnt his reconstructed paper, how pregnant with irony his answers had been at Vaux le Vicomte, and with what elegance he played the part of Allegra's discarded lover! "How he must have laughed at me, his jester!" he murmured.

The depth of his cousin's deception began to crystallize for Ivain during the night he had just passed with France. In the darkness he had found courage to ask her about the missing items in Le Plessis, and in New York; items so full of memories for him that he had even found it difficult to talk about them.

"What happened to the Hopper painting?" he had asked France, as he held her close to him.

"Fabian sold it," she had answered.

"And the Guardis? And the collection of drawings?"

"Fabian gave them to the Louvre," she had answered trembling.

"And the books? My collection of Roman history?" Ivain inquired, even though he felt that he could not go on asking questions that seemed suddenly foolish.

"They are gone," she said as she cried. But he could not stop asking one last question.

"And the small, white silk sofa? The one which used to be in the living room near the fire place? The one my mo –" he did not have the courage to finish the sentence, for he already understood everything, and when France murmured with infinite sadness, "Fabian had it burnt in the backyard," he felt no surprise. Fabian and the JanKam Co.! What a simpleton he had been!

Stung by the mockery of it all, Ivain now crumpled up the golden paper in his hand, and threw it on the ground, where it changed into a myriad forms, until it became a polished coin with the face of a Roman Emperor which Ivain immediately recognized. It was the coin he had found on the road to Rosay twenty-seven years before, the coin that had been the principal motive for his journey through the classical age of Rome, and his studies of Julius Caesar. He bent down, picked it up and put it in his pocket. "My good luck piece!" he said to himself. "The Emperor Tiberius himself." and he laughed out loud.

"What did I expect?" he asked himself. Had he not known that there was a circle of time around him and that the circle would eventually close with no hope of escape? After all, "The written script" called for the ultimate "Unwritten script."

He had to steady himself. There was a last time for everything and he was about to be sacrificed at the altar of a Godlet with two faces, two shapes, two shadows. He felt himself becoming a sacred object, like a lamb made ready for a ceremonial ritual.

Mme Kamiska had come closer to him, and she now took his arm under hers, showing an intimacy and cordiality that under the circumstances somehow shocked him.

"Where are you taking me?" he asked hurriedly.

"To the airport," she replied as she opened the door to the taxi. They both got in, and as he did so he thought, "Ah, that's how it's going to be done! A repeat of the first time. I should have guessed it."

In the taxi Ivain did not try to make any more conversation with Mme Kamiska. "What's the point," he said to himself, "she is the messenger, I am the distraction of a Godlet." And his thoughts wandered to fate, and he tried to understand how his life had been worked out in detail by the master writer of all playwrights. "Mine has been a life foretold," he thought. "But which life isn't?"

"Haven't I waited long enough?" he said angrily to Mme Kamiska. But as soon as he said it, he realized his own foolishness and fell silent. The Godlet was whipping him just as hard as men used to whip pigs to make their flesh more tender before killing them. Yet, yet he felt tremendous anger passing through him, like wave after wave of water rushing through a tunnel. He wanted to rebel again against "the script." He had done it once successfully when he had put on the toga of Julius Caesar and given Caesar the gift of life on opening night. Then he was the General who had saved the greatest of all Generals from the conspirators' daggers! He could take consolation in that. No one made him say that last all-important line. No one. Not the actors, not Mme Kamiska, not the Godlet himself. This was a triumph. A significant triumph. It left a little hole to breathe through. A straw to hang on to in the cascade of rushing water. But now – now it was different. He had played his part as far as he could go. It was not a play written by a man to be played just among men. There were other mysterious forces behind it. Therefore, the rebellion was not worth the effort. "The script" was there and he had to follow it, give in to it, and then everything would be so much easier.

He looked out of the window. A kite was trapped in a telephone wire. It had a trapezoid form with a long tail trailing behind. It was all white and blue and Ivain thought that comets must look like that, someplace in the Universe. He remembered how, on a sunny day, while he was passing through a gorge with high snowy mountains on either side, he had seen a group of young people throw themselves over a precipice, attached to their hang-gliders. They seemed like a flock of birds with motionless wings, who were airborne and moving gracefully. Their planes had soft pastel colors, light greens, light reds, light yellows, as if the sun had bleached them. A bit farther on, a young falcon high above the ground was moving with a tremulous flutter as he remained in the same place, hovering in the thin, clear air of the morning, looking intensely at something down below. What was it that Grandmother had said to him as a child in Rosay? "Look Ivain, look! Those beautiful birds have found a strange way to trap their prey. They put them to sleep by flapping their wings up and down, up and down."

"Ah, to sleep, to sleep!" said Ivain to himself, and wished he could go to sleep and not wake up again. And just then, he saw the bird swoop down and disappear in the high grass ahead of the car.

He sat up. "I'll open the door and jump out," he said determinedly, but he did not move. Mme Kamiska looked indifferent to his antics. She probably had gone through them since the beginning of time. It was all the same to her. And then he got it. He was supposed to say that. Supposed to feel that there might be a final escape. It was part of "the script," and he was playing it well. She must be proud of him. Out of the corner of one eye, he saw the old lady smiling to herself.

He wanted to shout, but he knew it would be completely and utterly useless. Like a condemned man he had to walk to the gallows on his own two feet or be dragged to it. He preferred to go with his head held high. "I won't run anymore," he said to himself. "I'll stay with the written word and give a good performance to the end." He arrived at the airport and was grateful that the rush of the first time was not repeated. Mme Kamiska had arranged things well. But then she knew the moment and the modality, didn't she? He became painfully aware of everything around him. The men and women pushing carts full of suitcases. The clothes they wore, even their hairdos, as he followed his executioner meekly wherever she led him. Dying a second time was the price he had to pay for living a second time, and therefore he must die as honorably as he could. He entered the gray building passing through one glass door after another, each one opening as if by magic. "Like the one at Mme Kamiska's stone house," he thought. He traversed corridors and more glass doors, until he believed the whole world to be one never-ending corridor, separated only by transparent doors. He turned right twice and left once, and then right again and left twice, and then left once more and right again, and then right again, and right once more, meandering through the bowels of the earth until he arrived at a spot where Mme Kamiska stopped.

He looked up and saw the escalator ahead of him, and at the same time he saw France talking quietly to her husband. She had her back to him, and was explaining something to Fabian, something he obviously did not understand. What was she saying to him? Was she telling him of her discovery? Their shared moments together? His return to Earth? Mme Kamiska's power of bringing back his dead soul? He saw he was nodding as he listened attentively. Ivain knew that Fabian knew, but France did not know it, and would never know. Ivain was still looking at them when he suddenly came to the escalator, and standing near it, hidden behind a large straw hat, he recognized Allegra. The hat covered almost all her hair, which she had let grow in its natural dark color. He saw too that the hat had a large, white band; printed on it in blue ink, he saw the name: "A. Cavalcore." And, all at once everything became clear to Ivain, even though the truth had been staring him in the face since his return to Earth. In a second he realized that Cagliostro had been Allegra's married name. The infamous Count of Palermo had been her husband, not her father, and Cavalcore had been her maiden name. And some far away memories came back to him about Count Cagliostro who, when his wife was twenty years old, would tell people she was sixty, and thus made a living by selling bottles of his elixir of youth. That had been one of her many lives! And he only just understood this. Yet France had known Allegra by that other name, and had silently reproached Ivain for his affair with her.

Meanwhile, he realized how little he really understood Allegra. He remembered that once she had mentioned a messy divorce, saying that she would never allow a man to treat her that way again. He also remembered her words at the very beginning of his second life, when they had just met outside Mme Kamiska's house: that he would die just moments before she would die. He now realized what this meant. Murder and suicide. That was the awfulness she had talked about! He noticed that she was holding something in her hand. It looked like a small, black umbrella, but it was certainly some sort of weapon, cleverly disguised to avoid suspicion. No more Libyans this time. No more Palestinians, Red Army factions, IRA terrorists, revolutionaries from all countries. It was to be a simple crime of passion. What the French call *un crime passionnelle*.

"A better ending," he thought, and felt that the way Mme Kamiska was looking at him called for a congratulatory note from him. Wasn't that a good rewrite? After all, the various terrorist theories had never quite convinced either the police or himself. The stray bullet, an imprecise aim taken by such expert hands was too coincidental. It made an implausible end. In Rome Terence had used extraordinary coincidences in his plays. In France Victor Hugo had done the same. But even then, those techniques had amused more than convinced. Unfortunate happenings could occur in life but were not probable. And in fiction, more than in real life, plausibility and logic were what counted, not reality.

He smiled to himself, thinking of the headlines in the papers the following morning, or even that same evening. The headlines would be about the tragic fate of a well-known actor, felled by a woman with an obsessive love for him – a love he had not returned, nor understood.

He also foresaw that Detective Petronio Pellegrino, in a rare leap of brilliance and touched by grace, would be able to link two different murder cases to the same assassin – through the ironclad ballistic proof of the arm used – a .22 with a small silencer – and through the fatal bullets recovered from the two bodies. And he was able to predict that Detective Pellegrino would also stamp two files "Closed," that of the late Professor Ivain La Baille, and that of the late John O. Elliab, and while doing so he would notice that they were both in their thirties when they died, both had dark hair and gray eyes, both were six feet tall, and had the same shoe size and, most amazing – each had a long scar on the same place on the left thigh. He also foresaw that Detective Pellegrino would feel impelled to write on the cover of both files, close to the name Cavalcore, the first words of an old saying: "Hell has no fury –" but would leave out the rest, believing it to be too obvious. However, he would not be able to show who Miss A. Cavalcore was or from where she came.

"The Detective," thought Ivain, "will no doubt also be astonished to find that his rather prudish, proper Latin Professor had had his own lover on the side, and will certainly wonder why he was never able to find any trace of this during his long inquiry." That was the only blemish in the otherwise perfect record of that outstanding Detective and humble servant of the state. No bureaucrat ever ended his career more successfully.

The irony of all this did not escape Ivain. "He will be stamping a murder case closed, that has not yet happened, yet it has already happened." He wanted to ask Mme Kamiska: "Was it a comedy that turned into a romantic tragi-comedy this time around?" but he said nothing. She, on the other hand, was being extremely polite, using repeatedly the words "please" and "thank you" as she blurted out – "Isn't it a shame that Time is such a great devourer?" Then, asking him to go first, she said she would follow. He hesitated for a second, taking a long last look at Mme Kamiska: the woman who had played the roles of the tongueless orator, and the blind tower guard, and was now the midwife in this new play. The woman who, with her capricious Father, had held him in their hands, as if he were a pretty toy, and he was on the point of saying, "Why was it not a dance of dolphins in clear blue water? Or a flight of swallows in an April sky?" but he kept it as a thought, for he feared it would become part of "the script" were he to utter it. But, as if she had read his mind, she stepped aside, and taking a dark scarf out of her pocket, she proceeded to wind it round her head, and simply said – "Once more, please." And as soon as she said it, he remembered that the same words had been uttered in the same place, by an old woman with a dark scarf on her head, on his way to his destiny ten years before. "That's why her face was familiar," he said to himself, and understood that in his case, the perfect circle of time, had spun around him an indefinite number of times. That explained the *déjà vu* of France. She'd seen his death before, because he'd died the same way before. That explained the presence of Fabian at the airport the first time around. He was meeting Allegra, only he, Ivain, had not known it then. Scripts don't change much. They just keep repeating themselves with some changes here and there. Practice makes perfect!

He stepped on the first step. Now he was being carried up, up, up. He had become a child again. No more struggles, no more fights. Someone was doing all the work for him. For some unknown reason he started to think of childhood rhymes of Mother Goose as his Parisian nurse in Le Plessis had recited them in broken English in front of the fire which was always burning, sometimes even on a warm August day. But now he mixed them up. Nothing was clear any more, nothing was simple. "Hickory Dickory Dickory Dock, Humpty Dumpty ran up the Clock, London Bridge is falling down, Hickory Dickory Dock."

The escalator was the longest he had ever seen or ever taken. "It will be a longer fall," he thought, and then he felt a punch on his side and knew he had been hit. He heard a great cry of alarm around him. He turned around and saw France looking at him as she raised her hand to her mouth to suppress a scream, no doubt. And then he saw her trying to run toward him, but Fabian was pulling her back, away from him. He closed his eyes and tried to straighten himself up as his body seemed to have acquired an immense weight of its own, but instead he felt himself pirouetting around twice on the toes of his shoes, as if turning on a large gyroscope or a colorful top, and knowing he would fall, he tried to fall carefully, as if life still mattered to him. But, unable to control his body, he fell forward as the people round him recoiled in inexpressible horror. Strangely, the pain was bearable. He knew this was the end and closed his eyes.

THE FINAL VISION

"Life is a matter of opinion."
Schopenhauer

As soon as Ivain closed his eyes he had a sense of falling through the stairs under him, through the cement that held the stairs, through the earth itself that held up the cement, through the core of the earth to the other side of the planet, coming out from the deepest oceans into the lightest atmospheres. Then he started to go around and around in a large circle while being pulled into a vortex. It was not an unpleasant sensation, something akin to flying without wings. He could see everything around him as if he had eyes within his forehead. "Inner eyes," he thought, "to see through the vortex that will bring me to the other side." But before he reached the vortex, he was back in Mme Kamiska's stone house where he noticed that the papyrus scrolls, historical tablets, and Chaldean and Etruscan drawings were no longer there. "They're already in the Library," thought Ivain without any sadness or regret. Then he looked up and saw that all the clocks which had been turning silently above him, as if they were aerial sculptures, were now ticking frantically; announcing the different hours, at the same exact moment, in a multitude of ways, including cuckoos, and tiny gnomes beating on red mushrooms with white spots. "*Amanita muscaria,*" said Ivain who now found that everything was pretty and that the air was filled with a delicate perfume of wild flowers, and an ecstasy came over him.

He was standing in front of Mme Kamiska who had become a beautiful young woman with an enticing smile, a Venus in fact; and this Venus, scantily dressed, was telling him that the play was about to end, and she congratulated him for his performance, and as a token of her gratitude she said she would grant him his request, that request which he had formulated the first time he had entered her stone house.

"And what was that?" he said, embarrassed not to remember what he had asked. It seemed such a long time ago and he had only the vaguest memory of it now. So she kindly reminded him, saying – "Before you return to the place where you came from, you'll know the answers to the questions that have been haunting you since your childhood, such as – Is the Earth the center of the Universe? What is the sky made of? And what is art?" And as soon as she said it, he realized that the Earth had always been at the center of the Universe because that was where he had been born, and where his consciousness appeared, and where he had loved France, and where he had died, and he asked himself how he could have missed it. At the same time he realized that the sky was made of stone. "Of course," he said, "it's made of marble." Marble that in the morning and at sunset took on the reflection of the city of Petra, soft hues of red and amber tones, and at midday changed from a deep blue Florentine marble to that fantastic white stone of Carrara, sometimes criss-crossed with veins of gray and pink. "Now I understand," he said to himself, "why as a young child I was always afraid that the sky would fall on my head!" And he felt an immense sympathy for the people who had believed all this in earlier times. He suddenly understood Heraclitus who said that the sun was no larger than his big toe, for with one finger he could blot it out. "How blind I was," he said, "for that is just so!" He looked to the side, and he saw the first man who carved a wheel out of an old piece of hard wood, chiseling it with two primitive stones. It was a Chinese with a loin cloth and no hair, and immediately another man replaced him, a Phoenician dressed in flowing robes, who kept looking up at the sky and writing down on the sand the magic circles of the planets. That round O by a leap of the imagination, became the missing link in mathematics. And for the first time, as a consequence of the invention of the wheel and the zero, Ivain realized that the O. in his John O. Elliab's name, meant at the same instant everything and nothing. That discovery led him to think of art, whose inner truth had always eluded him, and all at once, as if all knowledge was being poured into him, he understood the possibilities that art held, from Giotto's mysterious blue sky, to Pompei's inimitable red walls. In an instant he realized too that African masks were no less attractive than Michelangelo's sculpture, while the drawings of animals in the dark caves of southern France, or northen Spain, were no less extraordinary than the horses and goats of Picasso or Matisse or Chagall or Paolo Uccello. He understood also that wrapping up a building in "pink paper," or painting a white canvas with only "white zinc," and leaving it so, had nothing to envy in Piero della Francesca or Masaccio, or Morandi, or Carraccio, or Sol Le-Witt. They were all expressions of the human spirit, and therefore powerful experiences one and all.

"Go on," she said. "Go on. The wheel of Time is waiting for you," and he thanked her, though he did not know why he thanked her. Perhaps he was being too polite, perhaps it was just a reflex from his upbringing. After all, he had been taught to be always polite or perhaps it was because Mme Kamiska was giving him the chance to reconstruct the Universe in a new, contemplative light, without fear or bitterness or pain. And as he thought about it, he felt himself lifting from the ground and flying once more into the vortex. He was in the best of form again, he was handsome and clever and life was ahead of him, and he wanted to know everything there was to know. At the entrance to this vortex was a gigantic iron wheel, inlaid with bronze and silver motifs of wild mountain flowers, such as the edelweiss. He tried to steady himself and placed both hands on the wheel, and the wheel immediately began to spin at a prodigious speed, propelling him first into the future, where he witnessed the end of Time. That moment was revealed to him when he saw the cataclysmic collapse of our own Universe into a singular luminous point of nothingness. Immediately afterward, the wheel began to rotate at an ever faster and unimagined speed, and Ivain entered the past, going back to that same luminous point of nothingness that had begun the creation of our own Universe, while other Universes around him were simultaneously created and destroyed in a chaotic way among the intensely blue Quasars, and Black Holes. In going backward into Time he, himself, passed from being a human into all the forms that had preceded it, including the humanoid, the apes, the reptiles, the dinosaurs, the earlier amphibians, the primitive animals that looked like plants, then the plants themselves which mankind descended from, and the first molecules containing the D.N.A. that started it all. He realized then that those molecules had come intact and frozen inside the icy tail of a comet eight billion years ago, a comet that had landed in the mud and water already on our planet, which was the favorable condition needed to begin their reproduction. Earlier on, when Ivain was still going forward in Time, he got a look at the inheritors of the earth, and saw the earth taken over by gigantic flying insects, with flying fire ants as big as elephants, and on the ground, cicadas as large as whales. And the praying mantis and the wasp, all with their own beauty, all with enormous multi-faceted eyes, conscious of being the new owners of the earth. "This is how everything changes," Ivain thought. "The Mammals disappearing, as the other species disappeared before them." And finally he saw how evolution produced an Arachnid far more intelligent than any Mammal had ever been, who uncovered the one-hundred million year old bones of Homo sapiens, just as mankind had uncovered the dinosaurs, who philosophized better and more poetically than Plato and Socrates and Lucretius about this unusual discovery, which they called the unresolved question of the "small bones of past creatures," and who wrote melodious cantatas about them, while wondering what sort of catastrophe had overtaken the masters of that past world, for their world and their species had ended so suddenly and so mysteriously. He also realized that the only writing that had survived from that period, which went under the name of "The Tropical Age," was the writing found on the so-called "Allegra Stone." This was a large monolithic stone which had been uncovered in the Grand Canyon, engraved with both the words and drawing of the brief historical notes that Allegra herself had given Ivain, millions of years before. And he saw that the inheritors of the earth would finally come to the conclusion that in that enigmatic stone, and in those small petrified bones, the force of life itself had been turned to dust.

It was while traveling toward the end of Time that Ivain became aware of the innumerable planets similar to ours, scattered here and there in the large and small Galaxies, and their moons, sometimes consisting of pure diamond, sometimes of emerald and topaz, sometimes made out of vermilion ruby, so that when the light of a star hit them they became bright painted surfaces floating across a dark sea of silence. And in these planets he was able to discern the most extraordinary beings living there. But one particular planet struck Ivain, for it had all the names of the Atlas that Mme Kamiska had pulled out of her rags that day he met her on his walk on Riverside Drive. The day that she had granted him the chance to play Julius Caesar, for the first and only time.

He was amazed to see that there actually was the planet Sigellium and, flying closer, he was able to see that it had continents called Lilliput, Oz, Daddy Jones, Gondour, and so on. Equally amazing was the realization that on its shores he saw all the great characters of literature. He could actually see Sancho Panza trying to stop Don Quixote from hurling himself against the windmills, and Gargantua eating and eating and eating, and asking Ivain to sit at his table, which he politely refused, and the three brothers Karamazov crying together, and begging him to stop and listen to their story; and the three sisters, who said they had begun their walk to Moscow, while in the distance he discerned the delicate face of Anna Karenina walking toward a train. There was also a little man with a goatee who announced that he was Shakespeare, though the name Shakespeare was really an alias for his real name, which he proceeded to write in the air with a stick. He also revealed that he learnt his art of poetry as a scribe in the service of Marlow. So that Ivain finally understood that Shakespeare was not really Shakespeare, but someone else who called himself Shakespeare. He went on and saw Lady Murasaki and her Prince sitting in the Eastern Garden of the old Palace of Genji, the Nijo-in – and Ivain was amazed to gaze at her beautifully shaped face, and at her hair that reached the ground. He was able to perceive Jack and the beanstalk, and Alice in Wonderland, and the Golden Ass, and he even realized that the father of Pinocchio had not been Geppetto, but a distant cousin of the Godlet – called Wotan. And finally, he was given a papyrus paper by a regally dressed young woman, who held a handful of earth in her other hand, whom he knew to be Antigone. The papyrus was filled with commas and semicolons, colored in red and white, and though Ivain did not know in what language they were written, he was able to decipher it. In the papyrus he saw the answer to his question – How many sailors had sailed with Ulysses, which was 26 including the 10 pairs of rowers, and he realized that the *Odyssey* had been written before the *Iliad*, and Homer was older than Hesiod by more than one hundred years. He also saw clearly that only fifteen thousand angels and not one more would be able to fit on a pin's head, an exact count which pleased him, for it had always bothered him not to know.

It was after he had reached the end of Time that past Time came to be, and Ivain saw the past. He was able to see Tarquin, Prince of the early monarchical Rome, not seducing the young Lucretia, but being astutely seduced by her. And he saw Masinissa talking *sotto-voce* to his newly married wife Sophoniba under a trellis of perfumed roses, promising her an empire; just as Mark Antony, under the same trellis would later on promise the very same thing, using the very words of his predecessor, to his royal Egyptian mistress and wife.

And after that he saw the generals of all the ages, including Napoleon, Charlemagne, Pippin, Joan of Arc, Alexander the Great, Leonidas, Tutankhamen, Timor, and Suleiman the Magnificent, but not necessarily in that order, because Ivain had studied history, chaotically, through its poets or great writers, and not chronologically throughout its wars. And Ivain also saw all the Roman generals and Emperors, and there was one he fixed his stare on. He was then able to see the moment when a young and inexperienced Julius Caesar lost his virginity for the first time to a man, not King Nicomedes as historians assumed, but a young albino, hairless, sacred hermaphrodite, who lived within the antechambers of the King of Bithynia. And Caesar, sprawled on a gold cushion over resplendent cloth and dressed up as a slave boy, was that night initiated by the man-woman in the art of loving. The ceremony was almost sacred since the hermaphrodite had cleverly dressed himself as part-Venus, part-Mars. And as the king happened to wake up early, hearing the little cry of pleasure emanating from his sacred slave, rose and requested their company in his own bed.

Thus Caesar became King Nicomedes' favorite lover boy, even acting as his royal cupbearer. And it was during one such banquet with some debauched young men, which Ivain now had the possibility of seeing clearly, that the young Caesar was led to the king's bedchamber, where he lay on a gold couch, and where the sacred hermaphrodite played the lyre waiting for the king himself to appear. It was after that event that Ivain saw the envious senatorial handwriting on the Roman walls – "Caesar, husband to all wives, and wife to all husbands." And Ivain was surprised to see that Caesar, having learned all there was to learn in the art of love from the king, who knew one trick more than the madams of the best brothels, came back to Rome to teach it to a beautiful young bride in the Capital. Her name was Servilia, married off not for love, but for dynastic reasons to an excellent man. And Ivain saw how Caesar loved her. Loved her – not in spite of her coldness and her regrets, but because of them. And he saw Caesar not discouraging that coldness, since he loved a body that trembled under his but did not move. The feeling that he was her conqueror against her better judgment, the feeling that he could give her the biggest pearl, with the knowledge that ultimately she would boast publicly that he had seduced Cato the Censor's sister, and she, in return for the pearl, had given him a son – Brutus. Brutus, whom Servilia's husband recognized, to save his wife's and his own reputation. And at the very moment Ivain questioned whose son Brutus was, he understood the true motive of the parricide, not to save the Republic, but to avenge his family's dishonor.

Shaken by these revelations, Ivain looked still deeper into the past, and saw there the moment when Alexander decided to set fire to the greatest city of antiquity, Persepolis. It was when the prostitute Taide said the words, "Burn it, my Lord, to revenge the destruction of the Acropolis," and as she said it, she lifted her skirt to show him the place where her umbilical cord had been cut, 2500 years before Ivain was born, in the capital of the Archenemies empire, the new Takht-i Jamshid of Iran – where the golden vine symbol of life was kept. And he heard Alexander's last words as he lay dying in Babylon – "I should not have listened to Taide." And at the same time Ivain heard these words he saw the image of the young prince holding Taide's white, long-fingered, delicate hand while they threw the torch that started the cataclysmic fire. He also saw that, as soon as everything had been destroyed, the young prince sat among the ashes, weeping unrestrainedly; just as in the loneliness of his tent, Scipio Aemilianus had cried at the destruction of Carthage. He also saw the tears of Publius Cornelius Scipio, nicknamed the Africanus, who had wept after King Syphax had been brought to him in chains, and of Lucius Aemilius Paulus, when Perseus, King of Macedonia, entered his camp in bondage. He saw this as well as the moment when Julius Caesar was called Aegisthus by Pompey for having seduced his wife, and a moment later when Pompey, forgetting what he had said, had married Caesar's daughter Julia in a splendid ceremony. It was at that ceremony that Ivain now saw an ordinary citizen calling Pompey, "a greater cynic than Diogenes."

With a feeling of awe, Ivain now became aware of being a spectator to the burning of the last books of Sappho and the last books of Callimachus, full of poems so melodious as to be compared to the best songs of birds, burning in a fire made to roast chestnuts on a winter night, on a roadside, by people who lived by what they found.

And he saw how the ocean's waters had risen suddenly twenty thousand years ago, inundating the cities of Atlantis, built with stones inlaid with gold, lapis lazuli and turquoise. Atlantis, the greatest and most advanced civilization ever known, where bronze and iron were worked so well that women wore them as jewels, but gold was used for making daggers, and other instruments of war just for ceremonial parades, and amorous display. Ivain also understood that the sudden rise of the ocean had been due to a large ice comet with a long tail of white light that, passing too close to the sun, had broken up into pieces, a mile long, that fell upon the Earth. The earthquake that ensued was of such magnitude that all the world felt it, and the waves that followed it covered vast continents which disappeared forever under the green-blue wave.

Still further back in Time, he saw the moment the Atlantic ocean rose to such a height that it flooded the green valley of the Mediterranean, which until that moment had been incredibly fertile, with mammals that looked like birds for they had feathered skins, and birds that looked like reptiles for they had no feathers, only a scaly skin over their aerial bones. The coming of the Atlantic ocean inside the Mediterranean valley had happened when a huge wave, followed by another and another, had found a path between two mountain tops that joined Europe and Africa, and had cut a corridor there, through rock and snow, to become the most powerful cascade of water ever seen on earth. That cascade had first begun as a trickle, then changed into a small torrent that could not be stopped, and then had become a huge river. It created the sea that the Romans called *Mare Nostrum*.

And he saw that everything was moved by "cause and effect," but not necessarily in a one-two time sequence. He saw that the slapping of a child in India had direct consequences for another child lost in the forest that same day in North America. He saw that the killing of a beautiful egret in Africa had a clear effect on a man saving his dog from drowning in the family's pool, and then getting a cramp and dying himself. There was a link between the sneeze of a chimpanzee and the birth of a cockatoo, the making of an orange cake in England and the breaking of a table in China. He saw the link clearly, just as if you moved a chair from right to left and saw it before and after. Everything was related in some form to everything else in the Universe, only we didn't know how, since we didn't know the whole plan of the creation, only bits here and there. He also became aware that everytime we breathed, we absorbed ions of all the plants and all the creatures that had ever existed in the world, and one day, our quiet breath would join Alexander's and Caesar's.

And then Ivain saw the moon falling on the Earth, and the moment when Time stopped for our planet as we knew it. And he saw the wave it produced, a million times taller than the one that engulfed him outside the library, and he saw it as it began rolling over the planet, washing away all the millions, billions, trillions, quadrillions and quintillions of years that had been left behind, until there were only rocks and loose stones on the crust of the Earth. Then he heard a great wind beginning to blow, as the Earth's new craters opened, and saw that the wind was of such force and so swift that it caught up with the wave and then overtook it, picking up everything in its path that was still living and breathing, including all the trees, and the ruins of palaces, and homes, and huts, and flowers and insects, and the enormous Arachnid that had become wise and good and totally civilized. And finally he saw that the gigantic wave, propelled by the wind, left the Earth and returned into the upper part of the sky, and from there into the Universe, to become a radiant comet of ice and mud, and bring water and the molecules of earthly life to a hitherto unknown planet that one day would be filled with amazing beings, dressed in white silk and brocade, beings who would think, and walk and laugh, just as the inhabitants of the Earth had done once, and ask themselves where they had come from, and where they would go, when they died.

Then the vision stopped and Ivain realized that all the questions that had been haunting him had been answered with a truth that was as absolute as it was singular. A truth that was real only to him, and to no one else. A truth that was different from the truth he had lived his life by. A truth that had eluded him. A truth which he had finally found in all its facets. But ultimately, and most important, he was shown with infinite clarity, the enormous double deceit that had been played on him by both Heaven and Earth, Godlet and man.

"The ocean dies too," he whispered. "Take me," he continued, "take me to where there is infinite void, the nothingness, the empty hole, the wind through the skull, the rattling of dry wolves' skins, the elephant's cemetery, the luminous shells of the fireflies. Take me there, so that I shall not see, not hear, not touch, not smell, not be, since for now and forever and before the world was a thought in the Milky Way, I was a non-person, a non-being, a long lost-forgotten spark of light in a sea of darkness, that never was, that never could be, and never is. Take me and forgive the thought that I believed in my existence, that I was tempted to think that pain and joy were real, when everything and all that I have done is the same that was done since time immemorial, and nothing at the same time." And, as he said it, he became aware that his memories and thoughts were beginning to dissolve into the void he was about to re-enter. "The daughter of Time will make sure of that," he murmured, "for the sun must rise from the East and settle in the West."

His breathing was becoming more and more erratic, and his whole body was shaking, waving up and down. With the greatest effort Ivain opened his eyelids an imperceptible slit, saw the face of Fabian near his own, and thought of him as "The Virtuous Roman." He involuntarily caught one more breath and, feeling within himself for the first and only time the full force of the dying Caesar, he uttered: "Et tu, Brute! Then fall, Caesar," saying at last his exit line from that Shakespearean play he had so cleverly and so tenaciously avoided saying. And that was all he said, aware he was still following a script that was not his own, and could never be.